W9-BPK-489

3 9077 07198 0021

"IS THERE ANY SIGN OF ACTIVITY FROM THIS
TIMESHIP?" THE DIRECTOR WENT ON.

"No, ma'am," Dulmur said. "It's adrift. The subspace confluence seems stable."

"Then we have time to examine the records. I'm granting you full clearance to whatever classified DTI and Federation Science Council records from that period you believe may be relevant to your investigation. I'll request the equivalent clearance from Starfleet Command. And I'll tell you what I can remember about those early days."

"If it wasn't Grey," Lucsly said, "we should track down who in Starfleet would've headed up the investigation of the Enterprise's temporal incident. We know Starfleet undertook some reckless experiments with time in those early days. This must have been one of them."

"Then how did the ship end up with civilian markings?" Dulmur asked. "Department markings?"

"Don't get ahead of the process, Dulmur," Andos said. "To reconstruct the truth, we need to follow the chain of events from their beginning."

"And their beginning, as always," Lucsly said, "was James Tiberius Kirk."

STAR TREK®

DEPARTMENT OF
TEMPORAL INVESTIGATIONS

FORGOTTEN
HISTORY

CHRISTOPHER L. BENNETT

Based on *Star Trek*
created by Gene Roddenberry
and
Star Trek: Deep Space Nine®
created by Rick Berman & Michael Piller

POCKET BOOKS

New York   London   Toronto   Sydney   New Delhi   Regulus III

Pocket Books
A Division of Simon & Schuster, Inc.
1230 Avenue of the Americas
New York, NY 10020

This book is a work of fiction. Names, characters, places, and incidents either are products of the author's imagination or are used fictitiously. Any resemblance to actual events or locales or persons, living or dead, is entirely coincidental.

First Pocket Books paperback edition May 2012

POCKET and colophon are registered trademarks of Simon & Schuster, Inc.

For information about special discounts for bulk purchases, please contact Simon & Schuster Special Sales at 1-866-506-1949 or business@simonandschuster.com.

The Simon & Schuster Speakers Bureau can bring authors to your live event. For more information or to book an event, contact the Simon & Schuster Speakers Bureau at 1-866-248-3049 or visit our website at www.simonspeakers.com.

Manufactured in the United States of America

10 9 8 7 6 5 4 3 2 1

ISBN 978-1-4516-5725-8
ISBN 978-1-4516-5726-5 (ebook)

In memory of Fred Steiner

Those who would protect the past
may be obliged to reinvent it.
—Vaacith sh'Lesinas
On the Edge of Yesteryear

Prologue

U.S.S. Everett NCC-72392
Stardate 60143.8
February 2383
A Tuesday

Agent Teresa Garcia of the Federation Department of Temporal Investigations stared at the Starfleet officer across the table. "How can you be disappointed, Heather? We just spent a week in a pocket universe!" She laughed. "This is why I love this job. I keep saying sentences I never imagined I'd say."

Across from her, Commander Heather Peterson, the *Everett*'s strawberry-blond chief science officer, shrugged her slender shoulders. "I know, it should be amazing. And getting clearance to visit Elysia at all is a rare privilege, et cetera. Believe me, I was thrilled when we got the word." For over a millennium, the pocket dimension known as Elysia had been unknown to the outside universe, for travel through the interphase zone that led there—a region of space that humans had redundantly dubbed the Delta Triangle more from historical resonance than geometric accuracy—had been only one-way until just over a hundred and thirteen years ago, when Captains Kirk of the *U.S.S. Enterprise* and Kor of the *I.K.S. Klothos* had joined forces to break free of the dimensional trap. Soon thereafter, a safe method for two-way travel had been developed by the Starfleet Corps of Engineers, but the Elysians—the crews of the hundreds of ships that had been stranded there over the centuries, many of them enemies in the outside universe—had wished to minimize disruptions to the insular, peaceful utopia they had built from necessity, so their interactions with the outside universe had remained infrequent.

Peterson sighed. "It's just that it didn't quite live up to the hype. All the Elysians' talk about how time stands still there. The mystery of how they remain ageless. I mean, obviously it couldn't literally be that time doesn't pass there, or nobody could move, talk, think. I knew all the arguments from the skeptics, that it was some kind of metaphasic radiation that kept them young or something, but I wanted to believe there was something new to be discovered about the nature of time."

From where he sat between the two women at the round table in *Everett*'s crew lounge, Agent Ranjea spoke in his gentle, lilting tenor. "Well, we did gain insight into the differing laws of work and entropy in Elysia," the Deltan agent pointed out, tilting his hairless, brown-skinned head. "I find it fascinating. Less energy expended, less disorder created in achieving the same amount of work. So our bodies wear out less, and our healing mechanisms are far more effective."

"You find everything fascinating," Peterson teased. From what Garcia gathered, the science officer had come a long way since she'd first met the gorgeous Deltan man ten years, seven months ago, when she'd gone all giddy in his presence and striven desperately to impress him and catch his eye. It was normal enough behavior for humans around Deltans, excusable given the sheer potency of Deltan pheromones. Garcia was still embarrassed to think about her own desperate crush on Ranjea back when they'd first been partnered—and grateful to him for his patience and understanding in helping her overcome those feelings, allowing their relationship to mature into the stable, trusting partnership, and friendship, that it now was.

"With much reason, in this case," Ranjea replied. "Could this be part of why their society is so peaceful? If every action, even thought, comes more easily, the mind works better, endures less stress. It makes it easier to see constructive solutions, less common for distress or fatigue or frustration to cloud the judgment and provoke hostile or selfish choices. Imagine if we could find a way to replicate the effect here in our universe."

Heather looked abashed; there was still enough of that smitten young ensign left in her that she didn't like to risk Ranjea's disapproval. "Of course, I can see the potential, the importance of the research. It's just that it's not about *time*. That's what we're supposed to investigate, right?"

Garcia suppressed a smile at the thought of how Agent Dulmur, who'd sponsored her entry into the DTI, or his legendary partner, Agent Lucsly, would react to a Starfleet officer's presumption in speaking as though she were a member of the Department. *Everett* was a *Nova*-class scout ship attached to the DTI, providing transportation and scientific or logistical support when needed, but most career DTI agents found it an uneasy partnership at best, given Starfleet's reputation for stumbling into temporal anomalies beyond their expertise and threatening the integrity of the timeline through their well-intentioned but often reckless meddling.

"Well, I had a blast," Garcia told her. "The chance to study ships from over a hundred cultures stretching back over a millennium? To meet and interview people who were actually *alive* back then? I was in heaven!"

Peterson chuckled. "Still an archaeologist at heart. Do you ever wish you'd stayed with your studies? That you hadn't been—" She broke off, realizing she might have touched on a sensitive subject. Teresa had been on her way to graduate studies at the Regulus III Science Academy in 2366 when a spatial anomaly had flung her transport ship, the *Verity*, fifteen years into the future, to find Regulus devastated in an attack by a ruthless enemy called the Borg. Her shipmates had sought to return to their own time and warn of the oncoming disaster, but Garcia had stopped them, convinced that reckless, uninformed meddling in history could do far more harm than good. Ostracized by her fellow displacees, she'd been invited by Agent Dulmur to join the Department of Temporal Investigations, where he felt her instincts for protecting history at all costs would serve her well. She'd taken his offer because she'd had nowhere else to go in this new time, and hoped that working for the DTI would help her accept that she'd done the right thing.

And it had worked—mostly. She smiled at Ranjea. "No," she told Heather. "I'm exactly where I belong."

"Bridge to Commander Peterson." It was the voice of *Everett*'s captain, Claudia Alisov.

"Peterson here."

"Report to the bridge, please. Are Ranjea and Garcia with you?"

"We're here, Claudia," Ranjea told her as all three rose to their feet.

"We've detected a temporal anomaly forming about eight parsecs away, just beyond the Lembatta Cluster. We're changing course to investigate. Would you care to join us on the bridge?"

"It would be my pleasure," Ranjea purred. He didn't make a conscious effort to be suave, charming, and irresistible; it just happened. And every compliment and gesture of appreciation he offered was sincerely meant, if more platonically than their recipients often hoped. After all, for most humanoids, intimacy with Deltans had effects ranging from addiction to a permanent loss of self-identity, and most Deltans were far too considerate to exploit other species in that way.

"At last," Peterson crowed as the three of them hurried from the lounge, "something interesting!" There was that carefree Starfleet enthusiasm. But Ranjea and Garcia exchanged a solemn look. Disruptions to the normal flow of time could have devastating consequences. Consequences that DTI agents understood better than most—for it was their job to clean them up.

It took six hours, twenty-three minutes to reach the anomaly, in which time the DTI agents contacted their Aldebaran branch office and received formal clearance to investigate. Aldebaran sent their own scans of the anomaly to the *Everett*, as did the nearby Tandaran Institute of Temporal Studies, one of the Federation's leading temporal research centers. Neither set of scans was as clear as the *Everett*'s, but even the *Everett* could discern little through the subspace interference. "Odd sort of interference, too," Heather Peterson reported. "It's like two different sets of spacetime topologies and energy distributions were superimposed on one another."

Captain Alisov's cherubic features, framed by a mop of red-brown curls tinged with gray, drew into a frown. "You mean like a dimensional interphase?"

"There are interphasic aspects, but it's more than that. This isn't just an overlap with a parallel timestream; there's a spatial displacement as well. I'm getting gravitic and radiation readings through the effect that are consistent with a quiescent neutron star, but there are no neutron stars in this sector."

"We've encountered interspatial fissures that connected with other parts of the universe," Alisov said.

"But those interphases connected with subspace domains that allowed shortcuts between those regions. This is . . . more than that. It's like the region we're scanning doesn't just *connect* to a different place and time—it actually *is* both places and times at once."

"How could that be?"

"This subspace reading might be a clue. You know that space and subspace are different facets of the same manifold, right? The conditions in one shape the conditions in the other, and vice versa."

Alisov nodded, not confirming or denying that she knew that. "Go on."

"But the way in which they're interrelated isn't uniform. Mathematically speaking, there's more than one way that a given subspace topology can map onto a given set of spatial conditions. It can be affected by the larger-scale conditions—the position within the galactic gravity well, the subspace field density, and so on."

"And this is relevant how?"

"Captain, the subspace configurations I'm reading are *merging*—but they seem to be merging toward a configuration that can map perfectly onto *both* sets of spatial readings. They're becoming completely homeomorphic—pretty soon, as far as the universe is concerned, they'll effectively be the same place. Even though they're definitely widely separated places in space. Maybe even separate times, or even timelines."

Alisov blinked. "That latter part sounds more important to be definite about, don't you think?"

"I'm working on it, Captain. The computer turns up references to a theoretical construct called a subspace confluence. First showed up in some papers in the late twenty-two sixties. Stand by." Peterson spent a few minutes searching the theoretical physics database. "Odd. There's not much research on the subject . . . and some of the passing mentions I find are linked to references that don't seem to exist."

Alisov turned to the senior DTI agent. "Ranjea? Is this one of those ideas that the DTI, in its infinite wisdom, has decided is too dangerous to let people know about?"

Ranjea shook his smooth-skinned head. "If so, it's above my clearance level."

Alisov's eyes darted to Garcia, who shrugged. "Don't look at me, I'm the new kid."

"Captain," called the tactical officer, a coral-hued Saurian female. "Readings on the anomaly are growing clearer. There's some sort of ship in there."

"On screen." All eyes turned to the main viewer.

Only a vague gray blur appeared at first. "The image should improve as the ship comes into phase with our reference frame," Peterson said. Indeed, the resolution quickly increased. "Definitely getting time displacement readings now . . . similar to a slingshot signature."

"And that ship is in the middle of it," Garcia said.

Ranjea nodded. "Heather, is it generating any kind of energy that could be causing the anomaly?" Garcia understood his thinking. Timeships intruding on the present from other centuries were a perennial nuisance for the DTI, especially when they were operated by up-time scientists or temporal agents who insisted they knew better than the time police of a more "primitive" era.

"Its engines are generating power," she confirmed. "Basically a warp drive signature, with a chronitonic component . . . but with anomalies I haven't seen before. Not sure where the power's going, though. The ship has lost attitude control . . . No active sensors or comms . . . It's warm enough to be inhabited, but it's adrift." She frowned. "Still, that underlying signature . . . it's a little *too* basic. Like Federation basic."

Alisov rose and stared at the screen as the image became clearer. Garcia's dark eyes widened at the sight. It did have a familiar sort of shape to it, a cylindrical main hull with two nacelles rising from the rear on short pylons. Teresa turned to her fellow agent. "Temporal Integrity Commission again?"

"No," Ranjea said. "This design is far less advanced. It seems—"

"It can't be," Alisov interrupted. As the image came into full clarity, Garcia had to agree.

The main hull was a tapered cylinder with a glowing, recessed deflector dish on the front and a fantail rear. Navigational sensor domes were mounted on the top and bottom of the cylinder. Extending upward from the rear, on two short, boxy pylons, was a pair of cylindrical engine nacelles whose forward Bussard collectors were red domes with faint, swirling patterns of light inside them.

"My God," said Alisov. "It looks like someone took the engineering hull of an old *Constitution*-class ship and converted it to work on its own. Look," she said as the ship slowly tumbled to present its rear. "They've installed an impulse engine where the hangar deck would be. But it's inconsistent. The warp engines are a design from the sixties—sorry, twenty-two sixties—and the basic hull configuration fits that era. But the impulse engines, the deflector dish, the sensor domes, the hull plating, they're early seventies. Why keep outmoded warp engines and update the rest?"

The DTI agents traded a look. Alisov knew this technology firsthand. Like Garcia, she and many of the *Everett*'s crew were temporal refugees, trapped in a time loop for ninety years when they'd served aboard the *U.S.S. Bozeman*. The Department had a way of attracting strays. Alisov had been the *Bozeman*'s chief engineer, and had risen through the ranks on the types of starship she was describing.

"There's more," Peterson said, her voice hushed. "I ran a comparison on that warp signature. It matches one we have in our records."

"Well?" Alisov prompted when Peterson was slow to continue.

Heather swallowed. "The warp signature matches the configuration of the warp propulsion units used in the late twenty-two sixties by the *U.S.S. Enterprise* . . . NCC-one-seven-oh-one."

Garcia gaped at Ranjea, who looked uncharacteristically shocked himself. Teresa remembered the DTI joke that all temporal investigations eventually led to the *Enterprise*. It was an exaggeration, and was meant to apply to all starships of that name, which tended to have a disproportionate involvement with temporal phenomena. But it mostly applied to the Federation's first *Enterprise*, NCC-1701, whose captain—James Tiberius Kirk—was infamous in the DTI for having seventeen separate temporal violations attached to his name, a record unrivaled by any other individual in the DTI's files.

"But this doesn't make sense," Garcia said. Her training was recent enough that the lectures on Kirk's infamous ship were still fresh in her memory. "The *Enterprise* was never turned into . . . into this. It was refitted into a new configuration and served a dozen more years before Kirk scuttled it in the Mutara Sector."

"That's . . . not the only thing that doesn't make sense," Ranjea told her. "Look."

The ship's tumbling had brought its hull markings into view. Garcia read them, but couldn't process them. Couldn't believe them.

Timeship Two
FDTIX-02
United Federation of Planets

"'FDTI'?" Alisov echoed. "Federation . . ."

Ranjea nodded. There was only one thing those letters had ever stood for in Federation usage. "Department of Temporal Investigations."

DTI Headquarters
Greenwich, European Alliance, Earth
Stardate 60144.5
February 2383

"A DTI timeship?" Marion Dulmur asked, struggling to wrap his mind around the concept.

"Impossible," came the blunt reply from his partner, Gariff Lucsly. "It must be from a parallel history." Lucsly's gaze reflexively darted to the master timeline display that filled one of the DTI situation room's long walls, a holographic plot of known or suspected parallel timelines, their divergence and convergence points, their causal interconnections, and other relevant data. It was a sprawling chart, growing larger by the year, yet still frustratingly incomplete as a tool for predicting where or when the next temporal threat would come from.

"That was the first thing we tested for," Ranjea told his fellow agents over the subspace link from the

Everett. Ranjea was a good man, an accomplished investigator, and Garcia was shaping up well as his partner (Dulmur thought with avuncular pride), but they had both recognized that a find of this magnitude warranted calling in the big guns. *"The vessel's quantum signature is a precise match for our own timeline, correcting for the elapsed interval. Quantum dating puts the origin of its newest components circa 2275 Common Era."*

"You must have done it wrong."

"Lucsly," Dulmur said quietly. The blond, gruff-featured agent met Lucsly's eyes and shook his head fractionally. "We all know our jobs, partner. This ship is from our own past. And it's connected to Kirk."

"Kirk." Dulmur could practically see his taller, gray-haired partner's hackles rise when he said the name. Gariff Lucsly was a latter-day Phileas Fogg, a man who lived for order and precision. The purity of the timestream was practically his religion. And James T. Kirk, a Starfleet captain who'd gallivanted through time with more frequency than any captain before or since, was his devil. "Somehow he's behind this," Lucsly grated through clenched teeth.

"But how?" Teresa Garcia asked. *"How can a DTI ship have the* Enterprise*'s warp signature when we know the* Enterprise *stayed in Starfleet service until 2285?"*

"The *Enterprise* did," Lucsly replied, "but its warp engines didn't. The refit of 2272 to '73 replaced or upgraded everything but portions of the superstructure. Entirely new, state-of-the-art warp engines were installed."

"So what happened to the old engines?" Dulmur finished, seeing where his longtime partner was going

with this. "You know, given all the temporal displace-
ments that ship was involved with, you'd think the DTI
would've wanted to study them. Hell, the DTI *exists*
because of that ship."

"Because of its captain," Lucsly corrected. "Still,
you're right. There should be records about the fate of
those engines. I remember reading something in the
archives, long ago. But it's been decades." If Lucsly
couldn't pin it down to the day and hour, his recollec-
tion must have been vague indeed.

"Then maybe," Dulmur said, "we should ask someone who was there."

"I can't give you the answers," Director Laarin Andos
told Lucsly and Dulmur as they sat in front of her
desk. "Yes, I was present at the Department's beginnings, but only in a peripheral role. I was still an
adolescent at the time!" Of course, Dulmur knew,
Rhaandarites entered puberty at around a hundred
and thirty. The two-and-a-half-meter DTI director
was twice that now, in her healthy middle age, with
no gray showing yet in the pale hair that adorned her
bulbous-browed skull.

"Still, I heard rumors," Andos went on. "Or implications. Things people said or didn't say, or the way
they said them, that suggested a deeper story I wasn't
being told." Dulmur and his partner knew to take this
very seriously. Rhaandarites' gifts for processing social
dynamics made them experts at reading between the
lines. "Something to do with the *Enterprise*'s engines
and some kind of temporal experimentation."

Lucsly shook his silvery head. "No. Director Grey would never have authorized experimentation."

"Meijan Grey was not the only voice of authority in those early days," Andos told him. "The Department didn't spring to life fully-formed, with Starfleet readily heeding our counsel as they do now." Dulmur laughed at her sarcastic remark. Lucsly, being Lucsly, did not. But her point had been made.

"Is there any sign of activity from this timeship?" the director went on.

"No, ma'am," Dulmur said. "It's adrift. The subspace confluence seems stable."

"Then we have time to examine the records. I'm granting you full clearance to whatever classified DTI and Federation Science Council records from the period you believe may be relevant to your investigation. I'll request the equivalent clearance from Starfleet Command. And I'll tell you what I can remember about those early days."

"If it wasn't Grey," Lucsly said, "we should track down who in Starfleet would've headed up the investigation of the *Enterprise*'s temporal incidents. We know Starfleet undertook some reckless experiments with time in those early days. This must have been one of them."

"Then how did the ship end up with civilian markings?" Dulmur asked. "Department markings?"

"Don't get ahead of the process, Dulmur," Andos said. "To reconstruct the truth, we need to follow the chain of events from their beginning."

"And their beginning, as always," Lucsly said, "was James Tiberius Kirk."

I

"I think you're wasting your time here, Antonio," said Commodore Burton Kwan. "This story Kirk and his crew are spinning is just too ludicrous."

Commodore Antonio Delgado stroked his short, grizzled beard as he considered his colleague's words. "Did you verify it in the ship's computer logs?" he asked the younger man.

"Well, yes, but . . . the computer . . ."

"Yes?"

"It kept calling us 'dear.' If you ask me, the whole thing's an elaborate practical joke."

"Well, how else do you explain the *Enterprise* suddenly appearing in the Oort cloud, braking hard from high warp, just hours after disappearing without a trace from Sector 006? We've confirmed the presence of that 'black star' Kirk advised us of—it appears to be some new class of singularity. And we have found a passing reference in records from the period to an 'unidentified flying object' sighting by a Captain John Christopher, United States Air Force."

"So you're saying this is possible?"

Delgado hesitated. "I'm not saying anything on the record. And neither are you, is that clear?"

Kwan scoffed. "I'm happy to be left out of it. And even if I weren't, I know better than to cross someone who plays golf with Admiral Comsol himself." He came to a halt outside the door to Briefing Room 14. "They're in here, waiting for you. I leave them and their mess, whatever it turns out to be, in your capable hands."

Delgado shook his balding head as the younger commodore strode away. Kwan was the same kind of small-minded bureaucrat as the ones who'd dismissed the *Enterprise*'s first report of time travel earlier this year—an alleged seventy-one-hour backward jump resulting from a cold restart of the vessel's warp engines to escape the breakup of planet Psi 2000—as a mere time dilation anomaly. If Kirk's claim had been taken seriously sooner, valuable time might have been saved.

Delgado chuckled to himself. *Then again, if this pans out, I may have all the time in the universe.*

He entered the briefing room, and Captain Kirk and his first officer, the renowned half-Vulcan Commander Spock, rose to greet him. "Captain Kirk," he said, shaking the younger man's hand. "I'm Commodore Antonio Delgado, deputy chief of Starfleet Science Operations. Commander Spock," he appended, merely nodding at the Vulcan, who returned the greeting in kind. Despite his executive position, Spock wore the blue tunic of the science division rather than the command gold worn by Kirk and Delgado, reminding the commodore that he served as Kirk's chief science officer as well—a doubling of responsibility that would be difficult for anyone but a Vulcan to pull off. Delgado may have been second-in-command of Science Ops himself, but his role was chiefly administrative.

"Pleased to meet you, sir," Kirk said, though his impatience was clear. "If I may, I'd like to ask—"

Delgado held up a hand. "I know you're eager to get back to your ship. We've put you through enough of a runaround already, and I'm sorry to add to it. But I can tell you that this time, you will be listened to, and you will be believed."

Kirk's eyes widened, his stance easing. "I'm . . . glad to hear that. I appreciate that it's an extraordinary thing to ask someone to accept, but we've offered you the data from our ship's computers, and Mister Spock's sworn testimony as well as that of the rest of my crew." Kirk's tone conveyed particular disbelief and offense at having the Vulcan's account called into question. Delgado respected that level of loyalty and trust. It had been rare enough in his own experience. Political loyalty was something he knew how to bargain and barter for, but he knew it came and went as expediency demanded. Personal loyalty, the sort he sensed here, was far more elusive.

"Well, you understand we needed time to verify the corroborating evidence. It's essential to be absolutely sure of something like this."

"Naturally," Spock replied, his voice a rich baritone. "Extraordinary claims require extraordinary evidence."

"So with that in mind, I hope you won't mind going over your account one more time for me."

Kirk suppressed a sigh. "Of course, sir."

The three men sat around the polygonal briefing table and Kirk began. "As I said in my log, the *Enterprise* was en route to Starbase 9 for resupply when we were caught in an intense gravitational pull from an uncharted black star. Like a black hole, but different somehow."

"As though its gravitomagnetic effects extended into subspace," Spock added. "Even at warp, all subspace geodesics tended to spiral in toward the singularity. Only by employing maximum warp power were we able to reverse course and break free."

"We hurtled out of control," Kirk went on. "Most of us blacked out from the acceleration. When we recovered, we found ourselves inside Earth's atmosphere. We were lucky we didn't crash into the surface. Attempts to contact Starfleet Control failed, but my communications officer picked up a broadcast on an old EM band, announcing that the first manned moon shot would launch the following Wednesday."

"And from that," Delgado asked, "you concluded that you were in 1969?"

"Not from that alone, sir," Spock told him. "It only reinforced the conclusion I had already drawn from reviewing the sensor logs. Our trajectory on breaking free of the singularity was consistent with the theoretical predictions for a closed timelike curve around a Tipler object, which the dense, rotating mass of the singularity might well approximate. My scans of Earth and the Sol system revealed no traces of antimatter use or transtator-based technology, no orbital facilities or habitations beyond Earth, and no verifiable indications of extraterrestrial life on Earth itself. The configuration of the stars and planets established a date of July 12, nineteen hundred and sixty-nine Common Era in the Gregorian calendar—four days before the launch of *Apollo 11*."

"We then detected the approach of a military aircraft of the period," Kirk continued. "We attempted to retreat to avoid detection, but our systems were damaged, sluggish. The aircraft was armed with missiles, and from what I recalled of the tense political climate of the period, I knew we were in danger of being preemptively fired upon. I ordered the tractor beam activated to hold the aircraft at a safe distance."

"Were you aware that the aircraft might be damaged by the tractor beam?"

"To be honest, no, sir, it didn't occur to me," Kirk said. "Since the aircraft was small enough to fit entirely within the beam, I assumed it would simply feel a uniform attraction, no shear or strain."

"In the captain's defense, sir," Spock pointed out, "few people today are accustomed to dealing with non–antigravity-based aircraft."

"But you recognized the danger, Commander."

"Yes, Commodore. Considering the relationship of gravity, thrust, and lift in the operation of a fixed-wing aircraft, I realized that altering the effective gravity vector with our tractor beam would throw off the balance and cause the aircraft to tumble out of control. I promptly alerted the captain to the risk, but at that point the tractor beam had already been engaged, and the aircraft quickly began to break up."

Delgado turned back to Kirk. "So you felt you had no choice but to beam the pilot aboard."

"Captain John Christopher, yes. He was only in danger because of my mistake, sir," the captain told him. "I couldn't let him die."

"So instead you thought it was a good idea to give him a guided tour of a starship from centuries in his future. Thereby exposing him to knowledge far beyond what his society was ready for."

"Naturally I considered beaming him back immediately, before he knew what had happened. But if he arrived intact on the ground before his aircraft even crashed, I knew that would raise a great many questions."

"Did you consider sedating Captain Christopher until he could be returned to the crash site? Perhaps with some minor injuries consistent with ejecting from a crash?"

Kirk frowned. "With all due respect, Commodore, he was a human. A military pilot from the same country that first put humans on the Earth's moon. He was a spiritual ancestor, perhaps even a literal ancestor for all I knew. I'd wronged him enough tearing his ship out from under him. I wasn't going to knock him out and give him a beating as well." He took a breath, gathering himself. "I felt I owed him an explanation. And owed it to myself to assess what kind of man he was before deciding on his disposition."

"And the temptation to meet a 'spiritual ancestor' wasn't a factor?"

The captain gave a wry smile. "Would you have felt any differently, sir?"

Delgado's expression softened marginally. "Probably not, Captain."

As Kirk's account continued, it became more and more a comedy of errors. Every attempt he and his crew made to resolve the situation only made things worse, leading to the point at which a second individual from 1969 had been accidentally beamed aboard, Kirk had been captured and interrogated by the United States Air Force, and several USAF personnel had been attacked and rendered unconscious in order to rescue the captain. The only solution had been a total reboot. Spock had computed that the original "slingshot" effect could be re-created using the Sun's gravitational field, with the *Enterprise*'s warp engines configured to amplify the Sun's relatively feeble frame-dragging effects and re-create the closed timelike curve. In the process, they would regress further back in time before moving forward again on the escape trajectory. This would overlap Christopher and the sergeant with their own past worldlines, and Spock had had the inspired insight that beaming them into their own past bodies, superposing the same particles in two different quantum states, would cause those states to recollapse into a single individual apiece, with the quantum information incompatible with their reality—the experiences the two men had had aboard the *Enterprise*—erased from their memories.

"I'll be honest with you, Captain," Delgado said when the account concluded. "You bungled this situation in almost every possible way. Without Commander Spock's creative problem-solving, the consequences could've been disastrous." Kirk bristled and began to speak. "However," Delgado stressed, cutting him off, "I can't see that any other Starfleet officer in the same situation would've reacted any differently. I can't realistically expect you or any starship commander to be prepared for dealing with a time-travel scenario."

"It is an unprecedented occurrence," Spock agreed.

Delgado smiled. "Well . . . almost."

Kirk and his first officer stared. "Are you saying people have traveled in time before?" the captain asked.

"There are no records," Spock observed, "of any such occurrence prior to the *Enterprise*'s own experience at Psi 2000."

"You're right up to a point, Commander. The *Enterprise*—your *Enterprise*—is the first known Federation starship ever to travel through time under its own power. But—and this is classified information I'm about to give you—Starfleet has had evidence that time travel was a reality since the time of your ship's namesake over a century ago."

"Jonathan Archer's *Enterprise*?" Kirk asked.

"Yes. Archer became aware of the existence of individuals or groups from future centuries that were attempting to intervene in events of his own era through native agents and intermediaries, including Archer himself. A Temporal Cold War, they called it." Once he'd given Kirk and Spock a moment to take this in, he went on, "These interventions seemed to end around the time of the Earth-Romulan War. There's been virtually no evidence of visits from the future since the Federation was founded. But given the potential dangers of time travel, Starfleet Command of the time classified the knowledge that it existed as more than a theoretical construct, lest someone figure out a way to invent time machines of their own. There have been occasional isolated encounters with temporal phenomena in the century since, but nothing repeatable or controllable." He recalled all the case studies from Starfleet Intelligence files. A starship flung two years into its future by a natural warp that collapsed around them, almost crushing them and leaving them no way back. A Tellarite ship discovering ruins of what appeared to be a time portal on a remote planet, long ago smashed by a raiding party that came through it from the past. A civilian trader who'd gotten rich off future knowledge she claimed to have gained from an alien artifact, but who'd failed to predict her own death and the artifact's destruction in a firefight between Orion and Klingon agents seeking to possess it. "Starfleet buried the stories, and where evidence existed, it buried that too."

Kirk studied Delgado. "You don't seem to approve, Commodore."

"I think they were shortsighted fools. Imagine what we could learn about our history, our future. Imagine the potential for preventing or correcting great disasters. Captain, I've devoted much of my career to exploring the possibilities of time travel. That's why I left Starfleet Intelligence for Science Ops, so I could actually research the possibilities rather than just sitting on the knowledge that they existed.

"And now you've brought me the answer to my prayers, gentlemen. A starship that's actually traveled in time, on two separate occasions. And a science officer who's actually managed to achieve time travel on purpose."

"I hesitate to go that far, Commodore," Spock demurred. "Theory suggests that a temporal displacement creates a connection, known as a Feynman curve, between the displaced object and its origin point in spacetime. All I did, essentially, was determine how to follow that curve in reverse. Had it not been formed already by the initial accident, I would have had no way of creating it. There is still a great deal I do not understand about how the slingshot effect came about in the first place. The theoretical basis is a simple matter of general relativity, but by all rights, the unbounded accumulation of Hawking radiation at the horizon of the temporal warp should have vaporized the *Enterprise* before it could travel back in time."

"But the fact is, your ship has done it—three distinct times. Whatever made it work, it's repeatable."

Kirk furrowed his brow. "Commodore, if you're saying you want to take my ship apart for study, I must protest. We're in the middle of an active patrol tour. There are colonies out there that need our protection and support. Especially now, with tensions rising on the Klingon border. The *Enterprise* is needed on the frontier."

Delgado held up his hands. "Don't worry, Captain. I understand your obligations. But you'll need at least two weeks in port to repair the buckling your warp nacelles sustained in your return to the present."

"Three," Spock amended. "We also require a wholesale overhaul of our computer system to correct the . . . anomalous behavior resulting from its servicing at Cygnet XIV," he finished with a sour expression. Delgado remembered what Kwan had said about the computer's affectionate attitude, and suppressed a chuckle. It wasn't the first practical joke the Cygnetians had played on Starfleet, whose power structure they found insufficiently matriarchal.

"That would take three weeks at a *typical* starbase repair facility," Delgado countered. "But Earth Centroplex has the finest technicians in the Federation. If I authorize the resources and personnel, and order the *Enterprise* moved to the top of the priority list, you'll have her back to fighting trim within two weeks at most. And believe me, I can get that authorization with a single communication." There was no disbelief in Kirk's eyes; he knew how well-connected Delgado was. "All I ask in exchange is that you allow me and my team to study your ship and its engines and work with your science and engineering teams to learn what we can about how your journey through time was achieved. All right?"

Kirk looked reassured, even pleased. "When you put it that way, how can I refuse?" He smiled. "I have to admit . . . it was a thrill actually standing on Earth at the dawn of the Space Age, the time of the pioneers. What I wouldn't have given to meet Armstrong, Glenn, Leonov, Tereshkova."

"I envy you the experience, Captain Kirk. If we can reconstruct what the *Enterprise* achieved twice by sheer accident, it could open the door to a whole new kind of exploration."

Kirk's eyes turned outward in a thousand-year stare. "Just imagine the possibilities. . . ."

Starbase 12
Gamma 400 System
Stardate 3135.6
April 2267

When Antonio Delgado next met James Kirk, he found the captain a very different man. The commodore had rushed to Starbase 12 to debrief the crew as soon as Starfleet Command had received the log transmissions detailing the *Enterprise*'s great discovery. But rather than sharing Delgado's excitement at the find, the captain was subdued, closed off, leaving his first officer to do most of the talking. "Tell me what happened," Delgado said to the Vulcan.

Spock steepled his fingers before him. "Using the new chronometric sensor protocols developed in cooperation with your research teams, Commodore, we began to detect a series of temporal distortions propagating through space like ripples on a pond." Delgado nodded. The new protocols for detecting temporal anomalies had been the first payoff from studying the sensor readings taken during the *Enterprise*'s journeys through time. Delgado was thrilled to get positive results so soon. "Over the ensuing six days, we plotted multiple such ripples and were able to triangulate their source, a planet in an ancient, uninhabited red dwarf system. Our intention was to beam down a landing party to investigate the origin point on the planet's surface, once we had finished charting the distortion fields so the ship could navigate them safely. At that close range, the spatial distortions were quite pronounced and hazardous." Spock narrowed his lips. "However, our chief medical officer, Leonard McCoy, sustained an accidental cordrazine overdose as a result of the turbulence, causing paranoid delusions which compelled him to flee the ship via the transporter, which we had already locked onto the nexus of the time distortions.

"Pursuing the doctor, we discovered that the distortions originated from what appeared to be a simple megalith—a stone construct in the form of an irregular, upright toroid whose central opening was large enough to admit the passage of several humanoids. It seemed to pulse with energy, but I was unable to determine a source or method of generation.

"However, when the captain mused aloud as to its nature, the megalith . . . responded."

"Responded?"

"Yes, Commodore. It spoke in English, identifying itself as the Guardian of Forever. Though it was . . . evasive . . . as to its nature and origins, it became evident that it was in fact a portal to other times. It seemed eager to be used as such. Of its own volition, it offered us an accelerated display of Earth's history within its central orifice."

Delgado leaned forward. "But it was more than just images."

"Correct. It was an actual bridge through time, as we soon discovered to our peril. Doctor McCoy, still deranged from the cordrazine, leaped through the time vortex, and in so doing, evidently altered the entire history of the Federation."

"What do you mean?" the commodore asked, frowning.

Kirk spoke up at last, his voice taut. "The ship vanished. Between one eyeblink and the next, it was gone. According to the Guardian, our entire history was gone. Wiped out by McCoy's actions in the past."

"So why were you still there?"

Spock took a breath. "I can only surmise, sir, that the temporal effects emanating from the Guardian insulated it and its immediate surroundings from the transformation. In any case, this afforded us an option for repairing the damage. I had belatedly remembered to begin recording the Guardian's display on my tricorder shortly before McCoy jumped through. This enabled me to compute his approximate time of arrival in Earth's past. The Guardian claimed to be unable to alter the speed at which it displayed the past, but by asking it to restart and jumping at the correct moment, the captain and I were able to arrive shortly before Doctor McCoy."

Spock went on to explain how, by comparing the two sets of tricorder readings from the Guardian's displays before and after the historical alteration, he had discovered the nexus point that McCoy had altered, a social worker named Edith Keeler who, had she not died in a traffic accident in 1930, would have started a pacifist movement delaying America's entry into World War II and allowing Nazi Germany to perfect the atomic bomb and conquer the world. "At the crucial moment," Spock finished, "we were able to locate

Doctor McCoy and . . . negate his interference. With history restored to its proper path, the Guardian automatically returned us to our own time."

Delgado studied Spock. His account seemed uncharacteristically lacking in detail when it came to this Edith Keeler. "What specifically did you do to restore history? You said Keeler was supposed to die in an accident. Did you . . ."

"The details are of little relevance, Commodore. Suffice it to say—"

"I held him back," Kirk said.

Delgado turned to him. "Excuse me?"

"Bones—McCoy—he tried to save her. I had . . . I had to stop him. I held him back." He went on, haunted but deliberate. "I held him there on the sidewalk while he watched Edith Keeler die in front of him. I *let* her die."

The briefing room was silent for some time. "Captain . . . Jim," Delgado finally said, "I can't imagine how hard that must have been."

"No," Kirk replied. "No, sir, you can't imagine."

The commodore cleared his throat. "Still, it was clearly necessary. You . . . we all owe you a great debt."

"Then you can repay it," Kirk said, "by declaring that planet off-limits. Making sure nobody ever steps through that damn thing again."

Delgado was stunned. "Captain, think about what you're saying. Remember what we've discussed before. The possibilities for exploration, for discovery. Just the data in Spock's tricorder is going to improve our knowledge of Earth history immensely."

"And what about the possibilities for disaster, Commodore? A single well-intentioned gesture at the wrong moment, and billions of lives are wiped out. But how can you ask any decent person to go back and watch passively while good people die? No one should have to live through that."

Delgado sensed that there was something deeper beneath Kirk's words, that he'd gotten to know Edith Keeler rather more closely than Spock's account had indicated. He was tempted to pry, but decided it was none of his business. Whatever Kirk had felt, he had still placed his duty first and done what he needed to do. Delgado could respect that, and sympathize with the pain that came with it.

But that was exactly why he couldn't let the possibilities here go unexplored. What about the regrets and failures that *could* be undone? The suffering that could be prevented? Not his own, no; he accepted that it was too late for that, that he was too much a creature of duty and politics and would only make the same mistakes if he could go back and try to keep Elisa from leaving him, their daughter from hating him. But if he could master the power of time travel to help others undo their own failures and losses, maybe that would let him atone in some way for his own.

"Rest assured, Captain Kirk," said Delgado, not without kindness, "your recent experiences have underlined the importance of not rushing in where this Guardian of Forever is concerned. But ultimately it's Starfleet's call, not yours, what happens next. And in order to decide whether or not to use the Guardian, we must first study the Guardian. You say it's talkative, cooperative, even eager. Well, that means we can learn a great deal even without stepping through it."

"Perhaps not, sir," Spock said. "Its assertions about its nature are Delphic, couched in cryptic verbiage and needless poetry. It claims that its nature is beyond human or even Vulcan ability to comprehend." Had Spock not been Vulcan, Delgado would have said he was insulted.

"Still, the attempt must be made. Jim, I'd prefer it if you and your crew were involved, so we can maintain the circle of security."

"No," came Kirk's blunt reply. "Sir. I gave you the same answer last time. My ship is needed out there."

"The Klingon threat has subsided. The peace treaty is being finalized as we speak."

"There are always other threats, Commodore. The Romulans, the Tholians. We're still not sure where we stand with the Gorn."

"Yes, but—"

"Bottom line, Commodore, we're space travelers, not time travelers. I . . . respectfully request that you find someone else to study the Guardian. I want nothing more to do with it."

Delgado sighed. He was tempted to remind Kirk that he could make the captain's career very difficult if he so chose. But he didn't want to go that route. He still hoped to win Kirk as an ally. And he could be patient. "Very well, Captain. Commander Spock?"

"I am needed aboard the *Enterprise*, sir."

"Of course." He was unsurprised by Spock's ready

loyalty, given how carefully he'd protected his captain's feelings in his account of their sojourn in the past. One rarely saw that kind of empathy from a Vulcan, save toward those they considered family. Delgado was pleased, and a bit envious, to see that Kirk had at least one relationship he could rely on. "Still, I trust you'll compile a detailed report of all your findings and theories on the Guardian for the use of my research team."

"Naturally." Spock handed him a data card. "I anticipated your request, sir."

Delgado chuckled. "I admire your efficiency, Mister Spock. Your captain is lucky to have you."

"There was no random chance involved, sir. It was Captain Kirk's own choice to appoint me his first officer."

"Then he chose well." He wished he could prolong this conversation, but out of deference to Kirk, he said, "Thank you, gentlemen. Dismissed."

Once they'd left, he twirled the data card between his fingers, studying it. *The secret to mastering time could be right here. And I owe it all to those men.* Delgado couldn't believe it was the last time he would work with them on this project. Kirk's recent experiences may have made him reluctant to continue exploring the timestream, but Delgado hoped he would come around. That this single ship had made three such world-shaking temporal discoveries in the course of a single year . . . and the namesake of Archer's ship, no less. . . . Well, he wasn't one to believe in omens. The progression of the *Enterprise*'s discoveries made logical sense. According to his science team, whatever had happened to the ship's engines at Psi 2000 had probably enabled it to survive the Tipler slingshot at the Black Star; and it had been the data gathered in those two events that had led Spock to discover the Guardian. It would be foolish to read this chain of events as evidence of destiny.

But who knew? Time worked in mysterious ways. One of his lead researchers, Doctor T'Viss, insisted that the forward progression of time was an illusion arising from the lack of sufficient data to compute the entire wavefunction of the universe. And quantum theory had long proposed the idea of advanced waves, patterns of energy and probability propagating back from the future—usually canceled out by the retarded waves moving forward, but maybe, just occasionally, surviving and acting to determine their own past. So Delgado couldn't completely rule out the possibility that this string of discoveries was building toward something. Something quite extraordinary.

If that was so, Delgado knew, he would let nothing stop him from doing his part to bring it about.

II

U.S.S. Enterprise NCC-1701
Stardate 4742.9
April 2268

"Oh, no," Montgomery Scott declared to Commodore Delgado, stepping between him and the expanse of main engineering beyond as if to shield it with his body. "All due respect, Commodore, but you won't be subjecting my *Enterprise* to another o' those infernal slingshots. She barely survived the first two!" Beside him, Captain Kirk shifted his weight subtly as if tempted to join him in the symbolic blockade, a gesture Scott appreciated. Spock just stood calmly where he was, hands folded behind him, but that was Spock's way.

"But she *did* survive," Delgado replied, "and that's the point. All our unmanned probes have failed spectacularly, vaporized at the Cauchy horizon. Anything that is going back in time is doing so as random particles spread out across decades. We just can't figure how to counteract the runaway energy feedback."

The prim Vulcan civilian beside Delgado sniffed in evident annoyance. "The problem is not intractable," Doctor T'Viss said in disapproving tones. Though she was fairly young for a Vulcan—maybe mid-sixties, corresponding to thirties for a human—her manner reminded Scotty of a certain spinsterish schoolmatron whose disapproval he'd often incurred during his misspent youth in Aberdeen. Some people, he reflected, were just born old. "In theory, the divergent stress-energy tensor is little different from that found in the Cochrane warp equations, and should be manageable through the proper application of tetryon, verteron, or similar exotic-particle fields."

"Should be, but isn't, not yet," Delgado added. "Something is still missing, something our theorists can't crack, but that the *Enterprise* crew has already stumbled upon by pure chance." Beneath her Vulcan reserve, T'Viss seemed to take personal affront on behalf of the theoretical physics community. Scott had little sympathy; theory was all just abstract math until you put it into practice.

The commodore reached out and placed a hand on the master systems display on the wall of the engine room foyer where they stood, studying its shifting status lights. "So if we're to continue our experiments, they have to be with the *Enterprise*," he went on. "We need to observe its engines and systems in operation during a time jump, find out what's enabling them to survive the horizon passage. Is it some special modification you've made, perhaps some permanent change resulting from your cold restart at Psi 2000?"

"It could be anything," Scott told him. "A ship in the field is constantly bein' modified on the fly. We jury-rig repairs when we take damage. We learn the systems as we go, rig workarounds for the bottlenecks and inefficiencies. We stop at friendly alien ports for repairs or replacements. Aye, the cold restart could've been part of it. We had to reconfigure the magnetic constrictors to force a controlled implosion and align the plasma injectors just right to hold a manual phase lock without dilithium regulation. I've kept those modifications in place 'cause they boost our speed and efficiency. We now have the fastest warp drive in the Federation," he boasted. "But it could just as well be some property of the replacement plasma injectors that Balok fellow gave us after he forced us to burn out the old ones, or the articulation frame upgrades we made at Rigel XII, who knows?"

"Who knows, indeed, Mister Scott?" Delgado asked, moving out of the foyer into the main engineering chamber beyond. "Which is exactly why we need to find out."

"Do we?" Kirk asked as he and the others followed the commodore. "Need to? Haven't we established the great risks involved in time travel?"

"In fact, we have not," T'Viss interposed.

Kirk stared, halting next to the large, blocky reactor cap assembly in the center of the deck, the tip of the iceberg of the vast dilithium reactor that lay beneath them. "With all due respect, Doctor, I've seen it myself. Seen history changed, the past we knew wiped out."

"So it may have appeared to you. But your interpretation requires a physical impossibility. Any event that occurs is part of the wave equation of the universe. It cannot cease to have occurred. Any two alternative versions of a single segment of time are merely distinct quantum states of the universe in a coherent superposition. One does not replace the other; they coexist. What you perceived as the transformation of a single measurement history—'timeline,' if you prefer—must in fact have been your own displacement from one to the other. In both cases, you were within the influence of the temporal displacement mechanism at the time of the perceived transformations, whether your own vessel or the so-called Guardian of Forever. In fact, the mechanisms simply transposed you between two coexisting histories."

"You sound awfully certain of that," Kirk said, not as a compliment.

"It is the only logical interpretation of the evidence. You yourselves have observed direct evidence of the coexistence of simultaneous timelines—your encounter with a parallel version of Earth on stardate 2713 and your accidental exchange with your counterparts in an alternate quantum history on stardate 3639." Scott vividly remembered the latter incident late last year, when he, Kirk, Doctor McCoy, and Lieutenant Uhura had been switched with malevolent versions of themselves in a hellishly distorted version of the world they knew, where the *Enterprise* was a battleship in service to a warlike Terran Empire.

He had been less involved in the earlier incident, the discovery of an exact duplicate of Earth in a slightly off-kilter orbit around a star a few percent cooler than Sol. According to the landing party, which Kirk and Spock had led while Scott had remained aboard ship, it had even duplicated Earth's history up to a point three centuries back, when an experiment in life prolongation

had gone horribly wrong and released a plague that
killed off all the world's adults, leaving only children
who aged a month for every century and called themselves the Onlies. The landing party had been infected
by the same plague and stranded on the surface until
McCoy and Spock had devised an antidote. During
that time, the *Enterprise*'s science teams had surveyed
the planet from orbit, trying to determine how it had
come to exist. Sensors had revealed subspace anomalies
in the planet's vicinity, as if some other spacetime continuum had been overlapping their own. The planet, it
seemed, really was Earth, but an Earth from an alternate timeline, somehow transposed into this one. Federation science teams had been studying the planet ever
since—and evacuating those few hundred Onlies who
remained alive in scattered pockets across the planet
after centuries of feral living, starvation, gang warfare,
and disease had culled their numbers, not to mention
the climatological upheavals that had resulted from
the duplicate Earth's new, eccentric orbit and lack of a
moon. After all, there was no guarantee that the overlap
between realities was permanent.

Scott moved to the control stations along the starboard wall and clutched the ladder rail between them,
needing to feel the comforting solidity of his domain.
The idea of realities coming and going, of the history he knew being just one quantum variation out of
many . . . it was all a bit much. Give him simple engineering problems, where any equation had a single,
definite answer, any day of the week.

"It is true, Doctor," Spock was telling T'Viss, "that

parallel histories are a verified phenomenon. But there is nothing in the Everett-Wheeler equations that would preclude two coexisting timelines, once diverged, from reconverging once again, with one history erasing the other in the process."

"There is in thermodynamics, Commander Spock. Such a reconvergence would require decreasing the entropy of the entire system, a clear violation of physical law."

Spock nodded. "Granted. It would be astronomically unlikely. But not absolutely impossible. The overlap of the Onlies' Earth with our own reality demonstrates that some degree of convergence can occur."

"Confluence, perhaps, but not replacement. Both Earths still exist, and at a considerable physical remove."

"Theory is all well and good, gentlemen; Doctor," Kirk said. "But if theory were always right, we wouldn't need experiments to test it. No matter how you rationalize it, we'd be taking an enormous risk."

"Risk that can be managed, Captain," Delgado told him. "Rest assured, you won't be going back to intervene in historical events, merely to test the physics and engineering of the time jump itself." He led them up the ladder to the upper gangway, his excitement compelling him to stay in motion. The others had no choice but to follow.

"But you are asking us to conduct historical research," Kirk went on as they passed through the aft door to the maintenance gangway alongside the massive warp plasma conduits that ran up through the nacelle pylons, the same conduits visible through the large observation grille on the aft wall of the engine room. Scott took comfort from their warmth and deep, pulsing vibration, the heartbeat of the *Enterprise*.

"Yes, as long as you're there. Once you arrive in the past, you'll no doubt need a few days to assess the slingshot readings and perform any necessary repairs." Scott grimaced at the commodore's casual willingness to subject his bairns to damage. "So there's no reason not to use the opportunity to conduct some historical research. But only from orbit, I assure you."

"It sounds," Spock said, "as though you have already chosen the target destination."

"Yes," the commodore said. "To keep the variables consistent, we intend to re-create the Black Star slingshot and send you back to approximately the same place and time as before, Earth in the nineteen-sixties. Your deflectors can be adjusted to block radar scans, and a wide orbit with running lights doused should minimize the risk of visual observation. You won't be expected to interact or interfere with Earth history in any way," he went on as they reached the ladder at the end of the gangway and began to descend, "only take sensor readings and monitor transmissions."

The ladder took them down two levels to the main energizer monitor section, containing the secondary dilithium circuits that channeled warp power into ship systems. "A logical proposal," Spock said as he reached the bottom, high praise coming from him. "Captain, this would be a marvelous opportunity. The late nineteen-sixties were a particularly turbulent time in Earth's history, a time when the escalation of the nuclear arms race teetered on the edge of a catastrophic runaway. Historians are still baffled by how humanity managed to survive the decade."

"Vulcan historians, maybe," Scott replied as the group moved portward past the multiple banks of control computers, the nerve center for the *Enterprise*'s intricate systems. "We humans may be a hotheaded bunch, but I dinna believe we'd ever have chosen to blow ourselves up."

"Perhaps not, Mister Scott, but it was more than a matter of conscious decision. With so many weapons in play, so many forces both physical and sociological held so barely in check, the probability of a catastrophic accident sufficient to spark global war approached certainty. And there have always been those few who were sufficiently malicious or deranged to be willing to trigger the cataclysm intentionally. Whatever factor served to prevent such trigger events remains unknown." Spock turned back to Kirk. "Captain, direct observation of the era could reveal vital new insights into human history."

Kirk pondered his words as they reached the heavy, dome-shaped hatch to the engineering core below. "Your arguments are compelling, Mister Spock."

"I'm glad you feel that way, Captain," Delgado said. "Mister Scott, if you would?" He gestured at the hatch.

Scott suppressed a grumble as he nodded to Crewman Watkins to activate the hatch controls. *Self-absorbed Starfleet brass, expecting us to stop everything for a grand tour when there's work to be done. My engines aren't a bloody museum!* True, as long as the ship stayed in orbit around Starbase 9, the warp reactor was running at low power, so things were quiet enough that the tour would cause minimal disruption. But it was a matter of principle.

The group climbed down into the anteroom below, then moved onto the gangway above the long, horizontal cylinder of the warp reactor's intermix chamber. As they moved forward, the reactor gave a deep, seismic rumble beneath them, echoing loudly in the vaulted chamber even at its current low level of activity. The heavy conduits that rose on either side pulsed with light as warp plasma surged through them, heading toward the warp coils in the nacelles. The core was an awe-inspiring place, Scotty thought. He felt a momentary surge of regret that his work brought him here so rarely. When he needed to perform direct maintenance on the warp reactor, he generally used the maintenance crawlways alongside it. They were hot and cramped, and lacked this impressive view, but they allowed better access for his work, and that was what really mattered.

Kirk was still mulling over the commodore's proposal. "But weren't the Vulcans already observing Earth clandestinely around that time?" he asked Spock, raising his voice over the engine thrum. "Don't we run the risk of encountering them?"

"There were intermittent surveys, Captain, but none in that decade. Assuming we arrive on target—"

"That's a big assumption, Spock."

"I am confident that Mister Scott and I can successfully re-create the necessary conditions. Recall that on our return from 1969, we were able to calculate our target dates with great precision."

"Aye, Captain," Scotty added with pride. "You tell the old girl where you want her to go and she'll get you there, past, present, or future."

Emotions warred in Kirk's eyes. Scott remembered how haunted the captain had been after returning through the Guardian. Whatever had occurred back there had taken its toll on him. Yet Kirk was still an explorer at heart, and a devotee of history; the possibilities clearly intrigued him. Perhaps Scott would have felt the same had their target era been something more to his tastes, like Bonnie Prince Charlie's uprising or Isambard Kingdom Brunel's construction of the Great Western Railway.

But Delgado was growing impatient. "Captain, let me be clear: this is not a request. This mission has been authorized by Admiral Comsol himself. Your obedience is expected; your enthusiasm about it is your own affair."

Kirk stiffened, and Scott resented the commodore for throwing his weight around rather than allowing Kirk the dignity of coming around on his own, as it seemed he'd been about to do. Robert L. Comsol had been the commanding officer of Starfleet for over fifteen years, the man whose signature appeared on all the most important orders, from the death-penalty ban on travel to Talos IV to the mobilization orders for the abortive Klingon war last year. Invoking his name was a blunt instrument to enforce compliance. What bug was up the commodore's aft vernier to put him in such an all-fired hurry? If he got what he wanted, he'd have more than his share of time to play around with.

"Of course, Commodore," Kirk finally said. "But if I become convinced that my ship, my crew, or history itself is in imminent danger—"

"I have faith in your judgment, Captain—and your sense of duty."

It was the closest thing to an apology the commodore was about to give. Kirk nodded. "Thank you, sir." He sighed and turned to his officers, leading them back along the gangway toward the exit. Commodore's orders or not, he was still the captain and he would lead this crew. "Spock, Scotty . . . start your computations for the light-speed breakaway."

"Aye, sir," Scott replied. *And may God have mercy on us all. . . .*

Stardate undefinable

"Speed passing warp eight-point-five!" Lieutenant Sulu cried from the *Enterprise*'s helm, clinging tightly to the console as the ship trembled around him.

"Scotty, engine status!" Kirk barked.

"They're holdin' together, I dinna know how!" Engineer Scott's voice asserted over the intercom. *"We're matchin' their output as close as we can to the last time, but it's tricky!"*

"Spock, we're getting awfully close to the Black Star."

Spock declined to remind the captain that that was precisely the idea. Nor did he bother to observe the anomalous singularity's approach on the viewscreen; the sensor readings within his hooded viewer were far more informative, updating by the millisecond in complex, three-dimensional graphic patterns that Spock had customized for maximum information density. Instead, he simply announced, "Approaching breakaway point. On the countdown. Ten, nine, eight . . ."

"All hands, this is the captain. Brace for time displacement!"

". . . two, one—mark!"

Sulu activated the breakaway thrust without waiting for Kirk's order, as had been prearranged. So far, the maneuver was going precisely as the crew had rehearsed it under the guidance of Commodore Delgado's team. However, there were still many unpredictable factors, and Spock privately acknowledged sympathy for Doctor McCoy's sentiment as expressed before the maneuver began: *If they're so all-fired certain this is safe, why aren't they coming with us?*

Spock monitored the chronometers, which extrapolated the date from external astronomical observations and the emission cycles of known pulsars. They thus displayed the years racing backward at an accelerating pace. "It is working, Captain. Braking should begin on my mark." He counted down as before, and: "Mark!"

The ship heaved in deceleration. Spock saw the crew around him blacking out from the stresses, and felt his own consciousness fading. . . .

". . . some interesting experiences in store . . ."

"Spock, if you can't handle it, I'm going to have to trust . . ."

". . . talking about! Listen, you guys can't come in here!"

"If we ourselves do anything that changes history . . ."

". . . lovely animal, Captain. I find myself strangely . . ."

"*. . . destroy the Earth and probably yourselves, too.*"

"Spock? Spock!"

He blinked, forcing himself back to full consciousness, and noted that the bridge systems had remained on line this time thanks to the precautions he and Lieutenant Commander Scott had implemented. The crew had blacked out during their previous slingshot around the Black Star, so it was best to take no chances. "Checking, sir." He moved to confirm ship's status through his console. Yet he was distracted by the memory, already fading rapidly, of the sensory hallucinations he had experienced during the blackout. He could no longer recall any specific words or ideas, but he had the sense of having been on Earth in its past. Could he possibly have glimpsed his subjective future? Perhaps his later self's mind, returning along this same Feynman curve at the end of their mission, had entangled with his own now, allowing an exchange of memory?

No—this was baseless speculation. All he had was a vague impression that could easily have been formed of memories of his previous visit to Earth's past, blended with anticipation about what might lie ahead. He must still be disoriented or he wouldn't have wasted time on such conjectures. He refocused himself on the status check, and in moments the sensory aberration was forgotten. "All decks reporting in, Captain. No injuries, all critical ship systems functional."

At the engineering station, Lieutenant Leslie turned to report. "Engines read nominal, sir."

"*Nominal, he says,*" Scott declared from main engineering below. "*He means no worse than expected. It'll be at least three days before I'm ready to use these warp engines again."*

Sulu turned to the captain and displayed his habitual large grin. "We won't have to, sir. The automatic braking program did the trick. We're coasting north of Sol's ecliptic, about one-point-three astronomical units from Earth."

"Curious," Spock said, double-checking the readings. "That suggests we have arrived somewhat more than a year away from our previous arrival time— enough for the Sun and Earth to move that distance through space. Verifying . . . the date is April 4, nineteen hundred and sixty-eight." His eyebrow rose. "*Before* our previous arrival date. But still well within the critical period we are here to observe."

Kirk threw him a quizzical look. "Well, let's make sure we don't stick around long enough to run into our past selves. That would be a rather awkward reunion."

"Indeed."

They proceeded toward Earth at moderate impulse speed. Spock took the time to coordinate with Lieutenant Watley, the head of the science department's temporal analysis team, as she evaluated the sensor data gathered during the slingshot maneuver. Dierdre Watley, a physicist specializing in the temporal dynamics of subspace, had transferred aboard at the behest of Commodore Delgado, presumably in anticipation of temporal research missions such as this one. Her sister Elaine had already been part of the *Enterprise* crew at the time, having served as ship's historian since shortly after the departure of Marla McGivers from the post.

The current mission was perhaps uniquely suited to the combined talents of the Watley sisters. But Elaine Watley's contribution would come later, once they entered Earth orbit and collected scans of the events transpiring there.

It took slightly over an hour to reach Earth at this speed; any faster, and the plasma shock from their deflector shields cutting through the solar wind might have been detectable even to Earth astronomers of the 1960s. Once in extended orbit, however, their deflector configuration rendered them effectively invisible to all but chance optical detection. "Begin data gathering," Kirk ordered. "Conventional scans in passive mode only, subspace scans in active mode. Lieutenant Uhura, antennas to maximum gain. I want to pick up every last scrap of broadcast traffic, particularly the classified military bands."

"Aye, sir," the elegant communications officer replied, efficient as always.

An alarm sounded on the engineering board. "Captain," Lieutenant Leslie said, "we're getting energy leakage from the transporter emitters."

"Spock, is that something they could detect in this era?"

"Unknown, but quite possible, sir."

"Leslie, can you fix it?"

"Trying, sir," the big but soft-spoken lieutenant said. "No luck. The system must be damaged."

"Repairs can probably be effected from the main transporter room," Spock said. "As Mister Scott is occupied with the warp engines . . ."

Kirk nodded. "Go."

Moments later, Spock reached the transporter room, only to find Commander Scott already present. "Mister Scott, the engines—"

"Will keep. First let's make sure we stay hidden so we have space to work on 'em."

"Logical." Spock moved around to the other side of the transporter console and checked the readings. "The emissions have already stopped."

"I put the system in receive mode as a stopgap." Again, a logical choice. The emitters could not transmit a signal when they were set to receive one, even if there was no beam to receive.

Working together, Spock and Scott quickly diagnosed the problem, a fairly simple matter to repair. No sooner had they corrected the fault, though, than the ship shuddered as though struck by something. Seconds later, the alert indicator by the entryway began flashing red, though Spock almost unconsciously muted the klaxon so he could concentrate on the sounds of the transporter mechanism itself. Warning lights came on to indicate that ship's deflectors had been raised.

But the sudden activity in the transporter console told Spock that this was no weapons fire or meteoroid impact. The beam power readings surged even as the ship shuddered again, confirming the correlation. Spock hit the intercom. "Transporter room to captain."

"Kirk here. What's happening?"

"It appears we have accidentally intercepted someone's transporter beam, Captain." With the system engaged in receive mode, it had automatically locked

onto the signal and initiated materialization, pulling in
the beam before it could reach its destination—whatever that might be. Spock tried to abort the process,
but the sheer strength of the beam, strong enough
to render maximum deflectors useless against it, had
locked the system. "It is incredibly powerful."

"*That's impossible. The twentieth century had no
such—*" The ship rocked again, cutting him off. Unusual, flowing patterns of light began to form within
the field generator matrix along the transporter platform's rear wall, evidently an artifact of the alien beam's
distinctive field configuration.

"Captain . . . something is beaming aboard this
vessel."

**Starbase 9
Stardate 4744.8
April 2268**
Antonio Delgado listened in fascination to Kirk and
Spock's report of their bizarre encounter three hundred
years in the past. They had been hit by an alien transporter beam originating from over a thousand light-
years away, a beam powerful enough to affect them
like a weapon and overwhelm their own transporter
system. Yet the being who had arrived on the platform
had been a human calling himself Gary Seven, a man
possessing superhuman abilities and physiological perfection on a par with the Augments of the Eugenics
Wars, though predating them by a generation. He had
claimed to be indigenous to that time, raised on a secret
alien world and sent to help shepherd Earth through its

most critical period in order to ensure humanity's survival. Kirk had initially mistrusted the mysterious Mister Seven's tale, particularly when Seven had escaped from the *Enterprise*. Kirk and Spock had seen no choice but to pursue him to Earth; it was beyond their mission parameters, but Kirk had decided that the risks of Seven's interference outweighed the risk of accidental historical alteration. Though it had appeared his mission was to sabotage an orbital nuclear platform and send it crashing to Earth, it became evident that his goal was to detonate the warhead shortly before impact, in order to frighten humanity out of filling the skies with Damoclean death. When Seven had prevented his assistant from unknowingly threatening Kirk's life, the captain had chosen to trust him, and the warhead was detonated exactly as history recorded.

It seemed the mission had been more successful than Delgado's historians could have hoped. Gary Seven's intervention seemed to resolve the mystery of how so many looming disasters had been averted right at the brink—not all of them, surely, and not enough to prevent the Eugenics Wars or World War III; but enough to delay global nuclear conflict and guide humanity toward some degree of disarmament, so that when the war eventually came, it was limited enough to allow the species to survive and finally learn its lesson.

Delgado's colleagues in Starfleet Intelligence would surely be eager to investigate Seven's mysterious backers. Doctor T'Viss had been more intrigued by the physics of Seven's subspace transporter beam, which had exhibited properties that, in Engineer Scott's opinion, could potentially allow it to transport beings through time as well as space. But Delgado himself was more focused on the outcome of the *Enterprise*'s encounter with the strange Gary Seven. "So not only did your actions in the past not alter history," Delgado said with a smile, "but they were part and parcel of the original history itself. A self-consistent causal loop from future to past to future."

"With respect, sir," Kirk said, "I'm skeptical. First you tell me interacting with the past will split off an alternate history, now you say it can bring about our own history. How can it do both?"

Spock replied, forestalling the highly technical explanation T'Viss was about to give. "The same river can split into two branches or meander into a loop," he said, "depending on its interaction with the contours of the landscape. The same underlying physics apply in both cases, but the conditions under which they operate are different and thus produce different outcomes."

Kirk still frowned. "I have to wonder, though. Did we really just act out the part we were always meant to play in history . . . or did we change history, and our records and memories along with it, so that we only thought that was the case?"

"Jim," Delgado said, "T'Viss has explained to you why that can't happen."

"And Spock has said there's still room for doubt." He leaned forward, pausing to consider his words. "We were told we were only going back to observe, not to get involved. But despite our best efforts, we got pulled into the events of 1968 anyway."

Delgado sighed. "Jim, your caution is appreciated. It's good to have a skeptic as part of the decision-making. But my read of this event is that it only reinforces my belief that time travel can be managed safely. *And* that the potential for discovery more than justifies the risk. We'd still know nothing about Gary Seven's mysterious backers if not for this experiment." And though he wasn't ready to voice it aloud yet, he felt even more convinced that there was some physical process guiding events, though it would be melodramatic to call it "destiny." What were the odds the *Enterprise* would arrive in exactly the right time and place to intercept Gary Seven's transporter beam, and thereby allow this object lesson in safe, self-consistent time travel? Delgado felt that he, too, was being guided toward some important future event. He had to see it through; he might not even have a choice in the matter. "Thus, I'm going to recommend ramping up our research, both with the slingshot effect *and* the Guardian of Forever."

Kirk was reserved as he said, "You may need to go back to testing the slingshot effect with unmanned probes, sir. It still puts a great deal of strain on the ship, and Scotty is concerned that too many repetitions could seriously compromise our spaceframe."

"I know, I know, and the ship is needed in the field. Don't worry, Jim, I know your girl's been through a lot for us, and I'd say she's earned a rest. We still have a lot of data to analyze from this experiment. But sooner or later, Captain, I'll be calling on you again. Your ship and your crew are of unique importance to our efforts."

Even as he dismissed Kirk and Spock, the commodore began to wonder about the long-term possibilities. The *Enterprise* wouldn't be on patrol, or under Kirk's command, forever. All he had to do was bide his time and play his cards right . . . and sooner or later, those engines would be his.

III

Palais de la Concorde
Paris, European Alliance, Earth
Stardate 5318.1
January 2269

Vexam ko Nel, the Federation's new Secretary of Science, crossed her three arms over her chest, a complicated maneuver that distracted Antonio Delgado from the question she'd just asked. She was the first Edosian he'd met, and a far cry from her predecessor in the post, Ahmed Suleiman. Ahmed would have discussed business with Delgado over a fine Saurian brandy or across nine holes ("craters," as the wags called them) of Lunar golf. Vexam faced him from across her very neat desk in her very neat office, just recently stripped of all Ahmed's prized possessions and containing little in their place as yet. Had she been too busy with the transition between administrations to redecorate, or was this austerity simply the way she preferred it? Given the way her beady eyes peered at him from under the pronounced orbital ridges of her skull-like face, he was uncharitably inclined to assume the latter. Her yellowish-brown skin, pale for her species, only added to her cadaverous appearance.

"Well?" she said after a moment. "I have other appointments pending. I would think you'd appreciate the value of time."

Delgado tried to recall her question. He was vague on the specifics, but he knew he hadn't liked the implications. "Madam Secretary, the work my division is doing could be vital to the Federation."

"Or very dangerous. Don't you see the recklessness here? Sending ships back in time before you even have an adequately verified theoretical model of the possible impact?"

"Doctor T'Viss's analyses . . ."

"Are the ones you prefer to believe because they suit your agenda. And you've managed to convince the rest of your boys' club to go along with it, under the indulgent eye of President Wescott."

"Kenneth understood the potential benefits to the Federation. And the potential dangers if the Romulans or Klingons achieved this technology first."

"Well, 'Kenneth' is gone now, and I and the rest of President McLaren's cabinet have been tasked to rein in the excesses of his political cronyism."

Delgado suppressed a grimace. The members of Wescott's circle had had a good thing going. The two-term president's decision not to run for a third had felt like a betrayal. Delgado was past being surprised at having his friends turn on him, but not being hurt.

"Madam Secretary, you can't halt this research just because Lorne McLaren wants to make a show of cleaning house. I may have used my connections to facilitate the project, but the project itself transcends politics."

"It certainly should, Commodore. That's why *Presi-*

dent McLaren believes the project needs to be subject to independent oversight."

Delgado blinked. "Oversight?"

Vexam used her middle hand to press the intercom button on her desk. "Send her in, please."

A moment later, the door opened and a tall woman in a red pantsuit walked in. Her drawn, severe features suggested a blend of African and Asian ancestry: light tan skin, narrow eyes under arched brows, dainty lips, and a halo of tightly curled black hair with an incongruously frivolous streak of red running through it. "Commodore Antonio Delgado," Vexam said, "this is Doctor Meijan Grey, the noted xenoarchaeologist and xenohistorian."

Delgado shook her hand and offered a smile calibrated to make her feel more attractive than she was. "Doctor Grey. A pleasure to meet you."

"Commodore." Her voice was a sharp alto. "I look forward to working with you."

"Yes, the secretary hasn't quite filled me in yet on the particulars of our collaboration."

"Jan here," Vexam said, "is to be the head of a special advisory panel to the Science Council, known as the Chronal Assessment Committee." *Chronal?* Delgado thought. *Is that even a real word?* "This is an independent panel of experts whose task is to review your research methodology and findings and report its conclusions to the Science Council. While it conducts its investigation, any further experimentation with time travel is to be put on hold."

Delgado started to protest, but he could tell from these two females' stern gazes that changing their minds would take time and care. "I see," he said instead. "Well, I'm not afraid to submit my team's work for review. I'm proud of the work we've done and confident that a fair analysis will verify its safety and its importance. Doctor Grey, I welcome your oversight."

Inwardly, though, he seethed. Assigning an archaeologist to check his work rather than a physicist? Oh, he was sure the secretary had cobbled this committee together out of every discipline that might be seen as having some relevance to time travel, but Grey's specialties seemed to make her an odd choice for leadership. Which suggested her appointment was largely political, despite Vexam's protestations. McLaren and his cabinet were like any other administration, coming into office on a promise to transcend petty politics and find better ways to solve problems, but inevitably having to use the same political tactics as their predecessors, because that was how government actually worked.

And that gave Delgado hope that he could win Grey and her "Chronal" Assessment Committee to his side. If she was a political creature, then he could find a way to do business with her. He was confident that this would be only a temporary setback.

After all, this work was something that was meant to be.

Institutes of the Federation Science Council
Paris, European Alliance, Earth
Stardate 5344.7
March 2269

"This session of the Chronal Assessment Committee is now called to order," Meijan Grey said from her seat at the head of the large, rectangular Louis XVI table that dominated the committee's conference room. Grey thought the table's clean-lined, neoclassical style meshed well with the early Federation-era design of the conference room, whose lines evoked both classicism and forward-looking art deco optimism. On the sides of the table sat the other members of the CAC. At her left hand was Arthur Manners, retired science adviser to the Qasr administration, whose focus was the policy applications of scientific innovations. Beyond him sat the sociologist Crenfel, a Denobulan woman charged with evaluating the potential social consequences of time-travel technology. Opposite Crenfel sat Vaacith sh'Lesinas, the Federation's most acclaimed author of time-travel fiction. Finally, at Grey's right hand sat Professor Simok, former director of the Central Research Institute of Aldebaran III. The 140-year-old Vulcan was an accomplished administrator as well as an able quantum physicist, and it still surprised Grey that she and not Simok was running the show. Secretary Vexam had selected Grey for her achievements in xenoarchaeology and history, notably her development of computer models for simulating alternate historical development on alien worlds. In Vexam's view, this made Grey the closest thing available to an expert on how history could be altered by time travel. She had been selected as leader, she'd been told, for her dedication and objectivity—though in her private thoughts she understood that "dedication" translated to "almost total lack of social life to create distractions." Her near-exclusive focus on her work wasn't something she'd chosen, just something she'd fallen into through having little success in any other aspect of life. Still, if her work was all she had, she was determined to be her best at it.

After taking a few moments to get prior business out of the way, Grey turned to the man at the far end of the conference table. "Commodore Delgado, the floor is yours."

Delgado smiled his calculated smile, making sure to achieve eye contact with all the committee members in turn. "Thank you, Jan. Gentlebeings, we're here today to follow up on the recent discoveries made by the *U.S.S. Enterprise* at Beta Niobe." Several of the committee members smirked or sighed; they couldn't seem to get away from dealing with Kirk and his ship. "By now you've all read the logs, but to summarize for the record:

"The *Enterprise* had been monitoring the star Beta Niobe, which has been known for years to be on the verge of supernova. Their scans revealed that the supernova had become imminent, decades sooner than anticipated, leaving only hours for a final survey of the star's inhabited planet, Sarpeidon. A survey performed sixty-two years ago by the *U.S.S. Neumann* showed that Sarpeidon's humanoid natives had an industrial civilization, but were far from achieving space travel; with no other sizable bodies orbiting their star, they had little incentive to develop spaceflight. However, the *Enterprise* found the planet devoid of intelligent life, or of any active technology save for a single power source, which Captain Kirk and Commanders Spock and McCoy beamed down to investigate." Delgado's tone showed disapproval of Kirk's tendency to beam into danger himself rather than delegating the task to his officers. Grey, conversely, found it rather admirable that Kirk chose to lead from the front.

"To make a long story short, they discovered that the power source was a device identified to them as the *atavachron*."

"Greek for 'ancestral time,'" sh'Lesinas observed. "Whoever programmed their translators is an Earth classicist."

"Exactly. Kirk and his party discovered—by accident—that the device was a working time machine, which the entire population had used to escape into Sarpeidon's past. Somehow, in just six decades, a people with no space travel mastered time travel, jumped right past slingshot effects to something far more advanced and controllable. The device had properties we can't even begin to explain; for instance, when Commanders Spock and McCoy traveled through the atavachron and emerged five thousand years in the past, it affected Spock's behavior in a manner consistent with that of the Vulcans of the time, before the Reformation."

Simok frowned at the thought of a modern Vulcan reduced to the savage behavior of the past. Still, he said, "We cannot be sure that interpretation is correct. Perhaps the transportation process affected Spock's hormonal balance, with his resultant behavior only coincidentally resembling that of primitive Vulcans."

"You're quite right, Professor," Delgado said. "There's so much we don't understand about their achievement. How it worked. How it affected the minds of its travelers. The nature of the so-called 'preparation' that would adapt time travelers to their new eras and make it fatal for them to return."

"Allegedly," Crenfel said with a wide Denobulan grin. "Maybe they just told people that so they wouldn't change their minds and try to come home."

Grey spoke up. "We can speculate all we want, but we can't do much more than that. Sarpeidon no longer exists. All we know about the atavachron, all we can know, is what this report from the *Enterprise* tells us. So Commodore, what are you here to ask of us?"

Delgado leaned forward. "There is more we might be able to do, Jan. The planet is gone, but the radio signals its civilization generated are still expanding through space. We can send ships to intercept them, maybe reconstruct information about the atavachron and the physics behind it."

Crenfel pursed her lips skeptically. "Judging from these reports, the Sarpeidons never developed communication satellites. They relied on cables and short-range microwaves for most of their planetary transmissions. There's unlikely to be much signal leakage into space."

"Still, we have to try," Delgado said urgently. "Surely the very fact of what the Sarpeidons did is of the utmost importance. They sent their whole population, over a billion people, to live in times throughout their planet's past, and yet apparently caused no disruption or alteration to the timeline."

"Or did they?" Vaacith sh'Lesinas asked, the rakish cant of her antennae matching the smirk on her blue-skinned face. "Maybe the reason they achieved time travel so quickly is that they sent their physicists back to help boost its development. A self-causative loop."

Arthur Manners furrowed his high, hairless forehead. "Knowledge out of nowhere? How is that even possible?"

"As long as the event is self-consistent, it is mathematically permissible," Simok replied. "Quantum information can spontaneously emerge from the vacuum."

"Even so, it remains consistent," Delgado said. "No erasure or destruction of an 'original' history. If there were an original history where they didn't go back in time, how would they ever have achieved time travel at all, if Vaacith here is right?"

"Merely conjecture," Simok said. "We can say nothing for sure at this point."

"Which is exactly why we have to keep studying the Beta Niobe system," Delgado stressed. "What if there's some other explanation? What if they tapped into some natural spacetime warp that still exists?"

Sh'Lesinas's antennae tilted back thoughtfully. "Maybe a time rift caused by the supernova, propagating backward far enough that they could harness it to escape." She chuckled. "That's a good one. I can get a story out of that."

"In which case its existence might be impermanent," Delgado went on. "Time, pardon the expression, may be of the essence."

Grey sighed. She'd learned to be skeptical of Delgado's enthusiasms. Before the CAC had been formed, the commodore and his team had spent some time investigating the planet Omega IV, another *Enterprise* discovery. The natives there had reputedly recapitulated the political development of twentieth-century Earth superpowers, with a tribal people called Yangs even possessing exact duplicates of the flag of the United States of America, its Declaration of Independence and Constitution, and the Christian Bible—yet their warring civilizations had been wiped out in a global conflict millennia before any of those things had existed on Earth. Delgado had been convinced that the only explanation was some kind of time travel or alternate history. But once Grey had looked at the evidence, she'd seen the fundamental flaw in that idea. The American artifacts documented in the *Enterprise* logs and scans were far too intact to be thousands of years old; given the primitive conditions in which the Yang tribe had kept them, they couldn't have dated back much more than a century. A careful study of the logs revealed that the Yangs had never actually claimed that these "holy" artifacts were ancient; Kirk had simply jumped to that conclusion, as observers of indigenous cultures often made the mistake of assuming that their contemporary customs represented ancient tradition. With some further investigation, the committee had concluded that an Earth ship from the "space boomer" era, the *E.C.S. Philadelphia*, had visited Omega IV sometime in the late 2140s and then disappeared, probably dying from the same disease that had killed the crew of the *U.S.S. Exeter* twelve decades later. As far as Grey and Crenfel had been able to reconstruct, the *Philadelphia*'s traders, operating in the days before the Prime Directive of noninterference, had found the Yangs' traditional beliefs strongly similar to American democratic values and so had given them replicas of American paraphernalia to encourage them in their fight for freedom. The ideas were similar enough that the Yangs had easily embraced these writings as new revelations from their existing deities, seamlessly folding them into their culture as though they'd always been part of it. A fascinating sociological case study, but hardly a time-travel incident.

Still, Grey knew that not everyone on the committee shared her doubts. Delgado was a master politician and had been wooing all the committee members individually, trying to win them to his side. Manners and Crenfel had both fallen under his sway and were inclined to vote in favor of pursuing temporal research. Simok was immune to Delgado's persuasion, and sh'Lesinas had reacted rather negatively. Unexpectedly, the time-fiction author had proven reluctant to see time travel developed in reality; not only could she easily imagine the risks, but she feared seeing her novels rendered obsolete or made to look foolish by real breakthroughs. So Grey herself often cast the deciding vote.

The Sarpeidon issue was not one that came down to a divided committee. Simok was curious to see if more could be learned about the Sarpeidons' achievement, and even sh'Lesinas was intrigued to see what methods could be used to study a world after its destruction, in case she could crib something for her fiction. And though Grey felt Delgado was wasting his time on another wild goose chase, she couldn't see any harm in looking—unless they actually found something like an active time warp, in which case she might reconsider.

Delgado's next motion, however, was more divisive. "Kirk's encounter with the atavachron further underlines that it is possible to travel into the past and return without altering the timeline. Whatever uncertainties we may have about the theory behind time travel, the empirical evidence shows that it can be done safely, even when it occurs by accident. Imagine what we could achieve under controlled conditions—such as a carefully designed expedition through the Guardian of Forever."

"Let's not get ahead of ourselves," Grey advised.

"On the contrary, we've been lagging too far behind. The potential of the Guardian is too great to ignore. Why, we wouldn't even have to speculate about how the Sarpeidons developed time travel—we could just watch it happen through the Guardian."

"Well, that would take all the fun out of finding out, wouldn't it?" asked sh'Lesinas.

"Haven't your teams had problems getting detailed data through passive scans of the Guardian's playbacks?" Manners asked. It felt like a rehearsed question.

"That's right," Delgado said, sounding equally rehearsed. "The sheer volume of information is extremely dense, and it can be difficult to filter specifics out of the mass. Historically important events can stand out in the data, but the Guardian seems to have its own definitions of what's important. It's very stream-of-consciousness. Which underlines the importance of having historians to interpret events," Delgado said, meeting Grey's eyes. "Without that interpretation, the raw data can be very confusing. Especially when there's so much of it piled together, racing by so quickly that it's hard to tell what images go with what years or even decades."

"So you think we could learn more through actual expeditions," Crenfel prompted.

"I do. The value of observers on the scene cannot be overstated."

"Neither can the risks," Simok countered, "if the observers should inadvertently make a significant change. I remain skeptical of Doctor T'Viss's model of timeline invariance."

"Even so, there are ways that risk can be minimized," the commodore answered. "Our first expeditions could be to places and times that we know will have little effect on the future. As I said, Sarpeidon before its destruction is a possibility. Pompeii in the days before Vesuvius erupted. Galos Sigma before the dwarf planet collision."

"The dawn of Orion," Grey murmured, almost involuntarily. It was a longtime fascination of hers—an indigenous civilization undergoing its first great blossoming, only to be almost completely annihilated in a wave of alien invasions. The native Orions had been conquered and enslaved for generations, and though they'd finally overthrown their oppressors, by then their indigenous culture was lost, replaced with the language and customs of their former slavers. What little remained of their original, pristine civilization was an enduring archaeological mystery. What had the Orions been like before the event that so traumatized them as a people? What might they have become without the conquest? Even her simulations had been unable to provide useful answers, with so little data on Orion's dawn civilization to work from. Although Grey had eventually managed to bribe and buy her way onto Orion to conduct an archaeological dig, she'd been able to find little intact evidence. What the ancient invaders hadn't destroyed, centuries of Orion industrial development and internecine war mostly had. It was a gap in the archaeological record that she had despaired of ever filling.

"Perfect," Delgado said. "With your expertise, and that of any other experts you care to recruit, the expedition could be carefully designed to minimize any risk of historical disruption."

"This is premature," Simok warned. "There are too many unpredictable variables."

"But that's the beauty of it," Manners countered, no doubt repeating the words Delgado had already swayed him with. "Change the future of a place that has no future, and nothing is affected. Any alterations would just get canceled out."

Grey felt Delgado's eyes on her and knew she was being played. The prospect was enticing, but that was exactly why she had to approach it with caution.

Still . . . what if Orion history were to be changed . . . and the changes then canceled out, as Arthur says? Imagine if we could observe alternate histories for real, compare them against my models.

No—that kind of thinking was risky. Intentionally altering history, using real people's lives as an experiment? That was where the danger lay, in the sheer power to play God.

Still, she knew that Manners and Crenfel would vote for Delgado's plan, Simok and sh'Lesinas most likely against it. The deciding vote would be hers, and though she was reluctant to be the one to approve this plan, neither was she comfortable being the one who scuttled it altogether—not until she'd had more time to think about it. "I propose we table a decision until we've researched the proposal further. First we need to determine if a plausible methodology can be developed to minimize the risk of interference. If we can achieve that, then we can vote on whether to authorize it. Agreed?"

The motion passed easily, for after all it was just an agreement to discuss it more. Still, Grey saw the satisfaction in Delgado's eyes. He'd found her weakness now.

Time vortex system
Location classified
Stardate 5373.4
October 2269

"We are in orbit around the planet of the time vortex, the focus of all the timelines of our galaxy," James Kirk said into his log recorder. "Our mission is to assist a team of historians in the investigation of Federation history." Meijan Grey, who stood next to Kirk on the *Enterprise* bridge, declined to point out that she was more an archaeologist than a historian. After all, that was the least of Kirk's concerns.

The captain snapped off the recorder and turned to her. "It would be redundant, Doctor Grey, to restate my objections for the record. But I still consider this an unacceptably dangerous experiment."

"Believe me, Captain Kirk, I have considerable reservations about it myself. And I appreciate that no one understands the risks posed by the Guardian better than you and your crew. But taking risks in the name of

knowledge is what Starfleet is for, and the potential for
knowledge offered here is extraordinary." Alas, attempts
to probe Sarpeidon's past through the Guardian had
proved unsuccessful; whatever temporal phenomenon
made the atavachron possible seemed to create interference that the Guardian could not penetrate. Or perhaps,
as a member of the Guardian observation team had
proposed, the sentient time portal was simply jealous
of the competition. The Chronal Assessment Committee's decision on whether to undertake Delgado's
proposed expedition had been delayed for months as
other time-related incidents had taken priority, such as
the *Enterprise*'s second encounter with Gary Seven (in
the present, confirming that Seven's technology did
allow transporting through time) and the raid on the
Guardian planet by the race calling itself Clan Ru. The
latter event had brought the committee within a hairs-
breadth of abandoning the plan altogether, but Delgado
had won them over by citing the remarkable scientific
insights that had resulted from that affair, including
detailed documentation of the asteroid impact that had
triggered the death of Earth's dinosaurs. Delgado's
knack for exploiting his political alliances had played a
role as well; he'd recently managed to wangle a promotion to rear admiral and Chief of Starfleet Science Ops,
and had used that clout to push the mission through
over the Science Council's resistance, in exchange for
assurances from Starfleet that much more stringent security would be put in place around the time vortex planet.

Kirk rose and headed for the turbolift, summoning
Commander Spock to follow him. Grey continued her

speech as she joined them in the lift. "We've decided it's worth taking a chance, if we proceed with great care. Even knowing that nothing we do in Orion's past is likely to have any impact on its present, we still intend to limit ourselves to passive observation. No direct interaction with anyone in the past, not even physical contact with any person or object if it can be avoided."

"I understand, Doctor. But I'm imposing one more restriction. Only *Enterprise* personnel will travel through the Guardian."

"Captain!" Grey protested.

"As you say, Doctor, it's Starfleet's job to take risks. I'm not prepared to bring civilians along on a mission like this, not until we've been able to assess the dangers."

"Captain, civilian or not, I'm more than capable of approaching a site with caution and discipline."

"It's not just about that, Doctor," Kirk said as the turbolift discharged them onto the Deck 7 corridor. A faint shudder ran through the deck, the powerful spatial distortions of the time vortex making their presence felt even despite helmsman Sulu's deft orbital corrections to avoid them. "We don't know what hazards to life and limb there may be back there. My responsibility as a Starfleet officer is to protect Federation citizens."

Grey forced calm on herself, reminding herself again not to let her desire to visit Orion's past overwhelm her objectivity. "Of course, Captain. I'll brief you and your team on the approved procedures for interaction before you leave." She sighed. "Along with what vanishingly little I know about Orion's dawn culture."

"Thank you, Doctor." His military manner softened,

giving way to a boyish smile that must have gotten him quite far with the ladies. "And I promise, we'll bring you back the most detailed scans we possibly can."

"Oh, I hope for more than scans, Captain Kirk. It's your impressions I'll really want to hear. What it feels like to actually be there. What the atmosphere is, the dynamic of the people. History means stories, Captain. It's about constructing a narrative of the past."

"I understand, Doctor. I'll keep my eyes open."

Kirk's kindness reassured her that the mission was in good hands even if she had to stay behind. Kirk had a natural gift for winning people over, but there was more sincerity to him than to Admiral Delgado.

In the transporter room, the threesome met the rest of their team, one civilian, one Starfleet. Grey had brought along Doctor Loom Aleek-Om of the Institute of Galactic History, an Aurelian whose lanky, winged body was covered with golden feathers—and nothing else save a tricorder on a strap around his neck. Grey unconsciously tugged at the high, tight collar of her maroon jumpsuit. Whatever his sartorial choices, Aleek-Om was an accomplished historical scholar with nearly six decades of experience under his (strictly figurative) belt. Delgado had wanted to send one of his own people on the mission, but Grey had insisted that if this experiment was to go ahead, it should be with the participation of one of the Federation's most prominent historians.

The other team member was a square-jawed fellow whom Kirk introduced as Lieutenant Ted Erikson, the ship's historian. He was attired in a red uniform, like other starship historians Grey had met; for whatever reason, the Starfleet bureaucracy classified historians under operations rather than sciences. "Have you traveled through time before, Lieutenant?" Grey asked.

"No, Doctor," he replied. "I only came aboard in the last crew rotation. But I did my thesis on indigenous civilizations transformed by alien conquest, including the Orions. This is a great opportunity." Grey offered a faint smile, grateful that at least one trained historian would be on the expedition.

Kirk looked around the transporter room. "Where's McCoy? He was supposed to be here to update our immunizations." Heaven forbid the observers should bring back some long-dead disease from Orion's past, or contaminate it with one of their own. Kirk was just about to activate the intercom when the door slid open and Doctor McCoy came in. "Bones, you're late."

"Well, don't blame me," the doctor snapped in a tone Grey was surprised the captain let him get away with. "I'm not the one who decided to schedule this little jaunt in the middle of the annual crew physicals. I got away as soon as I could." He hefted his kit. "Now let's get this over with quickly so I can get back to work."

"No time," Kirk said, heading for the pad. "You know how tight the time planet's security is now. We've only got a limited clearance window for beam-down. You'll have to come down with us, Bones."

"Seriously? Go through that atom-scrambler twice just so I can—"

"Maybe that will teach you to be on time in the future. Come on." The doctor rolled his eyes and mounted the platform, grumbling all the way down.

After getting cleared through the security station, the team made their way across the barren, windy plain to the Guardian itself, during which time McCoy took care of the immunizations. The ovoid megalith was surrounded by crumbling ruins, oddly Greco-Roman columns and plinths that scans showed to be far younger than the Guardian itself. Perhaps some earlier civilization had settled here and built a facility around the Guardian, studying it, traveling through it. But how had their structure survived the turbulent time ripples? The planet was prone to seismic disruption, and indeed the local geology had apparently undergone some changes in just the couple of years since the planet's discovery, crumbling the ruins even further—though the Guardian itself, the eye of the storm, remained unaffected. Perhaps the ripples had not always been present. Perhaps they were a sign of some malfunction in the time portal itself.

Grey set aside her impulse to interrogate the Guardian about its own history, knowing that other researchers had gained no success along those lines. Instead, she went ahead with the final briefing for Kirk's team, then stepped forward to address the portal. "Guardian, can you hear me?"

"I HEAR ALL."

"These travelers wish to visit the earliest civilization of the world called Orion, or Tabit III. Eleven hundred years past, outside the largest city of the time."

Mist swirled in the Guardian's orifice and images began to cycle, glimpses of a lively agrarian city-state populated by humanoids with various shades of green, gold, and blue skin, a cultural nexus where members of the planet's various races crossed paths and engaged in trade. There was enough diversity of color and dress that even humans and a Vulcan could blend in if they stayed in the background. "THE TIME AND PLACE ARE READY TO RECEIVE YOU," the Guardian intoned.

Doctor McCoy frowned. "I thought this thing could only show the past at one speed, start to finish."

"One speed, yes," Aleek-Om told him in a reedy, slow voice. "But the observers recently discovered that the playback could be narrowed down to a particular range of dates and locations if one asked specifically enough."

Beside Grey, Kirk blushed. "I guess I never thought to try that."

"We had other things on our minds, Captain," Spock told him.

"There's still a fair margin of error around the specified time and place, though," Grey clarified. "As before, you'd need to observe the playback and time your entry precisely to hit a desired point within the cycle. But for this mission, it shouldn't particularly matter when you step through."

"Thank you, Doctor," Kirk said. "Gentlemen? Let's go." He threw a last glance at Grey, offering her a reassuring smile. "And remember not to step on any butterflies."

On Spock's cue, he, Kirk, and Erikson leaped into the vortex and disappeared along with it. Only empty gray sky and rubble now showed through the portal.

"All right," Grey said after a moment. "As long as we're here, we might as well conduct some historical

scans through the Guardian." Anything to distract from
her frustration at being left behind.

"Agreed," Aleek-Om replied. "Something routine,
something well-understood."

"Why bother?" McCoy asked as he packed up his
medkit. "Why not try to find out something new?"

But Grey understood her colleague's intent. "Because we still lack good algorithms for extracting meaningful historical data from the sheer sensory overload
the Guardian provides. By scanning a well-known
historical period, one we can compare against existing
records, we can establish a better baseline for decod-
ing." McCoy nodded in comprehension. "Let's make it
recent Vulcan history," she said. "Say, around the High
Council elections of YS 8878?"

"Any particular reason?" Aleek-Om asked.

Grey shrugged. "I read an article about the elections last week. I had some doubts about the author's
interpretations."

Grey asked the Guardian to access that time and
place, and she and Aleek-Om performed their scan.
It went smoothly, so they began discussing a second
target. "That's funny," McCoy said. "They should be
back by now. Before, we came back just moments after
we left."

Aleek-Om flexed his wings. "But then you were re-
storing history to its proper course—or returning yourselves to your proper history, if Doctor T'Viss's model
is correct. This is merely an observation mission, so
perhaps with no 'resetting' required, the relative time
flow is more, ah, equivalent, *cher-wit?*"

McCoy fidgeted a moment more, then called, "Guardian! Are the people who just stepped through you still alive and well?"

"THEIR EXISTENCE CONTINUES WITHIN ANOTHER STREAM OF TIME," the megalith replied.

"What's that supposed to . . . aww, never mind. I don't even know what I'm doin' here. I should be back on the *Enterprise* finishing up the physicals. If you'll excuse me, Doctors."

Grey and Aleek-Om barely noticed his departure. They remained engrossed with their routine scans for better than an hour, until an unexpected voice called, "Doctor Grey?"

She turned, startled, for it was Captain Kirk and Lieutenant Erikson who stood behind her. "Captain! How did you get there? And where's Spock?"

Kirk looked startled and relieved. "You know Spock?"

"Of course I do. What do you mean? Where did you come from? I didn't see you come through the Guardian!"

"I didn't," Kirk said, looking just as confused. "At least, not just now. We came through with Spock over an hour ago, except we were . . . in a different timestream. One where Spock had died as a child." He frowned at her tricorder. "Did you run scans of Vulcan's recent past? Around thirty years ago?"

"Why, yes," Grey said. "How did you know?"

Kirk fidgeted. "Because you . . . your counterpart in that other history . . . did too. Somehow it changed something. I'll explain later. But Spock needed to go through the Guardian to restore his own past. I stayed behind to wait for him, and I was just beginning to wonder what would happen to me when the timeline switched back . . . and then I noticed you standing in front of me. I was looking right at you, but I hadn't seen you appear. It was as if I just hadn't *noticed* you there until that moment."

"Captain, I don't understand."

"Neither do I. But I suspect the nature of time around the Guardian may be as mutable as within it." He pondered for a moment. "I don't want to take any chances. The rest of you, go back to the ship, now. With any luck, I'll follow with Spock in a few minutes."

Grey, Aleek-Om, and Erikson beamed aboard as ordered. Rather than waiting in the transporter room, though, Grey headed for the bridge to consult the temporal readings from the Guardian's vicinity, the others following. Indeed, there had been an odd quantum fluctuation registered at the time Kirk and Erikson had appeared—or, from their perspective, when she and Aleek-Om had appeared.

After a few minutes, Kirk's voice came over the comm channel. "*Enterprise*, this is the captain. Two to beam up." As Engineer Scott's voice acknowledged from the transporter room, Grey realized the second party must be Spock. She rushed to the turbolift.

A few minutes later, Grey and the others sat in the briefing room discussing the strange events that had just occurred—to the annoyance of Doctor McCoy, who had been eager to get Spock's physical over with but who, at Grey's insistence, would simply have to wait. "So you're saying," Grey asked Spock in horror, "that just by scanning the time of your childhood, I caused you to cease to exist?"

"Apparently so," Spock said. "History required my adult self to be present to rescue my juvenile self from a *le-matya* attack. My existence is the result of a self-consistent temporal loop. However, since that portion of Vulcan history was replayed while I was elsewhere in time, I was unable to play my role in those events, resulting in the alternate timeline where I did not survive to adulthood . . . nor did my mother," he finished, more subdued. Grey recalled Spock mentioning that in the alternate history, his human mother had divorced his father after Spock's death and had died while returning to Earth.

On one level, Grey was fascinated that so many events leading to this moment had unfolded exactly the same despite Spock's absence. It raised many questions about causality and free will. But most of her attention was on a more distressing matter. "My God. This means . . . the Guardian doesn't just display history . . . in some way it actually reruns history. Or connects with it as it flows. Even just by scanning it, we're interacting with it. There is no passive observation. My God, Spock, my carelessness could've cost your life!"

"On the contrary, Doctor Grey," Spock reassured her. "It was simply part of the necessary cycle of causality. Without my absence in Orion's past to cause my death in one timeline, I would never have known of the need to return to Vulcan's past to save my life, and my mother's, in this timeline. We seem to have discovered a new category of temporal loop, wherein the failure of an event to occur is necessary to bring about its occurrence. One could liken it to a Möbius strip."

"But what happened to that other timeline?" Erikson asked. "Does it still exist?"

"Our own timeline evidently carried on existing in your, *cher-wit*, absence," Aleek-Om observed in his slow, deliberate voice. "From our point of view, you were away for a period corresponding to the length of time you spent in that alternate history before the Guardian returned you to ours. This would seem to lend credence to T'Viss's parallel-history model of the Guardian's operation."

"And yet," Spock said, "the Guardian seemed capable of rewriting the very quantum reality around itself, merging the captain and Erikson in the alternate timeline with the doctors in this timeline."

"That occurred within the range of the Guardian's temporal field," Aleek-Om said.

"We know the Guardian's temporal energies extend parsecs into space," Spock countered. "If such a decoherence of separate quantum states can occur near the Guardian, it can occur elsewhere. Even if this timeline coexisted in parallel with the other for the duration of recent events, it does not guarantee that the other timeline still endures now . . . or if it does, it does not guarantee that every timeline must. As I said, this was a new and unprecedented form of causal loop, one where the original and altered timelines—and ours is, in fact, the altered one—are mutually dependent. That may require them both to survive to maintain the stability of the exchange. But that does not assure the mutual survival of interacting timelines in other circumstances."

Grey spoke with firming resolve. "Spock is right. These events have driven home that we understand temporal phenomena far less than we deluded ourselves into thinking. What we thought was a harmless, passive observation proved to have far more profound consequences. We're moving too fast here, with too little understanding of what we're doing."

She rose to her feet, taking in the others' gaze one by one. "And I think we need to stop."

IV

Excerpt from interview transcript: Spock, Cmdr., Ex. Off. *U.S.S. Enterprise*
Recorded on Starbase 23, Stardate 5578.1
Interviewer: Grey, Dr. Meijan, Chronal Assessment Cmte.

GREY: Commander Spock, you devised the warp intermix formula that enabled the *Enterprise* to move through time under its own power. You formulated the equations allowing the first controlled Tipler slingshot maneuver through time. You helped design the sensor protocols that led to the discovery of the Guardian of Forever, and have played a key role in discovering its potentials and effects. I think it's safe to say that you have more direct experience with the theory and practical application of time travel than anyone in the Federation.

SPOCK: I suppose that would be a reasonable assessment. Although I would question the accuracy of the term "practical" in this context.

GREY: Could you elaborate?

SPOCK: The word "practical" implies regular or reliable use. To date, our experiences with temporal displacement, whether accidental or intentional, have been notably irregular, and each attempt has revealed new, even apparently inconsistent ways in which temporal and paracausal processes can manifest. Practicality would require a degree of repeatability and controllability which we are far from attaining.

GREY: So what recommendation would you make to the Federation Council? Should we proceed with time-travel experimentation or suspend research?

SPOCK: Research, on a theoretical and observational level, should certainly continue. We cannot intelligently assess the risks and potentials of time travel if we do not understand it. But by the same token, active experimentation would be premature.

Excerpt from interview transcript: Scott, Montgomery, Lt. Cmdr., Chf. Eng. U.S.S. *Enterprise*
Recorded on Starbase 23, Stardate 5578.3
GREY: Then you would not recommend further experimentation with the light-speed breakaway or "slingshot" effect?

SCOTT: No, ma'am. Not with my bair—ah, my engines. It's too great a strain on the ship. You don't force a machine to do something it wasn't designed for.

GREY: So your only objections are technological? Do you have an opinion about the more . . . existential risks posed by time travel?

SCOTT: I don't know anything about that. That's for the philosophers and the theoreticians to hash out. I mean . . . aye, it's common sense that if the same day happens two ways, it's still the same day. The same time. And if two things happen at the same time, well, then obviously one hasn't replaced the other, but they're simultaneous. Side by side. Ah, if you see what I'm saying, ma'am.

GREY: As you've witnessed yourself in your crossing to the Terran Empire timeline.

SCOTT: Aye. Still, though . . . I've seen some things these past few years that make me wonder. That Guardian . . . when we saw history changed, it didn't say we'd just been shunted into a parallel track. It said our history was *gone*. That we had no home to return to. So I . . . I just don't know.

Excerpt from interview transcript: T'Viss, Doctor, Research Fellow in Quantum Physics, Cambridge University
Recorded at Starfleet Headquarters, San Francisco, Stardate 5534.8

GREY: Granted, Doctor, everyday logic says that an event cannot cease to have occurred. But haven't we seen compelling evidence that time travel defies everyday logic? Common sense used to insist that time and space were constant for all observers, or that one's own planet was the center of the universe.

T'VISS: My thesis is grounded in nothing so pedestrian, Doctor. It is a matter of detailed mathematics, a wave theory of the universe supported by extensive observational and experimental data. There have always been those who have sought to employ the counterintuitive aspects of quantum theory to justify beliefs in the irrationality or unknowability of the universe, but in fact, quantum equations are precise and deterministic. Every possible state of a particle and the relative probabilities thereof can be precisely described by its Schrödinger equation. The same can be extended to any ensemble of particles up to and including the entire universe. Any mystery or uncertainty we perceive is merely the result of incomplete information about the entire state of events. To the audience of a stage magician, an item may appear to transform or vanish mysteriously, but this is because they only perceive selected aspects of the performance. To one aware of the full scenario, the event becomes entirely rational and self-consistent. In our case, quantum linearity prevents us from perceiving more than one measurement history at a time. Could we but measure the entire universe at once, encompassing all contributing histories, all perception of paradox or erasure of events would vanish.

GREY: But the very act of crossing between timelines requires nonlinear quantum mechanics to exist.

T'VISS: To a limited extent. Still, each observer perceives only one outcome at a time, so unitarity is effectively conserved, and the mechanics are still essentially linear.

GREY: But if they remember a different outcome to an event . . .

T'VISS: Memory is classical. A mind can remember events that have no quantum existence, such as a dream.

GREY: So you remain convinced that there is no danger to our timeline from anything that a traveler might do in the past. All they would do is displace themselves from their own history into a different one.

T'VISS: There is no logical basis to doubt it. Any alternative models are grounded in hypotheticals and impossibilities.

Excerpt from interview transcript: McCoy, Dr.
   Leonard H., Lt. Cmdr., CMO *U.S.S. Enterprise*
Recorded on Starbase 23, Stardate 5578.4

McCOY: All right, let's say for the sake of argument that if you go back in time and foul things up, it won't affect your past, just create some other reality alongside it. Well, what gives us the right to foul things up for the people in *that* reality?

GREY: Any change wouldn't necessarily be for the worse, though.

McCOY: Maybe not, but who are we to decide that? Isn't that why we have the Prime Directive? To remind us we can't always judge what'll help and what'll hurt, so sometimes it's best just to leave well enough alone?

GREY: And yet your crewmates have always managed to correct whatever disruptions they caused.

McCOY: Maybe. (*pause*) What scares me, though . . . when I came to my senses back in 1930, after the Guardian threw me back . . . I'd lost my hand phaser. And the damn stone doughnut whipped us back before I could look for it. I've got no idea what could've happened to it. Ever since, I've been watching for signs that it changed something, that this isn't the world I started out in.

GREY: But you haven't found any?

McCOY: I don't know. How do I know what's a change and what's me forgetting my history lessons? I . . . I try to convince myself that I'm worried over nothing. The Guardian said everything was back to normal. Probably the phaser fell in an old-style sewer and washed out to sea or something. But still . . . something that powerful lost in a primitive world . . . it's scary to think of the harm it could've done.

GREY: So you don't think the risks of time travel are justified by the potential for historical research?

McCOY: No, I do not. What's so blasted great about the past anyway? Rampant filth and disease, primitive medicine little better than butchery, ignorance and hate everywhere. . . . They say people who don't study the past are doomed to repeat it, but in my experience, it's the people who can't let go of the past who end up repeating it.

GREY: I'm surprised, Doctor. The impression I've gotten is that you consider yourself an old-fashioned type, suspicious of progress.

McCOY: Oh, I'm suspicious of all sorts of things, Doctor Grey. Too much focus on the past *or* the future can keep people from making the right choices in the present. I don't appreciate old-fashioned values because they're old, but because they've stood the test of time and still have value today. You wouldn't want to drink a fine wine before it matured. No, Doctor—the value of time is that it moves forward.

Excerpt from interview transcript: Aleek-Om,
    Dr. Loom, Professor of Ancient History,
    Institute of Galactic History
Recorded in New Samarkand, Alpha Centauri III,
    Stardate 5708.0
ALEEK-OM: The importance of the past in our lives cannot be overstated. It can be difficult for you short-

lived races to understand this. But we Aurelians have strong ties to the past through the tales and insights of our elders, preservers of an oral heritage that stretches back over twenty thousand standard years. We look upon you humanoids, with your short lives and imperfect memories, and lament that so much of your past is lost to you, leaving you without a sense of direction. It is why I became a historian—to do what I could to help improve your sense of your past.

GREY: And you think that being able to go back and witness the past firsthand . . .

ALEEK-OM: Yes. It would anchor you to your history in a way otherwise unattainable.

GREY: Is that worth the risk that time travel might disrupt the past?

ALEEK-OM: I take a risk every time I fly to work in the morning. But I am trained in the use of my wings and my senses, so it is a manageable risk. There is hazard now, in the infancy of temporal research, but only due to ignorance. We are fledglings, tentatively venturing forth from the aerie and struggling not to fall. The more we practice, the more we stretch our wings, the surer and safer our flights will become.

Excerpt from interview transcript: Kirk, James T., Cpt., Cmd. Off. *U.S.S. Enterprise*
Recorded on Starbase 23, Stardate 5578.6
KIRK: As an explorer, I certainly appreciate the incredible potential for discovery that time travel offers. And I'd be lying if I denied there was a part of me drawn to the adventure of opening a whole new kind of frontier.

GREY: It's not the nature of a starship captain to be risk-averse.

KIRK: As a rule, no. Risk in the pursuit of knowledge is what Starfleet is all about. (*pause*) But it's one thing for this ship, this crew, to risk our own lives in that pursuit. Every one of us has chosen to make that gamble. But to risk the existence of others who don't have a say—let alone whole worlds, whole . . . time continuums that could be jeopardized without ever knowing why—is another matter altogether. That's not just a matter of our risk anymore. It's being reckless with the lives of other people, other civilizations. And my duty as a Starfleet officer is to protect those lives, not to gamble with them.

GREY: So in your best judgment, the experiments should stop?

KIRK: I know that once a thing is discovered, it can't be undiscovered. Our descendants will travel in time—that's a reality we can't avoid. But as for us, here and now . . . we're not ready. We're children playing with fire. And we've seen how little it takes for that fire to burn out of control. Someday we will master this, but now is not the time. We need to stop before we burn ourselves away.

The halls of power
May–July 2270

Admiral Antonio Delgado could see the writing on the wall as the interviews played before the joint session of the Science and Intelligence subcouncils. These fourteen Federation councillors would decide the fate of his temporal research based on the findings of Meijan Grey's committee, and it was clear that they were leaning toward an outright ban. As politicians, they had little grasp of the scientific arguments. And the testimony of the *Enterprise* crew, the very individuals with the most direct experience of time travel, was damning. Delgado couldn't help feeling betrayed as he listened to Kirk, Spock, and the rest of them forming a united front against the very research they had made possible. He had begun this with such high hopes of a long, productive partnership with these men, and now they had the sheer selfishness to pull the rug out from under him just because they'd had a few painful experiences or didn't want their precious ship to endure a few bumps and bruises.

No matter; Delgado had spent years cultivating friends on the Science Council. The seven-member subcouncil had been one of the Federation's most powerful legislative subdivisions from the start, overseeing the Institutes of the Federation Science Council, the leading state-sponsored research facilities in the known galaxy, as well as holding authority over Starfleet's scientific arms such as Science Ops and UESPA. And he still had Intelligence Council allies left over from his years in SI. He'd lost some supporters on both subcouncils in the recent elections, but he'd gone right to work on winning over the newest members.

"We can't close the door completely here, Maria," he urged the freshman Councillor Moi of Regulus III as he let her beat him at racquetball. "Imagine the insights into the nature of time and the universe that could be right around the corner. I've seen some of Doctor B'kash's recent papers," he added, citing the noted Caitian physicist from the Regulus III Science Academy, an institution in which the novice Science Council member took warranted pride. "He may be onto something important. Imagine the tragedy if his work were cut short."

For others, it was a matter of appealing to their relationship with the past. Councillor Chab jav Lorg of Mars longed to unearth more about the overlooked role the planet's small Tellarite population, his ancestors, had played in its colonial history, while his fellow Intelligence Council member Jard Elbir of Tiburon wished to recover ancient knowledge lost in the post-Zoran purges on his world.

Still, Delgado could tell that the majority of the councillors were concerned about the risks of altering the past. For them, he tried a different tack. "Time travel doesn't have to be one-way," he told two of the Science Council members, Danga Sitru of Ithen and Konahr Lutet of Makus III, as they dined together in one of Paris's finest restaurants. The two councillors made a striking contrast, Sitru a child-sized male with bright copper skin and a colorful fez and scarf, Lutet a strikingly tall female with mahogany skin and a hooded, multicolored robe. So Delgado had chosen a restaurant with privacy screens so they could talk without worrying about curious bystanders. "Imagine traveling into the future. Coming back with technologies that could push us centuries ahead of rival powers. Learning about wars and disasters before they happen, giving us a chance to prevent them."

"But if history can't be changed . . ." Sitru began.

"We couldn't erase those future timelines, but we could create a new branch for ourselves that would exist apart from them. We could shape the future however we wish."

During a round of Lunar golf with the Betelgeusian Science Councillor Chuu'iik Hru'uith and the Intelligence Councillors S'kaa of Sauria and Grace Murabi of Izar, he asked, "And what about our enemies? We've stumbled across time warps and portals by accident more than once—what's to stop the Klingons or Romulans or Tholians from doing the same? Imagine, say, the Klingons going back a week before an important conference, before security's in place, and hiding a time bomb. Or the Romulans traveling into the future to read about our classified military plans in a history book. We need to keep researching time travel so we can develop defenses against it." Hru'uith perked up at that; Betelgeusians thrived on competition, which was why Delgado only played golf against Hru'uith when he needed to persuade him of something. S'kaa and Murabi kept their own counsel, but he knew they were two of the most hawkish members of Intelligence.

"There must be laws, Antonio," said the chair of the Intelligence Council, Zhimen ch'Rhettel of Andor, as they took in Paris's most acclaimed multispecies burlesque revue along with freshman Intelligence member Lyo Morhas of Icor IX, whose purple skin flushed darker at the sights onstage. "You can't stop that. A lot of councillors and cabinet members are frankly frightened out of their wits by what they heard in Grey's reports. Either that or outraged that Starfleet has proceeded so recklessly with these experiments."

"I understand that, Zhim. But the question is, how far should those laws go? The Federation has laws against genetic augmentation, laws we both support, but I know how hard you've worked to make sure those laws don't become so draconian that they impede legitimate genetic medicine and research. That's how the Federation works. We seek a responsible balance, not absolutism and ideological purity. Even where we impose limits, we still recognize the value of pure knowledge, and of safe, practical applications of that knowledge within the limits we choose."

And so the legislation began to take shape. Temporal research within the Federation would be strictly regulated by the Science Council. The work of theorists studying temporal physics in the abstract would not be suppressed, of course, but any active experiments would have to be monitored and regulated in the name of galactic security. Any time machines or naturally occurring temporal warps discovered in the course of space exploration would be confiscated or secured.

But new law meant new bureaucracy to enforce it, so there would have to be a department established to carry out these responsibilities, under the aegis of the Science Council Institutes. (Ch'Rhettel had pressed for Intelligence or Starfleet oversight, but the Science Council chair, T'Nuri of Vulcan, had argued persuasively that this was fundamentally a scientific matter, one that the Science Council and its Institutes were best equipped to cope with.) Thanks to Delgado's lobbying, what was initially mooted as a Department of Temporal Regulation or Control was legislated as the Federation Department of Temporal Investigations—an agreeably ambiguous name, satisfying those who saw its mandate as criminal investigation to enforce the new temporal laws as well as those who saw it as scientific investigation of temporal phenomena and their applications. As for the general public, or those curious enough about government to notice this new line item in the Science Council budget, any guesses they might make as to its meaning would probably be off the mark, since who besides the crackpots would believe the government had a department investigating time travel?

The legislation passed in both subcouncils by a margin of ten to four, over the objections of those who found it too strict or too lenient. The closed-session vote in the general council was closer, though the reasons for opposition were different; many councillors simply couldn't grasp time travel as more than an abstraction and questioned what they saw as a frivolous allocation of resources. But it passed thanks to the clout of the two subcouncils that sponsored it and the willingness of the more reasonable councillors to defer to the judgment of those who actually understood the subject being legislated. And so, on Stardate 5886.7 (Sol referent), 7:08 PM Greenwich Mean Time on the twenty-second of July in the year 2270 Common Era—a Friday—the Federation Department of Temporal Investigations was created by law.

DTI Headquarters
Greenwich, European Alliance, Earth
Stardate 5909.3
August 2270
In Delgado's ideal world, he would have been appointed as the inaugural director of the DTI; but of course there

was no chance of that, given that the Council saw it as a civilian check on Starfleet's reckless experimentation with time. Besides, Secretary Vexam and the Science Council had felt the simplest way to staff it was to ask the Chronal Assessment Committee's members to stay on permanently. Crenfel declined, wishing to spend more time with her family, and sh'Lesinas already had her own career as a full-time author, though she agreed to remain available to the DTI as a consultant. So Mei-jan Grey, Simok, and Arthur Manners would form the core of the department's leadership. Its research staff would be drawn from those personnel within the Science Council Institutes who were most qualified to deal with temporal physics and technology.

"You need T'Viss," Delgado told Grey at their first meeting following her appointment as DTI director. Her private office was a small, spartan space within the equally austere headquarters of the novice, low-profile agency, which some whimsical Science Council planner had arranged to situate in a restored semidetached Victorian house just north of the Royal Observatory, sitting practically on top of the Prime Meridian. "She's possibly the finest, most experienced temporal physicist in the Federation."

"And one of the most hidebound," Grey said. "She lacks imagination."

"Is that a bad thing, Jan?" He smiled. "Take it from someone who's been in this business a few years—it's easy to let your imagination run away with you. I've seen personnel burn out or break down because they couldn't deal with the idea that our lives and histories are mutable.

I've seen them fall into depression because they were convinced that every decision was meaningless if it was just going to be made differently in an alternate timeline. No, the people who do best at this work are the ones with the most restrained imaginations. The ones who can focus strictly on the facts, the science, or their duties." He leaned closer. "Who don't let extraneous concerns or personal histories cloud their objective judgment."

He saw that Grey caught his subtext. "I'll talk to Doctor T'Viss," she conceded. "As long as she's able to work within a framework of caution toward the prospect of historical alteration . . ."

"Jan, let me tell you something about T'Viss. She doesn't care one whit about the applications of temporal theory. The pure science is all that matters to her, and everything else is beneath her notice. She may scoff at your operating assumptions, but she won't bother to get in your way. And could it really hurt you to have a resident gadfly? Caution is a sound policy, but for all we know, her models may still be the right ones." He spread his hands. "Or not. But that's a question for the researchers to hash out among them. And that's part of this department's mandate, isn't it? To oversee temporal research?"

"Theoretical research, yes. But I know what you're fishing for, Admiral," Grey told him. "You're hoping to convince me to allow further experimentation. No, don't give me the speech," she added, holding up a hand to forestall him. "Yes, you have made valid points about temporal defense, and about the possibilities of temporal observation of the future. But any experimentation this department might authorize would have to be along those lines. The Council is adamant: no more mucking about in the past."

Delgado found it significant that she pinned that decision on the Council, as if to distance herself from it. He suppressed a smile. He knew the yearning still existed within her. Delgado was content to develop temporal science for the greater good, as a positive legacy he could leave to atone for his mistakes. He believed there was a real chance that he was helping the universe work toward some specific goal, something that the forces of time themselves were pushing him toward; but he saw his role as that of a facilitator. Jan Grey, on the other hand, still yearned to visit the past she had spent her life studying. She was conscious of that urge, suspicious of it, determined to ignore it for what she considered the good of the Federation. But the urge still existed. Grey wasn't a bureaucrat afraid of the unknown, but a scientist, an explorer. More: he suspected she was a closet romantic. The way she streaked her hair or donned discreet jewelry to keep fashionable suggested that she still had aspirations beyond her cool professionalism, hopes that her unlikely yearnings could be made real. And he could tell from her body language, from the way she studied him when she thought he wasn't looking, that she might be more receptive to him on a personal level than she was professionally. If he played his cards right, there was a chance that this Department of Temporal Investigations could become a boon to Delgado's work rather than an impediment.

"Fine," he said. "The future it is. Or alternate presents, if we can find a way to reach them without going back in time and creating them." To date, his teams had had no luck re-creating the transporter accident that had accessed the Terran Empire timeline; it seemed to require unique spatial and subspatial conditions that were impossible to replicate with existing technology. And the subspace confluence, as T'Viss called it, that had brought the Onlies' Earth into this timeline remained maddeningly resistant to analysis. It didn't seem to be a natural phenomenon, but there was no sign of anything artificial that could be generating and sustaining it—not on this side of the confluence, at least. "But the Guardian refuses to show any era beyond the present—"

"The Guardian is off-limits anyway. No travel, no passive scans, no communication with it whatsoever."

"I know. I've read the legislation in great detail, believe me."

"Looking for loopholes?"

He deflected the question with a joke. "Well, the Guardian is a pretty big loophole. Or is it a knothole?"

Grey closed off. "If you ask me, it's a—it's just a hole. A big, empty hole."

Delgado winced at his poor choice of diversions. He hadn't appreciated how much she still blamed herself for, as she saw it, almost erasing Commander Spock from existence. It was a reminder that he'd have to tread carefully to win and keep her trust.

Which meant that trying to capitalize on her attraction to him would probably be a bad idea. He could be very persuasive with women, but holding on to their trust was a different matter. That could only be earned by giving them his own loyalty, but that meant placing them above his own agendas and ambitions. He'd had trouble enough doing that even with women he wasn't actively manipulating. If what he sought was a short-term gain, he could live with that. But he needed to cultivate Jan Grey as a long-term ally. So he'd have to approach her with delicacy, do what he could to cultivate her positive feelings toward him without complicating things with an actual relationship.

Which was just as well. He could do far better than this sour-faced woman who thought that streaking her hair like a "real now" teenager could make her attractive. In fact, he had a lively evening planned with the comely young Councillor Moi, in pursuit of political and personal gains that were entirely short-term.

So he wrapped up the meeting as courteously as possible and left. He chuckled as he looked around at the sparse facilities the DTI had been given, still full of storage cases waiting to be unpacked, consoles waiting to be hooked up, and seats waiting to be filled. Even this small space was virtually empty of staff, aside from Simok and a lanky, young-looking Rhaandarite female taking inventory of the cases. This handful of people in a small room was what the Federation Council hoped could prevent the perfection of time travel? He hadn't felt this good about his chances since the hearings had begun.

Still, with the Guardian interdicted, his choice of experimental subjects was essentially narrowed to one: the *U.S.S. Enterprise.* Or, more precisely, its special, time-capable engines. But Kirk and his crew had made up their minds; they wouldn't cooperate in any further temporal research. And with Bob Comsol's retirement last year, he'd lost his most powerful ally in Starfleet Command. The new commanding officer, Heihachiro Nogura, was not an easy man to get close to; prior to achieving his current post, he had been one of the Admiralty's senior military planners, and most of his work, sometimes even his whereabouts, had been classified from those without a need to know. His current post gave him a more public profile, but as yet, Delgado had not been able to establish a relationship with him. No doubt Nogura was a shrewd man, though, not easily manipulated. Delgado would have to proceed with care if he wanted to convince Nogura to give him access to the *Enterprise*'s engines.

But there were always options. If he recalled correctly, the *Enterprise* had been on its current survey and patrol tour for nearly five years, the recommended maximum interval between major overhauls. Knowing Kirk, he'd want to push his ship beyond that conservative limit. And given his enviable record of successes, he just might have the clout to pull it off.

So Delgado would simply have to find a way to bring the *Enterprise* home.

V

U.S.S. Enterprise
Stardate 6921.4
November 2270

Captain's log, Supplemental:
The situation on Pelos is worse than we could have imagined. With the sun dimmed by the cosmic dust cloud that has engulfed this system, agriculture has failed planetwide and famine grips the population. Worse, the pressure of the cloud triggers increased solar flares and suppresses the stellar magnetosphere that protects the planet from cosmic rays. Between the famine and the radiation, the Pelosians' immune systems are ravaged and plagues run rampant. The death toll is horrendous—and accelerating.

But the worst of it is not the natural disaster. The collapse of governments across Pelos has allowed the strongest nation, under the rule of Queen Palchelle, to conquer what remains of this world. Palchelle wields power by exploiting the Pelosians' belief that this disaster is punishment from their gods. And under her religion, only the gods may determine who lives and who dies. All forms of medi-

*cine have been outlawed, all the physicians rounded
up and executed. Spock and McCoy estimate that
without medical care, too few Pelosians will survive
the plagues to avoid extinction once the dust cloud
passes. This hardy, determined species could survive
the worst that the cosmos has to throw at them—but
their queen's fanaticism will destroy them.*

It was a great relief to Montgomery Scott when Lieutenant Uhura reported that Kirk was calling in from the
surface of Pelos. Scott had grown accustomed to keeping the center seat warm while Kirk went haring off into
danger, but it was not a job he'd ever want to hold on a
permanent basis, and certainly not as a result of Kirk and
Spock getting themselves killed on some godforsaken
rock in space. It was a particularly unwelcome task on
this mission, since Starfleet had sent an inspector, Commodore Harriet Griswold, to evaluate Kirk's request to
extend the *Enterprise*'s current exploration tour. Griswold was a staff officer rather than line, a classic desk-
bound bureaucrat resistant to the idea of lengthening
the tour beyond the recommended five years between
overhauls. Kirk had pointed out repeatedly that the
Enterprise had undergone a thorough overhaul at Earth
Spacedock less than four years ago, after that first to-do
with the Black Star, so the ship was entitled to at least
another year on the frontier. True, the crew was tired,
and a rest would be appreciated; but if the ship returned
home for a refit, it might be months before she set out
again and many in the crew might take other assignments. The captain had made clear his feelings that the

Enterprise's current crew was the finest he'd ever worked with, and he was in no hurry to see it broken up. Tired or not, Scott felt the same way, and he knew that nearly every man and woman aboard this ship did as well.

But Griswold, a small, pug-faced woman with tightly curled hair the color of old parchment, resisted any change from standard procedure, at least without a thorough performance evaluation of both ship and crew. Insisting that people as well as machines have their limits, she was watching the crew like a hawk for signs of excessive stress, fatigue, or trauma. It wasn't Scott's place to say so, but he had the feeling she was looking for any excuse to reject Kirk's request and order the crew back home. Between her and the recent visit from that DTI bureaucrat Manners—who'd questioned them relentlessly about the legality and necessity of their actions to rescue Captain Kirk when his consciousness was trapped in the past during the Skagway mission—Scott was starting to feel a bit persecuted.

Now Scott tried to ignore the commodore looming over his shoulder as he hit the intercom button on the command chair's arm. "Captain! We were gettin' worried, sir. When you didn't call in—"

"We're all okay, Scotty," Kirk's voice assured him. *"We had a little run-in with the queen's enforcers. Doctor McCoy couldn't resist trying to treat some plague victims, and that's apparently grounds for summary execution around here."*

McCoy's voice butted in. *"For someone who says life and death are in the gods' hands, she's awfully willing to deal out the latter herself."*

Kirk resumed his account. *"Which means, luckily for us, that there are a lot of Pelosians eager to see the queen removed from power. A band of rebels helped us escape the guards. We're with them now."*

"Glad I am to hear it, sir."

Griswold stepped forward, inserting herself into the conversation. "Captain Kirk, this is Griswold. Are you saying you have joined forces with the rebels?"

"No, Commodore, I'm saying they saved our lives and helped us elude capture. For now, at least. Mister Scott, ship status?"

"Holdin' steady up here, sir. We're keeping our orbit clear o' dust with the navigational deflector. And if I may, sir—Mister Chekov and I have been thinking that if we boost the deflector dish to maximum power, we could thin out this dust cloud quite a bit, maybe help the star get back to normal that much faster. We'd have to break orbit, of course, and it could take several days, but—"

"That's a great idea, Scotty. Proceed at your discretion." At the navigation station, the young Russian ensign turned to grin at Scott. *"But there's something we need first. The rebels have been doing what they can to provide medical care to the survivors, but they're stretched thin and their knowledge of radiation sickness is lacking. McCoy has a list of medications he'll need delivered to the surface. A long list. Tell Nurse Chapel to prepare to beam down with them."*

"Aye, sir." Scott didn't consider questioning the perils involved. He'd come to learn that was simply James Kirk's way. Pull him out of the jaws of death and he'd unhesitatingly leap back in if he thought he could pull someone else free.

But Commodore Griswold was another matter. "Captain, I must protest! Offering modern medical aid to a pre-spaceflight world is a clear violation of the Prime Directive."

"I don't agree, ma'am. We don't have to tell them where the medicines come from. Entire nations have been wiped out already. We can claim that we and Nurse Chapel are survivors from one of those areas, tell the rebels that our medicines are new breakthroughs that came just before the disaster struck. We can help them without revealing where the help is coming from."

"That is not how General Order One is supposed to work, Captain."

"General Order One is supposed to protect other cultures from harm due to outside interference," Kirk said. *"I don't see how preventing extinction qualifies as harm."*

"Captain—"

"With all due respect, Commodore Griswold, you are here as an observer only. The decision is mine, and it's been made. Scotty, you have your orders."

"Aye, sir."

"Kirk out."

Griswold turned to face Scott, her small gray eyes flaring in disapproval. "This is highly irregular."

"Welcome to life in space, ma'am. Now if you want to assess how efficiently we can do our jobs, then I respectfully suggest you stand back and let us do them."

She stared at him sourly for another moment, then turned and left the bridge. But she was scribbling fiercely on her data slate as she did so.

Imperial Palace, Pelos
Stardate 6922.8

Queen Palchelle's throne room was a shrine to excess. The queen adorned its rough-hewn stone walls and interior space with paintings, tapestries, sculptures, furniture, and adornments plundered from all over the globe, as well as slaves from all of Pelos's surviving ethnic groups. The Pelosians were basically humanoid, with a pair of small horns jutting from each temple and eyebrows that stretched out to merge with their hairlines, but their skin tones ranged from a light auburn to a rich maroon and the horns varied in size and sharpness from one racial group to another. The different populations had become jumbled together as survivors and refugees had congregated in the remaining stably governed lands, so McCoy's effort to disguise the landing party with an average Pelosian appearance had inadvertently created a look which the Pelosians saw as exotic. Far from being a problem, that had made it easier for Kirk and his party to pass themselves off as refugees from a far land.

The distinction didn't seem to matter to Palchelle now, though, as she gazed down from her ornate throne. Kirk couldn't help but notice how healthy she and her nobles appeared next to the slaves that attended them, let alone the refugee populations beyond. They showed little sign of the malnutrition, fatigue, anemia, hair loss, or susceptibility to infection that ran rampant through the population. True, the nobles had retreated to underground bunkers as soon as they had realized that exposure to the skies hastened the sickness, but that alone couldn't explain their robust health.

Palchelle flowed to her feet and sashayed down from the royal dais, her piercing blue-gray eyes roving over Kirk. She was a tall brunette, well-nourished enough to be voluptuous, a fact made vividly apparent by the translucent silks she wore. Elaborate jewelry, the plunder of a world, adorned her brow and body and shimmered in the glow of the throne room's oil lamps as she undulated closer. "So," she purred. "You are the leader of the heretics."

"You mean my friends?" he responded, keeping his tone even. "The ones you've sentenced to death for trying to save lives?"

"I merely carry out the will of the Originators," she said with feigned apology. "They have sent these ordeals to us as a test of our faith. If we do not trust in them to save us, then their wrath will continue until all unbelievers have fallen." She stroked his cheek. "I know it can be difficult to bear the suffering, but that is how we are tested."

"Are you so sure, Your Highness? What if the Originators are actually testing our initiative? Our ability to take care of ourselves?"

"You speak of matters you do not understand, Kirk. The plagues are a warning that we must renounce all sin and doubt, reaffirm our faith in Original law, or lose everything."

"And is that why you and your court are so healthy, Your Highness? Through faith alone? Not through the use of the medicines you confiscate?"

Palchelle lowered her hand, her gaze growing harder. "We are the Pure. Our faith has already been affirmed beyond question. And we are rewarded for our devotion." Catching herself, she softened her tone again, circling him at close range, close enough that he could feel the warmth of her body. "There is room for others who demonstrate the same devotion, Kirk. Who have not yet been damned by heresy."

He shrugged. "But I'm the leader of the heretics."

"Your followers have personally intervened in matters of life and death, but your own hands"—which she clasped now—"are not fatally tainted yet. You still have a chance to cleanse your soul. All you must do is tell me where to find the rest of your kind and the potions they create."

"There are no others," he told her. "We were the only survivors."

"Please do not waste your remaining breath on lies. These supplies in such abundance must come from somewhere. There are more of you in hiding, making these blasphemous substances. You can save your soul—and your life—if you tell me where they are." She squeezed his hands and leaned closer. "And there will be . . . other rewards . . . as well."

She kissed him, and he didn't fight it. He'd seduced female adversaries or let them seduce him to gain advantage in the past, and there were certainly pleasurable aspects to such an approach. But despite Palchelle's beauty and seductive manner, Kirk found little appeal in the idea of playing this game with her. She was a genocidal fanatic, a petty hypocrite who would damn her species to extinction in the name of a cause she didn't even believe in. She thought her small core of loyalists could wait out this plague, keeping themselves alive with hoarded food and medicine denied to the rest. But the remaining population base would be inadequate to recover from the disaster, particularly if it consisted only of pampered nobles with no skills in agriculture or industry. Palchelle and her inner circle would only delay their extinction by a few years at best.

Besides, he'd found himself tiring of these brief dalliances lately. He'd never wanted to become the kind of spacefarer who left a trail of broken hearts behind him, and his own heart too often yearned for something deeper than casual distractions or hollow seductions for the sake of the mission. Even as he pressured Starfleet to extend the tour another year, he found himself thinking that if he did go home, maybe he could finally find a beach to walk on and someone to share it with. Maybe he was growing up. Maybe he was just tired after five years in deep space.

So he pushed himself away from Palchelle's alluring form. "And what about their lives?" he asked. "You expect me just to throw them away?"

"Those who do not surrender to the Originators' will are doomed already, Kirk. At least I can make their end quick and merciful."

Kirk spread his arms. "Your Highness, I can tell you with complete honesty that there are no more of my people anywhere on this world. But even if there were, I wouldn't tell you where to find them. I have no interest in anything you're offering."

Her sensual manner dropped like the flimsy facade it was. "Then you will die with your friends."

"Better that than help you destroy this world with your petty hypocrisy."

"Throw him in with the others!" she told the guards. He sized them up as they advanced. There were three of them, big men forced to wear little clothing to indulge Palchelle's appetites, but they were not as healthy or well-fed as the nobles.

He let them lead him into the tunnel beyond, one grasping each arm, the third ahead. He played along meekly until they'd lowered their guard, then feigned tripping. He broke the guards' grip and drove his elbows into their guts, then whirled and took down the right-hand guard with a spinning kick to the head. The second guard was reaching for his sword, but Kirk delivered a haymaker to his jaw and the sword went flying. Glancing over his shoulder, Kirk saw the forward guard charging him, so he spun to intercept, rolled, and sent the man flying over his head. The other guards' bodies broke his fall, though, and he clambered to his feet. Kirk beat him there and launched into a flying kick that took him down.

Unfortunately, the drawback to the flying kick was that it left Kirk flat on his back once gravity had its say. Which was fine if you managed to knock out your last opponent before you fell . . . but not so fine if, say, a half-dozen other guards had come running in response to the commotion and were now converging around you with swords drawn while you were still lying on your sore backside. As six pieces of extremely sharp steel converged around his throat and chest, Kirk decided it was high time he reevaluated his fondness for the flying kick.

"Hurry up, Spock! It's getting hotter!"

"I am aware of that, Doctor," Spock replied. "And I assure you I have not been dilatory in my efforts until now." Indeed, McCoy's observation was atypically understated. The landing party and their rebel associates were currently incarcerated within a natural lava tube connecting to an active volcano near Queen Palchelle's capital. Iron bars on either side prevented their escape. This was Palchelle's preferred method of execution: since her prisoners' lives would be ended either by flowing lava, toxic gases, or lethal levels of heat, and on an unpredictable schedule, she could claim that their death was technically the work of the gods rather than the result of direct Pelosian action. Spock's attempts to persuade her guards of the flaws in her logic had proved ineffectual.

Luckily, Nurse Chapel had possessed the good judgment to hide her communicator in her medical kit upon their capture. The Pelosians' superstitions had made them reluctant to search the kit, and so the communicator had gone overlooked when the rest of the landing party's equipment was confiscated and when the medicines had subsequently been placed here to burn along with the prisoners. By itself, the communicator lacked the power to penetrate the layers of basaltic rock above them, but Spock was attempting to wire in the landing party's subcutaneous transponders, which McCoy and Chapel had extracted from all of their arms, to boost the communicator's power.

"Doctor," Chapel called. "Manti has lost consciousness."

"Damn," McCoy barked, followed by several harsh coughs. "Do what you can for her. I can't leave Lyban right now." Despite their willingness to use medicine, the Pelosian dissidents were still weak from malnutrition and were succumbing to the increasing heat and toxicity more swiftly than the *Enterprise* personnel.

"Captain," Spock said, "the communicator is ready. Insufficient bandwidth for voice, but an emergency beam-out signal should penetrate."

"Do it, Spock. And modulate the signal to let Scotty know it's nine to beam up, not just four."

Spock's brow rose. "Commodore Griswold will no doubt challenge that decision," he said, though he was already complying.

"Commodore Griswold is used to thinking of aliens as statistics. I'd like to think if she were here, seeing these people struggling for breath, she wouldn't just save herself and leave them here." He broke off, choking.

"I suggest you save your breath for when you see her, Jim." Spock's gentle words made the captain smile.

Spock monitored the emergency signal, aware that there was no way to be certain the *Enterprise* was in range to receive it, or could return to Pelos in time if it were. McCoy was right that the temperature was rising swiftly, as was the noise level. At best, with tri-ox from the medkits, the prisoners might endure a few more hours before suffocating. At worst, they would be consumed by lava rather sooner.

After a time, Nurse Chapel came alongside Spock to

administer a tri-ox booster. "No, thank you, Nurse," he said. "I can get by with considerably less oxygen than the others."

"Don't go Vulcan stoic on me, Mister Spock," she said. "We need you at your peak if you're to keep that communicator working. Basic triage: first save the person who can do the most to save others."

Spock nodded. "Logical."

Chapel administered the dose, then sighed and leaned against the wall. "Was there something else?" Spock asked.

"I just need to catch my breath."

Spock grunted in acknowledgment and resumed fine-tuning the communicator, ensuring the tenuous connections remained viable. But after a few moments, Chapel gave a wry smile. "Suddenly, going home doesn't sound like such a bad idea," she said. Since no reply seemed required from him, Spock said nothing. But Chapel continued. "I've decided . . . once we do go home, whether it's now or a year from now, I'm going to complete my M.D. training. I thought I was just going to postpone it until I found Roger, but then . . ." She trailed off. Spock recalled that she had given up a promising bioresearch career to search for her lost fiancé, Roger Korby. "Once I knew he was gone, I had no more reason to stay in Starfleet, but I . . . didn't think I had anywhere else to go. But now . . . it's time to move forward."

Spock hesitated. He and Chapel had only infrequently spoken beyond the demands of duty since the embarrassing incident with Harry Mudd's alleged love potion, but lately it seemed she had resolved to put it, and her unfortunate infatuation with him, behind her. Now it seemed she was reaching out and attempting to establish a new, more appropriate working relationship with him. That was something to be encouraged. "That is a commendable attitude, Nurse. I consider it likely that you will excel as a physician—provided," he could not resist adding, "that you do not follow Doctor Mc-Coy's example too closely."

"I heard that!" McCoy wheezed, and Chapel stifled a laugh.

"What are your plans for once the mission ends?" Chapel asked Spock.

He pondered how to reply. He was not ready to voice his plans just yet. He had become increasingly convinced that returning to Vulcan for the *Kolinahr* was necessary. Too often these past few years, his inability to resist emotional compromise had jeopardized the safety of his ship and his crewmates. Despite all his training, he had succumbed to the virus at Psi 2000, the spores on Omicron Ceti III, the effects of the atavachron on Sarpeidon, the siren song of the Taurean females, and other such disruptive influences over and over. Unless he could master his own mind, he would continue to be a liability to Kirk or any other commanding officer he might be assigned to serve. Thus, the only logical course of action, once his current duties aboard the *Enterprise* had been discharged, was to return to Vulcan and seek seclusion with the Masters of Gol to purge his emotions completely. But he knew that Kirk and McCoy would not understand this decision and would protest it fiercely. Now was hardly the time for that conversation.

That was the least of the reasons why it was fortunate that Spock began to feel the paresthetic effect of a transporter beam in operation upon his person. Moments later, he, Kirk, McCoy, and Chapel were in the *Enterprise*'s main transporter room. "Clear the platform, please, sirs," said Lieutenant Kyle in his crisp British accent, "so I can materialize the rest." Spock hastened to comply, assisting the weakened Chapel down the steps while Kirk did the same for McCoy. As soon as the five Pelosian dissidents materialized, McCoy and Chapel hastened to their aid. Seeing their condition, Kyle summoned further medical assistance.

But before a medical team could arrive, Commodore Griswold did, her reaction conforming closely to Spock's prediction. "Captain Kirk! Beaming pre-warp natives aboard the *Enterprise*? You've gone too far this time!"

"They were minutes from death," Kirk protested. "Look at them! What would you have me do?"

"People die all the time on primitive planets, Captain. We can't save all of them."

"But we could save these. And without violating the Prime Directive. They're barely conscious at best. They'll need to be sedated for treatment anyway. We can fix them up and beam them down to some remote part of the planet, far from Palchelle's reach. She'll never know they didn't get burned up in the lava with the rest of us."

"And how will you explain to them how they got there?"

Kirk shrugged. "I think they'll just be happy to be alive. These are pragmatic people, Commodore. They know how to keep a secret, and a low profile."

Griswold shook her head. "Do you even know how many regulations you've violated, Captain?"

"I probably know the regulations better than you, Commodore Griswold, because I have to interpret them in practice on a constant basis. Out here, regulations can't just be inert words on a screen. They have to be adapted, finessed to fit the unpredictable."

"That's not for you to say, Captain Kirk."

"If not me, then who? I'm the one Starfleet sent out here to make just those decisions."

Griswold stared up at him smugly. "If I have anything to say about it, mister, you won't be out here much longer."

Starfleet Headquarters, San Francisco
Stardate 6985.4
December 2270

Rear Admiral Antonio Delgado was pleased with the outcome of his maneuvers. After his first salvo, a DTI investigation by Arthur Manners, had failed to find cause for filing charges against Kirk in the Skagway incident, Delgado had persuaded the Starfleet Inspector General (during a fact-finding junket to Argelius, where they'd found any number of intriguing facts about the local women) to assign Harriet Griswold to review the *Enterprise*'s performance, knowing that she was a stickler for regulations who'd jump on any excuse to deny Kirk his mission extension. But he hadn't expected the captain to make it so *easy* the second time around. After the events at Pelos, Griswold had charged Kirk with violating the Prime Directive, and the *Enterprise* had been ordered back to Earth. Now, all Delgado had to do was convince Admiral Nogura to let him have the ship.

He found Nogura in the observation gallery of the courtroom hosting Kirk's preliminary hearing. Per Starfleet convention, the investigation was conducted by two command-level officers, Commodores William Smillie and T'Vran. The hearing was open to the public, and the press had turned it into a circus. Kirk was already notorious as the first Starfleet captain ever court-martialed, back when he'd been accused of negligence in the death of Lieutenant Commander Ben Finney. He'd been cleared when Finney had been found alive, of course, but the notoriety remained. Now that Kirk was on the verge of a second court-martial, the press and the public were obsessed with the case, examining all of Kirk's nonclassified actions over the past five years and harping on anything that seemed like a questionable command decision or a breach of regulations. Griswold had played to that appetite for scandal in her testimony, reporting on her own in-depth investigation of Kirk's record and attempting to demonstrate a pattern of contempt for the Prime Directive. In the wake of the debates that had led to the creation of the DTI, the Federation Council was still gazing on Starfleet Command with a wary eye, ready to pounce at the first sign of impropriety; so the brass was under pressure to examine all the doubts that Griswold raised.

But now it was Kirk's turn to testify before the panel, and the captain was defending his record with his usual eloquence. "Have I bent the letter of the Prime

Directive on occasion?" he said. "I have. But always in service to its spirit. When I have intervened, it's been to cancel out interference from other sources. On Beta III and Gamma Trianguli VI, I neutralized ancient computers that had held their civilizations in unnatural stasis for thousands of years. On Capella IV, Neural, and Omega IV, I removed interference from outside forces serving their own agendas, whether the enemy's or our own."

"What about Eminiar VII and Vendikar?" Smillie asked. "There was no external source of interference there. Everything they did was by their own choice."

"Yes, and that included marking the *Enterprise* as a casualty of their war and attempting to cause the death of its crew. That was a direct act of hostility against Starfleet personnel, effectively a declaration of war against the Federation. At that point, the Prime Directive ceased to apply. I acted in defense of my ship and its crew, and I did what was necessary to neutralize the Eminians' ability to take the lives of Starfleet officers."

Smillie didn't press the point further, but T'Vran asked, "And what of your intervention on Capella IV? The Ten Tribes' own customs called for the death of the High Teer's wife and heir following his own execution. The wife herself was ready to accept death under those customs. Yet you rescued her over her own protest."

Kirk thought for a moment. "Yes, I did. I saw a pregnant woman and her unborn child in mortal danger in front of me and I refused to accept it. Did I show disrespect for her people's customs? Probably. But I did what I felt I had to do in that moment. Given the choice between bending the rules to save an innocent life or obeying the rules and letting someone helpless be murdered right in front of me, I felt there was no choice.

"And that's why Starfleet sends men and women out there instead of machines. Because doing the right thing isn't about blind, robotic obedience to a programmed set of rules. It's about making choices. Choices informed by laws and regulations but tempered by wisdom and compassion, adapted to the unique right and wrong of every situation.

"Are those choices always right, always free from bias or impulse? No. We're fallible beings. We make mistakes. That's why we need a Prime Directive in the first place—to warn us against getting too sure of our own rightness, to stop us before we make well-intentioned mistakes that can devastate a culture we don't fully understand. The Prime Directive isn't about protecting other cultures from their weaknesses, but from ours. But they can make mistakes too. They aren't always right about what's best for them any more than we are. So we need the latitude to make choices of our own. It's a latitude that needs to be used sparingly and with careful thought. Believe me, I've seen what can happen when it's abused.

"But our laws were made by beings just as imperfect as we are, and they have their limits. We can't trust in them blindly, any more than we can trust blindly in ourselves. We need our laws and our individual judgments to balance each other, so that, hopefully, they can cancel out the worst of each other's imperfections."

The hearing soon took a recess for lunch, and Delgado caught up with Nogura in the HQ commissary. After arranging for an associate to call away Nogura's aide, Vice Admiral Lori Ciana, Delgado approached the commanding admiral and asked to join him. Nogura, a lean, grizzled man with heavy-lidded eyes, nodded serenely as he blew on his jasmine tea. "I think Kirk is making his case very well, sir," Delgado said.

"Mmm." Nogura's gravelly voice was untroubled. "Smillie and T'Vran have both been out there themselves. They know that Kirk's done no worse than any good captain before him."

"Agreed. There's no real chance of a court-martial."

"That's for the panel to decide, Antonio. But I will be surprised if they decide differently."

Delgado turned to the window overlooking the plaza in front of Headquarters, currently filled with protestors waving holographic signs. "Still . . . look at them. Half of them want Kirk's head on a platter, the rest want him to run for office. And both sides have councillors pandering to them. Either way this goes, there will be political fallout."

Nogura sipped his tea. "There's a way out."

"What's that, sir?"

"Promote the son of a bitch."

Delgado nodded in comprehension. "Of course. Bump him up to a desk job. It looks like a reward for his years of service, and it keeps him out of trouble."

"Something like that. But more. Kirk's made fine decisions in the field. He's a gifted commander, a leader who inspires great loyalty. Granting him responsibility over more than just one ship would be a genuine boon for Starfleet."

"And his gift for oratory, his celebrity, would make him a good face for Starfleet here at home," Delgado added.

"Yes, there is that." Nogura smirked. "Heaven knows the limelight is not something I crave. That's what I have Ciana for."

"It could work," Delgado said. He took care not to make his approval any more effusive, sensing that Nogura would not respond well to any appearance of sycophancy. After a few quiet moments, he asked, "What happens to his ship?"

"Ahh," Nogura sighed. "There we are. You want the *Enterprise*'s engines for yourself."

It was true what they said: the old man missed nothing. "The benefits to Federation science could be incalculable, sir. Not to mention the security benefits, if we can master time before our enemies do."

The admiral held out a hand. "No need to sell me, Antonio. I see the value in the research." He finished his tea and set down the cup. "But the *Enterprise* is the highest-profile ship in the fleet right now. If I just hand her over to you, it will attract the kind of attention that your project needs to avoid."

"If I may, sir, you've already found the answer to that. Make it look like a reward. Announce that, in honor of the great service done to the Federation by the ship and her crew, the *Enterprise* will be the first capital ship refitted with the new generation of engine and technology upgrades. I don't need the whole ship, sir, just the warp drive. The upgrade would involve a complete replacement of the warp assembly anyway, so its removal would appear to be simply part of the refit process."

Nogura pondered. "That's a little premature, Antonio. Michelson and Jennings won't be ready to proceed with a full-scale starship refit for months yet."

"That's the advantage of pitching it as a symbolic gesture, sir. People will accept that as a reason for waiting. And one other thing: I know Jim Kirk. He won't take easily to the idea of giving up his starship, settling down on one planet. But he loves the *Enterprise*, sir. It will make him more cooperative if he feels his ship is being rewarded."

The old man pondered. "It's a reasonable suggestion. If nothing else, taking his ship out of service would make his promotion to a ground post seem a more natural progression."

"So you'll approve it?"

Nogura rose, compelling Delgado to follow. "I know you want to travel into the future, Antonio, but don't start getting ahead of yourself yet. All this is hypothetical until the panel makes its ruling. I respect that, even if I know what they're going to decide." Delgado could understand that sentiment from a man as perceptive as Nogura. It seemed that he always knew what other people were going to do before they did it. The least he could do was extend them the courtesy of letting them actually do it before he reacted.

Still, Delgado found his response a little too noncommittal. "Sir, you already said you recognize the value of this research."

"I do, Admiral," Nogura replied, the title warning Delgado that any pretense of informality was over. "But I also recognize the risks. You're just a little too eager to get your hands on those engines. Can I trust you not to be reckless with them once you do?"

Delgado gave a wan smile. "You don't have to trust me, sir. Everything my team does will be carried out under the close supervision of Director Grey and her Department of Temporal Investigations."

"True, true. But they answer to the Science Council, and you have many friends there." Nogura's steely eyes locked on his. "So if I do give you the *Enterprise*'s engines, I think I will also keep a close eye on what you do with them."

Delgado swallowed. This was one man he had no chance of finessing or maneuvering.

Well, in that case, he thought, *I'll just have to make sure I bring him some very impressive results.*

VI

Earth Spacedock
Stardate 7061.9
May 2271

It broke Montgomery Scott's heart to see his beautiful *Enterprise* split open, her own heart in the process of being excised. The whole rear third of her secondary hull had been opened up along the top half, the roof and sides of the hangar deck largely removed, to facilitate the process of removing the warp nacelles, their pylons, the engineering complex below them, and the warp reactor below that from the ship as an integrated unit, gingerly eased free by a fleet of boxy yellow work bees.

Next to him, Commander Willard Decker clasped his shoulder. "Look at it this way, Scotty—it's not like we weren't going to do the same thing ourselves in a few months' time."

"Aye, I know," Scott replied, taking any sting out of it by smiling a bit beneath the mustache that Glynnis, his lass back home, had talked him into growing. Decker was a good man, personally selected by Admiral Kirk to supervise the refit process. He was command track, just off a four-year stint as first officer of the *Boston*, but he'd done his share of time in engineering and understood the meat and marrow of a ship. And as the son of the lamented Commodore Matthew Decker, whose sacrifice had helped save the Rigel colonies from an ancient doomsday weapon, he deserved respect.

And Decker was right. Breaking down a ship's hull, pulling out key components, and plugging new ones back in was a standard part of a refit process. The *Enterprise* didn't have the same bridge module, warp nacelles, deflector assembly, computer core, or hangar doors that she had possessed when Scott had first come aboard her six years ago. It was more than just the pieces that gave a ship her identity, her soul; it was the work put into her by her builders and caretakers.

"But this," Scott went on, gesturing out the viewport of the control deck where they stood, "it's not part of the job we're here to do. It's just . . . pulling out her guts so she can be stuffed and mounted." It would still be months before the refit was ready to begin. The prototypes of Michelson's new swirl-chamber intermix reactor design and Jennings and Minor's upgraded nacelles were still in testing, and Doctor Swansea was still refining her phase-transition bonding technique, which would allow the *Enterprise* to be given a shimmering new skin of superstrong crystal-tritanium plates. And in the interim, Starfleet wanted the *Enterprise* made accessible to a public still caught up in the mystique of its now-famous five-year mission, still fired by the controversy of Jim Kirk's Prime Directive hearing and his subsequent promotion to rear admiral. Once the engines and their control systems were removed, they would be replaced with old, non–flight-ready backups and the keel would be sealed again, so that the ship could spend the next several months on exhibit in the Smithsonian's orbital annex. "Put on display for the gawkers so they can tromp all over her decks, get their grubby prints all over her . . ."

Decker chuckled. "They are putting in partitions to keep the patrons away from the equipment. It's strictly look, don't touch."

"Aye, it was a figure of speech. Just the idea of it feels unclean."

"Funny," Decker said. "I would've thought you'd want to show off the old girl."

"Aye, I'd be glad to give a grand tour to anyone who can really appreciate her construction. But a bunch o' tourists who are just there because o' the nonsense they heard about Captain Kirk in the press . . ." He shook his head.

But Decker knew him too well. On the surface, Will was a Starfleet poster boy, clean-cut and golden-haired and cleft-chinned, but inside him was the soul of a poet. He had a gift for empathy, for making connections with people of all sorts. And he was a good enough listener to hear what people weren't saying. "Or maybe what's really bothering you is where those engines are being taken."

"Aye." Scott looked back out the window at the enclosed Spacedock bay beyond, its yawning volume atypically empty for security reasons, evacuated of all ships but the *Enterprise* and the tugs that would haul its engine assembly away. "An honorable retirement is one thing, but this . . ."

"Is better," came a new voice. Scott and Decker turned to see Admiral Delgado approaching from the other side of the control room, where he'd been supervising the dismantling. "This way, your remarkable engines can remain in active service, doing immeasurable good for the Federation."

"You mean bein' dissected and transformed into God knows what for your unnatural time experiments."

Delgado chuckled. "I wasn't aware warping space to travel faster than light was natural. Or walking and breathing inside a metal box in outer space. Time is just the next frontier."

"Don't mind Mister Scott, sir," Decker said to the admiral, trying to smooth things over and to gently remind Scotty to keep his cool. "This is an emotional moment."

"No hard feelings, Commanders," Delgado said. He moved closer to the Scotsman. "Indeed, I'd really like to assuage your concerns about what we plan to do with these engines, Mister Scott. I'd be glad to clear you to visit our research facilities. You know those engines and their quirks better than anyone. Your insights could help us immensely—and you could supervise the care and treatment of the engines, ensure for yourself that they're in safe hands."

The request was nothing new. Indeed, since the *Enterprise* had returned to Earth, the admiral had already poached a number of its personnel, including Bill Hadley, who had assisted Scott and Spock in the cold restart at Psi 2000, and Frank Gabler, Scott's assistant chief in the final year or so of the mission. "With all due respect, Admiral, I've said no before and I'll say no again. I've done as much mucking about with time as I care to. And it's not what those engines were meant for."

With an eye on Decker, he went on. "Besides, the *Enterprise* still needs me. Those engines . . . they aren't part o' her anymore. You've seen to that, sir. And the rest of the old girl . . . ohh, do we have plans for her." Scott and Decker shared a smile. Decker was a man with big ideas, and he'd inspired Scotty to take a good look at Michelson and Jennings's refit plans and then look beyond them. Their plans involved a substantial restructuring of the secondary hull of the ship: the new vertical warp reactor would be brought forward, connecting directly to the impulse engines as well as the new warp nacelles, with the pylons mounted farther forward and swept back to compensate. The navigational deflector dish would be replaced with a new inboard system with a dedicated fusion reactor, eliminating the need for the massive power transfer conduits that had connected the old deflector dish to the warp reactor; and the support struts and shock absorbers for the dish would be integrated with the hull superstructure, giving it a fuller, rounder shape toward the fore. A new torpedo launcher assembly would be installed at the base of the dorsal, taking advantage of the same structural bracing to allow a more powerful firing mechanism. All this would clear up interior space for larger hangar and cargo facilities, letting the ship go longer between supply layovers.

But the plan called for leaving the primary hull relatively unchanged, aside from an updated bridge module, weapons, sensor domes, and hull plating. Scott had found himself thinking lately that maybe that was a missed opportunity. Indeed, with more powerful engines, the warp geometry might even be better with a wider primary hull, allowing improved turboshaft and conduit placement as well as more extensive living and working space. He'd had some preliminary conversations with Commodore Probert of the S.C.E., a man with some cutting-edge ideas that he was eager to explore further.

Looking between them, Delgado sighed. "Very well, Mister Scott. I can see the two of you make a good team, and I have no desire to break up that kind of a rapport. But I just want you to rest assured, Commander, that I will treat your engines with the utmost respect. And I hope one day to convince you of the value of my work with them."

He extended a hand, and Scotty was enough of a man to accept the peace offering and mumble some polite words in return.

But later on, as he watched the detached engine assembly get towed out the Spacedock doors and off to parts unknown, Scott found himself more and more reluctant to let things stand.

Starfleet Headquarters, San Francisco
Stardate 7062.5
May 2271

"I'm sorry, Mister Scott," said Rear Admiral James T. Kirk. "There's nothing I can do about it."

Scott hardly recognized the man who faced him from across a desk cluttered with data cards, slates, and hard-copy printouts. Gone was the decisive, youthful man who'd skippered the *Enterprise*; in his place sat a subdued, distant, slightly harrowed figure. Scott pleaded with him, hoping to connect with some remaining spark of the Kirk he'd known. "But, sir, you're the chief of operations. Surely you can—"

"And Delgado is chief of Science Ops. We're equals, Scotty. I run my department, he runs his. I can't overrule him."

"But, sir, it's the *Enterprise*. There must be something you can do."

Kirk sighed, then rose and gestured at the big screen on the side wall, showing the deployment and status of all the ships and fleet resources he was responsible for maintaining and coordinating. "As much as I wish it were otherwise, the *Enterprise* is not my ship anymore. Now I'm responsible for the entire fleet. I have to decide where its resources are best utilized. I know how you feel about those engines, Scotty, but these days I have to consider the bigger picture."

"I see, sir," Scott said tightly. "Then that's why you delegated the refit to Will Decker instead o' seein' to it yourself?"

Kirk gave him a sharp look. "Why? Do you have a problem with Commander Decker?"

"Why, no, sir!" Scotty replied, wide-eyed. "He's a fine man, no question about it. It's just that . . ." *Just that you haven't even been to see her since you were promoted. Not even once.* "Never mind, sir. It's not important." He recognized how petty it sounded. The captain—the admiral—did have a lot of other matters on his mind. First the hearing, his reputation simultaneously dragged through the mud and exaggerated into a caricature of glory. Then Mister Spock's sudden departure. After the hearings, the crew had been given extended leave, and Spock had gone off to Vulcan and simply never returned, resigning his commission and (as far as Scott knew) sending only the most cursory of farewell messages to his former crewmates. Then Doctor McCoy had resigned as well, his way of protesting Kirk's removal from starship command, and though he'd stayed in touch, he'd spent most of the intervening time reconnecting with his daughter Joanna, and was now preparing to ship out on an extended research mission to study the advanced medical knowledge of the Fabrini. Scott supposed it hadn't been all bad for his former captain; in addition to gaining his new rank and responsibility and the ear of Admiral Nogura, he'd entered into a serious relationship with Nogura's aide, Lori Ciana. In principle, Scott was glad to know that Kirk had found someone, but looking at him now, it didn't seem to have made him any happier.

"Well, I'm glad to hear it," Kirk was saying. "In fact, I've been seriously thinking—based largely on your reports—of giving Will Decker the *Enterprise*."

Scott blinked. "Sir? You mean . . . as the captain?"

Kirk smiled, though there was a hollowness in his eyes. "He's eminently qualified. He's smart, dedicated, thinks big, and he's earned my trust as well as yours." The admiral spread his arms. "And who better to command this revolutionary new ship, once it's done, than the man who supervised its construction?"

"I . . . think that'd be a grand idea, sir." And that was true, as far as Decker was concerned. He would be a fine choice for the command of any ship, and Scotty would be proud to keep serving under him. But still . . . he wasn't James Kirk. And seeing Kirk talk about handing the reins of his ship over to another man . . . it felt like he was washing his hands of the responsibility. Like he was treating the *Enterprise* as an ex-lover who'd left him, going out of his way to avoid her.

No, that's not fair, Scott tried to tell himself. He was just upset because of Delgado's nonsense with the engines. To be honest, it was unusual for any officer to command the same ship for more than a tour or two. And even if Spock had stayed in Starfleet, he always said he had no wish for command, and Scott surely didn't either. So passing it on to Decker, who had become Kirk's protégé and Scott's friend, felt like the best way of keeping it in the family, even if Decker was a recent addition. Still, Captain Pike had held the *Enterprise*'s center seat for nearly a dozen years. It just didn't feel right for Kirk to surrender it after only five.

He realized Kirk had said something while he'd been distracted. "Come again, sir?"

"I said don't tell Will. It's not final yet, and I'll want to break the news myself."

"Oh, of course not, sir." He fidgeted. "So . . . there's really nothing you can do about Delgado?"

Kirk sighed again, resuming his seat behind the desk. "I can try to keep an eye on what he does. Though it won't be easy. It's a high-security operation, and Delgado's had little time for me since I spoke out against his project." He gestured at the clutter on his desk. "Besides, my own plate is full. We're still investigating the destruction of the *Zheng He*, plus I need to redraw the patrol routes to compensate for the loss, while at the same time making sure that doesn't compromise relief efforts to Mestiko and Sherman's Planet. On top of which, the Klingon-Romulan alliance seems to be disintegrating, and we need to be ready in case Federation worlds get caught in the crossfire." He threw up his hands. "I'm sorry, Scotty. Maybe I can assign someone to monitor the situation with the engines, but I just can't make it a priority right now."

Scott nodded grimly. "Aye, sir. I understand."

"Dismissed."

He nodded at his former captain and left. *Former indeed,* he thought. Even with all that had happened in recent months, all the promotions and departures and dismantlings, it hadn't truly sunk in until this moment how much—and how irrevocably—things had changed.

Black Star system
Stardate 7194.7
March 2272

Meijan Grey watched through the travel pod window as Warlock Station's engineering teams reattached the starboard warp nacelle to the prototype ship. Beside her, Antonio Delgado watched her face, gauging her reactions. But for the moment, her response was neutral. "The shortened nacelle struts don't critically affect the time warp metric?" she asked.

"No," Delgado replied. "Our analyses have shown

that multiple warp geometries can allow for a stable time displacement field. Otherwise we would've needed a full *Constitution*-class spaceframe."

"I see." Grey continued looking over the oblong shape that floated in the middle of an open drydock frame, trailing twenty kilometers behind the orbit of Warlock Station, the joint Starfleet/DTI outpost established to monitor the Black Star—one of Grey's first initiatives as DTI director. The station's name was a nod to one of sh'Lesinas's more obscure early novels—a fantasy about an early Andorian astronaut flung through a Kerr singularity into a bizarre alternate reality—and to the seemingly mystical temporal properties of the Black Star. The timeship prototype was being built here because it would be used here . . . assuming Jan didn't change her mind about authorizing a trial run into the future and back.

"That certainly looks like a complete *Constitution*-class lower hull, though," Grey said. "Aside from the impulse engine where the hangar would be."

"It is," Delgado told her. "The ship's built from duplicate components that were already on hand for repairs and refits. What with the new designs being phased in, they probably weren't going to be used anymore." Even though he'd already gotten what he wanted from the *Enterprise*, Delgado had kept abreast of the progress of its refit, since that project was competing with his for Starfleet's shipbuilding and personnel resources. Ever since Captain Decker and Commander Scott had persuaded Commodore Probert to join the refit team, the acclaimed starship designer had worked alongside them to rethink the modernization program from the ground up, convincing Starfleet to undertake an even more radical reinvention of the *Enterprise*, and if it panned out, of the entire Starfleet. This had meant delaying the refit by several more months and lengthening the reconstruction and testing process to an estimated twenty months, though Decker and Scott were confident they could complete it in eighteen. Starfleet had resisted keeping a heavy cruiser out of action for so long, but with the Klingons and Romulans expending most of their energies on battling each other in the wake of their disintegrated alliance, it seemed as safe a time as any. Probert had persuaded them that it was better to take the time to get the most advanced ship possible into service, rather than rushing and doing a half-baked job that would cost them in the long run.

"Besides, the engineering complex was designed to fit into a spaceframe of this configuration, and to power this type of deflector assembly," Delgado went on as the travel pod flew past the bronze-hued parabolic dish that protruded from the front of the hull. "It may not affect the time field, but it's better for the structural integrity of the vessel. Of course, we've added significant reinforcements to bolster the ship against the stresses of a slingshot passage—hence the shorter, thicker nacelles. There's even an experimental structural integrity force-field system that reinforces the molecular bonds within the hull—similar to the old hull-polarization system that was used before deflectors. If it works, the technology might be introduced throughout the fleet."

"What about the power flow dynamics?" Grey asked. "Shortening the struts, removing the entire saucer and neck . . . that's got to have an effect on the power distribution, the energy usage." She had clearly done her homework.

"Believe me, Jan, we considered all these questions in simulation and testing. We can compensate for all of that. The most critical factor is the chroniton emissions."

Grey lifted an arched brow at him. "Which gives me pause, considering that you still haven't fully figured out how these engines are generating them."

He winced. Although his efforts to cultivate her friendship had been moderately successful, she was not the type to let her personal life get in the way of her professional obligations—which was part of why she had so little personal life. They got along well enough that she was willing to give his ideas fair hearing, but she didn't hesitate to call him out on their shortfalls. "We understand the basics," he insisted.

"But not enough to know how to replicate the phenomenon, or you wouldn't have been so careful not to alter the engines any more than you could avoid. One breakdown and you could lose the ability to generate these chronitons forever."

"Except that these engines have been damaged, repaired, and modified many times and haven't lost the ability yet." His team's intensive study of the former *Enterprise* engines had largely confirmed the theory they'd devised in their earlier analyses: that the energy released in the controlled-implosion restart at Psi 2000 had transmuted a quantity of the hafnium in the interior lining of the matter/antimatter reactor chamber into a transuranic element provisionally called taranium; that the presence of this element, combined with the modified magnetic constriction and injector phase configurations Spock and Scott had put in place, altered the composition of the plasma stream sent to the nacelles; and that some idiosyncrasy of the warp coils' construction enabled them, when energized by that modified plasma stream, to generate a rare type of exotic particle as a side effect of warp field generation. These particles had sufficiently high mass and angular momentum to produce a gravitomagnetic field—a distortion of spacetime arising from a rotating mass analogously to the way a magnetic field arose from a spinning charge. They could amplify the frame-dragging effect that could turn a space warp into a time warp, and somehow, when emitted in proper proportion with the exotic particles the warp coils generated to stabilize the field, could generate enough negative energy to prevent the runaway Hawking radiation that would otherwise vaporize a ship at the horizon of a time warp. The theorists had given this "time-travel particle" the formal name *chroniton*, from the Greek for "time" and the Latin for "go."

But he had to admit Grey had a point. Naming the particles wasn't the same as understanding how to re-create the freak chain of circumstances that created them. Other warp coils from the same manufacturing run had been exposed to the modified plasma streams and had failed to generate chronitons. Perhaps the initial burst of energies from the controlled implosion had transmuted something in the coils as well as the

M/ARC, but there was no known way to replicate that accident. And they couldn't dissect the coils without risking the permanent loss of the only slingshot-capable engines they had.

Delgado suppressed a surge of resentment toward Spock and Scott for their unwillingness to participate in the project. He was convinced they both knew more than they were letting on. But Scott refused to leave the *Enterprise*, and Spock had vanished into the Mountains of Gol on Vulcan (perhaps to keep his time-travel knowledge out of Delgado's hands?). And so the research team was forced to start from scratch.

With the impulse drive taking up the volume where the hangar deck would normally be, the travel pod mated with a docking port on the starboard hull of the prototype ship—officially designated just FDTIX-01, though in Delgado's mind it was *Timeship One*. The admiral and the director disembarked into a pressurized corridor running along the inside of the hull toward the engineering complex. Relatively little of the timeship's interior would consist of habitable space even when it was completed and fully pressurized. The bridge would be fore and above, where auxiliary control was located in a conventional Connie, and there would be limited crew quarters and facilities aft of it. But the action was in engineering.

The engine room still looked much as it had when it had been part of the *Enterprise*. The status display panels on the walls had been modernized, but the controls remained essentially the same, like the components they regulated. Two engineers in heavy white hazard suits with ribbed black collars, the up-to-date design incongruous in this setting, stood at the master systems workstation in the engine room foyer and watched the upgraded systems display above it, which showed a schematic diagram of the timeship as well as a live video feed of the nacelle attachment procedure, now nearly complete. The senior officer, tall, brown-haired, and square-jawed, noted their arrival. "Admiral Delgado," he said, "and Director Grey, welcome aboard."

Grey shook his hand. "Commander DeSalle. A pleasure to meet you again." Vincent M. DeSalle, in command of the timeship's combined Starfleet/civilian crew, had been one of the few former *Enterprise* crew members to offer a guardedly positive opinion on the potentials of time travel during the CAC's interviews, acknowledging that mistakes had been made but seeing that as part of the learning process; so Delgado had been quick to recruit him.

Delgado gestured to the other officer, a craggy-featured, brown-skinned man who was still absorbed in his work. "And this is Lieutenant Commander Frank Gabler, the timeship's chief engineer."

Gabler glanced at her over his shoulder. "Ma'am."

"Mister Gabler." Grey looked between them. "You were both on the *Enterprise*, correct?"

"Not at the same time," DeSalle said, "but yes. Frank came aboard after I left."

"I've tried to bring aboard as many *Enterprise* veterans as possible for security reasons," Delgado said. "Particularly those who've actually been through time, as Mister DeSalle has."

"If you can call it that," the commander said. "I was on the ship when it happened, but I was too busy trying to hold her together against the stresses of the trip to notice what was going on outside."

Delgado clapped him on the shoulder, laughing. "Which is exactly what we want for this test flight, of course."

"And you, Mister Gabler?" Grey asked. "Have you been through time?"

Gabler smiled. "Just once, ma'am, and it's like Mister DeSalle says—I was too busy to take a look outside. But I'm here because I know these engines. I may have been a latecomer, but it didn't take long for me to fall in love with them. I figured they needed someone who knew them to, well, take care of them while Commander Scott oversaw the *Enterprise* refit. And the idea that they can do something unique, something no other engine can—I take a lot of pride in that, ma'am. And I want to help them keep doing it."

"Well said," DeSalle told him. "And we're eager to get started."

"How long until you're ready?" Grey asked.

Delgado answered with a sigh. "At least four more months."

"That's longer than you anticipated."

"Yes, well, I was hoping to finish before the *Enterprise* refit finally got under way, so there'd be no questions raised about the unavailability of engineers and resources. But the analysis phase took longer than hoped, and now that their refit's begun, I've had to let go as many personnel as we could afford—though natu-

rally they're sworn to secrecy. It will slow down comple-
tion, but it's more important to be quiet than fast."

"Quiet and safe," Grey replied.

"Of course," he said, smiling to reassure her.

Delgado allowed DeSalle and Gabler to get back to
work and led Grey out into the corridor. "You don't
need to worry about safety, Jan. As you can see, these
men care deeply about this ship. They won't let her
launch until they're certain she's ready."

"I don't know," Grey said. "They both seemed
rather gung ho about it."

"Can you blame them? The chance to glimpse the
future, find out where we might be going?"

It was the right thing to say, simultaneously reminding Grey of the diminished risks of a trip to the future
rather than the past and of her own barely restrained
excitement at the prospects of what might be learned.
The director relaxed somewhat and looked around.
"Can we see more of the ship? Or is there anything left
that isn't open to vacuum or crawling with engineers?"

Delgado smiled. He still had her hooked. "Well,
maybe I can point out a few things. . . ."

Timeship One FDTIX-01
Stardate 7260.8
September 2272

"Engines holding on full reverse," Lieutenant William
Hadley reported from the helm station. "Deceleration
curve nominal. Twenty seconds to target date."

"Engine stresses near redline," said Frank Gabler at
the engineering console. "Holding within tolerances."

In the command chair, Vincent DeSalle nodded. "Steady as she goes."

Seconds later, Hadley started the countdown from ten. Finally: "Two . . . one . . . full stop, Captain."

"Acknowledged," DeSalle said, liking the sound of the title. He didn't yet hold it by rank, but as the commander of the ship, he was entitled to be called "captain." His first command—humanity's first timeship. It was a heady feeling. True, it was officially a civilian ship under DTI supervision despite its mostly Starfleet crew, but the adventure that lay in store for this vessel more than made up for that.

But for now, he was all business. "Chronometer reading?"

At the science station, Lieutenant Dierdre Watley reported the stardate, then added, "Thirty-two days, eleven hours, fourteen minutes upwhen from our starting point."

DeSalle did a double take. "'Upwhen'?"

The dark-haired science officer displayed her radiant smile. "That's what Asimov called it in *The End of Eternity*."

"Yeah, but . . . shouldn't it be something like 'downstream'? I mean, if we're heading in the same direction time flows, like in a river . . ."

Watley shrugged. "It's a higher number, so it should be 'up.'"

DeSalle shook it off, aware that he was a little too eager for excuses to converse with the striking lieutenant. Not only was he her commanding officer, making any involvement inappropriate, but he knew full well that she had a thing for doctors. And he'd briefly dated her sister the historian back on the *Enterprise*, so it would be a bit strange. Still, she filled out her blue-gray Class-B jumpsuit quite distractingly, though it didn't flatter her as much as her old, miniskirted uniform had. "We'll sort out the terminology later. Hadley, hail Warlock Station."

"Aye, sir." The laconic, nondescript helm officer complied with his usual efficiency. Bill Hadley was the only member of this small bridge crew that DeSalle had known well, even though all four were *Enterprise* veterans. Hadley, among others such as Ryan Leslie, Angela Martine, and DeSalle himself, had been part of that cadre of junior officers who had been cross-trained in multiple shipboard disciplines and served as pinch hitters in whatever job was needed, either as part of command-track training or simply as a consequence of the vagaries of deep-space service. They'd been overlooked in the media blitz that had surrounded James Kirk and his command crew when the *Enterprise* had come home, but DeSalle knew that it was the steady, unsung service of folks like Bill Hadley, just as much as the leadership and inspiration of men like Kirk and Spock, that had kept the ship intact for five years. DeSalle was glad to have him on the team.

Moments later, the voice of Warlock's communications officer came over the speakers. *"This is Warlock Station. About time you showed up,* Timeship One. *You said you were just going out to get coffee!"*

The bridge crew chuckled. "Very funny, Samira. Warlock Station, this is *Timeship One* reporting a successful simulation run. Again."

The next voice he heard was Admiral Delgado's. *"Don't sound so impatient, Captain. It's only three more days until you do this for real."*

"Acknowledged, sir. But I can tell you, we'd all like to use this ship to jump through time to the day when we get to use this ship to jump through time."

"You've got it easy, Vincent. Keep in mind that the rest of us will have to wait a month for the results you'll know about within three days." He had a point. The DTI wasn't willing to risk a return jump at this early stage, so they would simply be making a one-way trip a month into the future. It would be a long, anxious wait for the people at Warlock.

"For now, though," the admiral went on, *"we've been at these simulations long enough. How about we break for dinner?"*

DeSalle looked around, seeing no objections. "Fine by us, sir. We'll meet you aboard in—"

"Sir," Samira Jalili interrupted, her voice sounding urgent. *"I'm picking up a distress signal!"*

A pause. *"Source?"* Delgado asked. DeSalle held his seat, as did the rest of the crew. This ship may have been secret, and the station did have others, but it was best to stand ready for any contingency.

There was a longer pause as Jalili tracked down the origin. *"It's just under four parsecs out, near Gliese 229."*

"Hadley?" DeSalle asked.

The lieutenant didn't even need to check the star charts. "That's a pretty empty region, but it's closer to Vulcan than here. I'm sure they've picked it up already."

"No, Lieutenant," Jalili said. "It's . . . er . . . not a general broadcast."

"What?" Delgado demanded. "It was beamed specifically here?"

"Yes. Sir . . ." Jalili was hesitant. "It's . . . on Timeship One's encrypted frequency!"

DeSalle was stunned. After a moment, he gathered himself and looked around at the bridge crew, all of whom were clearly in the dark. "We're not transmitting," Hadley assured him.

"Put it through," came the admiral's voice.

After a moment, a static-drenched voice began to speak. ". . . miscalculation . . . critical . . . braking thrust failed . . . we overshot by decades. Integrity field . . . inadequate . . . major structural damage. Hawking radiation . . . overloaded shields . . . lost half the crew . . . Hadley . . . Dierdre."

DeSalle spun to face Watley, who was staring back at him in horror. He saw in her piercing eyes what he'd failed to realize himself: that the voice he was hearing was his own.

"Couldn't let it stand," the voice—DeSalle's voice—went on. "Only chance . . . reverse slingshot. No way . . . survive a second trip . . . but had to warn . . . star nearby . . . gave the order . . . go back . . . warn ourselves . . . don't launch the mission! Don't launch the mission! For . . . love of God . . . don't . . ."

The voice trailed off into static. After a long moment, Jalili spoke into the void. "Signal power is fading, sir."

"Admiral, let us go," DeSalle pleaded. "We're faster than anything else at the station."

"No!" the admiral barked. *"We don't know what effects there might be. And I wouldn't wish that on you, Vincent."*

"Sir, we—"

"Stand down, Commander, that's an order. We're dispatching the Hypatia *to investigate."* A pause. *"For now, power down the ship and return to the station. Do you hear me, Mister DeSalle?* Get off that ship.*"*

Warlock Station
Stardate 7261.3
September 2272

As Meijan Grey had raced toward the Black Star system on the fastest ship available, she had hoped that the distress signal from *Timeship One* had been a hoax, some trick by Romulan or Tholian spies who had learned of the DTI's experiments and wished to scuttle them. But the updates she'd been sent throughout her journey, the images and data she'd pored over for hours and then relived in her nightmares, had been undeniable.

The *Hypatia* had found the timeship adrift fifty-eight hundred AUs from the dim red dwarf Gliese 229, its hull scarred and half melted from radiation, its superstructure warped and buckled from overwhelming gravitic stresses—even as the exact same timeship sat pristine and undamaged back at Warlock Station. The boarding party had arrived too late to find any survivors—and it was clear that even the faster *Timeship One* would have had no better success. The surviving crew had evidently tried to shield themselves by donning the surplus life-support belts from the timeship's emergency supplies, but the fierce radiation—both the runaway Hawking flux of the time warp and the more exotic radiations from the compromised warp reactor—had disrupted their force fields. Only the diminished bridge crew had been far enough from the engines for their belts to remain functional, but the miniature air tanks and carbon-dioxide scrubbers in the belts' dorsal packs had been damaged by the turbulence of the return trip and had failed shortly after Commander DeSalle's distress transmission. It was a textbook illustration of why the force-field belts had been phased out after less than two years in service—several fatal incidents had driven home the folly of trusting one's life to a system with no way of failing safely. Had the crew worn spacesuits, at least a power disruption wouldn't have instantly depressurized and suffocated them. But the timeship project relied heavily on surplus technology that Starfleet wouldn't miss, and it had been assumed that the belts would be adequate for whatever crises might arise in a "simple" test flight.

Maybe that underlines the overconfidence that went into this whole project, Grey thought as she surveyed the wreck of the timeship, now docked in the free-floating drydock berth several kilometers from Warlock Station, while the intact, earlier iteration of the timeship remained docked at the station itself. The theorists had no reason to believe the two ships—or rather, the two distinct spatiotemporal quantum states of the same ship—would spontaneously reconverge or blow up or whatever if brought together, but Delgado's team hadn't wanted to take any chances—an admirable, if belated, sentiment. Or perhaps they simply didn't want to force the occupants of the station to see the devastation of their dreams, the burned and broken remains of their colleagues and friends.

"Have you determined what went . . . what will go wrong?" she asked Delgado later as they met alone in the conference room, taking care not to put any flavor of accusation in it. She knew he'd cultivated her friendship for selfish reasons, but she could be selfish too; she enjoyed his attention, as far as it went, and it was better personally as well as professionally if their interactions remained cordial. Besides, she'd come to trust that, however manipulative his methods may have been, his motives for pursuing time travel were reasonably constructive and selfless. And frankly, she'd wanted the project to succeed too. She didn't want to be at odds with him over this.

"It's hard to say," the admiral replied. "The data banks are badly corrupted. It could take weeks to reconstruct what happened. Clearly they went much further forward than intended, though not nearly as far as the *Enterprise* journeyed back on two occasions. Our best estimate is twenty-six years." He shook his head. "It doesn't make sense. We've added more shielding, more structural bracing, than the *Enterprise* ever had. And the warp field, the gravitomagnetic field, it all checks out fine in the real . . . the original timeship. Maybe . . . DeSalle said it was a miscalculation, so maybe someone . . . ." He trailed off before he said something regrettable about the dead—the dead who were still living.

Grey furrowed her brows. "How long until the ship was meant to launch?"

"Thirty-two hours."

"What will you do when the time comes?"

"We have no choice but to suspend the launch. At least until we can understand what this . . . manifestation truly means. Or determine a way to prevent it."

"If T'Viss is right . . ." Grey began. "If time can't be changed . . ."

"No," Delgado reassured her, placing his hand briefly on hers. "Even if timelines can't be erased, they can still branch out. What we're seeing is just one possible branch. We just have to ensure we take a different one. The very fact that we received this warning shows that we're already on a new branch. We'll just . . . we'll wait, we'll study these ruins down to the atom until we determine what went wrong, and then we'll fix it." He mustered a tentative smile. "This could turn out to be a blessing in disguise, Jan. To be forewarned about a great disaster, to have an opportunity to make sure it never happens . . . it illustrates the whole reason I'm pursuing this."

Grey stared at him. "How can you look at . . . at *that* and be optimistic?"

He met her gaze soberly. "Because I have to. It's the only way I can face it. I have to believe the universe gives us the chance to correct our mistakes."

Wordlessly, she took his hand and tried to share in his hope.

The station's teams worked nonstop analyzing the remains—both of the ship and its crew—but for Grey, and for the timeship's crew themselves, the next thirty-two hours had the feel of a vigil, a long, still period of waiting for . . . *something*. T'Viss insisted that the moment would pass like any other, that there would be no tangible sense of change; indeed, if this timeline had already diverged from the one in which *Timeship One* was destroyed, it had done so the instant the vessel had been returned from the future. But to the non-Vulcans in the station's complement, the moment loomed like the sword of Damocles.

As the time neared, Grey, Delgado's core team, and the timeship crew all gathered in the station's control center, their eyes on the original *Timeship One* outside the port and its derelict twin on the main viewscreen. Even T'Viss was there, though she displayed no sign of interest in the vigil and was concentrating on the forensic analysis of the wreckage. Technically the moment of the timeship's scheduled launch from the station had already passed; with the ship powered down and the crew standing here aboard the station, there was no way they would make the slingshot jump at the same moment Jalili was counting down to. But that was the moment that carried the most weight for the watchers, the point of no return, and Grey could see Dierdre Watley mouthing the numbers silently as well. "T minus five . . . four . . . three . . . two . . . one . . . mark."

Grey looked around at the timeship crew, reassuring herself that they were still here, safe and sound. De-Salle and the others let out held breaths and began to chuckle in relief and embarrassment.

But then alarmed cries came over the comm channel from the drydock. Grey and the others spun to face the viewscreen—and saw only an empty scaffold. The duplicate timeship was gone! Grey turned back to the viewport—the original, intact ship was still there.

"Admiral, this is the infirmary!" came a new voice. *"All the bodies . . . they've vanished!"*

It took a few minutes to collate the reports and sensor readings. No one had actually noticed the moment of disappearance, and lack of attention couldn't account for it. Doctor ch'Venethes had been conducting a quantum scan on one of the bodies, looking right at it, and yet she had no memory of seeing it vanish, simply of realizing after a moment that it wasn't there anymore. And the quantum scanner no longer held any data from the scan in progress, as though it had never begun, even though more conventional recorders did still show the presence of the ship, equipment, and bodies, a presence which abruptly ceased at the moment the time jump would have occurred. The playbacks showed it all briefly blurring out, as though the readings became ambiguous, before it vanished without a trace.

Of all of them, it was the unflappable T'Viss who seemed the most stunned. "This should not have happened. It suggests . . . some form of quantum reconvergence . . . the alternative-state information collapsed, erased. But that would suggest . . ."

When T'Viss resisted saying it, Grey filled the void. "It would suggest that it is indeed possible to unwrite a moment in time. That any coexistence of two timelines may be temporary, with only one state winning out in the end." She looked around at DeSalle and his crew, at *Timeship One*, at everything. "If this had gone differently . . . if the ship had gone further back, made some broader change . . . it could've been our existence that ceased a moment ago. The existence of everything we know. Just like what Kirk described at the Guardian."

Delgado put a hand on her arm. "Jan, what are you saying?"

"You can't deny it anymore, Antonio. Don't let your dreams blind you to the facts. Traveling in time means putting our very existence at risk. It's too dangerous." She looked around the room, took in the stunned and sobered expressions, the terror and relief at dodging a bigger bullet than they'd realized. "I think most of us here can see the same thing. This experiment is over. We've found out what we need to know about the nature of time. We've found out how fragile it can be.

"I'm sorry, Antonio. But the DTI will support no further experimentation with time travel. I'm ordering this project shut down. *Timeship One* is to be dismantled."

Delgado was shaking his head. "No, Jan, don't do this. Don't rush into this decision. There's still so much we can learn, so much good we can do."

"I know, Antonio. I know. But we're not ready yet. We're not smart enough to handle this kind of power."

She took a breath, considering the ramifications of those words. A new understanding of her role was forming in her mind, and she only hoped she could make Delgado see it too, that they could stay on the same side in this. "The Department of Temporal Investigations was founded to regulate temporal research. But we need to do more than that. If we have the power to endanger the very fabric of reality, then we also have a responsibility to protect it.

"That's what the DTI's mission has to be from now on: preserving the integrity of history itself."

VII

"It doesn't make sense," Marion Dulmur told his partner once they and Andos had completed reviewing the records of the timeship incident. Andos has been called away to deal with the continuing bureaucratic fallout of the recent Split Infinite affair, so the two special agents were alone in the situation room for the moment. "The ship in the records was *Timeship One*, but the one Ranjea and Garcia found is *Timeship Two*. And it only jumped forward about twenty-six years, not a hundred ten years, five months, and thirteen days. And there was no mention of this subspace confluence effect."

"The ship's construction is different too," Lucsly said, calling up a schematic of *Timeship One* on the situation room's display screen, next to a sensor image of the other ship that the *Everett* had transmitted. "They're built on the same lines, but *Timeship Two* incorporates upgrades that were still in prototype as of 2272."

"Hmm, but the engine signature is still the same, allowing for minor construction variances. Those are the old *Enterprise* engines, the ones altered to create a chroniton field."

"So we're looking at a later variation on the same testbed," Lucsly said.

"But how? The records, even the classified records, show that the timeship and the *Enterprise* engines were dismantled. That the research was abandoned and Delgado's record was uneventful afterward . . . three more routine years in Science Ops, then a year as an adviser to President Lorg, then retirement."

"Records have been redacted before," Lucsly said. "And I have a hard time believing Delgado would give up so easily, even with Director Grey standing in his way."

"Yeah," Dulmur said. Then he frowned. "Although . . ."

He trailed off, and Lucsly turned to face him. "What?"

Dulmur hesitated. He knew how Lucsly idolized Meijan Grey. She was the foundation of everything the DTI stood for, and that was everything that Gariff Lucsly lived for. So he spoke carefully. "I'm just surprised that Director Grey was willing to authorize the time research in the first place. I always thought she was a lot more hawkish about protecting the timeline." Dulmur saw through the bullpen windows that Director Andos was returning to the room.

"And she was—after the timeship incident," Lucsly countered, predictably rising to his idol's defense. "It drove the risks home to her, shaped her into the leader she became. Even before then, she insisted on stringent precautions, traveling only into the future."

"It was a different time," Andos said. "There wasn't

as much temporal research then as now, in the Federation or elsewhere. Not as many people, or governments, were aware that time travel was more than a theoretical possibility. Aside from our work monitoring the Guardian and the Black Star, there was little need for active enforcement, so the DTI was more an institution for research and policymaking. I spent most of my early years there poring over historical records for evidence of anachronisms, or refining algorithms to extract data from old Guardian scans. Director Grey was a scientist first, so naturally she was open to experimentation until it proved too hazardous."

"But she was ultimately a practical woman," Lucsly insisted. "She made the DTI what it is today—never forget that."

"Okay, okay," Dulmur said, raising his hands in surrender. "Believe me, partner, I agree completely. I wouldn't think of saying a word against our founding mother. It's just . . . well, you know how it is. You dig closely into the past, you always find that things were more complicated than the history books say."

"Hm," Lucsly grunted.

"Hell, look at the testimony Captain Kirk gave for the Council hearings. Who would've thought James T. Kirk would be such a strong voice of opposition to temporal research?"

Lucsly grunted again. "Kirk was always good at giving speeches, but you know exactly how many of his seventeen temporal violations were committed *after* he gave that testimony. It's his actions that define him, not his words."

Dulmur frowned. "That's another thing that bothers me. Delgado's people were unable to make a slingshot work with anything but the old *Enterprise* engines. Sure, it's not easy to pull off a slingshot maneuver. Even if you have the right kind of engine and know how to configure it, it's still insanely risky. Otherwise anyone with a warp drive could change history on a whim. But we know Kirk's crew was eventually able to configure the later *Enterprise*s' engines to generate the right kind of chroniton field for a successful slingshot. They even did it with a Klingon bird-of-prey when they went back to retrieve the humpback whales."

"Mm-hm."

"So what did Spock and Scott know that Delgado's scientists—including T'Viss, by the way—didn't know?"

Before Lucsly could reply, the director's comm signaled. "Andos here," the towering Rhaandarite said.

"Signal from the Everett, *Director."*

"Patch it through."

A moment later, a melodious, Deltan-accented tenor came over the channel. *"Director, this is Ranjea."*

"Go ahead."

"Two troubling developments to report, ma'am. The subspace confluence zone around the timeship has begun to expand. Moreover, the ship has begun to emit a distress signal."

Andos and the agents traded a concerned look. "Can you tell whether this signal is detectable in the past as well as the present?"

"Yes, ma'am. Given the ship's power curve, such as it is, the signal gain is less than half what it should be. That

suggests that the majority of the signal energy is being emitted in some other reference frame."

"Would the signal still be strong enough to be detectable at interstellar distances?"

"Yes, ma'am. At its power levels, the propagation speed would be low, but we don't know how close it is to the nearest ship or subspace beacon in its own timeframe. We could have weeks before it's detected or only hours."

"Damn," Dulmur said. "If some ship on the downtime end picks up that distress signal and comes to investigate . . ."

"They could scan through the confluence, even travel through it, and gain knowledge of the future," Lucsly replied, his voice grim. Of course, his voice was grim even when discussing the weather—or would be if he ever discussed the weather—but this time it was *really* grim.

"I concur," Ranjea said from the *Everett*. *"This poses an imminent risk to the timeline."*

"Director, this is Captain Alisov," came a new voice. *"Do you want us to target the vessel?"*

"Negative," Andos said promptly. "We don't know the fate of this vessel or its crew in their own timeframe. Destroying them could alter history."

The next voice they heard was Agent Garcia's. *"Then we've got to beam over there and shut down the distress signal."* Even without seeing the grim looks the agents traded, she must have sensed their reticence—naturally, for she'd had the same training as the rest of them, and far more recently. *"Sure, that poses its own risk of timeline contamination, but it's better than the alternatives."*

Andos pondered it only briefly. "Agreed. Do what you can to minimize the exposure risk, but get that signal shut down!"

U.S.S. Everett
Stardate 60145.1

"I don't get it," Teresa Garcia said as she and Ranjea donned a pair of holographic isolation suits prior to boarding the timeship. Since the *Everett* was attached to DTI service, it was equipped for dealing with situations of potential temporal contamination, and thus it carried a supply of the suits, a technology normally used by Starfleet survey teams to study pre-warp worlds without exposing their presence. The silvery, hooded suits rendered their wearers invisible to conventional humanoid senses and masked their biosigns from standard sensors—hopefully including the timeship's intruder alert sensors.

"What is it?" Ranjea asked as he donned his own suit, which fit his frame far less baggily than the more diminutive Garcia's. Somehow the Deltan was even able to make it look dapper.

Garcia gestured to the padd he held, containing the briefing Lucsly and Dulmur had transmitted minutes ago. "The quantum convergence of the duplicate *Timeship One* doesn't make sense. I mean, I know how it's supposed to work. If you create an alternate timeline through time travel, it coexists with the original for the whole period of their overlap, up until the moment of the original time travel. Everything leading up to that event still has to happen, or there's a paradox. But after that moment, the timelines collapse together and only the altered one continues forward. The quantum information from the original is erased, and that includes any temporal duplicates like the other timeship and its crew."

"Generally, yes. Unless the duplicate becomes sufficiently entangled with its new timeline to survive."

"But that's for downtime travel. *Timeship One* went uptime. The furthest forward point of divergence should've been when it arrived twenty-six years in the future."

"But it wasn't there long enough to effect any significant change," Ranjea replied promptly. "They arrived and promptly returned. There was no interaction with the rest of the universe, so any local alterations didn't propagate and got damped out. The only significant change was the choice made in 2272 not to launch the ship at all. So that was the point of convergence."

Garcia nodded. "I get it. Sort of." The timeline was only split for three days, from September 6 to 9, 2272. A ship moving forward from either of the branches that had run in parallel for that three-day interval would've therefore found itself in the same singular future, like two roads merging into one. The reality was far more complex than that, but the straightforward analogy helped. At least it was a more useful explanation than "Time is just weird," though perhaps equally truthful.

Timeship Two FDTIX-02
Confluence 2275/2383
To minimize the risk of their arrival being seen or heard, Ranjea and Garcia materialized in a vacant cargo

bay near the keel of the ship. The holographic camouflage of their suits let them see themselves and each
other through their visors, so they were able to work
their tricorders to scan for biosigns and energy signatures. "So where's the best place to cut off a distress
signal?" Garcia asked her senior partner. "The bridge?
Engineering?"

"No. Somebody must be alive and conscious in one
of those places to have activated the signal," Ranjea
said. "Our best bet is the main subspace transmitter junction. We can rig an apparent malfunction. It
wouldn't seem out of place."

He led her to the door, scanned for activity on the
other side, then opened it and preceded her through.
The corridor was empty, so they were able to move
quickly to the ladder alcove at the forward end. Garcia gazed curiously at her surroundings. A student of
galactic archaeology with a focus on starfaring technology, she was familiar with the configurations of Federation vessels from past centuries. Although the exterior
of *Timeship Two* had been fitted with more advanced
equipment, the interior layout was still largely that of a
Starfleet vessel from the 2260s, albeit with a few mod-
ernizations here and there.

The three-sided ladder in the vertical shaft took
them into a horizontal Jefferies tube with bright red
and yellow power and supply trunks running along the
walls. Every few meters was an angular white archway
containing overhead and floor-level lights that flickered
unhealthily. It smelled clean, new, barely used, but
there was a whiff of burned lubricant and ozone. Ran-

jea had to crouch to avoid hitting his head, but Garcia was able to stand nearly upright. They made their way across to a more central, larger service corridor with a hexagonal shape and gray walls, stretching away in both directions. Ranjea checked his tricorder, looking back and forth between the two ends of the corridor. "The transmitter junction should be forward," Garcia said, "near the deflector dish."

"Understood," he said. "But I'm getting a strange power reading in the other direction, toward main engineering."

Garcia brought her own tricorder to bear. "You're right. Are those interphasic readings?"

"The distress beacon is a symptom," Ranjea said. "This could lead us to the source of the problem. The sooner we can get that information to the others, the better."

It struck Garcia as a Deltan way of thinking, giving a higher priority to sharing with the group than taking autonomous action. But that didn't make it more right or wrong. It was the diversity of the DTI's agents, the breadth of perspectives they brought, that gave the agency its strength—one thing they and Starfleet had in common. Besides, she trusted her partner. His perspective had proved very beneficial to her, both on the job and personally. "Lead the way, boss," she said. She rarely called him that anymore, since they had a more equal partnership now than when she'd first been assigned to him (was it really just seventeen months and eight days ago?), but she felt the affirmation was appropriate, for her own benefit at least.

Ranjea led her several dozen meters aft to another ladder junction, which led to a corridor near the center of the ship. Garcia gasped when she emerged and saw a number of humanoids lying crumpled on the deck, all of them clad in blue civilian jumpsuits. She instinctively moved forward, but Ranjea held her back. But she could hear the pain in his voice when he said, "Teresa, we can't intervene."

Regulations or not, she ran a tricorder scan. "They're alive . . . but they're weak. Neural activity is erratic."

"Yes," Ranjea said, checking his own temporal tricorder. "I'm detecting quantum phase variances in their nervous systems. It could've exacerbated the effects of slingshot blackout."

Garcia took that in. Take the acceleration-induced blackouts of a Tipler slingshot maneuver, then add to that the effects of phase variances in the brain and body—different parts of the self shifting subtly out of alignment with their home reality and losing contact with one another—and the consequences could be far worse. "Will they live?" she asked.

"If they get medical help in time."

"They've been here awhile, Ranjea. Help may not be coming."

"If that's what happened, we can't risk altering it."

She winced. "I know. I know."

They moved on down the corridor, turning a corner. The interphasic effects grew worse as they came nearer to the source of the readings. A Caitian female lay mewling and panting on the deck, eyes darting around in terror at things only she could see. Nearby, a human man covered in scratches consistent with the Caitian's claws was crying and banging his head against the bulkhead. Garcia recognized the effects of interphase psychosis, another consequence of the disruption of neural function. Farther along, a woman lay unconscious on the deck, her lower legs sunken into its solid surface. It must have phased out temporarily as she walked over it, trapping her. Judging from the swelling beneath her jumpsuit fabric, the woman's circulatory system was badly compromised by the deck molecules sharing space with her insides.

Walking past all these people in need and doing nothing was the hardest thing Garcia had done since she'd stopped her fellow passengers on the time-displaced transport *Verity* from going back through the temporal warp to save Regulus from the Borg. In a way, it was even harder. Far more lives had been at stake then, but they had been abstractions, too many for the humanoid mind to grasp as individuals. She hadn't had to look at their faces, to make the choice to walk right past them and do nothing to help. Garcia tried to remind herself that she was over a century removed from these people, that most of them were long dead already in her frame of reference. That what she saw before her was the past, its immediacy as illusory as a holodeck program.

It didn't help.

So she tried to distract herself by wondering about the corridor itself. On a standard *Constitution*-class ship of this vintage, this space would have been occupied by

the massive power conduits that fed the main deflector dish. But the more modern, more efficient dish
up front was autonomously powered, so the conduits
wouldn't have been needed. Still, the corridor was
significantly forward of the main engineering complex.
What took up the intervening space?

They found out when Ranjea opened the doors on
the corridor's aft wall and led her inside. Beyond was a
large, open bay three decks high, ringed by a catwalk
a level above them. The deck level was equipped with
a pair of freestanding, 2270s-vintage control consoles
mounted against a railing that surrounded . . .

"What the hell is that?" she heard herself asking.

Whatever it was, it bore no resemblance to any
Federation technology she knew. It was an intricate
spherical lattice at least eight meters across, with
softly glowing orbs at every node where the thick,
golden-brown arcs of the lattice intersected. Within
it were another couple of nested lattices, each about
three-quarters the size of the next one out but equally
intricate, connected to each other by radial tubes that
joined their luminous nodes. There appeared to be
a central core within, not quite half the radius of the
whole and hovering in the center with no physical connection to the lattices. It pulsed with blue-white light
and rotated slowly, revealing that it was not a perfect
sphere but a multilobed shape like the inside of a man-
darin orange or mangosteen. The whole thing looked
organic and extremely high-tech at the same time.

"Whatever it is," Ranjea said, "it's drawing power
from the warp engines." He circled the construct and

Garcia followed, taking care to avoid the jumpsuited personnel who lay unconscious—she hoped—around it. Now she could see the more conventional framework that held the giant bauble in place, the standard power transfer conduits that had been grafted onto its nodal spheres, an intrusion that seemed crude, almost obscene, against the diatomaceous beauty of the artifact. "And," the Deltan agent went on, "it's partly opaque to neutrinos."

Garcia stared. Neutrinos could pass through entire stars and planets without even noticing they were there. "There . . . aren't a lot of things that can do that."

"This is undoubtedly the source of the confluence effect," Ranjea declared. "And it is undoubtedly not Federation technology."

"It's so advanced," Garcia said, as much an intuition from its design as a deduction from the tricorder readings. "But it doesn't match the tech of any past or present supercivilization in the database. Could it be from the future? Our future?"

Ranjea tilted his elegant bald head. "There are more supercivilizations we don't know about than ones we do," he said, his tone hushed. "It's a big galaxy."

"Yeah, but if we don't know about them today, how could these guys have a piece of their technology eleven decades ago?"

Ranjea stared at the artifact—the drive?—a while longer. Garcia knew he must be admiring its beauty, a beauty he probably perceived more keenly than she could. But then he shook himself. "We should let the brain trust back home chew on that," he said, tapping the buttons to upload his tricorder readings to the *Everett*. "We need to take care of that distress signal."

DTI Headquarters
Stardate 60145.3
A Wednesday
It was the middle of the night in Greenwich, but time of day had always been the least important temporal referent for the DTI's personnel. Lucsly disliked the irritating tendency of reality to disrupt his neat, regular schedule, but he had long since learned to accommodate it, seeking order and regularity where he could. The timeless quality of the DTI's secure offices, located underground beneath an unassuming row of Victorian houses just off Greenwich Park and insulated from the diurnal cycles of light and dark that prevailed above, helped him to cope. So did the presence of the familiar faces who shared the large situation room with Lucsly, Dulmur, and Andos, colleagues he'd worked with for decades. They included Virum Kalnota, the Zakdorn head of research; Loom Aleek-Om, the department's senior historian; and of course Doctor T'Viss, who had been the DTI's senior physicist since shortly after its inception. Members of their respective staffs hovered in the background, ready to chip in or follow instructions as needed.

Aleek-Om had been brought in more for his personal history than anything else, for the elderly Aurelian, like Andos and T'Viss, had been there from the very beginnings of the department. But, as he had apologetically explained, he had been just a consultant at that early stage, often called on for assistance by his colleague Meijan Grey, but still maintaining his tenured position at the Institute of Galactic History on Alpha Centauri III. It had only been later, as the department's size and responsibilities had grown, that Director Simok—Grey's successor and the longest-serving director of the department—had persuaded Aleek-Om to come aboard full-time.

As for T'Viss, she had been unable to offer any insights beyond what the official records showed. Yes, she had liaised between her DTI employers and her former colleagues on Delgado's Science Ops team during the *Timeship One* project, but to the best of her knowledge, there had been no further research after the experimental vessel was shelved and eventually dismantled.

But then the *Everett* had transmitted the on-site agents' scans of the device in *Timeship Two*'s extra engine bay. A reconstruction of the device was projected holographically above the round, black-surfaced table in the center of the room, while updated schematics of the timeship showed on one of the wall screens, next to the screens showing the *Everett*'s sensor feed and subspace schematics of the growing confluence zone, and opposite the master situation wall, which displayed currently active investigations and agent deployments and the status of known temporal anomalies and unsecured artifacts. Distracted by the mysterious object, Lucsly was slow to recognize that T'Viss had fainted where she sat. The others' reactions to the event drew his attention. "Call a doctor," Dulmur was saying. While T'Viss's age of 181 standard years was well within normal Vulcan life expectancy, it was advanced enough that an episode of syncope, rare among Vulcans in any case, was worth taking seriously.

But T'Viss had already recovered consciousness and waved Dulmur off. "That will not be necessary," she said.

"T'Viss, you fainted," Andos said.

"No, Director," the physicist replied, as primly and severely as she would deliver any other correction to any other person. "I . . . withdrew. The sight of that object"—she gestured at the holographic image—"in combination with the ongoing confluence event, seems to have triggered a memory."

"You *do* know something about this second time-ship?" Kalnota asked.

"I believe I do. However, I do not yet know what I know." Andos's gaze alone made it clear she was awaiting further explanation, and T'Viss strove to provide it. "The memory is . . . hidden. It has been locked away from my conscious awareness for a very long time."

"A repressed memory?" Dulmur asked, shocked. "You mean someone, someone did this to you? Suppressed what you knew?"

T'Viss glared at him. "Had such a thing been forced upon me, the neurological consequences would have been considerable. It could not have remained hidden for so long. And it would have taken an especially formidable telepath in any case to overcome the Vulcan mind's resistance to tampering."

"So what you're saying," Lucsly said, "is that you did it to yourself."

"Correct, Agent. I chose to repress this memory."

"Why?"

"I do not yet know. I will need to meditate further to recover it fully."

"But if you had reason to hide it, even from yourself . . ." Aleek-Om began.

"I believe that reason is obviated by the exigencies before us. In fact, I believe it may be urgent that I recover the memory now. And I believe, Director, that I have knowledge that will be needed at the scene of the incident, once I have recovered it from my subconscious."

Andos never had to consider her decisions for long; both her centuries of experience and her Rhaandarite mental acuity enabled her to weigh all the variables with a swiftness Lucsly admired. To the Rhaandarite mindset, the rules of the universe were clearly laid out, and decision-making was simply a matter of determining and following those rules. Lucsly strove to lead his life by the same principle, but the universe he perceived had a way of being more chaotic than he wished. Andos's clarity reassured him that there was a deeper order after all, even if it was hidden from limited human minds. "Then you must go at once, as soon as I arrange transportation with Starfleet. You as well, Agents," the director added, her gaze taking in Lucsly and Dulmur. "All respect to Agents Ranjea and Garcia, but we need as much expertise on the scene as we can bring to bear."

"You are absolutely correct, Director," said T'Viss. "I am confident that this crisis is even worse than we are currently aware."

U.S.S. Capitoline NCC-82617
Stardate 60145.7

The *Capitoline* was one of Starfleet's precious few slipstream-drive ships, enabling them to reach the Lembatta Cluster in mere hours. By the time T'Viss completed her meditation, two hours and six minutes into the voyage, they were already past Davlos and skirting the Klingon border—something which was far safer to do now, in the age of the Khitomer Alliance, than it would have been in the era of Grey, Delgado, and Kirk.

But politics was irrelevant, Lucsly reminded himself as he and Dulmur sat down with T'Viss in the *Vesta*-class starship's most secure briefing room. If they didn't shut down the confluence quickly, all the history that had led to the current era of relative peace could be nullified and replaced with something impossible to predict. *Probably something worse,* he added, convinced that going against the natural flow of history never turned out for the better. Well, almost never, he grudgingly admitted. There were a few rare exceptions . . . but Lucsly was positive this was not one of them. He knew from certain sources that a major disruption of the past century's worth of history could have a devastating impact on the galaxy for many centuries to come.

So he was eager to learn what T'Viss had to tell him. The physicist appeared fatigued, drawn, almost alarmed—the opposite of what he would expect in the wake of meditation. "I have released the block," she announced. "I am still assimilating the memories . . .

but I believe it will help me to do so if I present them in a narrative fashion."

Dulmur leaned forward. "So you knew about the second timeship? Do you know who made it? Where they got that alien drive?"

He fell silent under T'Viss's withering glare. "It is generally the nature of a narrative, Agent, that it progresses linearly. I must work through this from the beginning—the earliest point of the repressed memories."

Dulmur leaned back, chastened. Lucsly simply put on his interviewer face and said, "All right. We're listening. Where does the story begin?"

The elderly physicist met his gaze intently. "Unsurprisingly, Agent Lucsly, it begins with the *U.S.S. Enterprise*. With Captain James T. Kirk . . . whose litany of temporal violations must now be increased to *eighteen*."

VIII

U.S.S. Enterprise
Stardate 7583.5
June 2274

Lieutenant Commander Hikaru Sulu stood at the bridge railing behind Captain Kirk's right shoulder, trying to look like he belonged there. Or at least trying not to glance around for a more comfortable place to be.

At the helm station that was normally his, Ensign Monique Ledoux looked over her shoulder. "Five minutes to coordinates, Captain," the tall Congolese woman said.

"Acknowledged," Kirk replied from the center seat. He glanced over his own shoulder at Sulu, who nodded and raised his wrist communicator.

"Bridge to sensor crews," Sulu instructed. "Begin ongoing scans on all subspace and gravimetric bands. Be ready for anything." He hoped he didn't sound nervous. It had been a while since he'd felt so uneasy about filling the role of acting first officer. But then, it had been fairly light duty until now. Since the refitted *Enterprise* had been launched in haste during the V'Ger incident late last year, the shakedown and testing process of the new design had been largely skipped over. Kirk, who had convinced Admiral Nogura to give him back his captaincy for the emergency, had subsequently made the impromptu decision to take the ship out on a "working shakedown," testing its systems in normal field use—and given that he and his crew (most notably Willard Decker, who had nobly sacrificed himself at the critical moment) had just saved the entire population of Earth from being digitized by a prodigal space probe with delusions of grandeur, Starfleet Command wasn't about to tell him he couldn't. But after six months in service, Kirk had finally given in to the pleas of Starfleet's engineering corps to bring the ship in for propulsion tests and systems analyses, assessing the long-term performance of the prototype technologies that were soon to be installed throughout the fleet. It had been easy duty for everyone but the engineers, and Commander Spock—who had given up his *Kolinahr* training and returned to service during the V'Ger incident—had taken advantage of the lull to join a rescue expedition that recovered a group of Vulcan refugees from a world on the Romulan border. Apparently Spock had become rather attached to one of the rescued children, for he had extended his leave of absence in order to tutor her.

As it happened, Sulu had been promoted to second officer just a few months earlier, once he'd decided to commit in earnest to the command track he'd only tentatively pursued before. He'd still been settling into that role, so having the responsibilities of a *first* officer suddenly thrust upon him had been a challenge. But things had been quiet enough during the system tests, and the *Enterprise*'s missions since had been fairly routine—colony supply runs, ferrying diplomats, and the like. It seemed that Starfleet wanted to show off its shiny new *Enterprise* around the Federation, now that it had passed its exams with flying colors. So the first three months of Sulu's tenure as acting first officer had been a relatively easy introduction to the post. The most excitement he'd had in the past month had been reading Crewman Spring Rain on Still Water's oceanographic reports from the *Enterprise*'s recent follow-up visit to the water world Argo, to verify the continued stability of the planet's newly un-sunken continent and to provide resources and rebuilding assistance to the native Aquans who had reoccupied its main city four years ago. Spring Rain was a Megarite who had a distinctive, poetic way of communicating, as well as a love of water that was rarely satisfied aboard a starship but was fulfilled in spades down on Argo. The combination made for some of the most lyrical scientific reports he'd ever read.

But then Admiral Delgado's orders had come in and Sulu had realized things were about to get complicated. The admiral had weathered the political storm over the collapse of his prototype timeship project, holding on to his leadership of Starfleet Science Ops by refocusing his efforts away from temporal research. But Delgado's orders—and the presence of the DTI scientist T'Viss, who stood to Sulu's left, hovering over Petty Officer Uuvu'it at the science station—showed that the admiral hadn't entirely given up his old tricks.

At the helm, Ledoux counted down the seconds to warp egress, then brought the ship down to impulse,

using the automatic course preset controls rather than
the manual override lever Sulu favored—but that
wasn't Sulu's place to judge at the moment, he reminded himself. On the main viewer, the prismatic flow
of warped starlight dissipated in a burst of light, revealing the glow of a G5 star, and in the foreground the
dim, small circle of their destination. Ledoux reached
over to the main viewer controls to magnify the image.
She'd brought the ship out farther from orbital distance
than Sulu would have—again, not his place to criticize.

Sulu had been on leave the last time the *Enterprise*
had been to this star system, but he knew the planetoid
on the viewscreen had not been there at the time. Once
he'd returned to the ship and been regaled by John Far-
rell and Janice Rand about the exact duplicate of Earth
they'd discovered here, he'd assumed they were joking
until he'd reviewed the log tapes and read the science
team's reports about the bizarre subspace anomaly
that had pulled the Earth of a parallel reality into this
one. He knew now that in the years since, Science Ops
and the DTI had been monitoring that anomaly—a
subspace confluence, as T'Viss called it—and judged it
unstable. Now the Onlies' Earth, as it was known, had
finally disappeared, presumably sucked back to whence
it came. Luckily, all the feral, near-immortal children
had long since been evacuated and cured of the disease
that would have killed them upon their long-deferred
puberty, though at the cost of reducing their life expec-
tancies to normal. And there had been enough warning
of the impending confluence breakdown (or whatever)
for the Federation researchers who remained on the

planet to get away in time, though it had been a hasty evacuation.

But when the Onlies' Earth had vanished, something else had appeared in its place. Something at once unexpected and strikingly familiar. Something Delgado and the DTI had both insisted the *Enterprise* investigate posthaste—and if they were on the same page again, that meant it must be big.

"Scanning," said Hrrii'ush Uuvu'it through the voder/translator that interpreted his high, chirping voice. The science officer was a Betelgeusian—tall, hairless, blue-gray, with pointed ears and a brownish triangular muzzle containing a beaklike speaking mouth above a fierce-looking eating mouth. Normally the bridge science station was not a posting for enlisted crew, but Uuvu'it was smart and driven, having swiftly worked his way up from crewman to petty officer, and he and Sulu had a good working relationship. Uuvu'it came from a predatory breed that relished competition, and he saw his scientific studies as a hunt for knowledge, chasing down answers and tearing them from the universe's throat. "Aha!" he crowed after a moment. "Confirming, Captain. The planetoid's atmosphere, surface spectra, and internal mass distribution are consistent with that of a Vedala planetoid! However, the atmosphere is tenuous, dissipating. No auroral illumination layer. Oceans receding. Surface vegetation is scant." Sulu could see that as Ledoux brought the ship into orbit and the sunlit side began to appear on the viewscreen. He'd seen a Vedala planetoid once before—making him one of the few humans who could say that, for there were only a few in known space and their inhabitants were notoriously reclusive—and it had been a beautiful worldlet covered in oceans and exotically colored vegetation, wreathed in an aura of blue light from the atmosphere layer that illuminated the sunless world. This one was mostly brown and red, covered in desert and dried ocean beds, with only small patches of liquid water and live vegetation remaining. Only the nearby star illuminated it. It reminded Sulu of the half-terraformed Mars, only in reverse. The immensely powerful artificial gravity generators and force fields that the Vedala used to hold in their worldlets' atmosphere and moisture must have failed long ago on this one.

"Life readings?" Sulu asked.

Uuvu'it turned to the life-forms detector panel in the retractable auxiliary console to his left, next to where Sulu stood. He raised the fine-tuning rod and played it like an instrument, refining the sensor scans with delicate motions of his talonlike fingers. But his body language had the intensity of a cat preparing to pounce on its prey. If there was any higher life hiding down there, Uuvu'it was determined to hunt it down. Finally, he let out a whistling sigh of defeat. "Nothing, sir. No Vedala, that's for sure."

"Are there any energy signatures consistent with technological devices?" T'Viss asked him.

"Some faint infrared hot spots beneath the surface, nothing more. Ooh, this is interesting . . . they line up with gaps in the neutrino background. Something down there is dense enough or exotic enough to absorb a fair number of neutrinos."

T'Viss turned to the center of the bridge. "Captain, I suggest sending landing parties to those sites."

Kirk rotated his chair to face her. "I'm still uneasy with that suggestion, Doctor. The Vedala are a powerful race. I'd rather not offend them."

"Attempts have been made to contact them about this planetoid's return to our local continuum, but they have taken no action. If they have abandoned it, then we are entitled to investigate it."

"The Vedala are not the most communicative race in the galaxy. Just because they haven't answered our hails doesn't mean they've abandoned this asteroid. They could be on their way to claim it even now."

"As could the Klingons or Romulans, Captain—neither of which would show your regard for other beings' property. If there are temporal or transdimensional technologies down there . . ."

"Understood," Kirk said. "We have to keep them out of enemy hands, if nothing else. I still don't like it."

Rather than lifting an eyebrow as Spock would, T'Viss merely narrowed her gaze. "Your personal gratification is hardly relevant."

Once T'Viss turned back to the science station, Kirk threw a wry look at Sulu, who could only shrug. He and the captain both understood what was at stake here, even if Sulu's understanding was secondhand. On that first visit to a Vedala planetoid, occasioned by the Vedala's summons of Kirk and Spock to address a reputed threat to galactic safety, the two officers had beamed down with the expectation of facing great peril, with Kirk leaving orders for Mister Scott in the event of their non-survival. That was the way it was with the Vedala; they were the oldest spacefaring race still known to be active, wandering the galaxy in their terraformed planetoids since the time of the Neanderthals, and the spacers' tales handed down from civilization to civilization universally agreed that if the fabled Vedala deigned to summon aid from other races, the dangers their champions faced would be epic indeed. And yet Kirk and Spock had returned within two minutes, saying only that the Vedala had "changed their minds." Sulu had suspected there was more to the story than met the eye, but the captain and Spock would say nothing more.

But now that Sulu was acting first officer, Kirk had filled him in for the purposes of this mission. At the Vedala's request, Kirk still couldn't reveal what had happened on their planetoid; indeed, they had somehow affected his mind so that his memory of the specifics had faded. But he had remembered one thing he deemed important enough to report to Starfleet Command: those two minutes from Sulu's perspective on the *Enterprise* had been nearly two days for Kirk and Spock. The Vedala had long been rumored to have the ability to manipulate time as well as space, and this seemed to confirm it. That was why T'Viss was here now on behalf of the DTI: if the Vedala could manipulate time, then there could be devices down on that planetoid—devices now abandoned and free for the taking—which could place the timeline in jeopardy. Thus, they had to be identified and secured at all costs, before the news of a derelict Vedala worldship triggered an interstellar feeding frenzy.

Still, Kirk had confided in Sulu that he was uncertain

about Admiral Delgado's motivations in this. It was unlikely to be a coincidence that a Vedala planetoid had materialized at the heart of the subspace confluence effect.
Those worldlets generally tended to drift in the spaces
between stars or take up temporary orbits in otherwise
empty systems, but they were occasionally known to vanish from one location and reappear in another with no
indication of the intervening passage. Either they could
move very fast or they could somehow jump across great
distances. The confluence event suggested they could
travel between timelines as well, or perhaps between
times. Was it possible that Delgado was still looking
for a way to achieve time travel? Had the DTI sent its
representative here to secure the technology against the
admiral as well as the Klingons and Romulans? And if so,
Sulu wondered, which side should the *Enterprise* be on?

At the science station, Uuvu'it tensed. "I'm picking up something more now, Captain," he said. "It
was hidden around the curve of the planetoid. Trace
subspace energy emissions coming from one of those
neutrino voids."

T'Viss studied the spectrum readouts in the radio-
metrics display above the science console. Sulu leaned
forward to examine them as well, drawing on his as-
trophysics training. The rounded viewer to the left of
the display showed a graphic of the planetoid with the
neutrino voids plotted, forming a regular array. "Those
subspace emissions look . . . erratic," Sulu observed.
"Like whatever's generating them is malfunctioning."

"A premature assessment," T'Viss declared. "There
may be some underlying periodicity we have not yet

discerned. Perhaps we are not receiving the full emission pattern. If the generating structure has components which block neutrinos, they may also be blocking portions of the energy pattern. I suggest a deeper subspace scan."

Uuvu'it gave a look to Sulu, who nodded and turned to Kirk. "Seems reasonable."

"Proceed," the captain said.

The Betelgeusian worked the wave analyzer controls with his right hand while using the other to program the library computer for in-depth analysis and comparison with known energy patterns. The power level gauges crept upward as the scans intensified. "Come on," Uuvu'it murmured. "You can't hide forever. Come out and let me play with your nice, juicy secrets." Sulu chuckled at T'Viss's scandalized expression. "There!" he crowed as the radiometric display lit up with more spectral data. "It's coming in . . . oh. No, that's not what I had in mind."

"Mister Uuvu'it?" Kirk asked, rising from his command chair and standing against the rail that separated it from the science station.

"We're not reading deeper, they're giving off more energy. Look, the thermal output has increased on the site we're scanning. And others around it. The subspace energy readings are surging as well."

"Surging?" Kirk asked. "That doesn't sound good."

"Ah, then I chose the right word."

Kirk and Sulu traded an alarmed look. This was technology powerful enough to move a dwarf planet, possibly even between realities. Not something you wanted to mess with. "Halt scans," Kirk said. "Ledoux, take us out to a safe distance."

T'Viss frowned. "Captain, until we have more data to base an analysis on—"

"It's best not to take any chances," he finished for her.

"Scans are halted, sir," Uuvu'it said, "but the energy is still surging!"

Radiation warning lights were blinking now. "Force fields and deflectors up!" Sulu commanded, a reflex he hadn't realized he'd picked up yet. He'd had nine months to get used to the new dual shield system, but he hadn't thought he was used to being the one who'd give the order.

The spectrum displays were lighting up more and more, filled across their entire bands, and Sulu spun to see the main viewer going white. On the bridge ceiling, the horizon disk in the attitude dome was spinning wildly, even though his last glimpse of the planetoid in the viewer had shown no change in the ship's relative orientation. But then Sulu felt as though his own internal gyros had lost alignment. The bridge spun around him, the deck rising up to meet him, and the blinding light gave way to black.

Sulu awoke to see Doctor Christine Chapel kneeling over him, scanning him with a medical probe. The side of his neck stung, telling him he'd been injected there with a spray hypo. "Christine, what . . . ?"

She helped him sit up. "Most of us passed out. Some form of interphase sickness. We've been reviving the crew with the theragen derivative Doctor McCoy whipped up that time we tangled with the Tholians." Sulu looked around to see Ron Liftig, a dark-haired lieutenant from the nursing staff, assisting in the revival of the rest of the bridge crew, including . . .

"Cella!" Chief Marcella DiFalco sat on the deck beside her navigator's station, a hand against her bloodied forehead. Sulu rushed to her side. "Are you all right?"

"I'm fine," she said, smiling weakly up at him. "It's just a scrape."

He clasped her shoulder. "Still, we should—"

"Mister Sulu!" Kirk's voice rapped from behind him. "Damage report."

Sulu shook himself, reminding himself of his priorities. He and Marcella had grown close in the months since V'Ger, sitting side-by-side every day at the forward console. But they had kept their romance relaxed and noncommittal, particularly once he'd become the acting first officer. They both understood that his duty had to come first. But he found it was harder than he'd expected.

Still, he had a responsibility to his captain, the one person he least wanted to disappoint. After giving DiFalco a tight smile, he stepped over to check the readouts at the damage control station, whose regular operator lay on the deck under Liftig's care. "Shields and propulsion are off line," he reported after studying the screens, "but no reports of serious damage. That surge burned out some of the sensors."

DiFalco had resumed her station after Chapel had sprayed plastiskin on her scalp wound. "Attempting positional fix, sir," she said in her faintly Italian lilt. Sulu trusted her to work around the damaged sensors while he coordinated with the repair teams below.

After a few moments, she had her report. "We're

still in orbit of the Vedala planetoid, Captain, but . . . we're sectors away from where we were. Sir, we're less than a parsec from Epsilon Eridani, practically in the Earth-Vulcan space lane."

Kirk turned to communications, directly across the bridge from where Sulu worked. "Uhura?"

The elegant communications officer shook her mahogany-skinned head. "I'm not picking up any Federation transmissions, sir."

"No navigational beacons, sir," DiFalco confirmed.

Kirk tensed in his chair. "Chronometer readings?"

DiFalco glanced at the time readout alongside the astrogation dome. "Stardate 7583.6," she said. "Same as before."

T'Viss stepped down to the lower deck, acting as if she'd never been affected by the blackout, though she bore a livid green bruise on her sharp chin where it had struck the deck. "Verify against pulsar referents."

Kirk nodded. "Do it."

The chief ran the check. "Verified, sir."

"So we're still in our own time," Sulu said to Kirk. "That's something."

"But not in the same place," the captain replied, rising from the center seat. "And if there are no Federation signals . . ."

"Yes," T'Viss said. "The most logical explanation is that the Vedala planetoid's drives have generated another confluence event. We have been transposed into another macrorealm. Another timeline, you would say."

"The same one the Onlies' Earth came from?" Kirk asked.

"Perhaps. Or perhaps a different one altogether."

"If we'd gone there," Sulu asked, stepping closer to them, "wouldn't we have swapped places with Earth again? Found ourselves in an empty orbit between Venus and Mars?"

"Not necessarily," said T'Viss. "The transposition appears to be independent of spatial coordinates. And since this confluence was most likely triggered by our sensor scans, the state of the mechanism that generated it may have been altered. We would need more data to narrow the possibilities." She sniffed. "This is the difficulty with *experimental* research. Too many messy variables."

Suddenly the proximity alert sounded, and the interception alarm lights began flashing on consoles around the bridge. "Multiple ships approaching!" Lieutenant Chekov called from the weapons and defense station, his Russian accent combined with his post-interphase wooziness to make him harder to understand than usual. "We are being scanned."

"Can you identify them?" Kirk asked.

"I . . . I'm not sure, sir."

Sulu crossed the bridge to look over his shoulder at the tactical display. "Those are familiar," he said after a moment. "They look like . . . Vulcan ringships from a century ago."

"Yes . . . you're right, sir," Chekov said, always remembering proper chain of command even though they were best friends off duty. "But their power curves . . . those are not the readings for antique ships. Reading highly sophisticated weapons and shields."

"What's our shield status?" Kirk asked.

"Half power on deflectors," Sulu told him. "Force field still off line."

"Then let's try to avoid a fight," Kirk said. "Uhura, hailing frequencies."

"We're already being hailed, sir." She gave him a look. "In Vulcan."

"Open a channel."

"Just a moment, sir," Uhura said, her slender fingers fine-tuning the translator controls. "It's an unusual dialect, not in our database. The computer's extrapolating."

Kirk frowned and glanced at Sulu. Before he could say anything, though, the viewscreen lit up with the image of a stern, gray-haired Vulcan male in a martial-looking uniform. *"I am Commander Sekel of the security vessel* Ahn-Woon. *On behalf of the High Command of the Vulcan Protectorate, I require you to identify yourself."*

Kirk stepped forward. "I am Captain James T. Kirk of the *Starship Enterprise.*" He paused, then added, "Representing the United Federation of Planets."

"No such government is known to exist." Sekel peered closer. *"What is your species? Halkan? Eminian? Zeon?"*

The captain blinked. "Human. From a planet called Earth. You're . . . unfamiliar with our species?"

But Sekel was looking over his shoulder now, noticing T'Viss. *"You have a Vulcan among you! Is she a member of the* Muroc's *crew?"* He noted the bruise on her chin. *"If you have harmed her in any way, you will face grave consequences."*

"Doctor T'Viss is a scientific consultant here of her own free will. I'm unfamiliar with this *Muroc.*"

"Your proximity to this Vedala planetoid argues

otherwise. The Muroc *was surveying an identical planetoid until shortly before that body disappeared. Now it
has reappeared and the* Muroc *has vanished. And you are
here with an injured Vulcan aboard your ship. And you
expect me to believe you know nothing of this?"*

"I assure you, Commander, we're here by accident.
I can . . . try to give you a partial explanation, though
we're still trying to piece it together ourselves. You see,
we come from—well, we were surveying this planetoid
because, until recently, its orbit was occupied by an
exact duplicate of our home planet, and . . ." On the
screen, Sekel was rapidly losing patience. "I know that
sounds a little strange, but you see, what we think happened is—"

*"Enough! Allow me to demonstrate the seriousness of
this matter!"* He gestured to someone offscreen.

"Incoming fire!" Chekov called. "Raising shields!"

But it was too little, too late. The ship rocked under
the impact. *"That will be your only warning,"* Sekel said.
"Return the Muroc *to us at once or face destruction!"* He
cut the channel, and the image of three red-brown ships
like spindles inside hoops took his place on the screen.

"Chekov," Sulu asked, "can we handle their fire?"

"Not for long in our current condition, sir."

"There's another concern, sir," Uuvu'it piped up
from sciences. "If the Vedala confluence devices were
triggered by our scans, what might weapons fire do? We
need to move the fight to more secure ground."

Another weapons discharge struck the hull, more
forceful this time. "I don't want there to be a fight,
Mister," Kirk said. "Not over a petty misunderstanding."

Uuvu'it's eating mouth grimaced; Betelgeusians hated to pass up a challenge. But he said nothing further.

On the screen, the ships were moving toward a tetrahedral englobement with the planetoid as the fourth vertex. "Ledoux, break for the opening before they close it. DiFalco, give her evasive options."

"Chekov," Sulu said, "concentrate deflector power to block their fire vectors."

The security chief complied, but still, the next few bolts rocked the ship hard. Ledoux threw Sulu a look. "No stable field," she said.

Sulu instantly understood. The weapons fire was disrupting the warp field before it could fully form. They needed a lull in the firing long enough to make their break. "Captain, we have to return fire. Break their formation."

Kirk's reluctance was clear, but he didn't hesitate. "Chekov, target their weapons."

"Aye, sir." Seconds later, phaser fire lashed out from the aft emitters. "No effect, sir."

"Ledoux," Sulu said, "pattern Sulu-Gamma."

Ledoux acknowledged, veering the ship to port and keelward. Chekov threw a grateful glance at Sulu, for as well as evading fire, the maneuver served to bring the ventral saucer and keel phaser banks to bear on the pursuers. One limitation of the new *Enterprise* design was that phaser coverage to aft was a little weak, just two single emitters over the hangar deck—plus a limited arc from the rearmost saucer emitters, but you had to be careful not to shoot your own nacelles. Some people said that wasn't a problem because Starfleet didn't run from fights; but of course the practical reality was that retreat was sometimes a preferable tactic even during a fight. So once Sulu and Chekov had identified the design flaw, they'd cooperated to devise a series of combat maneuvers to work around it.

With a larger number of phaser banks brought to bear, Chekov was able to break the pursuers' firing pattern long enough for Ledoux to launch the *Enterprise* into warp. "They're pursuing, sir," Uuvu'it said.

"Continue evasive," Kirk ordered.

Sulu moved to stand beside him. "Not very logical, are they? Pretty clear we're not in Kansas anymore."

"Yes . . . and that means we can't count on any help. We're on our own, and that means we have to shake those ships."

Right, Sulu thought. *First things first.* He was sure that Kirk was already plotting three or four moves ahead, but for now, he was keeping his crew focused on the immediate problem.

And a problem it was. The ringships were powerful, able to match the *Enterprise*'s speed in its weakened condition and keep pace with its evasive maneuvers. And now that the *Enterprise* had returned fire, the Vulcans escalated. "Sir," Chekov called, "they're firing what looks like Romulan plasma torpedoes!"

Sulu did a double take. He remembered the damage those had inflicted on the old *Enterprise* eight years before, in its first encounter with a cloaked Romulan ship. They were devastating weapons, but with limitations. They moved at high warp speeds, essentially compact soliton warp bubbles filled with superheated plasma, but they couldn't maneuver, so Chekov was able to pick them off with phasers, detonating them before impact.

Still, the pursuers kept on the *Enterprise*'s tail, and if this kept up much longer, the odds increased that the Vulcans would get a lucky shot in. But something was nagging at the back of Sulu's mind, and finally it came to him. "Captain, I have an idea."

Kirk met his gaze for a moment and nodded. "Take the helm, Mister Sulu."

Ledoux smoothly vacated the chair when Sulu tapped her shoulder, and he slid into it just as easily. It felt like coming home. Here, he had all the answers and the decisions were easy. And so was the maneuver, for he simply put the ship on a straight vector and held it there, easing the manual throttle forward.

After a few moments, DiFalco leaned over and hissed, "This is your plan? Just keep going straight?"

"All that zigzagging was slowing us down." He switched the main viewscreen to a tactical plot. "Chekov, for God's sake, keep picking off those torpedoes!"

"But we can't top warp seven in our condition!" DiFalco went on. "They're still closing in!"

"We just have to get fast enough," he told her.

"For what? Sir?"

The Vulcan ships were closing in now. They'd be close enough to synch warp fields and allow firing phasers within half a minute, and the plasma torpedoes were getting closer to the ship before Chekov was able to detonate them. He just had to hope the Vulcans hadn't made any radical theoretical breakthroughs in warp propulsion in the past hundred years. "See, the reason the Federation abandoned coleopteric warp drives—ringships—is that they resist course changes at high warp factors," he said, tapping in a course change on the console and hovering his finger over the execute switch. "Almost like a gyroscope. So all we have to do is get them going fast enough . . . and then . . ."

He waited until the last possible second, then hit the control, veering the *Enterprise* into the sharpest warp turn it could handle. The deep rumble of the engines rose to a high-pitched whine and stress alarms began to go off at the engineering console. The deck seemed to tilt beneath him as the shifting, asymmetrical warp field imparted an unbalanced gravitational vector on the ship within it, feeling uncannily like the *g*-forces imparted by a more conventional turn at sublight.

But after a few moments, the deck leveled out and the whine diminished. Sulu checked the tactical plot: the Vulcan ships were still heading in the opposite direction, decelerating and breaking formation as they tried to adapt to his maneuver. Sulu laughed. "There. We'll be a parsec away before they can reverse course!"

DiFalco smiled at him in admiration. "Which should be far enough to get out of their sensor range and lose them. Brilliant."

He grinned back, feeling more relaxed than he'd been in months. *Like coming home.*

Once the ship had successfully eluded pursuit for several hours, Kirk ordered Sulu to lay to in a small, nondescript brown dwarf system, using its compact belt of cometary debris for concealment. Then he assembled

Sulu, McCoy, Uhura, Chekov, and T'Viss with him in the main briefing room to sort out their situation while Scotty oversaw repairs. "There's no question," he began, "that we're in an alternate timeline. And since these Vulcans have never heard of the human race, it's a good bet that we're in the same timeline where the Onlies' Earth originated."

"A timeline where Earth's civilization fell over three hundred years ago," Sulu replied, seeing his point.

"So no Zefram Cochrane," Chekov added, "no warp drive, and no Federation."

"And no Jonathan Archer," Uhura said. "He was the Earth captain who helped the Vulcans recover the *Kir'Shara*, the lost writings of Surak."

"That's right," Kirk said, gesturing with a finger as he dredged up his old history lessons. He'd never paid as much attention to non-Terran history as he should have; embarrassingly, he'd once been introduced to an alien simulacrum of Surak, the founder of Vulcan logic and one of the most famous historical figures in the known galaxy, and had momentarily forgotten the significance of the man's name. In the wake of that, he'd tried to brush up. "Before then, the Vulcan High Command was practically a military government. Their fleet maintained order, policed this region of space, kept the Klingons at bay—but they also engaged in espionage, quashed dissident movements, and came close to war with the Andorians on more than one occasion."

"Indeed," said T'Viss. "The infamous Administrator V'Las escalated the militarization of the High Command and attempted to instigate a war with Andoria on false pretenses. T'Pau's recovery of the *Kir'Shara* . . . with *some* assistance from Archer . . . proved instrumental in the disgrace of V'Las and the dissolution of the High Command."

"As well as the social reforms that brought Vulcan civilization more fully in line with Surak's original teachings," Uhura said.

"Commander Sekel mentioned the High Command," Chekov said slowly. "So here, it never fell. T'Pau's reformation never happened. V'Las won. And so we get a universe where the Vulcans are just as warlike as he wanted."

"'Warlike' is a strong word," Uhura replied. "Even if V'Las wanted war, most Vulcans in his time still believed they were doing what was logically needed to keep peace and order. The Vulcans here may feel the same way. They do call themselves a protectorate, after all."

"Sekel didn't seem to have much use for logic," Kirk told her. "Consider how much Vulcan society changed in a century under guidance from Surak and T'Pau. These Vulcans could've changed just as much in the other direction. By now they could be little different from the Romulans."

He took in the others' gaze one by one. "And they're sitting between us and that Vedala planetoid. If we can't get back there and find a way to return home, we could be stuck here for a very long time . . . without a friendly port to be found."

IX

U.S.S. *Hypatia* NCC-S415
Stardate 7584.7

"Fascinating."

The ship Spock beheld on the *Hypatia*'s main viewer spoke of paths not taken by the Vulcans of his reality. Its spindle-and-hoop arrangement resembled a *Suurok*-class vessel from the era of the Vulcan High Command—an institution that had apparently survived into the present of this vessel's timeline of origin. Yet it was more advanced than the ships of that era in some respects—particularly weaponry and shielding—while in other respects was less sophisticated than present-day Federation ships of this timeline.

"Indeed," said Deputy Director Simok of the Department of Temporal Investigations, who stood next to Spock on the *Hypatia*'s old-style bridge. The *Capella*-class survey vessel, attached to the DTI, had already been on its way to join the *Enterprise* in its survey of the Vedala planetoid before both had vanished into the renewed subspace confluence and this vessel, identified in its transmissions as the *Muroc*, had appeared in its place. Director Grey had asked Simok to oversee the mission personally, given its potential importance. "I have spent decades refining our theoretical understanding of alternate quantum histories. Yet it is compelling to perceive firsthand proof of their reality. Is that illogical?" he asked, raising a brow with what Spock had come to recognize as self-effacing humor, for Simok was secure enough in his Vulcan disciplines to be untroubled by the occasional, justified exception.

"Not at all, sir," Spock replied with commensurate good nature. "A model may be soundly derived through logic and mathematics, but is still an unproven abstraction unless it is grounded in evidence. Logic is a means of evaluating fact, not supplanting it."

"Well spoken," Simok replied. "But you have had such firsthand experience before. What fascinates you about this vessel?"

"For one thing, how easily one may discern its timeline's era of divergence from its design. It is almost purely Vulcan, with no technological borrowings from other species, particularly humans. As a result, it is . . . limited compared to Federation designs. An illustration of the truth of *Kol-Ut-Shan*," he said, citing the Vulcan philosophy which humans translated as "infinite diversity in infinite combinations."

"The principle that we are stronger together than apart," Simok said, then nodded toward the *Muroc* on the screen. "Let us hope these Vulcans appreciate it as we do."

"Agreed," Spock said with an intensity he saw no need to hide from Simok. His curiosity about alternative engineering history aside, he found himself experiencing an unwonted impatience to resolve this matter, and not merely for the sake of his comrades

on the *Enterprise*. He disliked being away from Saavik
at this time. In the three months since he had rescued
the preadolescent Vulcan-Romulan girl from the abandoned Romulan colony known as Hellguard, she had
made considerable progress at overcoming the feral
behavior she had acquired there, but she still needed
close supervision. The colonists in whose care he had
left Saavik were neighbors who had established a cordial
relationship with Spock and his protégée, but they had
children of their own and might be overburdened by
the responsibility for tending to Saavik as well, particularly given their limited grasp of her special needs. He
made sure to correspond with her daily over subspace,
but it was far from the ideal situation. He would have
preferred leaving her in the care of his own parents on
Vulcan; indeed, Sarek and Amanda had already agreed
to take responsibility for the child's upbringing once
Spock decided she was ready to be integrated into Vulcan society. But the exigencies of the current crisis had
left him no time for that. By favorable happenstance,
the colony had been fairly close to the course of the
Hypatia, so the vessel had been able to pick him up
with a minimal delay in its rendezvous time with the
Muroc. But Vulcan was nearly two weeks away in the
wrong direction.

Moreover, Spock recognized that, in human terms,
he simply *missed* Saavik. At first, his decision to take
responsibility for the orphaned child had been logical,
though he would not deny an element of sympathy.
The girl had refused the genetic tests which would
identify her nearest Vulcan relatives, so she would

have been remanded to institutional care had he left it at that. Since he had been the one to discover her and convince her to return to civilization, Spock had concluded that would be a breach of his responsibility. Besides, he believed he might be uniquely qualified to assist Saavik. In a way, they were kindred spirits: children of two cultures, outsiders who struggled with emotional control. But Spock had an advantage he would have lacked in the past. Since his mind-meld with the vast cybernetic entity known as V'Ger, he had realized that a life of pure logic was barren, that emotion was necessary to create meaning and fulfillment. He had spent the subsequent months pursuing a new synthesis of logic and emotion—still mastering and regulating his feelings, for Vulcan passions were dangerous if unleashed, but accepting them as a component of his logical decision-making process rather than attempting to ignore or fight them. Given that Saavik had spent the first eleven years of her life either raised by Romulans or left to fend for herself in the wilds of Hellguard, she had none of the foundational training in emotional control that Vulcan children were given. So Spock had resolved that a conventional Vulcan education would be ill-suited to her needs. Instead, he had taken it upon himself to apply the lessons he had learned since V'Ger, attempting to train Saavik to come to terms with her emotional responses through acceptance and controlled release rather than suppression.

If anything, he had been learning as much from the experience as Saavik had. Keeping his emotions in a healthy balance had been difficult in those first months after V'Ger, but the need to set a good example for Saavik, and to remain patient with her frequent outbursts and misbehaviors, had brought him to a place of greater serenity. He did not consider Saavik a daughter, any more than he would consider her a sister if Sarek and Amanda were to adopt her later on. Those biological ties carried depths of meaning to a Vulcan that the human terms could not encompass, and adoptive or surrogate relationships were simply not seen the same way. But perhaps, as Jim Kirk was *t'hy'la*, the friend who was as close as a brother, Saavik might be *t'kam'la*, the student who was as cherished as a daughter. And so mentoring her had changed him in a way not unlike becoming a father. It was the only experience he had ever undertaken which was as rewarding as his service aboard the *Enterprise*.

And yet the *Enterprise* was still his home, so when Admiral Delgado had contacted him about the ship's disappearance, he had immediately requested to join the *Hypatia*. He believed Saavik had understood, for he had spoken to her often of his shipmates and the benefits he gained from Starfleet service. But the look in her eyes when he left had been one of fear, of doubt that he would return to her. Given her history, it was unsurprising that she feared abandonment. He was determined to resolve this matter quickly so that he could return to her and address whatever damage he had done.

He put such thoughts aside when the *Hypatia*'s Efrosian communications officer spoke up. "Captain, the *Muroc* is hailing."

"Onscreen." Captain Nijen Danehl was a Makusian female, tall and lanky with deep bronze skin and back-swept, winglike ears. She rose to her full, 1.9-meter height as the commander of the *Muroc* appeared on the viewscreen. "Greetings once again, Commander Satak," she said with the open warmth of her people. Spock raised a brow. In this reality, Satak had been a Starfleet officer, captain of the *Intrepid* when it had been destroyed by a spacegoing unicellular organism in the Gamma 7A system. It was perhaps not surprising that this alternate Satak had chosen a similar career path, given the same inherent aptitudes and inclinations. But it was gratifying to know that at least one incarnation of Satak still lived.

This Satak, however, did not seem gratified. *"Captain. You are behind schedule."*

"Apologies," Danehl said, "but as we informed you, we needed to divert to pick up a specialist." She gestured to Spock, who came forward. "This is Commander Spock, science officer of the *Enterprise*. He has prior experience with the phenomenon that displaced you into this reality."

Satak looked him over. *"Commander Spock. If you serve aboard the missing vessel, why are you here now?"*

"I was on leave at the time of its disappearance, Commander. But it is still my ship, my crew. As you can imagine, I am highly motivated to return them to where they belong."

Satak considered him a moment more, then nodded. *"I see that the Vulcans of your continuum still value loyalty as we do."*

"It is a value shared by most of the races of the Federation."

"This is not a sociological study, Commander Spock. You are here to coordinate with my science staff in order to bring about our return to our continuum. I suggest you proceed."

"Very well," Spock said. "I recommend you transport your science officer aboard the *Hypatia*, so we may evaluate the data contained in its computers."

"Agreed. Then we will proceed together back to the site of the anomaly."

"Excellent," Danehl said. "Let us know when your delegation is ready to beam over."

Satak cut the channel, and Danehl turned to her guest. "Mister Spock?"

Spock nodded. "Professor Simok, if you would accompany me? You as well, please, Ms. Watley." Dierdre Watley, now the *Hypatia*'s science officer, nodded and rose to join them. It had been years since Watley had been a member of Spock's science department aboard the *Enterprise*, but he had continued to follow her research into temporal theory and found her grasp of the subject incisive.

As soon as they reached the transporter room on Deck 5, the Caitian transporter operator told them, "The party from the *Muroc* is ready to beam aboard, sirs."

Though Spock was the ranking Starfleet officer here, he deferred to Simok's leadership of the mission. The older Vulcan nodded. "Bring them aboard, please."

Three columns of particulate matter shimmered into being on the transporter pad and solidified into

three Vulcans, two females and a male. Spock took in
all three faces, but then found his attention jerked back
to the lead female, who stepped down from the pad
with an imperious air. The shorter hair and utilitarian
jumpsuit had misled him for an instant, but he knew
that haughty poise as well as he knew her almond-
shaped eyes, her fine bone structure, her vivid scent. A
scent whose associations in his memory almost over-
whelmed his emotional restraint.

Parted from me and never parted . . . never and al-
ways touching and touched.

. . . As it will be for all tomorrows, I make my choice.

I came to know that I did not want to be the consort
of a legend.

The voice echoed in his mind, the same as the voice
that now addressed Simok. "I am Subcommander
T'Pring, chief scientist of the *Muroc*."

Spock told himself that his reaction to Subcommander
T'Pring was illogical. This was not the person he had
been betrothed to at the age of seven. This was not the
woman he had returned to Vulcan to marry when the
pon farr came upon him. This was not the woman who
had desired the company of another male instead, and
had thus ruthlessly manipulated him into the *kal-if-fee*,
the challenge to the death, against his own captain and
friend. The emotions that her face, her voice, her scent
evoked in him—emotions he was now able to face
directly and identify as a mix of desire, betrayal, resentment, and perhaps a touch of fear—were meant for
another person, her quantum counterpart in this reality.

However identical they may have been, this T'Pring had lived a different life, made different choices. In her universe, no human births had taken place in over three centuries, so Amanda Grayson had never been born, and thus neither had Spock. He had no history with this woman, no prior basis for mistrust.

But it proved difficult to let go of his prejudices when the subcommander was so clearly hiding things from him, Simok, and the rest of the team. Her explanations about the *Muroc*'s actions and circumstances prior to its arrival in this timestream were elliptical and evasive. And they failed to address a key question. With time being of the essence, Spock confronted her on that point. "Perhaps you would care to explain," he said, showing her a sensor readout of the *Muroc*, "what it is you have in your cargo hold that is able to create a void in the neutrino background."

Subcommander T'Pring stared at him tensely for a moment, as did her two aides. Then, unexpectedly, she relaxed. "I knew it was a mistake to keep this from you. It was Satak's order, for security reasons. I failed to convince him that openness would better suit our goals."

She inserted a data card into the briefing room's reader slot and entered a decryption code. The image of a large, intricate device appeared on the screen: a series of nested spherical lattices with a glowing, multilobed core. "We retrieved this mechanism from beneath the surface of the Vedala planetoid your *Enterprise* was sent to investigate, while it still resided in our continuum. We discovered only a few years ago that the planetoid had apparently taken the place of a Minshara-class planet in an uninhabited system."

"You mean Earth," Dierdre Watley said.

"Apparently that was one of the local names used by its civilization during our early surveys generations ago. But that civilization suffered a global biological cataclysm before it could achieve starflight, and thus we never made contact. Remote analysis suggested that Vulcans would be immune to the plague but could transmit it to other species. Thus, we interdicted the system and paid little subsequent attention to it. We only discovered the planetary substitution due to the minuscule gravitational anomalies it created in the orbits of nearby populated systems. Since normal-space gravitational effects propagate only at the speed of light, we did not discover the substitution until years after it had occurred."

Simok frowned. "You completely ignored the system after it was interdicted? You saw no benefit in studying it remotely to observe whether the survivors were able to rebuild their society or even continue to exist?"

T'Pring tilted her head in a way that was both haughty and embarrassed at the same time. "The High Command places a low priority on pure research. There was no practical gain to studying the system, so the Protectorate focused its attention elsewhere. However, once it was discovered that an apparently abandoned Vedala planetoid had replaced that world, study of the phenomenon became a priority. The *Muroc* spent several weeks surveying the planetoid and analyzing the strange subspace effect it was generating—what you call a confluence." She gestured at the screen. "We determined that these devices in its crust were responsible for the effect."

"So you removed one."

"Yes. And in so doing, we most likely precipitated what happened next. The other devices began going into shutdown. The confluence field began to dissipate. The *Muroc* had barely retreated before the planetoid disappeared and the original planet—Earth, as you call it," she said to Watley, "materialized in its place."

"Back in its original orbit?" Spock asked.

"Not quite, as a consequence of the displacement by a body of differing mass and the time it spent circling another star. Our projections show its new orbit will render the planet uninhabitable in the long term."

Watley appeared saddened by the fate of the planet. "How fortunate," Spock reminded her, "that all its surviving inhabitants were evacuated before its return."

"Maybe," Watley replied, "but what about all the animals? And still . . . it's home. At least, it was once."

Spock did not attempt to question her sentiment. He accepted that emotion could have value even if he could not fully agree with it. And he admitted that he could not predict how he might react to news of a similar cataclysm befalling Vulcan, even in another timeline.

T'Pring continued, disregarding the exchange. "The *Muroc* continued to survey the returned Earth for several days, until we could be confident the planetoid would not return. We then proceeded toward Vulcan, but soon after we passed Axanar, the device in the hold began to activate. And we found ourselves here."

"Intriguing," said Simok. "The devices from the Vedala planetoid—presumably their planetary drives—must share some form of quantum entanglement that transcends even the dimensional phase separation between timelines. That would explain why the planetoid's second displacement exchanged it with the *Muroc* instead of with Earth once again. The planetary drive aboard the *Muroc* attracted the confluence like a lightning rod, if I may be forgiven the crude metaphor."

"So why did it swap with Earth in the first place?" Watley asked.

"Perhaps mere chance. Under normal circumstances, with the drives all operating together, the confluence might exchange with any given location in another spacetime domain. But with one drive separated from the others, they attracted and exchanged with one another instead."

"In any case," Spock said, "we can gain little further understanding without studying the device directly. I recommend we adjourn to the *Muroc*'s cargo hold."

He held T'Pring's gaze, and to his surprise, she evinced no reluctance. "I agree. And I should be able to convince Commander Satak of the need, now that our possession of the drive is no longer secret."

It seemed her gaze lingered on Spock's for longer than was necessary. Was it possible that she . . . No. Spock dismissed the thought as illogical and irrelevant.

V.H.C. *Muroc*

"What does *Hypatia* mean?" T'Pring asked Spock once they arrived aboard her ship.

"Hypatia was a philosopher, astronomer, and mathematician on ancient Earth—a woman of great accomplishment in fields that women in her culture were almost completely excluded from. She was murdered as a consequence of a religious and cultural upheaval in which her civilization and its literature, art, and scholarship were largely destroyed. She is seen by many humans as a martyr to the cause of science and reason."

"Interesting," T'Pring said. "An emblem of learning, yet also of determination to strive against all obstacles—no matter the cost. It says much about your Federation."

"Hm. And *Muroc*?"

"The hero of Paan Mokar. When the Andorian occupiers murdered Ambassador Soval during peace talks, Muroc escaped and waged a guerrilla campaign against the occupiers that eventually succeeded in driving them off. He went on to become a fleet commander in the invasion of Andoria and proved instrumental in its conquest."

Spock permitted himself only a raised eyebrow. "Indeed."

Watley was looking around at the personnel who passed them in the Vulcan ship's corridors, noting that some of them bore unusually pronounced foreheads and showed less emotional restraint than the Vulcans. "Are those . . . Romulans?" she asked T'Pring in a hushed voice.

"Yes," the subcommander replied. "Is this a difficulty for you?"

"No, no," Watley said with poorly feigned lightness. "It's just . . . I wasn't expecting it, that's all."

Spock saw nothing to be gained by dissembling. "In this continuum, the Romulan and Federation governments have a hostile relationship."

"One which the Romulans instigated, no doubt. Have no fear," T'Pring told Watley. "Our Romulans were just as bellicose, once. They even infiltrated Vulcan and encouraged us to adopt a more martial value system, in order to prepare us for conquest and assimilation. But their efforts succeeded too well. When they attempted to conquer us . . . we conquered them instead."

"I see," Spock said, though at this point he was unconvinced that the distinction was relevant. These Vulcans might still embrace logic, but in many respects they were as martial as their Romulan offshoots. And that warrior's discipline combined with Vulcan logic and intellect might well make them more dangerous than the Romulans had ever been.

He wondered if that was the only reason he continued to be so agitated by T'Pring's proximity. He hoped it was.

U.S.S. Enterprise
Stardate inapplicable

"Force-field coils overloaded! Forward deflectors at twenty-two percent, starboard at forty-eight! Phaser banks four and five off line!"

"Hard to starboard! Target the lead ship!"

The *Enterprise* had managed to elude the Vulcans for just over two days before it came under attack again. A

fleet of ringships intercepted the vessel a parsec antispin-
ward of Coridan, a system that in this timeline was firmly
under Vulcan rule. Kirk had tried to hail them and talk
things out, but the Vulcans had fired preemptively, their
only transmission a demand for unconditional surrender.
Given the belligerence of these Vulcans, and the disquieting implications of their use of Romulan weaponry,
Kirk wasn't about to risk putting his crew at their mercy,
so there had been no choice but to retreat. But they'd
adapted to Sulu's maneuver, bringing too many ships to
allow the *Enterprise* to break for the straightaway.

"Sir! Torpedo incoming from starboard!" Chekov
cried.

"Roll sixty degrees starboard!" Sulu ordered
Ledoux. It would mean taking the hit on the dorsal
saucer grid, dangerously close to the bridge, but they
had little choice. Their phaser power and coverage were
inadequate to detonate all the plasma bolts.

But then Uuvu'it cried, "Captain! New ships incoming! They're firing on the plasma bolts!"

"And on the Vulcans!" Chekov added a moment
later. "The ringships are breaking formation!"

"Science officer, can you identify those ships?" Kirk
asked.

"Consistent with Andorian design," Uuvu'it said.
"But much of the technology seems almost . . ." He
hesitated.

"Incoming hail, sir," Uhura said.

"Onscreen."

A leering humanoid face appeared on the viewscreen—swarthy, thick-bearded, with sharp, stained

teeth . . . and a heavy ridge of bone down the center of his forehead. Uuvu'it completed his sentence, unnecessarily. "Klingon."

"I am Captain Tunzos of the Klingon-Andorian Compact," the Klingon intoned, grinning. *"I don't know who you are, but if the Vulcans don't like you . . . then I do."*

The Klingon's grin widened, and Kirk feebly tried to muster one in return.

Klingon-Andorian Compact Regional Capital, Chasav III

Stardate inapplicable

It took two days for the Compact armada to tow the damaged *Enterprise* to its spacedock facilities at Chasav—the Andorian name for the Regulus system. Any indication of Andorian influence in the KAC was reassuring to Kirk. True, they were a warrior culture themselves—particularly in this timeline, where they'd been hardened by a century of conflict with Vulcan—and they seemed to mesh well with the Klingons here. But at least Kirk knew that in his own history, the Andorians were an honorable people who had learned to trust and cooperate with the other races of the Federation, including their onetime enemies the Vulcans.

Indeed, although Tunzos was the battle leader of the KAC armada, it was under the overall command of an Andorian admiral, Revethanis ch'Naras. According to the *Enterprise*'s computer banks, the Revethanis ch'Naras of the home universe was a minor regional official in the Sheineth Province on Andor, unremarkable but known for his reliability. Kirk hoped this ch'Naras was as trustworthy, for he had no choice but to answer the admiral's probing questions honestly. He was hesitant to give the KAC answers about the *Enterprise*'s true origins or access to its technology, which was more advanced in many respects than the Compact's systems—the fruits of a century and more of cooperation and technological cross-pollination among dozens of Federation worlds. But the Vulcans' attacks had left the ship in dire need of repairs, and the Compact's assistance was the only option available. So it was better to be upfront about where the *Enterprise* and the humans aboard her came from, rather than try to hide it and risk their tenuous allies' anger if the deception were discovered.

At first, ch'Naras and Tunzos had been skeptical of Kirk's tale. Fortunately, thanks to the cosmopolitan leanings of the erstwhile Captain Decker, the refitted *Enterprise* boasted the most diverse multispecies crew currently in service, including several Andorian personnel. As it happened, one of them, security crewman Shantherin th'Clane, was the quantum double of a squad leader aboard one of ch'Naras's own ships, and seeing th'Clane brought face-to-face with himself had quite an impact on everyone involved. Another, sociologist Pasthemon sh'Levram, had a counterpart who had been married to the cousin of one of ch'Naras's fleet engineers prior to her death in a Vulcan raid two years earlier. The engineer had been to her funeral and had no doubt of her death. Ch'Naras was left with no choice but to accept Kirk's astonishing tale.

And so the *Enterprise* and her crew came to Regu-lus—rather, Chasav—as honored guests, with ch'Naras offering the full benefits of the planet's orbital drydock facilities. That night, once the most urgent repairs had been seen to, Kirk and his command crew were invited to a celebration in their honor, courtesy of ch'Naras and the planetary governor, a Klingon who introduced himself as Barak, son of Krase. To Kirk's surprise, he recognized Barak's name and face; the Captain Barak of his reality had commanded the *I.K.S. Amar*, lead ship of the battle group that had confronted V'Ger on its passage through Klingon space. It had been Barak's transmissions, intercepted by the Epsilon IX listening post, that alerted Starfleet to V'Ger's approach to Earth and enabled the *Enterprise* to launch in time to inter-cept it. In a way, the now-departed Captain Barak had been an unwitting hero of the Federation. Kirk hoped· that this reality's Governor Barak would be as helpful.

At the very least, the party they threw looked to be diverting, if raucous. Kirk had left Sulu in command of the *Enterprise*, wanting his ship to remain in trusted hands, and of course Scotty had refused to leave his baby while she was injured. So Kirk was accompanied by Doctor McCoy, Uhura, and Chekov. The security chief had brought th'Clane along as backup, figuring it was a good idea to have an Andorian in the group. McCoy had brought his own backup in the form of Reiko Onami, the ship's xenopsychologist. Although the two of them had clashed vehemently at first, McCoy had appreciated the dainty petty officer's will-ingness to ignore the niceties of status and seniority and tell him in no uncertain terms when she thought he was wrong—particularly when she'd turned out to be right and forced him to confront and rectify a serious limitation in his knowledge of nonhuman medicine. Since then, he'd practically adopted her as a junior McCoy, a fellow gadfly whom he trusted to keep him honest the way he kept Kirk and Spock honest—namely, by pestering and challenging them with a gleeful disregard for rank, tact, or propriety. Kirk had been wary about bringing her down to Chasav for that very reason, but McCoy had reassured him: "Reiko grew up on a planet where she and her folks were the only humans around. She gets along better with aliens than with her own species."

Indeed, Onami's deceptively delicate features were as happy and bright as Kirk had ever seen them as she took in the sensory tumult of the governor's private reception hall—though "barroom" was more the word. The garishly decorated hall was crowded with noise, bodies, and aromas both enticing and pungent. Most of the occupants were Klingon and Andorian, but Kirk saw others as well: Elasians, Troyians, Nausicaans, Lorillians, Aulacri, Suliban. Orion and Risan females, clad only in smiles, jewelry, and the occasional diaphanous veil, danced onstage or offered drinks, food, and other services to the guests. Ahead of Kirk, Captain Tunzos laughingly slapped an Orion serving girl's bare green rump and commanded, "Get me some meat!"

McCoy looked embarrassed on Onami's and Uhura's behalf, but Uhura maintained a practiced neutrality while Onami seemed to be enjoying herself. "Don't worry," she whispered to the others. "Orion females are a lot more in control of themselves than it appears." When the serving girl returned with a large platter of assorted meats for Tunzos, Onami joined him in tearing into them with gusto, and soon they were laughing together as the Klingon captain regaled her with accounts of his heroism in something called the War of Kentin.

Kirk found it more difficult to dine amiably with Klingons, and Barak noticed this as the evening went on. "And do you, Captain Kirk, have any great tales of combat with the Klingons of your universe?" he eventually asked. The captain fidgeted, and Barak gave a snarling grin. "No cause for shame, Captain. We are conquerors. We grow to survive, in any universe. That you stand against our time-spawned brothers to defend your territory does you honor. No doubt we would have warred with the Andorians as well had not the Vulcans given us common cause. That is the way of things. Neighbors fight for power, for territory, unless they have a common foe to join against."

"On Earth," Uhura said, "we once had a philosopher who believed the same thing. His name was Kautilya."

"Your Earth, or ours?" ch'Naras asked.

"He lived long enough ago that it would have been both. But here, his writings would have been lost along with the rest of humanity's lore and knowledge," she went on sadly. "Perhaps we could share some of that forgotten lore with you as a gift, to thank you for your repairs."

Kirk smiled at her, appreciating the sentiment—and understanding what drove it. Beyond any practical interest in deal-making with these allies of convenience, Uhura must share his anguish at the notion of a reality where humanity had effectively ceased to exist, where its great works had crumbled to dust, unknown to the rest of the galaxy. True, the Vulcans may have gleaned some fragments in their few clandestine surveys, but given Commander Sekel's complete ignorance of humanity's existence, any such information was probably buried deep in their databases, unknown to all but a few scholarly specialists.

"There is something more you can offer us," Admiral ch'Naras said, taking in all the humans' gazes. "You offer hope. You offer the vision of an Andor that is free." He focused on th'Clane. "I envy you, having known such a world, having walked its streets and known you were a free Andorian. Tell me of it."

Th'Clane happily regaled ch'Naras with tales of his life in Andor's capital city Laibok, dwelling particularly on the times he'd spent in his favorite park as a child. He broke off when he realized ch'Naras was weeping. "Forgive me," the admiral said. "I am moved by what you offer. Here, we have no such simple freedoms to enjoy. The people of my Andor have languished under Vulcan occupation for over a century. A puppet government offers a mockery of home rule while collaborating in the Vulcans' repression—helping their so-called Protectorate enslave our people, 'civilize' them with their barren, ruthless logic, and imprison any who resist." His voice trembled with bated fury.

Young th'Clane was dumbstruck. "That's . . . hard to imagine," he finally said. "The Vulcans I know . . . they would never tolerate that."

The admiral studied the security crewman a moment longer, then spoke to Kirk. "That offers hope as well, Captain. The knowledge that the Vulcans of your reality are . . . friends to the Andorians." It seemed a struggle to get the sentence out. "As difficult as that is for us to imagine, I must accept that it is a truth in your world."

"It is," Kirk said, "though it wasn't always that way. In our world, the Vulcans and Andorians had a history much the same as yours until a hundred and twenty years ago. But the invasion of Andor that happened in your world was avoided in ours. The Vulcans found they were being duped into a manufactured war by one ambitious ruler, and they turned away from that path. And before long, the Vulcans and Andorians were able to put aside their past disputes and work together for the common good.

"So I agree, Admiral. If it happened in our world, there's hope that it could still happen here . . . if both sides are willing."

Ch'Naras's antennae tilted skeptically. "Perhaps one day. But as things stand, the Vulcans have no incentive to come to the table. It would take much to change that. What I perceive, Captain, is a more immediate hope that *your* Vulcans can offer."

Kirk furrowed his brow. "What do you mean?"

The admiral nodded toward th'Clane. "As we have seen, many of the same individuals live in both universes. So surely many of the cruel Vulcans of this world must have more decent counterparts in yours. As th'Clane said, your Vulcans would not stand for what their twins have done here." Ch'Naras sat forward, speaking with growing intensity. "If we could establish a regular exchange between universes, then we could recruit the counterparts of key Protectorate officials. Use them to replace their doubles, infiltrate the Vulcan government and military as sleeper agents. With their help we could undermine the Protectorate from within and ultimately bring about its destruction!"

"*Qapla'!*" Tunzos cried. "More meat!" He slapped Onami on the back in celebration, but the formerly jovial xenopsychologist was now staring at ch'Naras as though concluding he was in dire need of her professional services.

Before Onami—or McCoy, who looked just as dumbstruck—could blurt out something that would get them eviscerated, Kirk tried taking a more diplomatic tack. "I'm sorry, Admiral, but that's out of the question. The laws of the Federation forbid us from taking sides in a military conflict. If we can establish ongoing contact, we'd be glad to provide humanitarian aid, or serve as a neutral mediator between the Compact and the Protectorate, help you end this conflict peacefully. Just the example we can provide of Vulcan-Andorian cooperation and its benefits could do a great deal to convince the Protectorate of the logic of making peace." He shook his head. "But military or intelligence aid is out of the question."

"Besides," McCoy finally spoke up, "you can't ask random Vulcans to turn spy just because they have important counterparts over here. What if they're school-teachers or artists? What if they just had babies? Not to mention that a lot of Vulcans on our side are pacifists."

"Those problems can be surmounted," ch'Naras insisted. "Given what is at stake, they must be!"

"Please understand, Admiral," Kirk told him. "We'll do everything we reasonably can to help. It's the least we can do to repay you for your aid and hospitality. But what you ask is not something we can legally or ethically provide."

"Think carefully, Kirk," Governor Barak said. "Your only way home is on a planetoid in Vulcan hands. By now it is surely under heavy guard and study. And who knows when they might accidentally trigger another jump, and send it forever beyond your reach? Without our aid in retaking the planetoid . . . you will never return home."

"And remember," Tunzos added, "we are Klingons. We are generous hosts to those who share common cause with us." The Orion serving girl arrived with another platter of meats. "But if we aren't given what we want—we simply take it!" He grabbed the serving girl's arm and pulled her roughly onto his lap, making her squeal and giggle. "Remember that," Tunzos told him with an amiable, sharp-toothed grin, "when you return to your powerful starship . . . which is in our spacedock . . . surrounded by many of our ships." He used the hand that wasn't pawing the Orion to grab a large, dripping drumstick and shove it into his mouth.

Kirk exchanged concerned looks with his crew-mates, then carefully rose. "With your permission,

Admiral, Governor, Captain, I think we should return to our ship. You've . . . given us a lot to think about." Ch'Naras nodded gravely, looking uneasy about the threats the others had made, but determined to let nothing stand in the way of his quest. Barak simply gave a confident grin.

"Mm," Tunzos said. "Good meat."

X

U.S.S. Hypatia
Stardate 7585.3

By their third day working together on the confluence drive in the *Muroc*'s hold, it was clear to Spock
that spending time with Subcommander T'Pring was
becoming a problem. He found himself distracted by
sensory input from her, focusing on the fullness of her
voice or the suppleness of her musculature when he
should be concentrating on the analysis of the Vedala
drive. It was becoming increasingly difficult for him to
concentrate on his thoughts. His emotions had become
more volatile, harder to control, than at any time since
the first days after his meld with V'Ger.

He had hoped—yet again—to be spared this.
Hoped that by relaxing his rigid emotional repression,
he would have somehow made it easier, less overpower-
ing, when the time came. And yet what burned in his
veins now was as intense as it had been before . . . seven
years ago.

So he retreated to his guest quarters aboard the
Hypatia and immersed himself in meditation. Hopefully he could at least defer the worst of it until he
could return to Vulcan and then . . . then . . .

What? He had given no thought to what he would

do when the *pon farr* came upon him again. He had known this day might come soon, but he had chosen to devote himself to Saavik's training anyway. Sometimes the cycle was irregular. Sometimes assuming responsibility for a child could postpone the hormonal surges that triggered the mating drive. Perhaps that was why it had kicked in so suddenly now—because it had been looming already, held in abeyance until he was separated from his young charge. Perhaps if he resolved this matter quickly and returned to Saavik, the urges would subside again until . . . until he could decide on a logical course of action.

Or until he died because he had been too foolish, too afraid even now of facing this onslaught of emotion, to develop a plan for it. To find someone he could turn to. To take a mate. Why had he avoided even considering it?

Spock became aware that the door signal had been sounding persistently for some moments. Then *her* voice, T'Pring's voice, sounded through the door. "Spock! Let me in!"

He did not mean to obey, but a moment later she was stepping inside, facing him. Her eyes caught his intensely. She trembled. Her skin was hot enough to feel across the small space that divided them . . .

He moved back, putting the length of the room between them, and turned to look out the viewport at the *Muroc* beyond. "You should not be here, Subcommander."

"Yes, Spock, I must. I must understand how this bond has formed between us."

"I . . . apologize . . . if it is inappropriate."

"No. I am unbonded." A pause. "My betrothed—Stonn—and I went into space service together, as couples so often do. But . . . he was killed in a Compact raid before our first time together came."

"I grieve with thee," Spock said ritualistically. Some part of his analytical mind that remained functional was fascinated by the degree of convergence between timelines, the tendency of the same individuals to follow similar life paths. In both realities, T'Pring and Stonn had come together. And now, somehow, the currents of probability had brought T'Pring and Spock together at a time of *pon farr*, even though no Spock had ever lived in her reality. Was there perhaps some kind of quantum resonance between timelines that led different iterations of the same individual along similar paths? But he was in no condition to assess the hypothesis now.

"When the need came upon me," T'Pring continued, "a fellow officer provided . . . his services. Yet he was bonded already and married soon thereafter. And so I remain unattached." She paused. "So why do I feel this . . . so strongly . . . toward you?" She stepped closer, but froze when she saw how he tensed. She retreated behind an elementary question—or so she must have thought. "Are you unbonded as well?"

Spock took several slow, deep breaths before daring to answer. "I . . . was bonded," he said. He still resisted facing her, but he glanced over his shoulder as he confessed, "To you."

She gave a soft gasp that only Vulcan ears could discern.

"Forgive . . . my inaccuracy," Spock went on. "Of course, I mean your counterpart. That T'Pring and I were bonded as children. When the time came, we met at the appointed place."

"We . . . were married?"

"She challenged. For she, too, desired Stonn." He repressed a surge of rage. "She maneuvered me into killing my closest friend—or so I believed at the time. I released her from her commitment to me."

There was a pause before T'Pring spoke. "Then that is why you resist this now. Is that logical, Spock?"

"This should not be. I react to you because you share her hormones and psionic signature. It has triggered this involuntary response. And my own hormonal and psionic influence is what you are responding to."

"Psionic?" she asked, startled. "You are a melder. This is something you are doing to me . . ." But her tone revealed disbelief in her own words.

Ahh, yes. Spock recalled that before the *Kir'Shara* had been rediscovered, most Vulcans had believed mind-melding to be a rare ability, socially ostracizing those who displayed it. The mating bond had been explained away as a purely pheromonal and psychological effect, its subtle psionic component glossed over. "All Vulcans have the capacity to join minds," he told her. "Some more strongly and instinctively, but in the rest it simply needs to be awakened through training." He saw her hesitation. "If you stay away from me, perhaps the effect—all of the effects—will subside for you."

This time, when T'Pring came closer, she did not

let his resistance stop her from touching him, turning him to face her. "But not for you. If we are mentally linked—never and always touching and touched," she went on, the ritual phrase carrying new meaning for her, "then that gives me a responsibility for you. Why should I leave you to suffer, perhaps to die, when I am ideally qualified to succor you?"

"Because I do not wish it!" he barked, seizing her arms and shoving her away.

But this T'Pring was a trained soldier. She grabbed his forearms and turned her momentum to her advantage, spinning around and flinging him onto the couch. A second later she was atop him, forearm pressing against his throat. His hands rose to clench her throat. Aghast, he caught himself, stopped them . . . and then watched them stroking her cheeks, her shoulders. He jerked them back, just as aghast.

"*Think*, Spock!" T'Pring cried, panting harder than exertion alone would account for. "We both need to be at maximum efficiency to save your crewmates. Logically, we should mate, and we should do it now. It is the optimal way to resolve this difficulty."

He pushed her off him, rising and seeking distance again, but she stood in the middle of the narrow room and there was nowhere to go. But did he resist so strongly because of his resentment . . . or because of the intensity of his desire?

"Spock, look at me," T'Pring said. He resisted. "You are being childish. *Look at me!*" Sullenly, he met her gaze. "I understand what you see, Spock. You see your betrayer. You see a cold, covetous manipulator.

But I am not that T'Pring. I could not be." Her voice softened. "Stonn was a part of me. And I lost him. Ever since, I have been incomplete.

"*She* could not understand that, if she was capable of making you kill your friend to satisfy her agendas. Perhaps then, when all I knew was desire for Stonn and its gratification, I would have been as selfish. But now I understand the . . . the immensity of loss. The profoundness of solitude."

T'Pring reached out the first two fingers of her hand, brushing them lightly against his. "I see that same solitude in you. You know the emptiness of being alone, and yet you seek it out, preferring it to the risk of making a bond. I find that an illogical waste, Spock. I would not see you condemn yourself—or your friends." She lifted his hand up between them, stroked his paired fingers more firmly with her own. "We can help each other, Spock. Let me help you . . . and then let me help your friends."

Let me help . . . He remembered how Jim Kirk revered those words. As Spock gazed into her dark eyes, as he sensed the timbre of her inner voice through her touch, he knew that her likeness to the T'Pring of this universe was superficial. The T'Pring he had known would see no logic in thinking of another's needs before her own. She could not be this generous. This kind.

So he could see no reason, logical or emotional, to refuse her generosity. Clasping both her hands, opening his mind to the untrained but instinctual touch of hers, he led her into the bedroom.

U.S.S. Enterprise
Stardate inapplicable

"Okay, so we have to break out of here," McCoy said. "Let's assume for the sake of argument that we can do that without getting blown to bits. But where will that get us? We'll still be damaged, and we'll have *two* fleets huntin' us down instead of one."

The doctor, Kirk, and Sulu were meeting in the officers' lounge at the rear of the bridge module—not the private meeting room with its holographic screens, but the public observation area, a cozy conversation pit with four large trapezoidal windows affording a spectacular view of the rear of the saucer and the back-swept, Art Deco warp nacelles. McCoy and Sulu sat in comfortable chairs on the port side of the lounge, the branches of one of the dwarf trees in the planter behind them tickling the doctor's head if he leaned back too far. Sulu took the seat closest to the windows, his knees blocking McCoy's view of the painting on the low wall beneath them, a representation of an Apollo astronaut on Luna with Earth over his shoulder. Assorted books and journals rested on the low table against the aft wall, left by various members of the crew for the benefit of their shipmates. Normally this lounge would have been more populated at this time of the evening, but the ship's officers were currently either busy with the round-the-clock repair schedule or sleeping off their exhaustion from same.

Kirk paced before the windows, gazing out at the claustrophobic drydock frame that contained the *Enter-*

prise like a cage, a dense clutter of scaffolds lit in the green hues that the Klingons favored, giving the *Enterprise*'s hull a sickly cast. "We can't stay here, Bones. I can't hold off ch'Naras and Barak much longer. Either we get out while we can or they take this ship by force."

"I'm not arguing that. I'm just asking, what the hell do we do next?"

"We try to convince the Vulcans we're not their enemies."

"*These* Vulcans? Jim, they're practically Romulans. You heard ch'Naras."

"We've heard his side of things. And we got off on the wrong foot with the Vulcans because they were concerned about their missing ship."

"And they're still Vulcans, Doctor," Sulu said. "Their history's only different for the past one or two centuries. So they still believe in logic. They should be open to reason."

"Vulcans aren't exactly known for their openness to new ideas, Mister Sulu," McCoy told him. "It took a hundred years for humans to convince them we didn't need mollycoddling." He turned to the captain. "And Jim, you and I know firsthand the kind of savagery the Vulcans barely manage to keep buried beneath the surface. And these Vulcans aren't tryin' as hard to bury it!"

"So what's your alternative, Bones?" the captain challenged.

"Hell, there must be some neutral worlds somewhere in this godforsaken reality. Someone who hasn't lined up with either side. Maybe Denobula, or the Betelgeusians."

"It could take weeks to find a viable ally, even longer to take the planetoid from the Vulcans and figure out how it works. We don't have time for that. The Vedala confluence drives might kick in again and leave us stranded here at any moment. Our only option is to work with the people who control the planetoid, who've already got a head start on studying it. We have to mend fences with the Vulcans." Once he saw that McCoy had no ready riposte, Kirk turned to his acting first officer. "Sulu? Any other thoughts?"

Sulu took a moment before responding. "I agree, Captain."

Kirk waited. "Anything else?"

The acting exec fidgeted. "No, sir. It's a sound plan."

"Very well," the captain said after a moment more. "Let's sleep on it and work out the details in the morning. Good night, gentlemen."

Kirk went up the short steps and headed through the dining area toward the exit. Sulu and McCoy followed, but the doctor stopped the younger man by the beverage dispenser as Kirk went on without them. "Hikaru, how about a little nightcap? It helps me sleep."

Sulu smiled, though with some confusion. "Sure, Doctor, if you like. But the captain . . ."

"Jim can manage. It's you I wanted to talk to."

"What about?"

Their drinks obtained, they sat at one of the tables. "Back there, when Jim asked your opinion, it looked to me like you weren't entirely sold on his plan."

"Why, no, Doctor!" Sulu said, shaking his head. "The captain knows what he's doing."

"You misunderstand me, Hikaru. The problem isn't that you weren't convinced. The problem is that you didn't say anything about it."

Sulu gave a nervous chuckle. "Doctor, you raised the objections just fine without me."

"Sulu, stop thinking like a helmsman. You're the first officer here, not me. Sure, I can tell Jim when I think something's a bad idea. But *your* job is to let him know if you have a better one."

McCoy sipped his drink while Sulu pondered that. "Think about it. Does Spock just sit there quietly and let Jim make the plans on his own?"

"No," Sulu said slowly. "If anything, Spock usually comes up with the plans. But . . . but he's Spock!"

"Yes, he is. And that's why Jim wants him as first officer, not just science officer. Because Jim doesn't want a yes-man or a rubber stamp. He wants a first officer who'll give him good ideas. Who'll come up with options he wouldn't have thought of on his own."

Sulu pondered his words, then finished his drink in one go, as if fortifying himself. "Thanks, Doc. Now if you'll excuse me, I think I need to see the captain."

McCoy raised his glass in a toast. "Attaboy."

"I think we should go to Earth, sir."

Luckily Kirk was still up when Sulu called at his quarters, doing some reading before bed. He set his book—Duane's acclaimed monograph on Vulcan history—on the couch beside him as he pondered Sulu's words. "You mean the Onlies' Earth?"

"Yes, sir. It stands to reason that it returned here. I know it's uninhabited now, but there were Federation relief workers and science teams living there for nearly eight years while it was in our timeline." He leaned forward, resting his hands on the table in the center of the living area, taking care not to disturb the antique armillary sphere that was its centerpiece. "And they left in a hurry. They may have left equipment there we can use to help repair the *Enterprise*, put us in a stronger position when we face the Vulcans."

"Hm." Kirk considered him. "And if they didn't?"

"If nothing else, sir . . . we know the Sol system better than the Vulcans or the Compact do. That would give us a defensive advantage if we needed to fight or elude pursuit. Sure, some of the inner orbits must have shifted by now, but we have detailed knowledge of things we could use for concealment or defense— Jupiter's magnetic field and radiation belts, Saturn's ring system, the geysers on Enceladus."

"It's an interesting idea, Mister Sulu," Kirk said after a moment. He rose, laying the book down next to an abstract crystal sculpture on the couchside shelf. "Which is why I already considered it before making my decision. You're right about the possibilities for repair and defense, but the bottom line is, we simply don't have the time. Fighting the Vulcans is not an option. We have to establish a dialogue with them—even if it means surrendering and throwing ourselves on their mercy."

"I understand, sir," Sulu said, disheartened. "I'm sorry I wasted your time."

Kirk came around the table and lightly clasped his arm. "Hikaru, a first officer never wastes his captain's time by offering an opinion—only by failing to do so. I need you to feel free to contribute ideas. Maybe the next one will be something I hadn't considered. Maybe it'll be something I would've rejected on my own but could be talked into by a persuasive enough argument. Who knows? Maybe I would've given more thought to going to Earth if you'd proposed it before I made my decision. But being a captain means sticking by your choices and not second-guessing yourself. So in future, Mister Sulu, I hope I can count on you to make your opinions heard up front."

Sulu straightened. "Yes, sir. I'll make sure of it."

U.S.S. *Hypatia*
Stardate 7585.8

The joining with T'Pring was at once more profound and more quotidian than Spock had imagined. Though their minds touched and flowed freely through one another, the resultant connection was not as deep, not as compelling, as that between mates bonded in childhood. It was impermanent, as it had to be, as they both preferred it to be. But it was what they both needed at this time, and its ephemerality, its particularness to this moment in their lives, gave it special meaning to them both.

The physical aspects of their interaction were certainly . . . fascinating . . . in a visceral sort of way. T'Pring had significantly more experience in such matters, more training and practice in the Vulcan arts of neuropressure which could be applied as a therapeutic art, a martial art as in the nerve pinch, or—as Spock learned now—a more intimate art as well. Yet she taught him the reciprocal techniques to ensure that the benefits of their interaction were mutually gained.

But what surprised Spock was how gentle and relaxed the interaction was. The burning, the frenzy, came from the frustration of the need for joining; once that need was met, the blood fever passed relatively quickly, the initial passion sated, though still remaining in a less urgent, more enriching form. Moreover, the intellect returned quickly, allowing them to take fulfillment from one another on a mental level as well as the primal, animalistic level he had expected and somewhat feared.

In short, they talked a great deal, in between and even during their more physical interactions. Spock found himself able to speak openly to T'Pring of things he had rarely been able to discuss with any but his closest friends and family, and sometimes not even that. She listened without judgment to things that most Vulcans in either universe would react to with scorn or shock, things that she herself might not have accepted in another state of mind.

"This new emotional engagement," she said to him at one point, "is something your father accepts?"

"It was difficult for him at first," Spock replied with an ease ill-fitting the words. "Sarek believes deeply in our traditions. He once refused to address me as his son for eighteen years after I chose to enter Starfleet instead of following the path he had carefully prepared for me. But we reconciled thereafter, and I believe he did not wish to repeat the same mistake. Once I assured him that I did not intend to abandon logic as his first son did"—for here, with her, he could speak even of forbidden things like the half brother that even his closest friends knew nothing of—"he proved able to keep an open mind. He still does not quite understand the path I have chosen. I can hardly blame him, for I myself do not fully understand it yet. But he accepts now that I am not he, and that the path I choose must be my own. He accepts that family is not conditional upon the fulfillment of preconceptions." He allowed himself a smile. "Of course, my mother is delighted. Although she would deny it, she has always felt on some level that my denial of emotion was a repudiation of the parts of me that came from her. Perhaps there was some truth to that, though I never wished it to be so. But it is no longer the case. I am what I am: Vulcan and human, logical and emotional. I should integrate both and be complete."

"It is a difficult perspective to conceive," T'Pring admitted. "I never knew what a human was until days ago. And I have never considered that the Vulcan way could have an equal, or could be permitted to merge with the philosophies of another, more emotional race. Yet you, Spock, are unlike any Vulcan I have known— and it certainly does not make you inferior."

"My Vulcan has taken a different path from yours," Spock said. "A path of peace, as Surak originally intended."

T'Pring grew subdued, nestling against him. "That you could know that for a fact . . . it is remarkable. My mother was denounced for endorsing that interpretation of Surak's doctrines. For teaching that melding was an act of harmony, not an assault. When my father discovered her attempts to awaken telepathy in me, he had her charged with the corruption of a minor. She was sent away for rehabilitation." She held his gaze. "I envy you for having a father who, even belatedly, was willing to accept your departure from the norm. My father annulled his marriage and took me to live on Coridan to escape the shame of my mother's acts. I had to learn to reject everything she had taught me lest I earn the disapproval of the only parent I had left."

"Is peace so shameful?"

"Passivity is. We are taught that it is our logical duty to create order, to protect the galaxy against chaos. And it is logical to use whatever methods serve that goal, including force."

Spock pondered. "Do you believe it was logical for your mother to be taken from you as a consequence of that policy?"

Here, in this safe space where inhibitions were on hold, T'Pring's eyes glistened with moisture. "My father conditioned me to accept that it was. But since Stonn was taken from me, I have grown less tolerant of loss." She pulled him closer. "If your Surak offered an alternative that would have let me keep them both, I cannot deny the worth of his words."

Spock stroked her hair and whispered in her ear. "He was your Surak too. You have simply forgotten. But perhaps that can be remedied."

U.S.S. Enterprise
Stardate inapplicable

The repairs to the *Enterprise* had become a cat-and-mouse game between the Compact engineers, who dragged their heels on repairs to critical systems in order to keep the ship hobbled while still offering the pretense of cooperation in case an alliance was still possible, and the *Enterprise* repair personnel, who tried to hasten repairs to critical systems while concealing their work from the Compact teams. On top of that, the Starfleet crew now had to prepare for their imminent escape without giving the Compact advance warning. It was an excellent exercise in strategic planning for Sulu, and for Kirk as well. But they were both master tacticians, and they had the resourcefulness of a brilliant crew to draw on as well.

The first stage came courtesy of Chief Theresa Ross from engineering, who devised a shipwide field that resonated with the crystals in the Andorian-issue chronometers worn by the KAC technicians, subtly speeding them up. Scott accelerated the ship's chronometers by the same amount. As a result, the morning shift broke for midday meal four minutes early, before the next shift had beamed to the repair dock. Noting the anomaly, the dock's Andorian transporter operator hailed the surface, but Crewman th'Clane had surreptitiously placed a signal interceptor under her console while flirting with her earlier, so while she thought she was reporting the problem to ground control, she was actually speaking to Crewman Shuuri'ik of communications, a Betelgeusian who had reprogrammed his voder to replicate the voice of the surface transporter chief and assured her that everything was being taken care of. Meanwhile, security hurried out the last of the stragglers and sealed the main gangway hatch behind them.

That left a brief window for assistant chief engineer Cleary to power up the impulse engines—drawing power solely from the fusion reactors that were already powering basic ship systems, so there was no spike to alert the dock personnel. At the same time, the rest of Scott's engineers were running the warp reactor through as much of its prestart process as they could without actually engaging the matter/antimatter intermix. Luckily the new warp reactor could more easily handle a cold restart than the old. Since it was a swirl-chamber design with the reaction proceeding gradually throughout the length of the dilithium-lined shaft rather than focused on a discrete dilithium matrix, it used colder plasma streams to begin with.

But the critical job belonged to the work bee crews under Sulu's coordination. Four of the *Enterprise*'s six single-operator maintenance craft were in use outside the ship at the time of the shift change, using their built-in waldoes or grabber sled attachments to replace deflector grid circuits and phaser emitters, rebond hull plates, and so forth. At the appointed moments, the work bee pilots locked their small yellow craft onto collision courses with the four connection points anchoring the *Enterprise* to the repair dock, primed the explosives they had installed in the stalwart craft (under protest, for the pilots were rather attached to the sturdy little vehicles), and signaled for beam-out. Chief Janice Rand beamed them all safely to the main transporter pad moments before the work bees made their noble sacrifice and blasted the *Enterprise* free of the connectors.

At that exact moment, Chekov raised shields and fired all four forward phasers to take out the clawlike protuberances blocking the *Enterprise*'s egress from the repair dock, and Sulu thrust forward at maximum impulse, shooting the ship out of the drydock like a torpedo. Chekov fired a spread of photon mines from the torpedo tubes to delay pursuit. They were set to home in on pursuing ships and detonate a good distance away, enough to blind them and hopefully damage their sensors or deflectors, but not destroy them. Although relations with them had quickly turned sour, the Andorians were largely victims here and Kirk wished them no harm.

Their initial course was tangentially outward from Chasav III's orbit, but under cover of the mine detonations, Sulu veered toward Regulus (for it was the same star whatever it was called) and took the ship into low warp. Regulus was a hot blue star, its habitable zone a considerable distance away, so the journey would have taken hours at high impulse. Even at warp 2, it wasn't long before the Compact ships began closing in.

As they dove toward the fast-spinning star, McCoy clutched the bridge rail behind Kirk and stared at it as it grew on the viewscreen, a distinctive orb shaped like a fat discus, hotter and brighter at the poles than the equator. "I hope you know what you're doing, Jim," he said. "The last thing we need is to get flung back in time on top of everything else."

"Unlikely, Doctor," T'Viss said from where she stood

nearby. "Mister Scott has calibrated the engines according to my computations, to negate any closed timelike curves. After all, without the unique properties of your old engines, this vessel could not survive a Tipler warp."

"Don't worry, Doc," Sulu said from the helm. "We're just using Regulus's frame-dragging effect to help throw off pursuit."

"You'll have to explain that to me sometime!" McCoy said.

"First things first," Sulu said. "Coming up on Regulus Ab. Slowing to impulse in five . . . four . . ."

Seconds later, the extrapolated image of Regulus on the screen gave way to a rainbow flash and a real-time optical image. Next to the looming main star, the white dwarf companion that hugged it at a third of an AU grew larger in the viewscreen. Sensor enhancement highlighted the thin atmosphere of hydrogen that had collected around the white dwarf, culled from Regulus's stellar wind by the powerful gravity of the dense remnant star.

"Pursuers have dropped to impulse," Chekov reported. "Three hundred thousand kilometers and closing rapidly."

"Range in five," Sulu said, and counted down.

"All aft sensors in shutdown," Uuvu'it announced from sciences.

"All antennae secured from pulse," Uhura reported.

"Fire!" Sulu cried.

As the *Enterprise* soared past Regulus Ab, Chekov fired a volley of torpedoes toward its surface, all concentrated on a single point. The impact triggered a fusion reaction in the dense hydrogen layer, a mini-nova that surely blinded the unprepared pursuers and would force them to break off.

But Scott had already calibrated the engines to take the nova energy into account in shaping the warp metric. As the *Enterprise* skimmed close to Regulus, Sulu threw her into warp again smoothly. Once the aft sensors were reactivated, Uuvu'it reported, "Good one, sir! That's pulled up a massive flare that should slow them further."

Sulu turned to the doctor. "And going to warp inside the frame-dragging zone should make it harder for them to predict our warp vector. The star's gravity pulls spacetime into a bit of a spin around it, and that introduces a random element—"

"Yeah, yeah," McCoy said. "I didn't mean it about explaining. Good grief, are all first officers required to be long-winded?"

But his ribbing was good-natured, for the maneuver had worked. The *Enterprise* had escaped the repair dock and eluded pursuit with no serious damage or loss of life, hopefully on either side. Kirk had rarely been more proud of his crew. He tended to think of Spock as the one indispensable man, but the personnel of the *Enterprise* had proved how capable and resourceful they could be without him.

Still, Kirk reminded himself, *what we just did was the easy part.*

V.H.C. *Muroc*
Stardate 7586.2

Assistant Director Simok had been unsure what to expect from Commander Spock when the half-Vulcan officer requested to join the *Hypatia*'s mission. Spock was a prominent figure among Vulcans for multiple reasons— he was a member of the clan of T'Pau, the son of Ambassador Sarek, the great-grandson of Vulcan's first ambassador to Earth, the first successful Vulcan-human hybrid, one of the first Vulcans to serve within a mostly human Starfleet crew, and an accomplished scientist in his own right. Moreover, he had been at the heart of the V'Ger affair, an event whose details and ramifications were still being discussed and debated across the Federation. It was well-known that Spock had failed *Kolinahr*, though such matters were normally kept private. And though few Vulcans would admit to engaging in anything so petty as the human "grapevine," an awareness had osmosed through Vulcan society that Spock's encounter with V'Ger had changed him, leading him to embrace the emotions he had so recently failed to purge. There had been murmurs that a pattern within Sarek's family was repeating itself, though none would speak openly of the renegade Sybok, Sarek's first son, long since disowned and banished. Yet in the subsequent months, Spock had done nothing overtly scandalous, and he remained in Sarek's good favor.

At first, when Simok had seen the intensity of Spock's reactions to Subcommander T'Pring, he had believed them to be a sign that Spock's acceptance of emotion was compromising his discipline and reason. He had been obliged to revise that hypothesis when he had noted the same responses from T'Pring—and recalled that seven standard years had elapsed since Spock's marriage to this timeline's T'Pring had failed to occur according to plan. Understanding that their Time was upon them, Simok had covered for them with the *Hypatia*'s captain and crew when they had gone into seclusion together for nearly two days. He had told Captain Danehl that the two were immersed in an in-depth examination of matters essential to the solution of the confluence problem. This had been reasonably truthful, for resolving their *pon farr* had been essential were they to remain capable of solving the problem, and they had surely examined one another in great depth.

Now that they had emerged from seclusion, both Spock and T'Pring were able to perform with their Vulcan control and discipline intact—though Simok could see the signs of continuing affinity between them which would be lost on a human observer. As the three of them and Watley continued their studies of the Vedala confluence drive aboard the *Muroc*, Simok found that, while Spock's emotions were evident as an undercurrent in his behavior, they did not impede his intellectual discipline or lead him to irrational actions or conclusions. Other Vulcans who had attempted emotional openness in the past had tended to let their passions overwhelm them, leading them in dysfunctional directions. Indeed, it was the dangerous intensity of Vulcan emotion that had required them to embrace Surak's disciplines in the first place. But Spock seemed to have achieved a synthesis that eluded most Vulcans. Simok had learned over his long years to maintain an open mind, and he began to contemplate the possibility that, while Spock's half-human neurology might have undermined his capacity for conventional Vulcan methods of emotional partitioning and sublimation, it might actually be a boon to his current efforts at emotional engagement, tempering his Vulcan fire to the more manageable intensity of human emotion.

In any case, Spock and T'Pring were now functioning with considerably greater efficiency. Not only was the distraction of incipient *pon farr* no longer an issue, but they meshed quite smoothly as a team, functioning almost as one mind with the combined knowledge and experience of two. It substantially enhanced the science team's efforts to understand the confluence drive.

Although that was not saying a great deal, for their understanding of the drive was very limited. Simok was well-versed in the relative state formulation of quantum mechanics and its consequence of parallel histories, as well as in the ways in which quantum gravitational theory applied in subspace domains. And yet an understanding of how the Vedala device achieved its effects eluded him. He had some theoretical grasp of how it could generate a subspace manifold that operated as a bijective map between two domains of normal spacetime, rendering them effectively isomorphic so that a particle occupying one domain would simultaneously occupy the other, even without any spatial fold or wormhole connecting them. But the specifics of the mechanism the drive employed, the way it directed energy to achieve the effect, remained beyond him. And he could not grasp how the device could simultaneously achieve an interphase between parallel timelines. Insofar as Simok could understand the mechanism, its configuration should be incapable of that.

It was Spock who had the key insight. "Perhaps the

reason this particular confluence drive lacks interphasic capability is that it is not the drive responsible for achieving the interphase. Consider: it was one of multiple such devices implanted in the Vedala planetoid's crust. It is entangled with its sister devices on the other side of the dimensional divide, and that is why the *Muroc* was transposed with the planetoid when *it* jumped between timelines. The logical conclusion is that the drive units that are configured to permit an interphasic confluence— whether through design or through malfunction— remain on the planetoid in the Protectorate's timeline."

"Oh, no," Dierdre Watley said. "That would mean the only hope of getting the *Enterprise* back is on the other side."

"Which is not cause for pessimism," Spock told her, growing animated. "We may assume with a fair degree of confidence that Captain Kirk and the *Enterprise* crew, along with Doctor T'Viss, have been studying the Vedala planetoid and its confluence drives."

"That seems unlikely," T'Pring replied. "The Protectorate would surely have sent ships to investigate our disappearance. As an unfamiliar craft that could not account for its presence, the *Enterprise* would surely be detained, its crew interrogated."

"I am sure the attempt would be made," Spock said. "Which might require us to revise the expected timetable. My own absence from the *Enterprise* could well delay things further. However, Captain Kirk is not a man from whom it is logical to expect failure. He will most likely find a way to gain access to those drives, if he has not already done so. My science team, Mister Scott's engineers, and Doctor T'Viss will be studying them and are likely to discover a means of reactivating the confluence effect."

"So we just have to sit back and wait for them to fix things?" Watley asked. "Seems a little too easy, doesn't it?"

"The previous confluence," said T'Pring, "occurred through no action of the *Muroc*'s crew. The drive activated spontaneously and transferred us here."

"Still, we cannot rely on that happening again," Spock told her. "Quantum entanglement can be an ephemeral thing. The more interaction these drives have with their respective continuums, the weaker the link between them may grow. Through our own investigations of the drive, and those performed on the other side, we may have weakened the connection."

"And given the evident interconnectedness of these devices," Simok said, "the drives on the planetoid may not function unless this one is in the quantum circuit with them."

"Yes. We need to reinforce that connection through coordinated action with the *Enterprise* team on the other side."

"Which would require communication with them," T'Pring said. "While the entanglement may be weakening . . ."

"It may remain sufficient to allow a limited form of communication," Spock finished. "Are you familiar with the concept of an ansible transmitter?"

"I am aware of the research in that field."

"Excellent. Let us begin."

Yes, Simok reflected as they went to work. *Quite an effective partnership indeed.*

XI

Vedala planetoid
Stardate inapplicable

Once the *Enterprise* entered Protectorate territory, Uhura began transmitting a message to the Vulcan fleet declaring the vessel's nonhostile intentions and requesting assistance in defense against the KAC. The message included the *Enterprise*'s sensor logs of their escape from Regulus, including their detonation of Regulus Ab's hydrogen shell. Part of Captain Kirk's reason for that flamboyant gesture was to send up a flare bright enough that the Vulcans' subspace monitoring posts could not have failed to register it. It served as independent verification of their story.

When they were intercepted by Commander Sekel's fleet hours later, at least they weren't shot at on sight, which was a promising sign. "By now," Kirk told Sekel over the viewscreen, "your scientists have probably deduced some of the essentials about where the Vedala planetoid and our vessel came from—and where the *Muroc* most likely ended up. Commander, we have a common goal: figure out the Vedala drive so we can get both ships back where they belong. Aboard our ship," he said, gesturing to T'Viss, "is one of the most gifted physicists of our universe, and many of the finest scientific minds in Starfleet. Whereas your scientists already have a headstart studying the Vedala drives. It's . . . logical . . . for us to combine our efforts."

Sekel agreed the logic was sound, though he voiced some skepticism about T'Viss's qualifications, given that the T'Viss of his timeline was apparently a reclusive artist living in the Vulcan desert, devoting her life to the construction of intricate, ephemeral sand sculptures that no one understood. Doctor T'Viss's scandalized reaction to the news was a thing to behold.

And so it was that, a day later, the *Enterprise* was back in orbit of the Vedala planetoid, flanked by Protectorate ringships as Montgomery Scott and T'Viss joined the Vulcan teams who had unearthed several of the confluence drives buried beneath its surface.

Scott had never beheld any technology quite like the Vedala drive that loomed above him now, an intricate, eight-meter-wide sphere of nested lattices around a dimly glowing, organic-looking core. The drive hovered in the center of a spherical chamber over twenty meters wide, with narrow spines extending toward, but not physically touching, the illuminated nodes on its outer lattice. Gravity in the chamber behaved oddly, pulling radially outward in all directions, so that Scott and the Protectorate scientists could walk freely around the entire inner surface of the sphere. Looking above him now, he could see assorted Vulcans, Romulans, and the odd Denobulan or Mazarite standing over his head at odd angles, their definitions of "down" differing from his. Normally the gravitational field inside a uniform spherical shell, whether naturally or artificially generated, would cancel to zero at any point, Scott thought. So either the chamber's artificial gravity effect dropped off after a few meters' distance like starship gravity plating, or the drive in the center was as opaque to gravitons as it was to neutrinos.

The *Enterprise* team was briefed by the head of the Protectorate research team, a Vulcan named Sornek who appeared to be roughly the same age as Spock's father. "This drive, like others around it," Sornek explained, "was damaged by radiation from a massive explosion that struck the planetoid some decades ago. It is unclear whether this was a natural impact event or an attack; we know so little of the Vedala that we cannot rule out the possibility that they have enemies." The thought of enemies mighty enough to overwhelm the Vedala was intimidating to Scott. They were a non-aggressive, highly reclusive race, but their power was known to be vast. But then, that made it unlikely that they'd be caught off guard by a mere asteroid impact, didn't it? Unless they'd already abandoned the planetoid for some other reason.

"The *Muroc* chose to sample an undamaged drive from the other side of the planetoid," Sornek went on. "However, our study of identical drives shows no capacity for the kind of interphasic transfer we have observed. Further investigation has revealed that the radiation from the impact event altered the quantum-level circuitry of this and other adjacent drives in a manner analogous to a biological mutation. The drives appear to have some capacity for self-repair, and while they were able to restore themselves to functionality, they did so in an altered way that somehow permits the interphasic effect."

"All o' them bein' mutated the same way?" Scott asked. "That doesna seem likely."

"Given the interconnectedness of the system, we theorize that the drives take their repair cues from the nearest functional drive they can interface with. Presumably one of the drives was 'mutated' in a way that left it functional yet altered so as to produce the interphasic effect, and the others reconfigured themselves to match. A single such drive would be insufficient to transpose an entire planetary body between quantum histories, but the combined array can certainly do so."

"But you say the drive aboard the *Muroc* is unaltered," T'Viss said. "This means that they will be unable to return unless we initiate the transfer here."

"Well, then, we'd better get on with it, hadn't we?" Scott asked.

And so they did. Luckily, Sornek and his people knew their stuff; they had already made significant progress, if not in understanding how the technology worked, at least in tracing its interface and control circuitry. With the added insights T'Viss and Scott brought, they were soon able to interpret their readings of the drives' activity and begin to construct a model of how they could reactivate the universe-jumping effect.

But soon enough, Scott noticed something else in the readings, a fluctuation in the quantum circuitry that T'Viss and Sornek could not account for but Scott soon recognized. "It's an old Starfleet binary code, sir," Scott told Kirk over his wrist communicator. "One designed for basic text and numerical communication over very low-bandwidth systems. The message is prefaced with the string 'S one seven nine two seven six SP,' sir."

A moment of silence. *"Spock's serial number!"* Kirk cried.

"Blasted long-winded Vulcan," McCoy grumbled in the background, but his relief was clear. *"Why not just send his name?"*

"Standard procedure," Kirk replied. *"He needed a unique identifier so we'd know for sure it was him."* The captain laughed. *"I should've known he'd come running as soon as he heard we were missing. Scotty, what does the message say?"*

"Basic instructions for how to coordinate communication with, er, the other side, sir, so we can reinforce the connection that allowed the switch to happen—the same connection he's sendin' the message through. He says we and the *Muroc* need to activate our drives at the same time. They're ready whenever we are, sir—ours are the ones that actually cause the universe jump, with them along for the ride, so they just have to flip the switch when we tell them to. But we still need time to sort out the details on our end."

A longer pause. *"Better make it fast, Scotty. Commander Sekel informs me that a Klingon-Andorian fleet is incoming—a big one. They'll be here in less than three hours."*

"We'll need more than that, sir," Scott said, and it was no exaggeration. "You and the Vulcans'll have to hold them off as long as you can."

"We'll make sure you have the time, Scotty. Kirk out."

Scott shook his head. "He makes it sound so easy." He looked up at the barely comprehensible, almost living piece of technology that loomed over his head— that would always be over his head no matter where he stood in relation to it. He tried not to see that as a symbol of the hopelessness of the task. *After all, we basically just have to turn the blessed thing on. How hard can that be?*

Still, he said a silent prayer before getting to work.

U.S.S. *Enterprise*

"The Vulcans have lost another ship!" Chekov cried from the tactical station. "A Compact vessel is going for the gap!"

"On viewer," Kirk ordered. "Stand ready." It was frustrating having to watch passively while dozens of Protectorate and Compact starships battled for control of the Vedala planetoid. But the *Enterprise* had to stay in orbit to ensure it was taken along when the confluence drives engaged. So the best they could manage was to serve as a rear guard, maintaining control of the planetoid's orbital space. On the plus side, that passive position let them avoid overtly taking sides in a battle that, according to the Prime Directive, they should not be involved in at all. Yet it was frustrating to have the fate of his ship and crew depend on others. A part of him was almost hoping the KAC vessel would break through and engage the *Enterprise*.

But on the viewer, the incoming ship was struck by a barrage of phaser fire and broke off. Sekel's flagship swooped into view and harried it back out to a higher orbit. Kirk hit one of the intercom switches on the command chair's left arm, opening the channel assigned to the flagship. "Commander Sekel, this is Kirk. Thank you for your assistance."

"Personal thanks are illogical, Kirk. I act to ensure that Vedala technology does not fall into the Compact's hands. Ensure that you continue to do the same."

McCoy leaned down over Kirk's shoulder. "Jim, if this works and the *Muroc* comes back, then Vedala technology's gonna fall into the so-called Protectorate's hands. How is that any better?"

Kirk had been asking himself that very question, and he didn't like the answer. But he voiced it anyway. "There's nothing we can do about that, Bones. We don't have the right to decide these people's fate."

"But isn't that what we're doing? Giving the Vulcans the edge so we can get our own butts home?"

"Anything could happen once the *Muroc* gets back. And at least they'll only have one isolated drive, not a whole planetoid filled with Vedala technology." He gestured to the screen. "That's a lot of Klingon-Andorian ships out there. We'll be lucky to get out of this ourselves."

McCoy grimaced at the reminder. "In that case, I should be down helping Christine get sickbay ready for casualties."

Kirk smiled up at him. "I'll do my best to disappoint you."

The doctor nodded back. "You do that."

As McCoy left, Kirk hit the channel to the surface. "Scotty, how's it coming?"

"Another ten minutes at least, sir. These Vedala soft-ware protocols are the devil's own tangle."

"Sir!" Chekov called. "Another Vulcan ship down!"

"Scotty, we may not have ten minutes."

"Ach, do we ever, sir? I'll let you know. Scott out."

From his place at the helm—since Kirk had wanted his best pilot there if it came down to combat—Sulu studied the flow of battle. "Captain," the acting exec said after a few moments, "I have an idea. We can blind the Compact's sensors like we did before."

"But, Commander," Chekov said, "we have too few photon mines remaining. And they would be a hazard to the Protectorate ships."

"Not with mines—with shuttlecraft. We can remote-pilot them around the Vulcan ships, then detonate them in front of the Compact ships. We could distract them, maybe disrupt their shields and sensors enough to take away their advantage."

Sulu offered the suggestion without hesitation, with the confidence needed in a first officer. Kirk caught the man's eyes and offered a nod that approved of more than just his proposal. "Do it, Mister Sulu."

With only a quick grin of acknowledgment, Sulu got on the comm to the hangar deck crew and gave them instructions. The wedge-shaped modular shuttle-craft would first need to be outfitted with impulse en-gines and weapons pods, but the deck crew had been well-trained under Sulu's guidance as chief helmsman, and so all four modular shuttles were on their way within three minutes, plenty of time for Uhura to brief the Vulcans on the plan. As their remote pilots bobbed and weaved them around the Protectorate ships on the viewscreen, Kirk reflected that this adventure was costing them most of their support craft. Well, there would be plenty more where those had come from, assuming the *Enterprise* managed to return to its own universe.

The shuttles soon engaged the Compact ships, their phasers barely more than an irritant—but the warrior's pride of their Klingon (and, to an extent, Andorian) officers compelled them to retaliate against the insult. The shuttles led them on a chase that maneuvered as many of them as possible within range of the four small craft before they detonated their impulse engines, flooding the enemy sensors with radiation—sensors that had already been the true targets of the phaser fire, softening them up for the final blow. It was too early to say how much they'd been impaired by the blasts, but the shuttles had drawn them out of formation and the Vulcans had taken advantage of the disruption. Kirk didn't approve of the ruthlessness with which the Protectorate ships demolished the opponents Sulu's maneuver had left vulnerable. But it had given him a fighting chance to get his crew home, and that had to be his priority.

"Scott to Enterprise*!"* came a welcome voice from the surface. *"We're as ready as we're goin' to be down here, and the* Muroc *signals ready on their side. Sornek and his people are beamin' back to their ships. My team will stay here and—I hope—ride through with the* Enterprise. *On your signal, sir."*

"Good man, Scotty! Uhura, general hail!"

"Open, sir."

"Attention, all vessels in the vicinity of the Vedala planetoid! This is Captain Kirk of the *Enterprise*. In a moment, the interspatial drives on the Vedala planetoid will begin to engage. These drives will generate a spatial distortion field which we estimate will be at least ten thousand kilometers in radius. Any vessel caught within this field when it activates will be transported to a different space-time continuum. Be advised: if you ever wish to see your homes again, then do not approach the planetoid. Kirk out." He switched channels. "Scotty, go!"

"Drives engaged, sir!"

"Kirk to all personnel! Secure for interspatial transfer!"

Which was basically a more dignified way of saying *"Hang on to something."* The crew had been given precautionary injections against interphase sickness, but there was still the disorientation to contend with. All around the bridge, the seated crew lowered their armrests around their thighs, securing them in place. The standing crew secured their stations and sat on the deck.

"Subspace energy surging," Uuvu'it confirmed a moment later. "The confluence drives are active."

"Vulcan ships breaking formation and retreating," Chekov said. Would the Compact see this as a trick? Would they take the opportunity to make a dash for the planetoid and strand themselves in the Federation's timeline? "Compact ships . . . are pulling back." Apparently not. The energy surge from the planetoid must have convinced them to seek the better part of valor.

The screen went white, and Kirk felt himself spinning, blacking out . . .

. . . but only for a moment. The shot must have done some good. He looked around, seeing the rest of the bridge crew recovering as well. "Status?" His eyes went to the screen. To his relief, the planetoid was still there . . . and the star patterns were different. But were they the right patterns?

"Scott to Enterprise, Scott to Enterprise! Are ye there, sir?"

Mister Scott is still with us, Kirk's memory echoed. He hit the intercom after a couple of false tries. "Kirk here, Scotty. The ship made it through."

"No, ah, no Protectorate . . . or Compact ships in sensor range," Chekov managed to report. "But . . . there is a ship. . . ."

"Sir," Uhura said, "incoming hail." Her grogginess gave way to a joyous grin. "From the *U.S.S. Hypatia,* sir! It's Mister Spock!"

Cheers went up among the crew, and Kirk's fist triumphantly struck the arm of his seat. "Onscreen, Commander!"

Uhura hastened to comply, and a long-missed visage appeared on the viewer. "Mister Spock," Kirk said, grinning. "Are you ever a sight for sore eyes!"

Spock raised a brow. *"While my eyes are experiencing no discomfort, I am gratified to see that you and the* Enterprise *are well. I believe 'Welcome home' is the proper sentiment, Captain."*

"It is indeed, you sentimental fool, you." Spock looked mildly scandalized. "Sorry. It's been a long week."

"Indeed. I look forward to hearing more. What I learned of the Vulcan Protectorate from the Muroc's *crew was . . . intriguing, if disturbing."*

"You should talk!" came a new voice—McCoy, fresh from the turbolift. "At least your species still *exists* over there. And what were you doing while we've been fighting for our lives? Sitting around solving equations, I imagine."

"If you say so, Doctor." Spock was oddly reticent to rise to the bait, and Kirk and McCoy exchanged a concerned look.

But that would have to wait. "Spock, status of the *Muroc* and its personnel?"

The Vulcan took on a distant look. *"The vessel and all its crew vanished at the moment you and the planetoid appeared in the same space, Captain. Mister Scott on the planetoid should be receiving confirmation via ansible signal if they have returned safely."*

McCoy shook his head. "I still don't like it—them getting to keep one of those Vedala drives."

"Do not trouble yourself, Doctor," Spock said. *"The matter is well in hand."*

V.H.C. *Muroc*
Stardate inapplicable

Commander Satak stared at the surging power readings in stern disapproval, as if the sensor displays were somehow deserving of chastisement. "You must halt this buildup, Subcommander," he told T'Pring. "With the planetoid gone, we must secure this confluence drive for the Protectorate."

"There is nothing I can do, sir," T'Pring told him. "The drive may have been damaged in the transition. The energy buildup is irreversible. We have no logical option but to jettison it."

Satak glared at T'Pring, but she stared back serenely. Finally he relented. "Very well. Jettison the drive. Helm," he ordered into the intercom, "once the Vedala drive is ejected, take us to a safe distance."

T'Pring efficiently operated the jettison sequence, gratified that she at least had been able to send the confirmation message so that Spock would know of her safe return. They had already made their farewells before returning to their respective ships—and she knew that they had each given the other something they would carry with them forever. Although what she had gained from Spock could prove far more meaningful.

Minutes later, the confluence drive erupted in a burst of subspace energy so intense that sensors showed it damaged the very structure of subspace. "The High Command will be displeased," Satak told T'Pring. "That Vedala technology could have given us the power to defeat the Compact forever, to ensure the peace against all threats. We had it in our hands, and now we have lost it all. What will I tell them?"

T'Pring pondered for a moment, remembering the thoughts of another mind. "Tell them that having is not so satisfying a thing as wanting."

"That is not logical," Satak said.

T'Pring heard Spock, from within, saying the same thing. "I disagree," she replied. "Logically, one cannot truly assess the benefit of a possession one does not yet have. Thus a saying that is popular among the humans of the Federation: 'Be careful what you wish for; you may get it.'"

"Be wary, Subcommander," Satak warned. "Some might interpret that as sedition."

"Indeed," T'Pring replied. *And they would be correct.* Each of T'Pring's statements about the drive malfunction had been truthful enough in isolation; it *may* hypothetically have been damaged in the transition, even if it had in fact been sabotaged afterward. And once she had begun the drive's buildup to destruction, there had been nothing she could do to reverse it. Even if there had been, it would have remained true that she could not ethically have stopped it. She understood now that the Protectorate could not be allowed access to such an enormous advantage over their neighbors.

At least, not as the Protectorate now was. Not so long as they were still the Vulcans of V'Las and Muroc, the ones who saw coercive force and suppression of unpopular ideas as a logical way to protect civilization. The ones who saw the joining of minds as a perversion. The ones who claimed to follow Surak's will but forgot, more and more with each generation, what that truly meant.

But it need not be that way forever. For Spock had given her something that would mean more to the Vulcan people than any mere stardrive. He had given her Surak's true words—the *Kir'Shara*, whose text they had studied together in their time on the *Hypatia*. He had given her a copy for her personal database, so she could continue to study and contemplate its layers of meaning.

And most importantly, he had told her where the

Kir'Shara had been found in his reality. There was every chance that on her Vulcan, it was still there . . . just waiting for her to rediscover it and begin the redemption of a world.

U.S.S. Hypatia
Stardate 7586.7

"Has there been any response from the Vedala yet?" Simok asked Director Grey, whose image flickered with subspace interference on the monitor in his VIP quarters. They were quite far from Earth, and it took considerable power to maintain a real-time communication.

"Still nothing," Grey told him. *"At this point I'm not sure they'll even want it back."*

"Unlikely. The Vedala have always been intensely protective of their technology."

"Well, they're not answering our calls, Simok. We can't rely on them showing up to reclaim the planetoid themselves. With the Enterprise *called back for debriefing, the* Hypatia *will have to stay on-site to guard against scavengers. I'll see what I can do about assigning another ship there."*

Simok nodded. Spock had accompanied the *Enterprise* to starbase; he hoped the debriefing process would be swift, since Spock had demonstrated an eagerness to return to his young pupil, Saavik. Simok could sympathize, having long ago discovered the fulfillment of imparting knowledge and insight to the young. Now he found similar fulfillment in helping the members of the young Department of Temporal Investigations determine how best to fulfill the unprecedented responsibilities they had taken on. He thought of Meijan

Grey as his own protégée in a sense, and strove to offer his calm guidance and support when she struggled with the challenges of her post.

"The Science Council also wants you to study the Vedala drives," Grey went on. *"Learn as much as you can about them before the Vedala claim them—if they ever do. Just the normal confluence drives, for their potential propulsion applications. But I insisted that the research be under DTI supervision, just in case."*

"A logical precaution."

Grey paused. *"What's your assessment of the drives' potential? Do you think there are time travel possibilities as well as interdimensional?"*

"The potential for one implies the potential for the other, Director. However, we would need a theoretical understanding of how they create the confluence effect before we could extrapolate how they might generate a temporal warp. Should these drives fall into the hands of the Klingons, the Romulans, or . . . certain irresponsible parties within the Federation . . . it might take generations to understand these mechanisms well enough to build new potentials into them."

Grey pondered his answer. *"Understood."*

"However," it occurred to Simok, "it is possible that certain potentials of the drives such as we can understand and exploit could be combined with known technologies to achieve temporal effects." He was silent for a beat. "For our purposes, it will be preferable if the Vedala reclaim the drives in the near future. There are those within the Federation who may not be content to research the propulsion possibilities alone."

Grey's dainty lips narrowed. *"Don't worry about Delgado, Simok. I can manage things with him."*

"I do not worry, Meijan," Simok assured her. "And I have no doubt that you can."

Starfleet Headquarters
Stardate 7589.3

Antonio Delgado had spent a long day reviewing reports from dozens of Starfleet research vessels participating in an ongoing project to catalog ion storm categories throughout known space—a valuable project, to be sure, but a tedious one. He often strove to reassure himself that there was still plenty of satisfaction in his work as chief of Science Operations even without pursuing the mysteries of time. That the destiny he'd once imagined was guiding him had been wishful thinking, or at least that it had now moved him along a different path. But on days like this, it was difficult.

He was just about to turn in for the evening when a communication came in on his terminal. The signature gave its point of origin as London, where it was much later at night. Who could be calling him at this hour?

He opened the channel, and blinked in recognition at the dumpy, bald man who appeared there. "Mister Manners," he said. "What can I do for you at this . . . very late . . . hour?"

Arthur Manners of the DTI offered a conspiratorial smile. *"The question, Admiral, is what I can do for you."*

Delgado listened with fascination. Maybe destiny hadn't abandoned him after all.

XII

"How much time did you spend on the planetoid?"
Agent Lucsly asked T'Viss.

"I personally spent most of my time in the *Hypatia*'s science labs, performing simulations and refining our theoretical models," T'Viss clarified. *Of course,* Dulmur thought. Far be it from her to dirty her hands on actual machinery, even machinery as amazing as the Vedala's creations. "However, the analysis teams remained on-site for five weeks and three days in total. I speak in the aggregate, for individual personnel were relieved and replaced. I believe at least one other Federation vessel arrived and departed during that interval, though I paid little attention to such things.

"At the end of the cited interval, the Vedala finally arrived to reclaim their planetoid."

Dulmur leaned forward. "What were they like?" Few Federation citizens had ever interacted with the Vedala directly, even before their migrations had led them away from Federation space. They had always guarded their privacy intently.

"There was no visual communication," T'Viss said,

deflating him. "But a second Vedala planetoid materialized at the first planetoid's L1 libration point and transmitted instructions for our teams to evacuate immediately. Captain Danehl complied. They further required us to turn over all the data we had gathered about their technology. When I objected, the *Hypatia* lost all power. When power resumed, all our documentation of the confluence drives had been deleted from our computers.

"The Vedala further required the Science Council and the DTI to turn over all duplicate records in their possession. It was unprecedented for the Vedala to be so . . . emphatic in their interactions with the Federation."

"But there were legends," Dulmur said, "of what happened to civilizations who managed to make the Vedala angry."

"Indeed. Not wishing to take the chance that those legends were accurate, the Federation Council as a whole required the Science Council to turn over all data. Moreover, to accommodate the Vedala's demands for secrecy, the entire affair was classified. The very fact that it had occurred was deleted from our records." She raised a brow. "Many in the Federation Council were still in emotional distress following their near destruction by the V'Ger probe ten months earlier. They were afraid to risk the animosity of other entities whose power far exceeded our own."

"But you went further," Lucsly said. "You repressed your own memory of the event."

"It is against my nature to allow a counterfactual statement to go uncorrected," T'Viss said primly . . . though she went on in tones that, for her, were practically abashed. "I concluded that the only way I could be assured of keeping the secret was if I concealed it even from my own awareness."

"You keep plenty of secrets, T'Viss," Dulmur said. "It's part of the job."

"I have gained a great deal of experience in the intervening decades, Agent Dulmur. At the time, I was far younger and less corrupted by the practice of deceit."

Dulmur struggled to imagine a T'Viss who was even more blunt and uncompromising than the one he knew today. He shook his head, refocusing on what was important. "Anyway, none of this explains why that timeship is here today. If the Vedala reclaimed all their technology, how come that ship has a confluence drive on it?"

Lucsly grimaced. "Kirk. He must've taken one aboard the *Enterprise* and run off with it before the Vedala got there. Probably took it right to Delgado."

"Wouldn't the Vedala have known?" Dulmur asked.

"They weren't omniscient," Lucsly said. "They didn't seem to know about the return of their planetoid until the Federation got their attention. The downside of isolationism," the agent went on, oblivious to the irony of those words coming from him of all people. "Kirk and Delgado might've told the Vedala that the Protectorate took the drive."

"Hold on, partner. T'Viss says another ship came and went after the *Enterprise* left. Besides, if it's a Starfleet project, how come it's got DTI markings and a civilian crew?"

"Protective camouflage. They wanted to pin it on the DTI if anything went wrong."

Dulmur stared. "Aren't you getting a little paranoid there, pal?"

Lucsly's gaze was intense. "This is *Kirk* we're dealing with. I put nothing past him."

Timeship Two
Confluence 2275/2383

"Okay," Garcia said as she closed the panel on the subspace transmitter junction. "That should do it."

Ranjea checked his tricorder to confirm. "Yes. The distress beacon is neutralized. We can only hope it was in time."

"Hey, I worked as fast as I could. Studying old technology in texts isn't the same as actually operating it."

"No criticism intended, Teresa," he said, stroking her shoulder, though she could barely feel it through the isolation suit. But his keener Deltan senses noted her tension. "We should get back to the *Everett*."

"No, Ranjea. Not yet. I've been thinking . . . we should find a library terminal and download the crew manifest. If we know who these people are, we can check against the *Everett*'s database, find out whether they lived past 2275."

"Teresa . . ."

"Listen! We're here, now. That makes us part of these past events whether we want to think we are or not. So maybe we have a role to play in history. Maybe we're *supposed* to help these people. Maybe we *have* to in order to ensure our own history. A good old retro-causal Novikov loop. It's possible, isn't it?"

His hand pressed her shoulder more firmly, com-fortingly. "Yes, it's possible. But we can't be certain. Teresa, I understand how urgently you wish this could be an opportunity to save people in the past as you couldn't before. But we have to play this by the book. You know that. It was what your own instincts told you back on the *Verity*, when you chose not to intervene in the past."

"I know, I know," she said, putting her hands on his own broad shoulders. "But listen! The reason we don't take chances like that is because we don't have enough information about the past. All I'm saying is that we have an opportunity to *get* more information! At the very least, let's read that crew manifest before we jump to any conclusions that could be catastrophic!"

She couldn't clearly read his expressions in the sen-sor image on her visor's heads-up display, but she could feel him studying her, contemplating her words and the emotions that drove them. Ever since their close call with Deltan-style intimacy in the Axis of Time last year, there'd been a lingering empathic connection between them, and sometimes they could sense each other's state of mind, especially at moments of strong emo-tion. After a moment, she felt the warmth of his smile. "You're right, of course, Teresa. I'm sorry."

She punched his shoulder. "Hey, no mushy stuff, boss. There's work to be done."

They made their way back through the service corridors to a data junction servicing the bridge, and

Ranjea tapped into its feed with his tricorder. But before he could access the personnel records, an alarm drew his attention. "Oh, no," he said.

"What?"

He struck his combadge. "Ranjea to *Everett*. We have a problem."

"Ranjea, this is Lucsly aboard the Capitoline. *We're eight point seven minutes away. Report."*

"Gariff, hello. There's a ship incoming from the 2275 side of the confluence zone. It's sending hails in response to the timeship's distress beacon. We were too late."

"Can you identify the ship?"

Ranjea hesitated. Garcia stared; it was unlike him to be unsure of himself. "Yes, Gariff, I'm afraid so. It's the *U.S.S. Enterprise* . . . NCC-1701." He sighed. "It's Kirk."

"Madre de Dios," Garcia breathed. "We're doomed."

XIII

"What got into you, Hrrii'ush?" Hikaru Sulu asked Petty Officer Uuvu'it when he found him in Reiko Onami's counseling office. "Starting a fight with Crewman Worene? What could've provoked you to do that?" As aggressive as the Betelgeusian was by instinct, such behavior was out of character for him. Even in his early days on the refitted *Enterprise*, before he'd learned to channel his intense need for challenge and competition in constructive ways, he'd acted out more through sophomoric pranks and reckless stunts than direct confrontation. True, the *Enterprise* had been on a rather tedious milk run for the past few weeks, a make-work mission from Starfleet Science Ops to update the star charts in a little-traveled sector toward the northern rim of the galactic disk, but Uuvu'it had handled tedious assignments before without taking it to this level.

Uuvu'it looked up at him defiantly, though the attitude faded when he saw that Sulu was in full-on second officer mode at the moment, not friend mode. "Well, if I'd started the fight with Ensign Nizhoni, I might've hurt her. Besides, she outranks me."

Onami gave a loud bark of laughter. "You? Hurt Mosi?" She laughed some more. "I'm sorry," she finally managed to get out, recognizing Uuvu'it's wounded expression. "I know your ego's in a delicate place right now and all, but . . . damn, if you'd seen Nizhoni in action last month when the Gatherers tried to storm the Acamarian peace conference . . ." She dissolved into laughter again.

This is how Onami handles her therapy sessions? Sulu thought. The dainty xenopsychologist had been brought aboard as part of Willard Decker's initiative to diversify the crew, on the theory that such wildly disparate species would need some degree of expert assistance in order to mesh smoothly. After a year and a half of mostly smooth crew interactions, it seemed she was doing her job well. But Sulu was sometimes at a loss to see how.

Uuvu'it bristled. "There's nothing delicate about my ego! I have no insecurities about my malehood, my work performance, or anything else!"

"Then why are you throwing temper tantrums just because Spock came back and kicked you off the bridge?" Onami challenged.

"He did not . . ." Uuvu'it tempered his tone, and the voder translation came out commensurately softer. "He did not 'kick me off.' I still man the science station on gamma shift."

"Really?" Onami asked, not tempering her own confrontational tone at all. "On a 'Geusian argosy, getting bumped from alpha to gamma would be pretty shameful, wouldn't it? You'd feel you had something to prove. That you'd have to fight the guy who displaced you for dominance. Or, failing that, fight anyone tough you could find to stand in for him."

"We're not on an argosy!" Uuvu'it fired back.

Onami sat back and smiled. "No, we're not. Are we?"

The science officer stared at her, blinking his hawk-like eyes a few times. "No. I suppose not. It's Starfleet. More egalitarian. I haven't lost status, simply moved laterally."

Sulu smiled, recognizing now what Onami had done. Betelgeusians were a competitive people, so she'd chosen confrontation to deal with him, forcing him to take sides against himself and thereby make himself see reason, whereas he might've been more resistant hearing the same arguments from someone else. *Psychological judo,* he thought. *Who knew?*

"You're damn right, Mister Uuvu'it," Sulu told him. "You're still a valued member of this crew. But you always knew the post was temporary until Spock came back. Just like I did."

"That's different," Uuvu'it said. "You weren't comfortable being first officer. You were good at it, very good, but it was always obvious you were holding Spock's place for him. But me, I got comfortable in that chair. And I was good too. I should be moving upward, not sideways."

The science officer's words struck a nerve. "Hrrii'ush, sometimes you have to accept that advancement takes time. You have to know what you're ready for, and when. There's nothing wrong with taking it slow. I mean . . . it's Mister Spock. Why be in a hurry to stop learning from the master?"

Uuvu'it studied him closely, and Sulu tried not to feel like a rabbit being sized up by an eagle. "Is that really how you feel?"

Sulu pondered for a moment. "Yes. Yes, I do," he said with growing realization and contentment. Being first officer had been exciting and enriching. But the *Enterprise* just hadn't been the same without Spock around. Now that the Vulcan had returned from his year-long leave, it felt like home again. Someday Sulu would move on, move up the ladder, but there was still so much he could learn from Kirk and Spock in the meantime. Besides, he had more time now to spend with Marcella DiFalco.

The Betelgeusian let out a chirping sigh. "Well, then I suppose I can feel the same. For now," he added. "Until a better opportunity comes along."

"Um." Onami threw Sulu a look. "Assuming Worene doesn't want to press charges."

Sulu chuckled. "No. Lucky for you, Hrrii'ush, you chose an Aulacri to pick a fight with. She thinks you were flirting with her."

Uuvu'it looked up in alarm. "Don't tell me she's . . ."

"Sorry, pal," Sulu said, stepping to the door and holding it open. "You're free to go. And you're on your own."

Uuvu'it paused to check the corridor outside before bolting from Onami's office. Sulu and Onami watched his departure from the doorway. "I'll tell Worene to go easy on the kid," Onami said. "Though not too easy. He could use something to burn off that nervous energy."

Sulu was still trying to figure out how to respond when he felt the engines ramping up to a higher warp factor. His eyes went to the annunciator display in the corridor ceiling. The changing pattern of colored, blinking lights in its black panel alerted him to the change in ship's status just as communications officer Auberson's voice came over the intercom. *"Senior officers, report to the bridge, please."*

Sulu made a quick farewell to Onami and headed for the nearest turbolift. He reached the bridge to find the rest of the senior staff either already there or arriving in the opposite lift. Uhura had relieved Auberson and was reporting to Kirk. "The distress signal is coming from a neutron star system three light-years away."

Chief DiFalco was checking the astrogator display as Sulu took the helm next to her, giving her a quick smile. "We can be there in six hours at warp nine, Captain," she said before smiling back.

"Set course and prepare to go to warp," Kirk ordered. "Uhura, origin of the distress signal?"

"I can't identify it, sir. It's in Federation Standard language and protocol, but there's no ship identifier, and the message is automated."

"Course plotted and laid in, sir," DiFalco said.

Kirk nodded. "Ahead warp nine, Mister Sulu."

"Warp nine, aye."

"But Chekov, keep your eyes open as we approach. In case they have a reason for not identifying themselves."

"Aye, sir," Chekov said from tactical, though of course he would have done so anyway.

Sulu launched the *Enterprise* into high warp, pushing her easily to pseudovelocities that would've torn the old ship apart. After a few minutes, Spock turned from the science station that was now his again and reported, "Captain, I am picking up anomalous subspace readings from the vicinity of the neutron star."

"What kind of readings?"

"Jim . . . they are consistent with a subspace confluence."

All eyes turned to the Vulcan. "A Vedala drive?" Kirk asked.

"All known Vedala drives are on record as having been returned to the Vedala, sir. I can only say the readings are consistent. Except for one thing."

"What's that?"

Spock's eyebrow lifted. It was amazing, Sulu thought, how much you missed the little things. "Sir . . . there is also a temporal reading."

After the surprise subsided, Kirk's features grew hard. "Spock . . . am I very much mistaken, or were our orders for this routine survey cut by Admiral Delgado's office?"

"Your memory is accurate, Captain."

Kirk turned his seat forward to face the viewscreen . . . and whatever lay ahead. "What are you up to this time, Admiral?" he murmured.

According to Spock, the neutron star was an unremarkable, quiescent one that they had charted during their initial survey of this sector over five years ago. There had been no surviving planets, no unusual activity, nothing to draw Federation interest to such a remote system. But that made it an ideal place for unauthorized time-travel experiments, especially if they involved a stolen Vedala drive.

It wasn't too surprising, therefore, that Uhura received no response to her hails until the *Enterprise* drew close enough to the system to allow real-time communication on a low-power, short-range subspace band, one unlikely to be intercepted by anyone else. The short-range signal emanated from a research station in a wide orbit of the neutron star—unlike the distress call, whose source was a vessel in a much tighter, more eccentric orbit. The confluence zone remained centered on the vessel as it orbited, but it was slowly growing.

When Uhura put the signal from the research station on the viewer, it came as even less of a surprise to Kirk to see Admiral Delgado's face. *"Captain Kirk. We appreciate your punctuality."*

"Credit where it's due, Admiral. You assigned us to this sector. You wanted us on hand in case something went wrong with your latest time-travel experiment, because we're already within the circle of secrecy."

The admiral made no effort to deny it. *"And because your crew has the greatest experience and expertise with temporal and cross-dimensional phenomena, Captain. Including the particular technology being researched here."*

"'Researched' is a euphemistic word, Admiral, considering that you've actually put lives at stake." Kirk gestured toward Commanders Spock and Scott, who stood flanking his command chair. "And according to what my people tell me, that ship out there is built around the *Enterprise*'s old engines—the ones that were supposed to be dismantled over two years ago—and appears to contain an interphase-capable confluence drive stolen from the Vedala."

"Captain, there will be abundant time for recriminations later—and let me remind you that you're no longer my equal in rank. That timeship is in danger. Perhaps even the timeline is in danger. And we need your crew's expertise to resolve the crisis. Your people know these engines, and they've studied the confluence drive."

Spock stepped forward. "Granted, Admiral. However, in order to address the problem, we will need to understand just what it is you were attempting to do with these propulsion systems."

Delgado sighed. *"After* Timeship One, *the Council refused to permit any more time-travel experiments. But the potential for knowledge was too great to abandon. Rather than dismantling the timeship engines, we cached them in the event of future need."*

"But you lied about it to the Council," Kirk said.

"Sometimes what's politically comfortable and what's strategically necessary are at odds, Captain. And your discovery of the Vedala confluence drives created an unprecedented opportunity. It might be too risky to time-travel within our own timeline, but what if we could travel to the past or future of independent timelines?"

Kirk blinked. "What would be the point?"

"We could learn a great deal about historical pro-

cesses through observation of alternative paths. We could observe possible futures and be alert to the threats that might arise, such as natural disasters or invasions from without—things that would occur regardless of the shape of local history. If nothing else, it would be a way to explore the potentials of time travel without risk to our own timeline.”

"Good heavens!" Scott cried. "So it's not enough to risk forcin' more slingshot jumps on those poor engines, you thought you'd throw in a confluence effect and see what happened?"

"Mind your tone, Commander. We spent months simulating and testing the combination."

"And you concluded," Spock said, "that you could send your timeship simultaneously to another era *and* another timestream."

"Naturally we aimed for the future, just in case. But the confluence field interacted with the slingshot in a way we didn't anticipate. Our calculations showed that the combined effect would transpose Timeship Two *with a point in the future of a different timeline. Instead . . . something else happened."*

Spock turned to Kirk. "Captain, our sensors detect stellar spectra through the confluence field that are consistent with the Lembatta Cluster, a small open star cluster several hundred light-years from our location. Extrapolating from its Doppler shifts and the luminosity curves of its variable components, we are detecting the Lembatta Cluster as it will be over one hundred years from now."

"Spock, what are you saying?"

"That apparently the operation of a Vedala confluence drive during a slingshot maneuver did not merely transpose two regions of space and time, but connected them. Overlapped them, if you will. The timeship, and everything else within the confluence zone, exists in two places and times simultaneously. The zone thereby forms a crossing point between those places and times. Light and information can travel through it, and presumably so can material objects."

Kirk stared. "But are they in different timelines as well?"

"Since the Vedala drive clearly did not operate as intended, it is unknown whether the interphasic effect engaged. The only signals we can as yet receive through the interference are astronomical readings which would presumably be identical in alternative histories. This could as easily be a conduit to our own future as to a separate one."

Kirk held his gaze grimly. "And that means anyone who stumbles onto it in the future could change what's supposed to be."

But Spock was more contemplative. "Captain . . . we cannot say what is 'supposed' to occur in the future. There are many possible paths the future could take— and undoubtedly will take, given the established reality of spontaneously branching alternative histories. The potential for knowledge here cannot be overlooked."

Kirk gave it thought, but then shook his head. "No. We wouldn't want people from the past putting our history in danger. Those people on the other side deserve the same consideration. So keep your scans of the confluence zone to short-range readings. Only what we need to know to rescue that ship's crew and shut down the confluence."

Ever the professional, Spock acknowledged without protest. "Aye, sir."

"Well, now that you've got that settled, Captain," Delgado said, *"we need to determine how to make that happen. We haven't been able to make contact with the crew, even after they triggered that distress call. They might be incapacitated by interphasic effects, or worse."*

And even though they might've been dying, Kirk thought, *you still refused to talk to us until you could do so without jeopardizing your precious secrets.* Although, he had to admit, there was nothing the *Enterprise* could have done until they were closer. And they were still twenty minutes away, so Delgado's late explanation hadn't yet cost them anything . . . probably. So he simply said, "Agreed. Send us all your telemetry from the timeship prior to the . . . accident."

Spock and Scott began to coordinate with the research station's staff—all of whom were civilians, though some of them had a disciplined bearing that marked them to Kirk as ex-Starfleet. But in the background, Kirk recognized Arthur Manners, the DTI policy director he'd met late in his previous tour aboard the *Enterprise*. *That must be how Delgado arranged to spare the timeship engines,* Kirk thought, aware that the DTI had been responsible for overseeing their dismantling. *He had a man on the inside.*

Finally, Spock and Scott made their report. "Captain," Scott said, "there's only so much we can learn from out here, and nothing we can do remotely. Our only shot is to beam aboard that misbegotten Franken-stein ship and shut its drives down from there."

"And to beam aboard safely," Spock added, "we must take the *Enterprise* into the confluence zone along with the timeship."

"Is that safe for the ship?" Kirk asked. "The crew?"

"If we stay on the periphery of the zone, the in-terphasic effects should be minimized. I believe I can adjust the shield harmonics to ameliorate them further, thanks to my studies of the confluence event last year."

"All right," Kirk said, standing. "Scotty, get your best people and join me in the transporter room in ten minutes."

"Captain," Spock said, "as the one with the greatest grasp of the physics involved, I should be . . ."

"No, Spock. Scotty's fingerprints are on every piece of those engines. He knows their quirks better than anyone."

"I was not questioning Mister Scott's presence."

Kirk held his gaze. "Whatever they've done to it, that's a piece of *my* ship over there. So it's my responsi-bility." He softened his tone, giving Spock a gentle smile. "Besides, if we manage to get ourselves whisked away to some other reality again, I'd rather have you here to find a way to bring me back. You seem to have a knack for it."

Spock's expression barely changed, but in his own way, he smiled back. "Acknowledged. Good luck, Jim."

Kirk headed for the lift. "Captain," Chekov said, rising from his station. "If that ship is in interphase, the crew could be . . . unpredictable." He spoke with discomfort, still embarrassed by how the interphase madness in Tholian space had affected him all those years ago.

"Don't worry, Mister Chekov, you're invited too. But keep the security detail small; we've got enough people going over as it is. Uhura, have Doctor McCoy report to the transporter room as well, and have him bring his theragen derivative for interphase symptoms."

"Aye, sir."

The captain paused at the doors. "And Mister Spock, while we're over there, you get DTI Director Grey on subspace, secure channel. I think she needs to be brought into this discussion."

U.S.S. Capitoline NCC-82617
Stardate 60145.9
February 2383

The *Capitoline* completed its approach at standard warp rather than slipstream, lest the still-experimental drive system have some unanticipated effect on the confluence field. The sleek *Vesta*-class starship dropped out of warp and moved into station-keeping fifty kilometers off the flank of the much smaller *Everett*. No sooner did Lucsly, Dulmur, and T'Viss arrive on the *Capitoline*'s bridge than their fellow agents aboard the timeship sent a transmission on an encrypted channel beyond the detection capability of 2275 Starfleet technology. *"Ranjea here. We've intercepted signals from the downtime end of the confluence. Captain Kirk and his chief engineer are preparing to beam aboard* Timeship Two. *Repeat, Captain Kirk is coming aboard."*

"Of course he is," Lucsly grated. "He could never leave well enough alone."

"So what do we do about it?" Dulmur asked, trying to refocus his partner away from his animosity and toward constructive solutions.

"Kirk needs to be watched closely," Lucsly said. "But a matter this sensitive calls for the most senior agents on the scene."

Dulmur met his eyes, gauging him. "Which would be us."

"Mm-hmm."

"Ranjea," Dulmur called, "you and Garcia beam back to the *Everett*. We'll be taking point."

"Acknowledged," Ranjea replied. *"To be honest, I'm happy to pass the buck on this one."*

Lucsly asked the *Capitoline*'s captain to have two isolation suits ready for them in the transporter room, and then the two agents headed for the turbolift. "Doctor," Lucsly said to T'Viss, "you beam over to the *Everett* and coordinate with Ranjea and Garcia."

"Very well," she said as she joined them in the lift.

Soon the two veteran agents were in the transporter room, donning the claustrophobic isolation suits over their plain gray business suits while T'Viss transported over to the *Everett*. Dulmur tried to control his breathing. In his seventeen years, five months, and twenty-four days as an active DTI agent, he'd hardly ever traveled any significant distance into his past or future; that was something DTI agents were supposed to prevent, not participate in. Technically, the ship he was about to beam to was still in his relative present;

but it also existed, and originated, a hundred and seven years, eleven months, fourteen days, twelve hours, and thirty-three minutes in his relative past, according to the chronometer readings Ranjea and Garcia had taken. Stepping into history like this was a last resort for any DTI agent, and Dulmur was terrified that, even cloaked in the isolation suit, he might do something wrong. He glanced over at his partner, who looked as cool and businesslike as ever while he donned the suit. As he so often did, Dulmur drew strength from Lucsly's example. The important thing was to follow the rules. The rules existed to maintain order amid the chaos of temporal disruption. Too much imagination just got in the way of doing the job calmly, efficiently, and safely.

His center found once more, Dulmur climbed onto the transporter platform next to Lucsly. The older, gray-haired agent threw Dulmur a stern glance. "Looks like you finally get your wish," Lucsly said without humor. "You'll get to meet James Kirk."

Dulmur rolled his eyes. "It was one little comment to Captain Sisko, nearly ten years ago. Are you ever going to let me live that down?"

"Probably not."

XIV

Timeship Two
Confluence 2275/2383
Kirk, Scott, McCoy, and Chekov materialized on the timeship's bridge, accompanied by an Edosian medtech and a helmeted security guard. It was located where auxiliary control would have been in an old-style *Constitution*-class ship, but outfitted with modern consoles, like a scaled-down version of their own bridge. Their immediate reaction, though, was to the blue-jumpsuited personnel who lay motionless around the bridge. "Bones," Kirk said, and the doctor and his medtech hurried to tend to the crew.

"Sir," Scott said, "most of this is civilian equipment, but it's as good as Starfleet issue." Indeed, the differences in design were subtle, so Scott could easily work the engineering console. "Aye, they've wired something alien in here. Probably a Vedala drive. It's in a bay just forward of main engineering."

"Go, Scotty. I'll meet you there when we've seen to the crew. Chekov, go with him." Scott and Chekov acknowledged the order and left, while the other guard remained, assisting with the timeship crew.

"Jim," McCoy said. "Most of them are comatose or dissociated. But this one, the captain . . . she's in a cataleptic state. Her breathing's slowed." The woman frozen in the command chair was statuesque and dark-haired, her large eyes staring blankly. McCoy took something from his medkit and injected her.

"I know this woman," Kirk said after studying her for a moment. "Tracey Amritraj. She was a captain in Starfleet Intelligence. She's supposed to have retired."

"This is a civilian ship, sir," Chekov pointed out.

"At least it's supposed to be. But Delgado probably called in a lot of old favors to get this done. Bones, can you bring the captain around?"

"I can try. But the best thing for all these people is to beam them back to the *Enterprise*, get them out of this interphase field."

"All right," Kirk said. "But command officers, department heads, anyone healthy enough to be revived and knowledgeable enough to help us find out what's going on here, should be treated here."

McCoy glowered. "I'll do what I can. But we need to start beaming the rest back right away."

"Go to it, Bones."

"Thank God," Teresa Garcia's voice came over Dulmur's suit speaker. He and Lucsly stood at the command junction in the service corridor right beneath the timeship bridge, monitoring the activities of the *Enterprise* away team there. (No, he recalled, the twenty-third-century term would be a boarding party.) *"They're getting help."*

"With no intervention from us," Lucsly reminded her. Had Dulmur said it, Garcia would've talked back, but Lucsly tended to intimidate junior agents (and sometimes senior agents), so only her silence indicated that his point was taken.

Dulmur leaned forward and peered at the bridge security display on the junction screen, watching the guard who was putting spare wrist communicators on the bridge crew—minus the captain, on whom McCoy was working—so the *Enterprise* transporter could lock onto them. "That's Joaquin Perez," he realized. "Shouldn't he be on the *Bozeman*?" That ship had been attached to the DTI's service for years following its ninety-year displacement into the future, and many of its crew still worked with the DTI on its successor, the *Everett*. Though Dulmur couldn't remember if Perez was one of those—in which case he would be in transporter range of his younger self at this very moment.

"He transfers there the following subjective year," Lucsly said.

"Mm."

On the screen, Kirk was trying to get answers from Captain Amritraj, but the woman was only muttering, *"Distress . . . need assistance . . . please respond . . . distress."*

"I guess we know who it was who sent that distress signal," Kirk said, mirroring Dulmur's own thoughts. *"She must have been alert enough to activate it, Bones. Can't you do more for her now?"*

"Not here, Jim, I'm sorry. She needs to go back to the Enterprise."

"Do it," Kirk ordered after a moment. Dulmur studied his features, his voice. Kirk wanted answers badly,

but he wasn't willing to put this crew in jeopardy to get them.

"Captain," Engineer Scott's accented voice came over the intercom. *"I'm in the engine bay. You need to come see this, sir. And bring the doctor."*

Kirk only needed a second to reflect. *"I'll be right there, Scotty."*

"We should follow him," Lucsly said. "Wherever Kirk goes, we need to be there."

Once he secured the junction and followed his partner aft down the service tunnel, Dulmur asked, "To do what? Kirk or no Kirk, you know the regs. Technically nothing here is an anachronistic influence except us."

"I know."

"So logically, anything Kirk does here is what he did anyway in our own past."

"Unless it's a predestination paradox. Unless our intervention is what prevents Kirk from undoing our timeline."

"Whoa there, partner. You know there's a reason we hate those."

Lucsly threw a look over his shoulder. "It's Kirk. We need to be ready for anything."

Dulmur hurried to keep pace with his older but longer-limbed partner, wondering if the more volatile element here was Kirk or Lucsly himself.

Kirk unthinkingly followed the route that would have led from auxiliary control to main engineering on the old *Enterprise.* But in place of the corridor outside the main engine room, he and McCoy found themselves on a catwalk a level above the floor of a large bay. The bay was mostly filled by a bizarre spherical construction that Kirk recognized as a Vedala confluence drive. While McCoy directed Medical Technician Rixil to see to the unconscious personnel on the deck below, Kirk circled the Vedala device, trying to get a handle on it. Once he reached the aft wall, he saw it was hooked into the warp reactor by the same heavy power transfer conduits that would normally have led forward to the deflector dish.

"Aye, it's impressive," Scott's voice came from a doorway at center aft of the catwalk level. "But that's not what you need to see, sir." He raised his voice. "Doctor McCoy, I need you in here too!"

"Soon as I can!" the doctor called.

Kirk followed Scott through the doorway and found himself in the foyer of a far more familiar space. The consoles and readouts might have been upgraded, the configuration modified as it had been so many times before, but Kirk felt it immediately: this was the old *Enterprise* engine room. The control center of the engine complex that had been carved whole out of the old ship's body and had this new one built around it.

Scott's eyes met Kirk's in brief acknowledgment of their shared sense of homecoming, but his attention was mainly on the radiation-suited man who slumped against the master console in the foyer. "It's Frank Gabler, sir!"

"McCoy!" Kirk called, moving over to Gabler and trying to gauge his condition. He seemed oddly peaceful, as though merely asleep, but he wouldn't wake up. Kirk noted that Chekov was tending to the other two engineers in the main chamber beyond, slipping wrist communicators on them for beam-out.

"Good Lord." It was McCoy, frozen in the entryway and staring at the engine room as though he'd seen a ghost. But a moment later he shook it off and went to his patient.

"Can you wake him up, Bones?" Kirk asked after a minute.

"Maybe. The effect of the interphase varies from person to person. If we're lucky, a simple paratheragen shot should work in his case."

The doctor injected the nerve-toxin derivative into the dark-skinned engineer's neck. A few moments later, Gabler began to stir, opening his eyes. They took a moment to focus. "Captain . . . Kirk?" He convulsed a moment later, as though suddenly alarmed.

"Easy, lad," Scott said. "It's me, Scotty."

"Scotty! It's . . . I'm . . . When'd you grow a mustache?"

Kirk grabbed the young engineer by the shoulders. "Mister Gabler!" he barked in his best command tone. "Report!"

Gabler came to a semblance of attention, though his eyes still drifted. "We . . . test flight. We made a test flight. Slingshot trajectory . . . activate confluence drive."

"For heaven's sake, man," Scott demanded, "what possessed you to try doin' both those things at once? There's no tellin' what could happen."

"Necessary . . . no risk . . ." Gabler shook his head, struggling to focus. He stared at the master situation display as if drawing strength from it. "Sir. The idea was that . . . we'd cross timelines during the slingshot passage. So we wouldn't . . . risk interacting with our own future. Safer that way."

"Safer for the timeline, maybe, but for the ship?" Scott asked.

"Calculated risk . . . sir. But as you can see . . ." Gabler sighed. "The drive got . . . stuck. Stuck in the middle. 'It isn't really anywhere, it's somewhere else instead.' And . . . we can't shut it down."

Gabler sagged, winded from the exertion of speech. "We should get you to the *Enterprise*," McCoy said.

"No," Gabler insisted. "My engines . . ." He laughed. "Sorry, Scotty. *Our* engines. I'm not leaving 'em. You need me."

Scott clasped his hand. "Aye, lad. That I do." His gaze shifted to McCoy. "Doctor, anything you can do to get him on his feet . . ."

"I'll do what I can, Scotty. But you need to give him a few minutes."

"All right. But if we could have the console . . ."

Kirk helped McCoy move Gabler's seat out of the way, and Scott gave the console a quick going-over. "Look here, Captain. This is the master regulator for both the warp engines and the confluence drive." He called up a schematic on the circular screen, studying it sadly. "Och, look what they've done to my poor bairns. Like tryin' to graft an elephant's head onto a racehorse. They've turned the *Enterprise*'s heart into somethin' it was never meant to be."

Kirk clapped his shoulder. "Scotty, if anyone can restore the lady's honor, it's you. Let's get to work."

On the catwalk above the starboard consoles, the cloaked Lucsly and Dulmur watched as Kirk, Scott, and the recovering Gabler attempted to diagnose the problem. "You think they can figure it out?" Dulmur asked his partner.

Lucsly was studying his temporal tricorder. "The subspace metric is a mess. The best I can figure is that since the confluence was engaged in the middle of a slingshot jump, the effect is somehow 'trapped' inside the inverted spacetime between Cauchy horizons."

Dulmur nodded. He wasn't great with the math, but he'd had the basic principles drilled into him enough back in T'Viss's training courses. The gravitomagnetic field of a rotating black hole, or the milder one of a rotating star amplified by a chroniton field from a warp-driven ship, tilted the space and time axes in the vicinity so that moving through space locally would send you through time relative to the rest of the universe. The inverted spacetime was a sort of bridge connecting past and future, and the Cauchy horizons were the boundaries between that bridge and the normal space beyond, roughly analogous to the mouths of a wormhole. "So instead of passing through from past to present, the timeship is caught in between—and the Vedala drive is merging the two horizons, making them interchangeable."

"Something like that. Plus the interphase effect on top of it. I'm reading quantum signatures of a parallel timeline." Lucsly threw his partner a concerned look.

"I'm not sure twenty-third-century physics is up to solving this metric."

"Couldn't they just shut off the power? Cut the cables to the Vedala drive?"

"No," Lucsly said. "That would be very bad."

"How so?"

Before his partner could answer, a voice came over their comms. *"Ranjea to Lucsly and Dulmur,"* the Deltan agent said, sounding excited. *"There's something you've got to hear."*

"What is it?" Lucsly asked.

"We're intercepting a signal from the Enterprise *in 2275. They're within the fringes of the confluence zone so we can receive it."*

"Is this important?"

"Gariff . . . Spock is talking to Director Grey herself."

Lucsly straightened, as though coming to attention. "Patch it through," he said, his usual deadpan giving way to a hushed, almost reverential tone. "Patch it through now."

U.S.S. *Enterprise*
Confluence 2275/2383

On the bridge viewscreen, Meijan Grey listened with quiet concern as Spock filled her in on the events taking place at the neutron star. The *Enterprise*'s powerful subspace transceiver, one of the many upgrades of this new design, allowed them clear real-time communication with Earth even from this remote sector. *"Thank you for bringing this situation to my attention, Commander,"* Grey finally said when Spock was done. *"I'm gratified to hear that the crew is alive and under your doctors' care. And rest assured you'll have the full cooperation of the DTI's best scientists should you need it.*

"*As for you, Admiral Delgado,*" she went on, speaking to the man whose visage filled the other half of the split viewscreen, "*I expect you to cooperate fully with the* Enterprise *in resolving this situation. Hold nothing back, do you understand?*"

Delgado lowered his bald head gravely. "*I understand, Director. I knew there would be consequences for this if it went wrong. I'm willing to accept them.*"

"*Thank you, Admiral,*" Grey said. "*But recriminations can wait. For now, we need to focus on resolving this disaster. Commander Spock, do your sensors show any evidence of starships or transmissions on the other side of the confluence? Either from the future or from a parallel timeline? Or both?*"

"Negative, Director. However, Captain Kirk ordered the sensors set to short-range only, as a safeguard against anachronistic information coming into our possession and potentially affecting the future course of events."

Grey's angular brows drew together. "*I'm not sure how wise that is, Commander. If something is approaching from the other side, we need to be alerted. Any knowledge we might gain as a side effect could be contained, classified.*"

Spock raised a brow. "Our knowledge of Vedala confluence technology was supposed to have been classified or erased, Director. Yet here before us is a Federation vessel employing a Vedala propulsion device."

"Yes, and there will be an investigation into how that came about."

"Director, the vessel bears DTI markings."

Delgado interposed. *"Call it wishful thinking, Mister Spock. Or protective camouflage. It was Arthur Manners's idea. He wanted the markings there so that if future incarnations of the DTI detected the timeship's arrival in their eras, they would know it was civilian and friendly in origin. As for myself, I hoped that if these experiments panned out, the Council might relax its restrictions and* Timeship Two *could be recognized as a legitimate temporal research vessel. Perhaps I was getting ahead of myself, Director, but it's something of an occupational hazard."*

"Admiral, I hardly think this is an occasion for frivolity."

"No, Director. I apologize."

"Nor is it an occasion for incomplete truths, Director," Spock told her. "The Department of Temporal Investigations was responsible for the dismantling of the first timeship prototype. Yet the dismantling did not occur and the records were forged. The DTI was also responsible for securing the Vedala planetoid and ensuring the return of all Vedala technology to its owners. Yet a confluence drive was removed and, again, records were forged or altered to conceal the fact. In fact, Director Grey, this timeship could not exist without the complicity of your department."

"I'm very aware of that, Mister Spock. The investigation will not exclude our own people."

"Spock," Delgado said, *"this was my doing. I subverted Manners into redirecting the matériel and*

concealing the evidence. But do we really have time for recriminations when there's an emergency to resolve?"

Spock stepped forward around the helm console, folding his hands behind him. "Before we can resolve it, Admiral, Director, we must have total candor about the origins of the drive and the circumstances of its integration into the timeship. Director Grey, I understand your desire to protect the reputation of your agency. And Admiral, I am surprised, yet impressed, by your willingness to, as they say, 'take the fall' for another."

"Spock, let it go," Delgado urged.

"Under the circumstances, sir, I cannot. Director Grey, forgive me. But you are well-known for your meticulous attention to detail and your ability to discern patterns from fragmentary evidence. They are among your leading qualifications for your post. And with all due respect, the number of individuals actually employed by your department is rather small, as is the number of distinct matters for which you have responsibility. It is inconceivable that an undertaking as significant as this could have completely evaded your notice, Director—and unlikely that it could have remained secret without your direct complicity."

Timeship Two

"What is he saying?" Lucsly said. "He can't be saying what I think he's saying."

"Partner, listen," Dulmur urged.

"He's—he's covering for Kirk. That's the only thing that makes sense."

"Lucsly! Be quiet and listen!"

The older agent blinked. "She's not saying anything."

"That's right. Why isn't she?"

When Grey's voice came over the channel again, it was subdued, heavy. *"You have to understand, Mister Spock. We were careful. We did everything we could to ensure the timeline would be in no danger."*

"You broke Federation law," the Vulcan replied. *"You stole technology from the Vedala, potentially jeopardizing our tenuous relations with the oldest active spacefaring race in the known galaxy."*

"No," Lucsly breathed.

"I had a higher responsibility, Commander. Someday, someone will master time travel. Maybe us, maybe our enemies. Maybe some other civilization we've never even met yet that could go back and wipe us out of existence without ever knowing we were here. Look at what happened with V'Ger. According to your own reports, Commander, the Voyager 6 *probe somehow survived a slingshot around the Black Star—traveled a vast distance through time and space, giving it plenty of time to evolve into the form that almost destroyed the Earth. We thought nothing but the old* Enterprise *engines could survive a slingshot, certainly nothing without warp drive. But that primitive space probe did, somehow. It means the possibilities are broader than we thought, and our understanding is less than we thought. That made it necessary to learn more. To keep experimenting."*

"Jan, don't take this on yourself." It was Delgado's voice now. *"I pushed for this. I talked you into it."* Yes, that made sense. Delgado had been a master manipulator, Lucsly knew.

"Don't sell me short, Antonio. Or yourself. I chose to do this. I realized, Mister Spock, that our best defense against time travel was to create a safer alternative. A way to explore time without jeopardizing one's own history. If we could perfect that, make it available, it might protect the timeline from future threats."

"A noble sentiment," Spock said. Lucsly grabbed at that. *Yes. Noble. She was trying to protect the timeline, as she always did.* Yet it slipped away, a lifeline with no solidity. *"But you nonetheless felt compelled to rush into the experiment. To launch the timeship without a complete theoretical understanding of how the confluence drive would interface with the slingshot phenomenon. Was it perhaps because you hoped to achieve results before the Vedala discovered your crime?"*

Lucsly felt his fists clenching. He wanted to strike out at the Vulcan for speaking to Grey in such tones. He wanted to strike out at Grey for betraying his faith in her. But there was nothing he could do but listen helplessly as everything he'd believed in was torn down around him.

"I took a calculated risk," Grey went on. *"I did it to protect the timeline."*

"And yet, Director, it has had the opposite effect. If we wish to preserve the timeline now, you must hold nothing more back. Any information you have about the origins, acquisition, and handling of the confluence drive may be critical to diagnosing its malfunction."

"All right," Grey said after a long pause and a sigh. *"I'll share all the information I have."*

Lucsly couldn't listen anymore. He shut off the

comm channel and strode through the door at the aft end of the catwalk, not caring if Kirk and the others below heard it open. What did it matter now? The history he knew was a lie.

The roar of the massive power conduits that fed into the warp nacelles muffled Lucsly's shouts, the blows of his fists against the wall. He didn't even register how much time passed before he noticed Dulmur standing nearby as he sat slumped against the catwalk rail. He *always* kept track of time. But that had been when time, history, and the Department had made sense to him.

"Are we all just a lie?" he finally asked. "Is everything we fight for just a self-serving facade?"

"Get ahold of yourself, partner," Dulmur barked. "Come on, get up." The younger man took his wrist and pulled him to his feet. Normally Lucsly would have let go right away, but now, suddenly, he needed to hold on. Through their visors, Dulmur held his eyes, startled.

An awkward moment or two later, they both let go. "Look," Dulmur said after several seconds more (*how many?*). "You know as well as I do that history gets rewritten. People take messy, ambiguous history and clean it up. They idealize some people, demonize other people . . . they make it into a myth to suit their own needs, whatever the facts may have been. They focus on the parts of the truth that matter and ignore the rest."

"So Director Grey, the one who made us what we are . . . she was a myth?"

"She was a person, Lucsly. A human being no better than anyone else. And that means she screwed up. That's what human beings do—even DTI agents. We're the ones who made her into a myth. But there had to be a reason for that. Whatever screwups history hid from us, we chose to remember the part where Meijan Grey founded the DTI and defined our mission to protect the timeline. That's our reality, Lucsly: the job we do. The job we *have* to do. And if the myth of Meijan Grey gives us the strength and the focus to keep doing this impossible, thankless job without losing our minds . . . well, maybe that's her redemption for that one big mistake." Dulmur took a breath, then another. "And maybe by getting back out there and doing our job, we're helping her redeem herself a little more."

Lucsly absorbed his words silently for a moment. "Okay, partner?" Dulmur asked, his patience thin.

Gariff Lucsly set his jaw. "Whatever happened in the past . . . we have a present to protect. Let's get back to work."

XV

Timeship Two
Confluence 2275/2383

Kirk was startled when Spock relayed the gist of his discussion with Meijan Grey. He'd always found the DTI director to be a reasonable, responsible woman, and smart enough to see through Delgado's manipulations. What could have motivated her to support a project like this?

But that would have to wait. What mattered was what they could do now. According to the classified DTI records Director Grey provided, the confluence drive had been salvaged from near the site of the impact event that had triggered their dimension-jumping malfunction. Scans of its activity in situ had indicated a feedback process among the different drives, serving to regulate their activity and correct errors and malfunctions. "We tried to replicate that," Gabler explained to Kirk, Scott, and Chekov. The security chief had finished evacuating the rest of the timeship crew and was now drawing on his old engineering training to help out. "We . . . we echoed its own signals back into it. Not in real time, of course . . . could give runaway feedback. But ordinary signals, an 'all's well' kind of thing. To keep it calm." He chuckled. "That's how we talk about it. Sometimes seems alive."

"Indeed," Spock replied over the communicator channel. *"Given the sophistication of Vedala technology, we cannot assume that is entirely a metaphor. And given the location of the stolen drive, it may have suffered additional damage beyond what our science can detect, damage that the mutual error correction among the drives was not able to undo."*

"Or," Scott suggested, "that could've been compensated for by the rest o' the drives if they were still workin' in tandem. But operatin' on its own, it canna get the corrections it needs. And we don't know how to modify the feedback signals to tell it to reverse the confluence."

"Can't we just cut the power to the drive?" Chekov asked.

"Not on your life, lad," Scott replied. "The confluence means we're in two places and times at once—maybe two timelines at once too, judgin' by the interphase effects. The confluence drive makes them essentially the same place, the same quantum coordinates. If you just cut it off, sure, the different pieces o' space and time would go back to normal—but the particles of the ship and our bodies couldn't tell *which* o' those places and times they were supposed to stay with, so they'd be divvied up randomly between the two. It'd tear the ship apart. Worse—it'd rupture the antimatter containment, and the resultin' explosion in the middle of an interphase would probably create a *permanent* interspatial rift between times and dimensions. There's no tellin' what damage that could do in the long run."

Kirk pondered. "Could we jettison the antimatter pods, rig an automatic shutdown for the Vedala drive, then beam off?"

"The drive itself has a lot of stored energy. It could blow up just as easy when its atoms got torn apart."

"Captain." Spock's voice on the open channel was urgent, and a red alert siren sounded behind him. *"A vessel has just entered the confluence zone. It is firing—"* A rumbling sound and static came over the channel, and a second later, the timeship itself trembled and rang from a weapon impact, sending Kirk and the others reeling.

"Spock, report," Kirk barked, running for the master console to get an external sensor reading.

"Minimal damage, but I believe that was simply a warning shot. The vessel is highly advanced, Captain, beyond our technology. Its configuration is familiar, however." A pause. *"Captain, we are being hailed."*

Kirk checked the external communication controls. "Us too." He opened the channel.

"—dentified vessels. Stand down and prepare to be boarded. You are now prisoners of the Klingon-Andorian Compact."

U.S.S. Enterprise

"It's definitely a KAC design, Mister Spock," Sulu reported from the helm position. "But those engines, that hull plating . . . it's unlike anything the Compact had when we encountered them before."

"Same with their shields and weapons," reported Ensign Mosi Nizhoni from the weapons and defense station. "If this becomes a fight, sir, I'm not sure how long we can hold out," the young Navajo woman continued.

Spock pondered. It was logical that the confluence drive would connect to the same parallel timeline it had transposed with twice before. And the advancement of this ship seemed to confirm that the slingshot curve connected it with the future of that timeline.

"Hail them," Spock said to Uhura. A moment later, she nodded, indicating that the channel was open. Spock stepped in front of the helm station to address the screen. "Compact vessel. This is Commander Spock of the *U.S.S. Enterprise.* Our intentions are nonhostile. However, the region of space you have entered is dangerously volatile. Please cease firing, for your own safety."

"*Enterprise?*" The face that appeared onscreen was that of an Andorian female-equivalent, most likely a *shen,* judging from her strong build. "*So you* are *the ship from the old records. The one from another universe. But a Vulcan in command?*" Her tone conveyed considerable contempt toward Vulcans, suggesting that the Compact's enmity toward the Vulcan Protectorate continued in the future this vessel evidently came from.

"I am Spock, an officer in the Starfleet of the United Federation of Planets," he informed her. "Whom do I have the honor of addressing?"

"*I am Captain Pava ek'Noor sh'Aqabaa of the Compact warship* Thorn of Justice,*" the Andorian replied. She seemed young to hold such rank, but the scars she bore on her face and neck, including a nick in her left antenna, suggested she had distinguished herself in combat. In a hybrid Klingon-Andorian culture, that could have earned her rapid advancement. *"Whoever you serve, Vulcan, you will obey my command or be destroyed. Surrender and prepare both your ships to be boarded!"*

"As I have explained, that is not possible. The other vessel is experiencing a dangerous malfunction, and we are in the process of rescue operations. Time is of the essence." *In more ways than I care to explain at the moment.* "And any weapons discharges in this immediate vicinity could be hazardous to the integrity of local spacetime."

"Do you take me for a fool, greenskin? Your flimsy excuses will not spare you. Now drop your shields or we will batter them down!"

Captain sh'Aqabaa vanished from the screen. Spock turned to the defense station. "Ensign Nizhoni. Can you extend our force-field envelope around the timeship?"

"If we move in closer, sir. Ideally within ten kilometers."

"Mister Sulu?"

"I can get us even closer, sir," Sulu replied, and Spock had no reason to doubt him.

But as soon as the ship began to move, it came under fire from the *Thorn of Justice*. "Status of the timeship?" Spock asked.

"Taking fire too, sir," Nizhoni said. "Should we return fire?"

"Negative." He turned to the engineering station. "Mister Mercado, attempt to repel the hostile vessel with a tractor beam."

Sulu leaned forward and spoke sotto voce. "Mister Spock, is that the best we can do?"

"We cannot risk firing weapons, lest we hasten the destabilization of the spacetime metric."

"Even to stop them from firing?"

"Our odds of successfully doing so are limited, Mister Sulu. We would only add to the problem."

"Then what can we do?"

Spock raised a brow. "We can shield the timeship . . . and thereby give Captain Kirk and Commander Scott time to find a way to deactivate the Vedala drive."

Timeship Two

"Holy crap, they're shooting at us," Dulmur gasped. Even though the *Enterprise*'s force field—the spheroidal shield envelope that was the forerunner of modern deflector shields—surrounded the timeship and kept the KAC vessel's fire from getting closer than a few hundred meters, the radiation from their energy beams was intense enough to make the ship's hull tremble from sheer thermal shock. Down below, Kirk's people were taking it in stride, still trying to work out a way to shut down the confluence drive. But Dulmur was a government man, not a soldier. He'd been in some tight scrapes before, been shot at by hostile time travelers or technology thieves, but few of his cases had put him under fire from starship weapons, weapons powerful enough to vaporize whole cities. Dulmur's thoughts went to the holo of his mother that he carried in his pocket, reminding himself of why he did the job. It helped.

If Lucsly was similarly alarmed, it barely showed. "Lucsly to *Everett*. The situation has escalated to a full-blown prochronistic incursion. The timeline is in jeopardy. At this point, we need to consider every possible option." Dulmur stared at his partner. Now that there was imminent danger of the past being altered, it meant the DTI agents were authorized to intervene in events. That would be an absolute last resort, but still, the prospect was even more disquieting than the trembling of the ship's deck.

"*Understood,*" came Ranjea's voice. "*We stand ready to assist.*"

"*Captain Alisov here. Can we warn off the* Thorn of Justice? *It's from our own time, technically.*"

"No," was Lucsly's emphatic reply. "That would expose the *Enterprise* crew to knowledge of our existence." The ship shuddered as though struck by something. The irradiation must have grown intense enough to flash-vaporize the surface of the hull, rocking the vessel like an explosion. "Is there any way we can safely deactivate the confluence drive without exposing ourselves to them?" Lucsly began descending the gangway to the main deck—a wise precaution under the circumstances. Dulmur followed.

"*T'Viss here, Agent Lucsly. There is a possibility. I have been applying the Manheim and Vard equations to the confluence metric and devised a potential solution that would have been unavailable to twenty-third-century observers.*"

"Just tell us!" Dulmur shouted as he reached the deck.

"*In order to shut down the Vedala drive without de-*

stroying the timeship, you must employ phase discrimination to associate the particles of the vessel with their proper spacetime coordinates."

"They didn't have phase discriminators in 2275!"

"I believe the effect can be approximated using the chroniton emissions of the timeship's engines. By generating a gravitomagnetic field of like phase and opposite polarity to that of the neutron star in the 2275 timeframe, you can employ said neutron star as an anchor, if you will, to draw the ship back into its proper frame of reference when the confluence collapses."

"Can you instruct us on the procedure?" Lucsly asked.

"I am transmitting the instructions to your tricorders, gentlemen. I advise haste."

Another blast rocked the ship. "Gee, never would've thought of that," Dulmur growled, grabbing for the ladder railing.

But his hand went *through* the railing—and disappeared into the adjacent console!

Dulmur yelped, yanking back his tingling hand. "Interphase!" he cried. "The ship's going into interphase."

He and his partner exchanged a look. Lucsly said it out loud, for the benefit of the listeners in their own timeframe: "If we don't act fast, we may not be able to work the controls. Come on."

They made their way across the floor, dodging around Gabler as he ran between consoles, oblivious to their presence. Dulmur counted his blessings that the gravity plating in the floor spread its phase out enough to keep it solid beneath their feet. But the controls they needed to operate were in the emergency manual monitor, a raised booth opposite the catwalk where they'd been, and the main access was via ladder. Luckily their shifting phase stayed in sync with that of the ship long enough for them to get up it, though Dulmur felt the rungs losing solidity just as he stepped off into the monitor booth. As a manual backup, the EMM had undergone minimal refitting, still containing the same angular, black-and-red control console it must have held when it was a part of the *Enterprise*.

Studying his tricorder screen, Lucsly attempted to enter the commands, but his gloved fingers kept slipping through the controls. "No use. The phase variations are accelerating. We can't stay in phase long enough."

Dulmur tried to snap his fingers, but the gloves of his isolation suit muffled it. "The phase discriminators in our tricorders. Maybe we can lock onto the time-ship's phase and ride through the shifts with it."

"Worth a try." They adjusted their tricorders, and soon the console became mostly solid to their touch, only phasing out for brief moments. They worked as swiftly as they could to program the sequence, but the ship was still trembling under fire, and soon the controls lost substance beneath their fingers once again as the phase shifts worsened. "No good!" Lucsly grated. "If there were some way to rig a remote interface . . ."

"Wait." Dulmur was staring out the window grille at the group below. "It's Kirk! He's coming up here!"

The agents moved to the corner farthest from the console and held very still as the captain ascended into the room. They stood face to face with James Kirk himself. *I thought he'd be taller,* Dulmur thought. The captain paused for a moment, taking in the surroundings with a look of surprise giving way to a faint, nostalgic smile. Then he shook it off and moved to the console, working the controls. "All right, Scotty," he said into his wrist communicator. "The manual jettison controls are responding."

"Then there's a chance we can eject the antimatter pods, sir," came a Scottish brogue over the device's speaker. *"But it's a huge gamble. We still can't be sure the Vedala drive itself won't blow."*

"It's all we've got, Scotty. Stand by."

Dulmur gestured to Lucsly to follow him down the ladder. It was hard for their phase discriminators to keep them solid long enough to descend safely, but they were still sufficiently in phase to be heard, and the isolation suits' sound dampeners weren't meant for such close quarters.

Once they were out of Kirk's earshot, Dulmur said, "Kirk can still work the controls. His people are still in phase with the ship. Must be since they're from the same time."

Lucsly stared in horror. "You can't be saying . . ."

"Lucsly, it's our only chance."

"It's *Kirk*. Giving him knowledge of future technology is like giving a flamethrower to a pyromaniac!"

"Are you sure?" Dulmur urged. "Or is our image of Kirk as big a myth as our image of Director Grey? Think about what we read in those records. If anything, the James Kirk in those logs and transcripts understood the dangers of tampering with time as well as anyone in his era could have."

"Seventeen violations, Dulmur! No, eighteen! Maybe more!"

"That doesn't mean he was reckless. It means he was *experienced* enough with time travel, thanks to the accidents that got him involved with it in the first place, that he became Starfleet's first choice for dealing with it." Dulmur laughed, a bit hysterically. "Hell, who are we to judge him at a time like this? We've spent our whole careers trying to avoid time travel! We're out of our comfort zone! But this is old news for Kirk! He's the expert here! I say we trust him!"

But Lucsly still resisted. "Lucsly to *Everett*, have you been monitoring?"

"*. . . here, Lucs . . . barely rea . . .*"

"Please advise. Can you suggest *any* other options?"

But the *Everett*'s signal dissolved into static—a type of static Dulmur thought he recognized. "Lucsly, doesn't that sound like—"

"Lucsly to *Everett*, come in, please!"

A new voice barked at them—in Klingon. It must have been an unusual dialect, for it took a moment for their translators to catch up. "*—authorized to be on . . . channel! Let alone speaking . . . outlawed language! Identify yourself, human slave!*"

The agents exchanged a look. "Another Compact ship?" Dulmur asked, knowing the answer.

"No," Lucsly said, checking his tricorder. "It's from our side of the confluence. Our own era. And I'm not reading our ships there."

"Can Kirk's people hear it?"

"I think it's mostly out of their phase, like us." He worked the tricorder. "I'm jamming the signal. Nobody with twenty-third-century tech should be able to hear it."

"Attention! Your signal has been traced and vessels . . . route to apprehend you! Explain . . . you come into possession of a Federation relic and perhaps we . . . not annihilate you along with it!"

"Our timeline's been overwritten," Dulmur realized. "The Compact, they must've gone through into the past, given modern technology to the Klingons of that time and let them conquer the Federation!" The ship trembled again, still under fire from the Compact ship, but that didn't matter. They might be subjectively experiencing a point in time before the Compact ships broke through the confluence into 2275, but the occurrence of that event would be in the past of the 2383 side. The agents were protected within the confluence zone, just as Kirk had been within the Guardian's influence . . . but everything they knew was gone.

"But the quantum interference is still there in the signal," Lucsly said. "That means the timeline's still in flux, the merger hasn't resolved yet. The original quantum information of our timeline is still present, just suppressed. As long as we have the opportunity to prevent the change in *this* timeframe, our own timeline state is still retrievable."

Dulmur prayed his partner's grasp of temporal theory was as sound as ever. "But you know what that means, partner." He glanced up the ladder. "The only person who can help us now is—"

"All right. Don't rub it in." Lucsly sighed. "Only one of us should make the contact. Minimize the variables."

Dulmur could practically hear him grinding his teeth. "You want me to do it?"

Lucsly set his jaw and began to remove his isolation suit. "No. I'm not going to hide from this. Besides, I want to keep a very close eye on him—just in case."

"Okay," Dulmur said, hoping this was the right choice. Who knew? Maybe it would do Lucsly good to face his personal demon.

But he was glad Lucsly was unarmed.

Kirk stared in dismay as his fingers passed through the manual controls as if through water. A moment later they were solid to his touch again, but he knew they might not stay that way. He still had nightmares about being trapped in the interspace void, helpless to defend his crew against the Tholians. "Scotty, the ship's going into interphase."

"Aye. We've got to work fast, sir. The longer we wait, the shorter the time we'll be able to touch the controls. Pretty soon we'll have to evacuate no matter what."

Another burst of disruptor fire punctuated Scott's sentence. "If we even last that long," Kirk muttered. Normally he had every confidence in Spock, Scotty, and the rest of his crew. But this Vedala technology was so far ahead of them. He had to face the fact that there might be nothing they could do to prevent a rift from forming. If it did, maybe there was a chance they could defend it. He began to catalog the resources available on his side: the *Enterprise*, Delgado's station, the neutron star itself. Maybe there was a way—

He whirled, reacting to movement in his peripheral vision. A man stood there, a tall, narrow-faced man with wavy gray hair, gray eyes, and a dark gray civilian suit in an unfamiliar style. "Who are you?" Kirk demanded, knowing all the timeship's personnel had been accounted for. "Where did you come from?"

"I can't tell you that," the man said. The look in his heavy-lidded eyes was oddly reluctant, reminding Kirk of the look in his brother Sam's eyes when their father had ordered him to muck out the stables. "All I can tell you . . . is that there is a way to return this ship to your own timeframe."

Kirk furrowed his brows, seizing on that. "*My* own timeframe? Are you saying you're from the future?"

The gray man winced. "That's not important, Captain. Time is of the essence. I can show you the procedure, but you must act before you lose phase synchronization with the timeship."

"Can't you do it yourself?" Kirk probed.

"No," the gray man said. "For many reasons. Please . . . I need you to trust me. Just as I need to trust you not to reveal any of this."

Kirk studied the man's eyes, gauging him. He was reluctant to hold Kirk's gaze, but not from dishonesty; it seemed more like anger, even fear. The man desperately did not want to be here, and it seemed that Kirk himself was a large part of the reason why. But nonetheless he *needed* to be here, needed to make this contact, even though it was the last thing he desired.

Whoever he was, there was as much at stake for him as for Kirk.

"All right," the captain said. "Tell me what to do."

Reluctantly, the gray man showed Kirk a device in his hand. It looked like a type of tricorder, but smaller, more advanced than Starfleet issue. "The instructions are here. I'll talk you through them."

Kirk moved in to study the small screen, forcing himself to focus on the instructions rather than the questions he was dying to ask. Under the guidance of the gray man, he operated the controls as best he could, though the moments in which the console lost tangibility were growing longer. He began to grasp that the plan was to use the old *Enterprise* engines to create a field that would anchor them to the neutron star—an elegant solution. Scott's voice came over his communicator. *"Captain, what are you doin' to the controls?"*

"No time to explain, Scotty. Just follow my lead."

"Aye," Scott breathed a moment later. *"I see what you're tryin' to do. If it works, it could draw us back right enough. But how—"*

"Questions later, Scotty, that's an order."

While Kirk adjusted the engine output with the manual controls, Scott, Chekov, and Gabler worked below to transfer power, adjust the intermix balance, and do whatever else was necessary to keep the new configuration stable. The gray man's tricorder beeped encouragingly. "We've got field coherence," he said to Kirk. But after a moment he frowned. "But it's not enough. The resonance with the neutron star is too weak. Damn it, it's not going to work!"

The ship rocked, sending Kirk staggering into the forward wall. The gray man fell forward, his flailing arm passing clear through the console, confirming Kirk's suspicions about why he couldn't make the adjustments himself.

"*Enterprise to Captain Kirk,*" came Spock's voice over his communicator. "*Force-field power is down to thirty percent. And the instability of the confluence zone is worsening. Recommend we beam you aboard and retreat.*"

"No, Spock, we're close to a solution. Stand by." The gray man was clambering to his feet. "Sorry I can't help you up," Kirk said after shutting off the outgoing channel. "Is there still a chance? Any way we can intensify the field?"

"The problem isn't on this end," the mystery man told him. "There isn't a strong enough anchor on the other side."

A thought occurred to Kirk. "Is there any chance you could generate a field like this on your end? Pull the ship into your timeframe after my people evacuate?"

The gray man fell very still. "There's no help coming from that quarter, Captain." He slumped. "We've failed."

Kirk grinned. "I don't give up that easily, mister." He worked his communicator. "Kirk to *Enterprise.*"

"*Spock here, sir.*"

"Spock, are you scanning the gravitomagnetic field this ship is generating?"

"*Yes, Captain.*"

"Is it possible to create a field of the same phase and opposite polarity with the *Enterprise*'s current warp engines?"

The gray man stared. "What are you doing?" he hissed.

"The only thing I can," Kirk murmured back.

"Difficult, sir," Spock said after a moment. *"As you know, the parameters that enabled our former engines to generate such a field were unique."*

"Spock, it was your theoretical restart formula that turned them into a time machine in the first place. If anyone can do it again, it's you and Scotty."

Now Scott's voice came over the open channel. *"We can sure as hell try, sir! Mister Spock, the others can handle things here. Beam me back aboard!"*

"Do it, Spock."

"Acknowledged." Kirk glanced out the grille and saw Scott dematerialize. Since both ships were inside the *Enterprise*'s force-field bubble, there was no need to lower it first.

The gray man was staring at Kirk, aghast. "Do you realize what the consequences will be if they succeed in duplicating these engines' unique properties?"

"I do, sir. And that's something I'll have to deal with when the time comes. But I have a suspicion that you realize, better than I do, what the consequences will be if they don't."

The gray man tugged uneasily at his gray collar.

U.S.S. *Enterprise*

It was most inconvenient, Spock thought, to be forced to contend with the effects of enemy fire while attempting to formulate and apply new principles of physics.

The problem before him was most fascinating, its ramifications far-reaching. The new warp configuration that Captain Kirk had somehow known to program into the timeship's drive system, which Commander Scott had relayed to Spock on his return, offered new insight into the frustratingly incomplete models of chroniton generation that the DTI and Admiral Delgado's scientists had managed to formulate over the past eight years. The specific way in which the timeship's engines had been modified to produce the desired alterations in their gravitomagnetic field suggested underlying equations that, assuming they were correct, pinpointed which properties of those engines' plasma stream interacted with which properties of the warp coils to induce chroniton emissions. And with such a mathematical model, it became possible to extrapolate how to generate a chroniton field with a *different* set of warp engines.

That was what he and Commander Scott were attempting to do now. While Scott and his engineers worked on the main engineering level to adjust the injector timing, chamber pressure, and magnetic field configuration to create resonance pulses within the intermix chamber that should result in the appropriate plasma stream modification, Spock was a level above in the engineering computer bay, attempting to tune the flux constriction, coil synchronization, and temperature within the warp nacelles to emulate the coil configuration of the timeship's nacelles.

Unfortunately, it was difficult to make such delicate adjustments when the controls beneath his hands and the deck beneath his feet repeatedly shuddered as disruptor impacts on the force-field bubble induced feedback pulses in its generator coils, and as the ship's power surged and shifted unpredictably in response to the ever-increasing power demands of the shields and weapons. Given the imminent threat, Spock had authorized the firing of torpedoes against the *Thorn of Justice*, on the principle that the energy release from a torpedo would be localized at a greater distance from the timeship than a phaser discharge and thus do less to destabilize the confluence field. But the maximum safe yield for the torpedoes was low, and though Ensign Nizhoni's reputation as a sharpshooter was well-earned, the hostile vessel's weapon ports were abundant and quite effectively shielded, and she had only managed to disable a fraction of them.

A new shock to the vessel caused Spock to lose his balance. Staggering back, he spun and caught himself on the rail surrounding the scintillating intermix shaft. He raised an eyebrow, realizing the sound and sensation was that of a beam impact against the ship's conventional, skintight deflector shields. "Force field is beginning to fail!" Lieutenant Cleary called from the foyer console, confirming Spock's analysis. "Partial penetration of enemy fire!"

"Concentrate power to forward deflectors!" Sulu ordered from the bridge. Spock winced at the loud bark of the torpedo tubes directly over his head launching their projectiles toward the hostile vessel.

"Mister Spock!" Scott called up from the warp drive control console adjacent to the intermix shaft. "Even if we can keep up the force field long enough to complete the adjustments, you realize we'll have to leave the confluence zone to give the timeship the anchor it needs!" Another hull impact came close to pitching Spock forward over the rail. He braced himself more carefully. Another torpedo discharge assailed his sensitive hearing. "They'll be defenseless!"

"Scotty," Kirk's voice came over the exterior channel, *"we're doing what we can to regain shield control over here. Gabler's trying to shunt impulse power to the deflector grid, but this damned chimera of a ship wasn't put together with that in mind."*

"Spock, we've got to fire everything we've got at that futuristic behemoth!" Scott cried. "It's not like it can make things any worse at this point!"

"It would leave us with insufficient power to ensure the success of the engine modifications, Mister Scott," Spock replied. "There are still many uncertain variables in play. We need as large a cushion of available power as possible."

"Aye, there is that," Scott conceded. "But what can we do to protect the timesh—"

The next impact struck even harder, and a power surge blew out a deflector coupling on the level below Scott. An engineer screamed and fell to the deck, his hands and face burned, and Chief Ross called for a medical team while Crewman Chezrava moved in with a fire extinguisher. The lights in the engineering section flickered. "Force field down to eleven percent!" Cleary called, and Spock considered that a more fundamental question was, *What can we do to protect our own ship?*

As Spock might have expected, Kirk had an answer to that. *"Uhura, patch me through to the* Thorn." A moment later: *"Attention,* Thorn of Justice. *This is Captain Kirk of the* Starship Enterprise. *In a few moments we will begin to collapse the interspatial confluence our ships now occupy. If you remain within this zone when that occurs, your ship will most likely be disintegrated. At best, you will be trapped in a place and time not your own."* A bluff, since they could not engage the process until after the *Thorn* stopped its attack—but Captain sh'Aqabaa did not know that.

"We will take our chances!" the proud Andorian commander declared. *"There is nothing left for us there in any case, unless we take your ships!"*

More impacts rocked the ship. White-hot droplets of molten metal rained down the shaft from above; the status screens on the walls of the computer chamber showed that the impulse deflection crystal at the top of the shaft had sustained damage. Now they would be unable to move except on thrusters—insufficient to evade the *Thorn* even if they could abandon *Timeship Two.*

But then Sulu called from the bridge. *"Mister Spock! Another ship is incoming from beyond the confluence! It's not KAC . . . sir, it's firing on the* Thorn!"

Spock stepped onto the lift platform and rode it down to the main level. "Transfer it here, Mister Sulu." Cleary made way for Spock as the main viewer feed appeared on the circular monitor of the foyer console. The incoming vessel firing on the *Thorn of Justice* was merely an indistinct blob of light at first, but its effect on the other vessel was evident. Bright flares erupted on the *Thorn* and its disruptor fire first transferred to the new ship and then died out altogether. *"Nice!"* called Ensign Nizhoni. *"Sir, it's precision fire. Taking out their weapons and propulsion . . . minimal damage otherwise. I'd like to meet their gunner."*

As sensor resolution improved, the configuration of the new vessel became evident. It was a silver-hued cylindrical vessel ringed by a toroidal propulsion system. *"They're Vulcan!"* Sulu breathed.

"Indeed," Spock said, noting the advancement of the design. "And evidently from the same future era as the *Thorn*."

"Sir, they're hailing," Uhura said.

"Onscreen here, Commander," Spock told her.

The face that appeared on the viewer was unexpectedly familiar, yet even more unexpectedly different. *"Greetings, Spock,"* the gray-haired Vulcan woman said in a rich contralto roughened by time. *"I thought that might be you . . . though I am fascinated by how little you have changed."*

"Greetings to you as well, Commander T'Pring," Spock said, recognizing the rank markings on her uniform. "I am gratified to see that you remain in good standing within the Protectorate."

"There was some uncertainty on that count at first," the aged T'Pring told him. *"But in the final analysis, you enabled me to give my people something far more precious than the confluence technology we denied to them."*

"The *Kir'Shara* was found, then?"

"With some difficulty. V'Las bombarded the T'Karath

Sanctuary in our world as in yours. When we excavated the artifact, it was damaged, incomplete. But the copy you provided allowed us to reconstruct the rest. And Surak's true word has transformed the Protectorate over the past century. We have learned that control of others is a poor substitute for control of ourselves—and that peace within ourselves facilitates peace with others. Even the Romulans among us have benefited from this message. We are more unified than ever."

"Indeed," Spock said. The idea that the Vulcans' long-lost cousins had the potential to be restored to the family, as it were, was a compelling one. "However, it appears that your enmity with the Compact remains."

"Only the extremist splinter group to which your attackers belong, Spock. They refused to accept the peace treaty the Compact signed with us, even after we granted Andor its independence. But they are few, and their acts of terrorism are usually averted and have little impact on the peace."

"Fascinating. You have even achieved peace with the Klingons?"

"It became necessary for them to accept our aid when—" T'Pring broke off. *"I should not say more. Our past may not be your future, but there may be certain commonalities. Our own experiences with time travel have shown us that the future is best discovered at its own pace."*

"A wise principle," Spock told her. "And one we hope to act upon in short order, thanks to your intervention. We are engaged in an operation to dissolve this confluence and should be ready to begin within minutes. I recommend that you and the *Thorn* evacuate the area immediately."

"We will take the Thorn *in tow."* T'Pring lifted her brows. *"It is gratifying to see you once more, Spock. But I understand why it cannot continue."*

"Yes." It was a sigh of regret. But she had given him hope, in more ways than one, and he was grateful for that. He raised his hand in the Surakian salute. "Live long and prosper, Commander T'Pring of the Vulcan Protectorate."

She returned the salute, and there was an incongruous warmth in her eyes. *"I have done both, Spock. Thanks to you."*

Timeship Two

"We should be ready to synchronize fields within two minutes, Captain," Scott's voice came over Kirk's communicator. *"Even with the walloping we've taken, Spock says we can still make it work now things have quieted down. We're movin' out of the confluence zone now, ready to anchor you in normal space."*

"Good, Scotty. We're ready on this end."

While Kirk's attention was on the monitor room controls, Lucsly glanced down the ladder to Dulmur, who had deactivated his isolation suit and removed the helmet so Lucsly could see him. His partner gave him a thumbs-up as he talked on his communicator, no doubt to the restored *Everett*. Lucsly released a tightly held breath. The timeline was safe again.

Thanks, he reluctantly admitted, to James T. Kirk.

He turned back to Kirk and found the man's eyes

on him. "We'll be collapsing the confluence in a few moments," the captain said, his voice surprisingly gentle. "You should . . . go back to where you came from."

"Gladly," Lucsly said. "But you have to give me your word that you will reveal nothing of what you saw here."

"Of course," Kirk said, and it was startling to Lucsly to see how truthful, how natural, the promise was. Kirk had never had any intention of abusing the knowledge Lucsly had exposed him to. "And don't worry," Kirk went on. "Only Spock, Scotty, and I know the details of what we did to generate the time field. We'll keep it to ourselves."

Lucsly nodded. "Thank you." He hastened down the ladder to join his partner.

"I heard what he said," Dulmur told him softly. "So that explains it. That's how Kirk and his people were able to slingshot in other ships. Because we showed them how."

"Don't remind me," Lucsly said. "Let's get back to the *Everett* before I throw up."

XVI

U.S.S. Enterprise
Stardate 7675.8
March 2275

After the tumultuous buildup, collapsing the confluence field was rather anticlimactic. Once Spock confirmed that the two ships' gravitomagnetic fields were correctly aligned, it was a simple matter of cutting power to the Vedala drive. All that happened at that point was that the timeship did *not* disintegrate, detonate its antimatter stores, and tear the fabric of space a new hole. Instead, the *Enterprise* towed the timeship out of the confluence zone and the crew watched as the disturbed patch of spacetime gently settled back to normal.

Shortly thereafter, Kirk received orders from Starfleet to place Admiral Delgado and his crew under arrest. Delgado offered no resistance; his latest failure seemed to have taken the fight out of him, and he ordered his people to cooperate with the *Enterprise* crew as they scanned and surveyed the research station and *Timeship Two* to gather evidence for the criminal proceedings to come.

All of that had to take a back seat late the following day, however, when the *Enterprise* sensors detected another confluence effect forming near the station. "Is it coming from the timeship?" Kirk asked as he rushed to the bridge, sharing the turbolift ride with McCoy.

"Negative," Spock's voice replied. *"A much larger confluence field forming a hundred and ninety thousand kilometers off the starboard bow."*

"Could it be the Protectorate again?" McCoy mused.

"Their T'Pring destroyed their confluence drive, remember?" Kirk asked.

"Oh, right," McCoy grumbled. "This keeps up, I'll need a scorecard . . ."

The lift doors opened onto the bridge and Kirk came up short at the image of the shimmering blue orb that now appeared on the main screen. "Captain," Spock reported as he ceded the command chair, "it is a Vedala planetoid. An inhabited one."

Uhura turned from her console, holding a hand to her earpiece and speaking in a stunned hush. "Sir . . . message from the Vedala. They're requesting the presence of yourself, Mister Spock . . . and Admiral Delgado. They've provided beam-down coordinates."

"Spock," Kirk said with a gesture toward the turbolift. After all, when the Vedala made one of their rare invitations for a visit, you accepted. Especially under circumstances like these. "Mister Sulu, you have the conn."

"Aye, sir."

"Well," Kirk said once he and Spock were in the lift. "Here we go again."

Spock's brow lifted. "This time, however, I very much doubt the Vedala will be requesting our aid."

Vedala planetoid

When the Vedala had recruited Kirk and Spock for a mission five years before, their concern for secrecy had been so great that they had caused their recruits to forget its details not long after they were returned to their respective ships. But Kirk still largely remembered his time on the Vedala worldlet before and after the mission, when he and his teammates had first met and later said their good-byes. He didn't remember what had been discussed, but he remembered his teammates Sord, Em-3-Green, and especially the striking huntress Lara. And he remembered the setting, a blue-carpeted forest clearing surrounded by purple trees, red bushes, and giant multihued mushrooms. He had seen no devices of any kind, and yet their Vedala host had been able to show them holographic images and transport them . . . somewhere . . . with nothing but a gesture. Perhaps their technology was so advanced as to be invisible, and they chose to live in a natural environment. Or perhaps they had restricted their visitors to the forest glade in order to maintain their strict privacy.

This time, however, Kirk, Spock, and Delgado materialized on a rocky plain ringed by low hills, mostly barren aside from patches of the familiar mossy blue ground cover growing in cracks in the stone. The aurora-like atmospheric glow that was the planetoid's primary source of light gave a blue tinge to the entire landscape. The hills were close; on such a small world, they would have to be in order to be visible past the horizon.

"Welcome again, Captain James Kirk and Commander Spock," came a soft feminine voice. Kirk spun. The speaker was a Vedala, all right: a white-furred felinoid in an orchid-hued jumpsuit, resembling a bedraggled lynx rearing up on its hind legs, its head hanging below its shoulders like a cartoon caricature of dejection or hunchbacked old age. The gray fur that formed tabby-like stripes atop its head and rings around its golden, slit-pupilled eyes looked familiar to Kirk; could this be the same Vedala he had met five years before, or were the patterns a common species trait? His memories of his first visit were not clear enough for him to be sure. "And thank you for coming, Admiral Antonio Delgado. We will be joined by two others shortly."

Kirk turned to see that Delgado was contained within a transparent rectangular prism. "Why is the admiral being confined and we are not?" Kirk asked the Vedala.

"You have made your integrity clear by reversing the damage caused by the abuse of our technology, Captain. An abuse for which the admiral's responsibility is to be investigated." The Vedala pricked up its large ears at something unheard. "Along with one other."

She raised her forelimbs and made a snarling cry, and a flash of golden light filled Kirk's view. When it faded, two other humanoids were present: T'Nuri, the long-standing chair of the Federation Science Council . . . and DTI Director Grey, confined in the same glassy box that held Delgado. The box had doubled in size to accommodate them both with room to spare. "Welcome, Councillor T'Nuri and Director Meijan

Grey," the Vedala said. "Thank you for attending voluntarily."

"Fascinating," Spock murmured to Kirk. "The power required to transport them here directly from Earth . . ."

"Now we know why nobody turns down an invitation from the Vedala," Kirk whispered back.

"Councillor," said the Vedala, "you are here as a witness, as are Captain Kirk and Commander Spock. Since the crime committed here defies your laws as well as ours, you are entitled to question the accused, and once the truth is established, they will be remanded to your care and disposition." *Naturally,* Kirk thought. The Vedala were so isolationist that they would prefer to let others handle their own wrongdoers.

The Vedala turned to the confinement box. "Director Grey, Admiral Delgado, you are here to explain your continued possession of Vedala property in breach of your earlier promises. Be sure to speak the truth, or we will know."

Delgado had been about to speak, but at that last sentence, he fell silent, trading an awkward look with Grey—an apology? Spock had told Kirk how the admiral had seemed willing to take the blame onto himself to protect Grey—something Kirk was hard-pressed to understand.

Grey stepped forward. "The responsibility is mine," she said. T'Nuri showed no surprise at the revelation; by now the councillor had been briefed on the confession Spock had elicited from Grey. The prisoners had no trouble breathing or being heard from within the glassy box, suggesting it was some kind of force-field construct. As Grey spoke, the Vedala lowered herself into a quadrupedal stance, resting on the knuckles of her hands. It seemed to be the posture their bodies were best adapted for, the bipedal stance perhaps being a courtesy to bipedal visitors.

The DTI director went on to explain how she had sent a special team to the abandoned Vedala planetoid to retrieve one of its damaged confluence drives, and how she had conspired with Arthur Manners and Delgado to arrange for its disposition in secret. Delgado joined her in explaining how he had drawn on his political and intelligence connections to organize a sub rosa revival of the timeship project, employing personnel who had previously retired from the service or who then did so as cover for the project, and reallocating excess starship components manufactured for the massive fleet-conversion project that was still under way so that *Timeship Two*, even as a civilian craft, would have the most modern technology available to maximize its ability to withstand the strains of slingshot. "Fortunately," Grey explained, "the admiral's lobbying had thrown up enough red tape to delay the dismantling of the first timeship prototype. It had remained in its hangar at Warlock Station until . . . well, until I decided to help Antonio."

"But why?" Kirk asked her. "Why would you of all people want to assist Delgado in tampering with time? What did he say to bring you around? What kind of . . . incentive did he offer you?" He noted her use of his first name, the affinity she seemed to show toward the man who had once been her rival. He knew Delgado was a manipulator and a ladies' man—and Grey was the kind of woman who might hunger for that kind of rare attention.

Grey smiled. "Nothing, Captain. He convinced me by asking nothing." She grew wistful. "I know what you think of him, and it's not without truth. He spent years cajoling me, trying to play me. Flirting with me just enough to make me feel flattered without going far enough to make his intent obvious—or so he hoped." She smirked. "I'm a realist, Captain. I always knew a man like him could do better.

"But then . . ." She sighed. "We were in the middle of an argument when V'Ger came. This giant, living ship filling the sky, surrounding the planet with deadly weapons, shutting down all our planetary defenses as effortlessly as we would brush away a gnat. It looked like the end."

Delgado put his hand on her shoulder. "And at that moment, when I thought I was about to die, I had nothing left to push for, no agenda to pursue," he said. "No reason to play any more games. I . . . I dropped my guard. Maybe for the first time in my adult life, I let someone else in. And she was there for me. She comforted me, and asked nothing in return."

"It wasn't romantic, Captain, if that's what you're thinking," Grey went on in a tone of subtle chastisement that Kirk had to admit was warranted. "But from that point on, we were friends. There was a bond of trust."

She blinked away tears. "Something else happened that day."

"My daughter died," Delgado said. "She was serving on one of the orbital defense platforms when V'Ger shut them down." He shook his head. "I don't even know why Angela joined Starfleet, when she hated me so much for putting it above my family. Maybe she wanted to prove it wasn't Starfleet to blame, just me. But I'll never know. She made a spacewalk—incredibly risky with no power to the airlock or the sensors, but she had an idea to try to jump-start the platform's weapons." He squeezed his eyes shut. "It didn't work. We still don't know exactly what happened, but she . . . she went out, and never came back in."

Grey held his hand in silence for a moment, but then remembered the Vedala listening impatiently. "After that, I kept expecting him to push harder to restart the time-travel research, so he could go back and save her. But he never asked."

"I couldn't," Delgado said. "That was the sort of thing that drove my family away in the first place. Every time I tried to manipulate matters to fix things, I just made them worse. I couldn't risk asking that again—and I couldn't risk jeopardizing this fragile new thing I had with Jan. This honesty."

"But I saw how it ate him up inside," Grey went on, "knowing he'd never have closure with Angela. So when we learned about the confluence drive last year, I had a thought that . . . maybe if we could master timeline-jumping, it would give him a way to find her again. Maybe find a version of her that still welcomed him in her life." She gave a little scoff. "Well, that and all the potential scientific gains, of course. The potential fascinated me. I've spent so many years simulating alternate histories that the prospect of visiting them was compelling. Between that and my concern for Antonio, I convinced myself that it could be done safely."

Grey released Delgado's hand and stepped forward as far as the clear walls around her permitted. "But obviously I was wrong. I allowed my objectivity to be compromised by personal considerations and betrayed my responsibilities as DTI director. And I stand ready to accept justice for my crimes."

"As do I," Delgado said, moving up alongside her again. "Maybe I didn't ask her for this, but I was eager enough to go along when she offered it."

"Your confessions are appreciated," Councillor T'Nuri told them. "However, there will still need to be legal proceedings back on Earth."

The Vedala rose up again and turned to her. "That may be difficult," she told the Vulcan council chair. "We cannot allow the United Federation of Planets to retain knowledge of our technologies. As before, all records of these events must be purged. All technical details of our propulsion engines will be deleted from your computers and from your minds. The very fact of their existence must be absent from your governmental and historical records. We appreciate that this will impede the normal operations of your justice system, but it is necessary. Surely recent events demonstrate that you are far from ready for the knowledge we possess."

T'Nuri pondered. "I shall discuss the matter with President Lorg. At the very least, Director, Admiral, you shall both be required to resign your posts.

Though not simultaneously, for that could raise questions. Perhaps one of you could be transferred to a sinecure position for a time, with no responsibility and under close monitoring. And there shall be a detailed audit of the practices of both the Department of Temporal Investigations and Starfleet Science Operations."

"That's only fair," Grey said. "My greatest regret is the damage I've done to my department's reputation. I pray that the DTI as a whole doesn't pay the price for my foolishness."

"This is satisfactory," the Vedala said. "If that is all, Councillor T'Nuri, we now permit you to escort the prisoners back to Earth."

"Thank you, Madame Vedala," T'Nuri said, raising her hand in the Surakian salute. "Peace and long life to you."

"That is most likely," the Vedala assured her. Again she raised her forelimbs and growled. The golden light seemed to emanate from her body and engulf the councillor and the prisoners. When the light faded, only Kirk and Spock stood with the Vedala on the barren plain.

Kirk cleared his throat. "Rest assured, ma'am, you will have my crew's full cooperation in removing your drive mechanism from our spacecraft."

"Thank you, Captain, but that has already been done." She gestured, and a hologram appeared in the air before them: the confluence drive within a spherical drive chamber, being tended to by more Vedala than Kirk had ever seen in one place (or in total) before. "The drive is already back with us. We will heal it and restore its purpose."

"Fascinating," Spock said, brows climbing high. "Then you do not consider its ability to transcend temporal dimensions to be a useful purpose?"

"It is not what these drives are meant for," she replied. "It hurts them. It leaves them lost." Did she mean, Kirk wondered, that they already had other mechanisms for doing the same thing—and more?

Kirk took a step closer to the Vedala. "We apologize for any . . . distress we caused. We didn't know."

"That is the nature of the young. Your apology is appreciated, as is your willingness to amend your mistakes. It shows promise for your civilization."

A small smile played across Kirk's lips. "Thank you."

The Vedala rose higher. "But we elders are slower to adapt . . . slower to forgive. We have trusted your Federation in the past, but that trust has been shattered. You, James Kirk and Spock, will be remembered for your services to the Vedala. But your Federation will not see us again. Not until you have outgrown your impetuous youth. Farewell."

She roared, and the golden light was the last thing James Kirk ever saw of the Vedala.

U.S.S. Enterprise
Stardate 7695.0
Montgomery Scott personally operated the tractor beam controls to decelerate *Timeship Two* out of orbit of the neutron star. It was the least he could do for his old bairns. There was no formal scuttling ceremony for the vessel, for it had never been a commissioned Starfleet craft and had no legal right to exist in the first

place. But the bridge crew all stood at respectful attention as they watched it spiral down under the neutron star's pull, faster and faster until it was torn apart by the tidal stresses. Blinding flashes of light erupted on the neutron star's surface as fragments of the craft struck the surface at high velocity, accelerated by its mind-boggling gravity. The soft X-rays of the flares were essentially harmless, but the light show, which would continue for several minutes as the fragments continued to rain down, would serve as a fitting memorial pyre for the erstwhile *Enterprise* engines.

"I hate to spoil the mood," Doctor McCoy murmured as he stood alongside Scott, Kirk, and Spock watching the pyrotechnic display. "But destroying the old engines doesn't really change anything, does it? We have the formula for making a time field with any engines."

"But no one has to know that, Doctor," Scott told him. "And it's best for everyone if the Federation thinks the secret o' time travel died with those engines."

"*We* still know it," McCoy said. "How soon before the temptation to use it becomes overwhelming?"

"There may come a time when it's needed, Bones," Kirk said.

McCoy stared. "That you of all people would say that . . . surely it's clear by now that time travel causes nothing but trouble."

"But time travel has also enabled us to solve those troubles, Doctor," Spock said. "Someday there may come a crisis that cannot be solved any other way."

"I don't like it any more than you do, Bones," Kirk said. "But I'm a soldier. That means it's my job sometimes to do things I don't like for the greater good. Delgado wasn't wrong that our enemies could discover time travel someday. So it's worth keeping the knowledge we have in reserve—just in case."

McCoy glowered and made a skeptical noise. Scott turned to him. "And you're wrong, Doctor, to say that doesn't accomplish anything," he told him, gesturing at the blaze of glory onscreen. "It lets my engines rest in peace at last."

"More than that, Scotty," Kirk said. "It restores their honor. And maybe the Federation's as well."

Epilogue

"Meijan Grey's departure from the post of director will be little remarked by the greater world," said Deputy Director Simok—*Director Simok now*, Laarin Andos corrected herself—"but its impact within these walls will be keenly experienced. I know many of you are concerned that Director Grey's decision to resume her field studies, and the impending retirement of Arthur Manners, will leave our already small department critically shorthanded. However, I have confidence that those of you who remain are capable of rising to the new responsibilities placed upon you."

Andos hoped Director Simok was correct. Until now, the young Rhaandarite had been the most junior clerk in the DTI, and she had little real expertise in its fields of study; she had been assigned to the department at its founding only because she had happened to be cataloging past temporal research for the Science Council when it had been formed. But she had applied herself diligently to her assigned duties, for accepting one's duty was the way of her people. And now, at the tender age of 154, she had reached the rank of junior researcher. Director Grey had even told her she had potential for an administrative position one day—not surprising, for such tasks came naturally to Rhaandarites, but still a gratifying affirmation from her superior.

Yet now the comfortable hierarchy of the DTI had been disrupted, two of its founders leaving the young organization within weeks of one another. It puzzled Andos, for there had been no prior warning of the change. Or had there? Grey's microexpressions and body language had often seemed uneasy, even secretive, in recent months. And Manners's activities and location had become difficult to track. Still, it was the nature of the DTI to deal in classified matters. Andos knew she would need to gain multiple levels in status before she would have clearance to know everything that went on in the department. And Simok had always been a reliable, reassuring administrator. His words now brought her comfort.

"Many of us have also come to perceive Director Grey as synonymous with the DTI," Simok went on, and Andos noted his shift to the first person plural to create a note of empathy. For a Vulcan, he was perceptive of the needs of emotive species. "There is concern over whether our goals and ideals can survive now that she has taken a different path. But Director Grey laid down those goals and ideals in the very foundations of this department. From the beginning, she was motivated by the need to understand not only the laws and mechanics of time, but our own responsibility for their safe management. This has been a learning process, and like any learning process, it has not been smooth and effortless." Beside Simok, Grey lowered her eyes, her cheeks flushing. It almost seemed like guilt to Andos, but Grey had never been the easiest human for her to read. More likely a very human sense of self-recrimination about past performance. On that score, Andos felt Grey was being too hard on herself.

Indeed, Simok proceeded to put Andos's thoughts into words. "But Director Grey brought the department through its turbulent beginnings and guided it to a place of stability. So if she believes her work here is done, we cannot refute that conclusion. We can only pledge to move forward—and to pay close heed to the lessons we can learn from Meijan Grey's choices and actions."

Yes, Laarin Andos thought, joining the rest of the small audience in a spontaneous round of applause in tribute to the outgoing director. Grey's example had always inspired Andos, and she had a feeling it always would.

"And so, in that spirit," Simok continued, "as the second director of the Federation Department of Temporal Investigations, I pledge to recommit this organization to its vital purpose of monitoring the timeline and guarding it against threats to its integrity. This will not be an easy task . . ."

DTI Headquarters, Greenwich
Stardate 60159.8
February 2383
A Monday

"*. . . for there is still much that remains beyond our control and beyond our understanding. All that can be asked is that we pursue the task with diligence, dedication, and patience; that we honestly accept our own limitations and not blame ourselves for failing to achieve the unachievable; and that, above all, we never lose sight of the founding principles laid down by those who came before us.*"

"Wow," Marion Dulmur said, leaning in to study the image on the situation room screen. "Director Andos was a lot shorter then."

"Yes, I was," Andos said as she strode through the door. Lucsly paused the playback.

"Uhh, sorry, ma'am," Dulmur said. "I didn't mean anything . . ."

"No offense taken, Marion. Why, look at that gawky child! I didn't really grow into my features until, oh, around a hundred seventy."

The director studied the image on the monitor and sighed. "I remember that speech vividly. But now I hear it in such a different way."

"Yes," Lucsly said. In the five days since the *Timeship Two* incident, Lucsly had despaired of ever understanding why Meijan Grey had chosen to compromise her principles and help Delgado. The facts had been too thoroughly buried—as irretrievable as the Vedala themselves, who in their own languid way had drifted out of known space altogether, so gradually that it took decades for the Federation to realize they were leaving. But now, watching this familiar speech in a new light, he realized that maybe he didn't need to know why she'd strayed. "I always assumed Simok was pledging to follow in Director Grey's footsteps. But now I realize . . . he was creating the myth of Meijan Grey, for the good of the Department. He didn't want our image of ourselves to be tarnished by her mistakes. He wanted the DTI and its actions to be defined by the good side of her legacy, not the bad."

Dulmur stared. "That's the most philosophical thing I've ever heard you say, partner. Meeting James Kirk must've really had an effect."

"Well, you know what the old stories say." It was Teresa Garcia, breezily entering the room with Ranjea close behind. "Once you've been with Kirk, you're never the same."

The others laughed, but of course Lucsly didn't. "That's hardly appropriate."

"Aww, come on, Lucsly," Garcia said, leaning across the table, her dark eyes wide with interest. "We're all dying to know. You met James Tiberius Kirk! The Time Pirate himself! You talked to him! You've got to tell us what he was really like."

"Yes, please do, Gariff," Ranjea said. "All we know are the legends. You've seen the truth. You could tell us so much. What was it about him that made you trust him with the knowledge you shared? What was it that convinced you, Gariff Lucsly, to do the one thing none of us ever imagined you would do?"

Lucsly pondered the question in silence. The truth was, he no longer knew what to think of James Kirk. On the one hand, Dulmur had been right; Kirk was far more responsible, more concerned for the integrity of the timeline, than he was painted in DTI or even Starfleet lore. Yet it had been Kirk's impulse to use the future knowledge Lucsly had given him and contaminate his own time with it. But under the circumstances, there had been no other choice, had there? And Kirk's crew had used that knowledge to help the Federation in later years, most notably to retrieve the humpback whales whose communication with a powerful alien probe had been necessary to save Earth. If Kirk hadn't violated his promise to Lucsly and used that knowledge, then Lucsly might never have existed. It was all very confusing.

But one thing Lucsly knew: uncertainty could be fatal for a DTI agent. Maybe that was the value of the myths that had grown up around the department's origins: they replaced messy reality with clear, inspiring messages. Just as the myth of Meijan Grey motivated Lucsly and his fellow agents to guard the timeline with quiet, solemn discipline, so the myth of James T. Kirk served as a cautionary tale, reminding them of what was at stake if they ever relaxed their scrutiny.

"Trust Kirk?" he finally said. "Not a chance. The man was a menace. I had to use all my training and control to avoid revealing any unnecessary information about the future. If I hadn't ridden tight herd on him every step of the way, we would've all been doomed. In fact, I wonder just how many other temporal crimes Kirk managed to keep out of the history books . . ."

U.S.S. Enterprise
Stardate 7677.4
March 2275

Kirk was in the botanical garden on Deck 20, sitting on the bench beneath his favorite Centauran oak and staring out at the prismatic streaks of the stars in warp, when Spock found him. "The latest updates from Earth have arrived by subspace," Spock informed him. "Among them was a notation that Simok has officially taken over as director of the Department of Temporal Investigations."

"Hmm," Kirk said, taking it in. "You've worked with him, Spock. What's your take on him?"

"He is an excellent physicist and an excellent administrator. I have no grounds to doubt his diligence or his integrity . . . with the proviso that his discretion can be relied upon when the cause warrants it."

Kirk threw him a sidelong look. "So you'd say . . . the future of the DTI is in good hands?"

Spock tilted his head. "Were you attempting a pun, sir?"

"No . . ." Kirk did an annoyed double take, then let it go and went on. "Never mind, Spock. Just thinking about what might lie ahead."

Who was that mysterious, drab man who helped me shut down the confluence? Kirk wondered in the privacy of his own mind. Spock had deduced that Kirk had gotten help from the future, but it was not Kirk's place to reveal the specifics; he was a man who kept his promises, even when he didn't know to whom he'd made them. But was it possible that the gray man represented some future incarnation of the DTI, that odd little government department that seemed to have been created specifically to second-guess Kirk when he stumbled across something time-related? Could that explain why the gray man had seemed so . . . so *angry* at him?

"There you are, Jim." It was McCoy, strolling across the footbridge spanning the brook that burbled through the botanical section, just this side of the little pool where Crewman Spring Rain splashed her webbed feet happily. "Spock."

"Doctor."

"Jim, I thought we were gonna meet for dinner."

"Oh, sorry, Bones." Kirk rose from the bench. "I lost track of time."

McCoy took in where they were standing, one of Kirk's favorite spots for contemplation. "What were you lost in thought about this time?"

"Apparently the future," Spock supplied. "Understandable, given recent events."

"Hmp. I've thought enough about the future lately to last a lifetime."

"But Doctor, the rest of your lifetime will be in the future."

"Not at all, Spock. Every second of it will be in the present."

"Doctor . . ."

"Gentlemen," Kirk said, leading them toward the exit. "Dinner."

They followed, but Kirk stayed quiet, lost in thought. Once they were in the turbolift, McCoy said, "My, you are preoccupied tonight, Jim. What is it about the future that you're so worried about?"

"Oh, this and that," Kirk replied with feigned breeziness. "For instance . . . do you ever wonder what people will think of us in a hundred years or more? How we'll be remembered?"

The doctor let out a puff of breath. "Is this about your reputation again? I thought you'd gotten over that. I say don't worry about it. History will always get things wrong. The truth gets lost under the exaggerations and the oversights and the self-serving lies. For instance, the future will never know about what Delgado and Grey almost did. Hell, even the Vulcans forgot what Surak really taught until his real writings turned up, in either universe." He scoffed. "For that matter, I'm not convinced our Vulcans have the whole story even now."

Spock's gaze was stern. "Doctor, the *Kir'Shara* was long ago authenticated as the actual writings of Surak."

"Maybe so, but those writings are still subject to interpretation. People always pick and choose the parts of history that support the myths they want to believe, and forget the rest. Vulcans as much as anyone."

"Then how do you explain the swift reformation that swept through Vulcan society as soon as the *Kir'Shara* was revealed?"

The turbolift doors opened, but McCoy went on unheeding. "How do *you* explain that there are still Vulcans who act like they did a hundred years ago and don't really buy all that diversity stuff?"

"Spock! Bones!" Kirk clasped their shoulders and led them out into the officers' lounge. "If you ask me, sometimes it's better not to have too many answers about the past. And I think we can all agree that the past is best left where it is."

James Kirk smiled. "So let's focus on building the future instead."

Acknowledgments

Forgotten History is both a sequel and a prequel to my previous novel, *Star Trek: Department of Temporal Investigations—Watching the Clock*. Readers curious about the scientific basis for the principles of time travel depicted herein may learn more in the acknowledgments of that book or on its annotations page at http://home .fuse.net/ChristopherLBennett/DTI_Annot.html. This novel is also both sequel and prequel to my debut novel, *Star Trek: Ex Machina*, whose post–*Star Trek: The Motion Picture* continuity I also revisited in *Star Trek: Mere Anarchy—The Darkness Drops Again*.

Agents Lucsly and Dulmur were introduced in the *Star Trek: Deep Space Nine* episode "Trials and Tribble-ations" (script by Ronald D. Moore and René Echevarria, story by Ira Steven Behr and Hans Beimler and Robert Hewitt Wolfe). The timing and circumstances of the DTI's formation were informed by the two DTI-related stories in *Star Trek: Strange New Worlds II*: "Gods, Fate, and Fractals" by William Leisner and "Almost, But Not Quite" by Dayton Ward. The Chronal Assessment Committee was mentioned in *All Our Yesterdays: The Time Travel Sourcebook* from Last Unicorn Games, which also loosely inspired the Simok character.

The episodes of *Star Trek* from which this novel's

events are drawn include "The Naked Time" (written by John D. F. Black), "Miri" (written by Adrian Spies), "Tomorrow Is Yesterday" (written by D. C. Fontana), "The City on the Edge of Forever" (written by Harlan Ellison), "Amok Time" (written by Theodore Sturgeon), "Mirror, Mirror" (written by Jerome Bixby), "Assignment: Earth" (teleplay by Art Wallace, story by Gene Roddenberry and Art Wallace), "The Tholian Web" (written by Judy Burns and Chet Richards), and "All Our Yesterdays" (written by Jean Lisette Aroeste). The episodes of *Star Trek: The Animated Series* (TAS) informing this novel include "Yesteryear" (written by D. C. Fontana), "The Time Trap" (written by Joyce Perry), and "The Jihad" (written by Stephen Kandel). Grey, Aleek-Om, and Erikson are from "Yesteryear." Gabler is from several TAS episodes, notably "Once Upon a Planet" (written by Chuck Menville). For their first names, and for the background of the Vedala civilization, I have drawn selectively on Alan Dean Foster's *Star Trek Log* series, which adapted and expanded on TAS. Heather Peterson is from *Deep Space Nine— Invasion!: Time's Enemy* by L. A. Graf. Watley is from "Trials and Tribble-ations." Kirk saving the Pelosians from extinction and the five-year mission ending in 2270 were established in *Star Trek: Voyager*'s "Q2" (teleplay by Robert Doherty, story by Kenneth Biller), and *Ex Machina* established additional details of those events, which I expand on here.

The name Robert L. Comsol for the commanding officer of Starfleet during the 2250s–60s was seen on the General Order 7 paperwork in "The Menagerie,

Part 1" (written by Gene Roddenberry), and also referenced in dialogue in that episode. Thanks to Memory Alpha, the *Star Trek* Wiki, for bringing this to my attention. The name Satak for the captain of the *Intrepid* comes from the *Star Trek Concordance* by Bjo Trimble, most likely based on an early script draft for "The Immunity Syndrome" (written by Robert Sabaroff). The name Barak for the Klingon captain played by Mark Lenard in *Star Trek: The Motion Picture* is based on Harold Livingston's 1977 first-draft script for "In Thy Image," the television pilot episode that was reworked into *Star Trek: The Motion Picture*. Tunzos and his love of meat are from a 1980 *Star Trek* newspaper comic strip storyline by Thomas Warkentin.

Thanks to Doug Drexler and Rick Sternbach for technical input. My portrayal of the innards of the pre-refit *Enterprise* is based heavily on Drexler's cutaway schematic at http://drexfiles.wordpress.com/2009/10/11/1701-cutaway/. A version of this schematic appeared onscreen in *Star Trek: Enterprise*'s "In a Mirror, Darkly, Part II." I have also attempted to reconcile the onscreen engine room and the Drexler cutaway with the engineering locations depicted in *The Animated Series*. My description of the main energizer monitor section combines the engineering computer room seen in "Beyond the Farthest Star" and other episodes with the small engineering set seen in "The Alternative Factor," and my description of the warp reactor core blends the core layout from the Drexler cutaway with the alleged "antimatter nacelle" interior from TAS: "One of Our Planets Is Missing" (written by Marc Daniels). The timeship's service corridors are based on those from "In a Mirror, Darkly." The *Star Trek: The Next Generation Technical Manual* by Rick Sternbach and Michael Okuda provided insight into warp technology. The dual deflector/force-field defense system of the refit *Enterprise* was established onscreen and in production notes for *Star Trek: The Motion Picture*. The limitations of ringship propulsion were explained by Michael Okuda in the centerfold to the *Star Trek: Ships of the Line 2011 Calendar*. The *Capella*-class survey vessel is a design from Masao Okazaki's Starfleet Museum website at www.starfleet-museum.org.

Gary Seven's second encounter with Kirk's crew was depicted in the novel *Assignment: Eternity* by Greg Cox, and Clan Ru's raid on the Guardian planet is from *First Frontier* by Diane Carey and Doctor James I. Kirkland. The Skagway mission occurred in *The Rings of Time*, also by Greg Cox.

About the Author

CHRISTOPHER L. BENNETT's tenure as a distinct entity within the space-time continuum commenced several months after the *Enterprise* crew first encountered Gary Seven. Nearly half a Jovian year later, he discovered *Star Trek* and fell in love with space, science, and science fiction. After earning bachelor's degrees in physics and history, he went on to author such critically acclaimed novels as *Star Trek: Ex Machina* (January 2005), *Star Trek: Titan—Orion's Hounds* (January 2006), *Star Trek: The Next Generation—The Buried Age* (July 2007), *Star Trek: Titan—Over a Torrent Sea* (March 2009), and *Star Trek: Department of Temporal Investigations—Watching the Clock* (May 2011). He visited alternate timelines in *Places of Exile* in *Myriad Universes: Infinity's Prism* (July 2008) and "Empathy" in *Mirror Universe: Shards and Shadows* (January 2009). Shorter works include *Star Trek: S.C.E. #29: Aftermath* (July 2003), *Star Trek: Mere Anarchy: The Darkness Drops Again* (February 2007), and the e-novella *Star Trek: Typhon Pact: The Struggle Within* (October 2011), as well as short stories in the anniversary anthologies *Constellations* (original series' fortieth), *The Sky's the Limit* (TNG's twentieth), *Prophecy and Change* (DS9's tenth), and *Distant Shores* (VGR's tenth). Beyond *Star Trek*, he has penned the novels

X-Men: Watchers on the Walls (May 2006) and *Spider-Man: Drowned in Thunder* (January 2008) as well as several original novelettes in *Analog* and other science fiction magazines. His first original novel, *Only Superhuman*, will be published in fall 2012 by Tor Books. More information and annotations can be found at http://home.fuse.net/ChristopherLBennett/, and the author's blog can be found at http://christopherlbennett.wordpress.com/.